ALSO BY PEGGY BLAIR

FICTION

The Beggar's Opera
The Poisoned Pawn

NONFICTION

Lament for a First Nation

HUNGRY GHOSTS

PEGGY BLAIR

Simon & Schuster Canada

New York   London   Toronto   Sydney   New Delhi

Simon & Schuster Canada
A Division of Simon & Schuster, Inc.
166 King Street East, Suite 300
Toronto, Ontario M5A 1J3

This Simon & Schuster Canada edition June 2015

SIMON & SCHUSTER CANADA and colophon are registered trademarks
of Simon & Schuster, Inc.

For information about special discounts for bulk purchases,
please contact Simon & Schuster Special Sales at 1-800-268-3216
or CustomerService@simonandschuster.ca.

Interior design by Lewelin Polanco

Manufactured in the United States of America

10 9 8 7 6 5 4 3 2 1

ISBN 978-1-4767-5794-0
ISBN 978-1-4767-5795-7 (ebook)

FOR RODDIE BLAIR (1916–2013)

Ah, if only I had brought a cigar with me!
This would have established my identity.

—Charles Dickens

HUNGRY GHOSTS

The Inuit of the far north have dozens of words to describe snow, the quantity of snow that falls, its different hues and textures. Surprisingly, they have no word for snow itself.

To the Ojibway of Northern Ontario, snow is goon. Goonikaa *means there is a lot of it.* Ishkwaapo *means it no longer falls.*

Snow no longer fell from the night sky. It dropped in clumps from branches bent over by its weight. It rested in the boughs of pine trees that two centuries earlier would have been cut down and shipped to Halifax as masts for tall ships.

A hare stood frozen against a drift, ears alert.

Harsh winds had blasted snow into deep sculpted waves. Otherwise, there would have been enough goon *to hide the woman's body until spring.*

1

Inspector Ricardo Ramirez whistled as he carried a battered kettle to the washroom on the thirteenth floor of the medical tower. He pushed open the swinging door and was startled to find a half-naked man admiring himself in the cracked mirror above the sink. It took Ramirez a few seconds before he realized the man was dead.

The apparition turned to face Ramirez. He bent his elbows and held out his hands, palms up. Ramirez recognized the gesture, a kind of universal "why me?"

For years, Ramirez had been shadowed by ghosts. His Yoruba slave grandmother had prophesized that messengers would come, sent by Eleguá, the god of the crossroads. They began to appear shortly after Ramirez's promotion.

At first, he thought he was suffering from the same rare dementia that took his beloved grandmother's life. But on New Year's Eve, Hector Apiro found her decades-old autopsy report and told Ramirez she'd died of natural causes.

Ramirez was no longer sure what to believe. If the visions were real, then so were the *orishas*, and that conflicted with the Cuban government's official policy of atheism.

Besides, Ramirez had no way of knowing if his clean bill of health was accurate. After all, his friend had attempted a diagnosis without full disclosure. Ramirez hadn't told his best friend, or even his own wife, that he sometimes saw the ghosts of the murder victims from his unsolved files.

The dead man followed Ramirez back to Apiro's cramped office. The small pathologist was busy grinding coffee beans he had purchased on the *bolsa negra* that morning. Real coffee was the one treat that Apiro allowed himself daily, and he was always happy to share.

The dead man walked over to the window. He placed his hands shoulder-width apart on the ledge and stared out at the turquoise ocean.

Hector Apiro's office was not much larger than its occupant, but it had a spectacular view of the Malecón. Rolling waves smashed against the seawall, drenching scores of *turistas* who strolled along Havana's famous promenade.

The dead man shook his head sadly. Ramirez made note of his stylishly cut black hair, his white sleeveless undershirt and briefs, the thick braid of gold around his neck. That single piece of jewellery cost more than most Cubans earned in a decade. The fact he was wearing it suggested he hadn't been robbed.

There were no obvious causes of death—no blood, no bullet holes—only dark purple bruising on the side of the man's face and a red welt on his forehead. The ghost's clothing, what little there was of it, looked new.

The spectre turned slowly, as if he'd remembered something. He held out his hands, like a child showing his mother his clean fingernails. His nails were short, manicured. There was no wedding ring, no white line to suggest he'd ever worn one. Ramirez observed red marks around the wrists, deep lines that cut into the man's flesh. The same raw impressions circled his ankles.

Ligature marks.

Ramirez exhaled. He handed Apiro the kettle to plug in. He removed the stack of well-thumbed medical textbooks that tilted crazily on one of Apiro's wooden stools and placed it carefully on the floor. While Apiro fussed about preparing the French press he used for his coffee, Ramirez sat down and pondered his latest vision.

The dead man had obviously come from a place with expensive shops and good hair stylists. He couldn't be Cuban, Ramirez decided. But a dead *extranjero* would be a problem, particularly one tied up and beaten before he died.

"Ready in a few minutes, *asere*," said Apiro. "It smells wonderful, doesn't it?" The doctor lowered his voice conspiratorially. "I found the beans *por la izquierda*." Through the left hand, on the black market. "I even saw a small piece of steak. I thought the vendor might charge me for admiring it."

Apiro cackled, his laugh resembling the sound of a night gull. He seated himself in his worn swivel chair and reached for his pipe. The chair had once been upholstered, but the fabric had worn through. Tufting poked through its seams like the hair in old men's ears.

Apiro often joked that smoking could hardly stunt his growth at this late stage. Mother Nature had done that long before. Apiro suffered from—or, more accurately, lived with—achondroplasia. Dwarfism. For this reason, the stools in his office were short and his many medical degrees and certificates hung low on the stained plaster walls.

"So how is bachelorhood, Ricardo? Is Francesca enjoying her holiday?" Apiro struck a match. He put the pipe stem in his mouth and puffed until the tobacco caught. A coil of fragrant smoke rose to the ceiling. He pursed his lips as he exhaled, forming a series of perfect smoke rings that floated towards the open window. The dead man waved them away.

"I'm sure she is. But I'm slowly starving to death," said Ramirez.

"You should learn how to cook," Apiro said. "I'm teaching Maria." When he was satisfied the coffee was strong enough, the surgeon poured some into a cracked mug and handed it to Ramirez. He reached beneath the pile of papers on his desk for a second mug and poured some for himself.

Ramirez accepted the drink gratefully. It was almost impossible to find genuine, unadulterated coffee in Havana. Their rations were cut with chickpea flour as effectively as if the government bureaucrats responsible had been coached by Mexican drug dealers.

Only *turistas* had easy access to real Cuban coffee. Sometimes they were careless and left a foil bag in their luggage when they passed through airport security. Whenever that happened, Customs shared the treat with Major Crimes. Feed the horses, thought Ramirez, and the sparrows eat too. Spoils of Fidel Castro's war against capitalism. A war that could never determine who was right. Or who was left, for that matter. Only those left behind.

"I have to call Francesca tonight before the children go to bed," Ramirez said. "I'm sure they're at the stadium now." He sipped the hot coffee slowly, savouring its rich taste and smell. The ghost sniffed the air. He looked dejected.

"Was Edel able to find a baseball glove?" asked Apiro.

"No," said Ramirez. "But the other boys will share."

Ramirez's son had no equipment. His team played with balls made of rags and with sticks instead of bats. The fielders had no gloves; the catcher no mask.

"It's probably a good thing they're away," said Ramirez. "There's a full moon this Saturday. It could be a busy weekend. And you know how much Francesca hates it when I have to work late." The ghost shrugged helplessly, as if to say it wasn't his fault someone killed him.

Ramirez reached in his pocket and removed a cigar. He fumbled for a match.

"Here," said Apiro, and slid one across his scratched wooden desk. "You know, Ricardo, there are quite a number of scientific studies on the question of whether there is a correlation between the full moon and aggression. The results are contradictory, although I remember from my days at the emergency ward that patients were unusually agitated whenever one appeared. A full moon, that is, not another study." He shook his large head and chuckled. "These days, of course, the majority of my patients are rather more passive."

Apiro was the pathologist on call to the Havana Major Crimes Unit. He often joked that being a surgeon was much easier when his patients were dead. Less fear of complications.

"I always assumed the crime rates went up during a full moon because the criminals could see better at night," said Ramirez. He looked at the ghost again and wondered when his body would turn up.

About eight hours later, as he and Detective Espinoza watched security videotapes at the museum, two children playing on the beach answered that question.

2

Celia Jones looked out the kitchen window at the mountains of snow that surrounded her parents' home. Her father was outside pushing the snow blower, trying to carve a path from the driveway to the side door. His breath formed clouds above his head. Jones inhaled deeply and again tried to mask her frustration. "What do you mean, we can't adopt her?"

"I'm sorry, Mrs. Jones," said the woman from Children's Aid. "We can't process an adoption request for a child from a foreign country unless that country has a licensed agency in Ontario. Cuba doesn't have an adoption agency here. Those are the rules."

"But this is insane," said Jones, gripping the phone tightly. "The Cuban government would never establish an adoption agency in Canada or anywhere else for that matter. They have a policy against foreign adoptions. This was an exception. The acting president, Raúl Castro, signed the papers himself."

"I'm sorry," said the bureaucrat. "We can't work with an agency that doesn't exist. The child entered Canada on compassionate medical grounds. When she's well enough to leave, she'll have to go back to her legal guardians."

"But she *has* no legal guardians. Her father is a political dissident. He's stuck in a Cuban jail. Her only other relative was her grandmother, and she was murdered. That's why Beatriz was in the orphanage in the first place; she has health problems. No one else could care for her."

"That makes her an unaccompanied minor, and I'm afraid that's out of our jurisdiction. She'll have to apply for refugee status if she wants to remain in Canada."

"Refugee status? What does that involve?"

"She would have to prove to a federal immigration board she has a genuine fear of persecution if she's returned to Cuba."

"Oh, for God's sake," said Jones. "She's only three years old. How is she supposed to testify—with hand puppets?"

"I'm sorry, Mrs. Jones. You'll have to talk to the appropriate federal officials about those kinds of procedural matters. Is there anything else I can do for you?"

You could shove your procedure up your ass, thought Jones. "No, thank you. You've done quite enough."

"Have a nice day."

Jones was glad her parents had an old-style phone. She smashed down the receiver with a resounding thwack. Then she took another deep breath, picked it up, and called an old friend.

Paul Cloutier was an immigration lawyer and former classmate from McGill University's Faculty of Law.

"Well," Cloutier said, after she'd filled him in. "I guess technically, she's right. An unaccompanied minor means a child who enters Canada without a legal guardian or parent and claims refugee status."

"But she didn't come here to be a refugee, she came here so we could adopt her. As far as Cuba's concerned, she *has* been adopted, but Ontario won't recognize Cuba's paperwork. The idiot I spoke to said Beatriz would have to leave Canada as soon as her surgery is over."

"Well, I don't think they can do that. They're not supposed to return a minor back to a foreign country unless there's a legal guardian there to receive her. Wow, this is starting to sound like a law school exam, isn't it? It's a real catch-22."

"What are we supposed to do? It's like she doesn't exist."

"I think the biggest problem, Celia, is that she didn't leave the country illegally. The usual basis for a refugee claim is a fear of persecution if the claimant returns to their original country. If the Cuban government agreed to let her go voluntarily, that could be hard to prove."

"How about the fact that if she's sent back there, she could die? She developed all these heart problems because of the American trade embargo. They didn't have the antibiotics they needed to treat her."

"I know you won't like this, Celia, but that embargo applies to all Cubans equally. It's not targeted against this little girl specifically. In refugee law, that's a problem."

"What about the political route?"

"I don't know how far you'd get. There are forty or so Cubans warehoused at Guantánamo Bay right now that Canada has refused to accept, even though the Americans keep asking. As far as Canada's concerned, they're on Cuban soil, which means they don't qualify as refugees under our laws. The U.S., needless to say, has a different position. They consider Guantánamo Bay to be an American territory, under their exclusive sovereignty." Cloutier sighed. "Where is she now?"

"She's at home while Alex gets her strong enough for surgery. I'm up north at my parent's place for a few days, but I'll be back at work on Tuesday. Alex thinks we might have a month or two before she's ready. That's not much time to sort this out."

Celia Jones wouldn't have left Ottawa at all if her father's call hadn't been so desperate. He needed to find home care or a nursing home for her mother soon, he'd explained. Her condition had deteriorated to the point where he couldn't leave her alone while he looked for help.

"Don't worry, Celia," Cloutier laughed. "This whole process is so cumbersome that by the time they get around to dealing with her, she'll be an adult."

"Then we find a way to get around the law," Alex said when she called him with the news. Normally, Alejandro Gonsalves was a happy, easy-going man. The tightness in his voice betrayed his anger.

"I can't do that, Alex," Celia said. "I'm an officer of the court."

"Celia, how do you think I got into this country? I broke Cuban laws when I left without an exit permit."

A ninety-mile journey across the Straits of Florida took Jones's husband eighteen months. President Bill Clinton had agreed with Fidel Castro to "normalize" migration, but Alex was aboard a tugboat heading for Miami when the Americans changed their minds. They would no longer permit Cubans intercepted at sea to land on American soil. The Cubans en route weren't refugees anymore; they were illegal immigrants.

The Cuban Coast Guard sprayed the tugboat with fire hoses, then rammed it until it sank. Alex managed to keep afloat by grabbing onto a body until someone pulled him out of the water. He was detained at Guantánamo Bay, with thirty thousand other Cubans, while Castro and Clinton negotiated what to do with them. Clinton finally agreed to take the Cubans on stringent entry terms. From Miami, Alex made his way to Montreal, where he finished his medical training.

"I know how much this whole thing upsets you, Alex," said Jones. "Believe me, I'm upset too. But there are laws."

"We had laws too, Celia. Those laws put me in a detention camp.

Laws almost killed me. I won't let some crazy, arbitrary law take our daughter away."

"We'll find a way to keep her," Jones pleaded. "I know we will. We'll talk about the options when I get back. Please, Alex. I don't want to fight. I have enough to deal with, between this and my mother."

Alex took a deep breath. "I'm sorry, sweetheart. I didn't even ask. How is she doing?"

"Not good." She described her mother's new symptoms.

"Celia, that may not be Parkinson's. That doesn't usually cause mental confusion."

"Then what could it be?"

"I don't know," he hesitated, "but it sounds like Alzheimer's."

3

The English-speaking guide stood with her tour group inside the massive front doors of the Museo Nacional de Bellas Artes.

At the centre of the building was a vast atrium. Five floors above, a Tiffany stained glass ceiling spanned its entire length and breadth. Coloured sunlight danced like butterflies against the cream-painted walls, which were topped with intricate plaster mouldings of flowers and carved figures. Balconies flanked by columns overlooked the magnificent space.

It was the last group of the day and the tour guide's feet were tired, but she managed to inject enthusiasm into her voice.

"The national museum is actually housed in two buildings," she explained to the group of attentive tourists. "We are in one of them. The Asturian Centre, or rather the former Asturian Centre, was built in 1927. It has been completely restored. It holds valuable artifacts from around the world, including thousands from Egypt, Mesopotamia, and Greece. We have a wonderful collection of art on permanent display as well, including paintings by famous European artists like Goya and Gainsborough. We are also very fortunate to have a visiting exhibition with us at the moment of Italian master-pieces."

A uniformed *policía* burst into the foyer. "Out of the building," he shouted in Spanish. He pushed a rather large and somewhat overweight male *turista* towards the massive front doors. "Everyone. Get out now."

"What is it?" the guide said. "What's wrong?"

The other tourists gaped, confused.

"There's a bomb on the fifth floor," said the policeman, his voice high-pitched with stress. "Take your group outside quickly. You," he said to the closest security guard, "evacuate the building. Once you're outside, make sure everyone is kept back. The police and fire trucks will be here soon. I'm going up there to see if I can find out where it is. I'll check the floors on my way down to make sure the building is empty."

"What is it?" a female tourist asked the tour guide. "What's going on?"

"We have to leave the building. Come," the tour guide said, her legs quivering, "I'll explain outside."

Another security guard jogged over to the policeman. "I'll go with you. Our policy requires that more than one person check the building."

"No," said the policeman. "It's too dangerous."

The security guard hesitated. "Are you sure?"

"You want to risk blowing yourself up?" said the policeman. "*Move.* Get everyone out of here. And make sure your colleagues block off the streets."

Scores of *turistas* and museum staff poured onto the sidewalk, running for their lives as word of the bomb threat spread. The museum director, Romero Garza, sprinted to the end of the block with Carlos Hernandez, the head of security. Once he recovered his breath, Garza paced back and forth.

At least a dozen security guards stopped traffic at each intersection while others milled around.

"Oh my God, Señor Garza," said one of his staff, weeping. "If a bomb goes off, it will destroy all our beautiful art."

Garza hugged her briefly. "Don't worry. The important thing is that everyone is safe." He released her and chewed his lip. On the other side of the giant wooden doors, he heard the piercing sound of a fire alarm, then a second one, so loud his eardrums vibrated.

"Where is the bomb squad?" his staff member said. "What's taking them so long?"

"I don't know," Garza said, worried.

Moments later, sirens blasted. The line of security guards parted and a half-dozen white Peugeots blew through. The police cars pulled in front of the museum, blue lights flashing. "What are they doing?" said Hernandez. "They're too close, those *monados*."

Another siren yelped. Security guards leaped out of the way as an aging fire truck careened through the intersection of San Rafael and Monserrate. The truck barely missed smashing the row of police cars as it squealed to a stop. It left a long streak of rubber on the steaming asphalt.

Firemen scrambled out. They wore red helmets with orange ear protectors and black rubber boots. Sweat poured down their foreheads.

As they raced towards the marble stairs, Hernandez waved frantically: "You can't go inside. There's a bomb!"

The fire chief shouted at his men to stop. He held up a gloved hand impatiently. "What are you talking about?"

"A policeman told us to empty the building," Hernandez explained.

"What policeman?" asked a young *policía*. He hitched up his pants as he joined them.

"I don't know his name. A foot patrolman, I think," said Hernandez, recovering his breath. He tried to remember if he'd seen a patrol car when they ran outside. "It's on the fifth floor."

The policeman glanced at the fire chief.

"Move the cars," he yelled at the other patrolmen as he pulled out his radio. "And you, get that fire truck out of here."

The fire chief clenched his jaw. "I was sent to a fire, not a bomb," he said. "While we're standing here talking, the museum could go up in flames."

The young policeman shifted his feet. "If what this man says is true"—he nodded his head at Hernandez—"we need to wait for the bomb squad." He radioed his dispatcher, puffing out his chest to compensate for his uncertainty. "No one goes inside until we have more information. And, *compañero*, let's carry on this discussion a little further away from the building, okay?"

The fire chief glowered. "You'd better hope it's not a fire," he said, and ordered his men to move back.

Garza grabbed the fire chief by his heavy jacket sleeve. "I'm the museum director. The art in there is priceless. Please do whatever you can to save it."

An *extranjero* materialized from the crowd. At his side was a woman who looked to be in her thirties. The foreigner looked directly at the fire chief. "Do you speak English?"

The fire chief nodded, watching the building warily.

"I am the Italian curator responsible for the exhibition on that floor. I'll give you and each of your men one hundred convertible pesos if our paintings are brought out of there unharmed."

The tourist pesos were worth roughly seventeen times more than domestic pesos. It was a fortune to a man who earned less than ten dollars a month. The fire chief narrowed his eyes and set his jaw.

The *policía* clicked off his radio. He turned to Hernandez, bewildered. "I don't know who you spoke to, but our dispatcher has no report of a bomb. No foot patrolman has checked in from this location. I'm the first policeman to call in."

"Then get out of the way and let us do our job," said the fire chief. He motioned to his men. They ran up the wide stairs and inside the building, carrying a heavy grey hose.

The young policeman looked at the museum director and made a sign of the cross. "I hope he's right," he said. He gripped his radio, training his eyes on the fifth floor.

A few minutes later, the alarms stopped ringing. Another twenty minutes passed before the fire chief came out.

"There was no fire," he said, disgusted. "Not even any smoke. Someone smashed a fire alarm on the fifth floor. The second alarm went off when the emergency exit door on the same floor was pushed open."

Garza exhaled slowly. "Thank God nothing's damaged."

"I didn't say that," said the fire chief. "There's red paint all over the place. I'm assuming it wasn't there before."

Garza gasped. "Are the paintings all right?"

The fire chief shrugged. "I'm no artist."

"The foot patrolman, where is he?" asked Hernandez.

The fire chief shook his head. "The building is empty. We checked all the bathrooms, the coatroom, everything."

"Empty?" Hernandez frowned. Then his expression shifted. "It was a diversion. He was alone in there for at least ten minutes, maybe more. It has to be a theft."

He started to run towards the museum entrance but was stopped by the young policeman. "No one goes in until I say so. This is a crime scene. You heard the man. Willful destruction of state property."

"What's going on?" the Italian curator demanded. Garza translated for him.

"*Merda*," the Italian said. "That's not Cuban property; those paintings belong to Italy. If any of our paintings were damaged . . ."

The policeman put his hand in the air. "Enough. Everyone stop talking." He pulled out his radio a second time and called the dispatcher. He spoke rapidly for a few minutes before he clicked the radio off.

"Detective Espinoza is on his way from Major Crimes. No one leaves until he gets here. That means *no one.*" He looked nervously at the fire chief. "Not even you."

———————

"We should have set a fire ourselves; we could have rescued the paintings," the fire chief said to the fire truck driver as he rolled himself a cigarette. They watched the younger firemen coil up the hoses. "What were you going to do with all your money?"

"Me?" The driver spat on the ground. "Fix the fucking brakes."

4

Celia Jones listened anxiously to the news as she cleared away the detritus from her mother's second attempt at cooking dinner. CBC television was predicting another twenty or thirty centimetres of snow. Her father planned to take advantage of the short window of good weather to go into White Harbour for groceries to replace the burned burgers, the scorched buns.

Emma Jones sat transfixed before the TV. The men wearing bandanas over their faces frightened her, but she wouldn't let Celia change the channel.

The CBC reporter spoke excitedly as wind whipped the hood of her parka, leaving her stiff, sprayed hair intact.

"Standing behind me are a dozen Mohawk Warriors who joined the lines late last night in a show of support for the Ojibway protestors who have blocked the access road to the mill. The Wabigoon River Pulp Mill is in the traditional territory of the Manomin Bay First Nation. And that's the problem. The natives are unhappy with what they say is a lack of consultation by the government. They're afraid their traditional fishing grounds will be devastated once the mill reaches capacity."

Behind the reporter, dark smoke twisted in the wind from oil barrels filled with burning firewood. Around thirty Aboriginal men dressed in camouflage held rifles. They stood around the open fires, bare hands extended over the flames.

The camera cut to an interview with the chief of the Manomin Bay First Nation.

"Of course we feel betrayed," Chief Wabigoon said. He sounded more puzzled than angry. "Forty years ago, the government promised my father that this mill would never open again. Now we find out it's been open for months. The white man has a short memory. The government has a fiduciary duty to us, to our treaties, but they don't care. No one even told us."

The camera cut back to the blockade. Two yellow school buses lay on their sides obstructing the road. HONOUR YOUR TREATY PROMISES, read a banner strung along the side of one of them. The red, yellow, and black flag of the Mohawk Warriors flapped above it.

An Ojibway elder sat on a green lawn chair with a small hand-lettered sign in his lap: I DIDN'T FIGHT IN WORLD WAR II TO PROTECT *YOUR* LAND.

Ontario Provincial Police cars lined the gravel road, their motors idling. Exhaust was carried upward by the wind. A dozen or more protestors stood warily across from them, stamping their feet to stay warm.

"If you can hear that drumming behind me, Peter," said the reporter, "the natives have built a sweat lodge behind the barricades." She pulled a grim face and pointed to a structure behind the overturned buses. "It looks like they're here to stay. I had a moment to speak with the CEO of the pulp company, Malcolm Byers, for his reaction to the occupation."

The camera cut to an executive in a white shirt and striped tie.

He looked relaxed, tanned. He sat behind an expensive-looking wooden desk.

"We have a provincial permit to proceed with our mill and we're going to do what the law says we can. These are Crown lands. What we're doing is legal, and believe me, the residents up here need the work. You remember the scene in *The Graduate*—the future's in plastic? Well, wood fibre, that's the real future. Recycled paper. Every time you see a picture of a dead bird strangled by a plastic bag, we have a marketing opportunity."

When Celia Jones arrived in Manomin Bay, her father took her aside, out of her mother's earshot. It was her first time home in a year. She saw the lines in her father's brow, the grey tinge of fatigue. Eric Jones was frightened too. But not of native protestors disguised with bandanas.

"She let herself out about an hour before you got here. I found her wandering down the gravel road towards the reserve. She said she saw a broken down truck from the upstairs window and wanted to go over to see if she could help. But there was nothing there when I found her, just some old red plastic pylons."

"Cripes, Dad," Celia said. "She could have been hit by a car. There are no lights on that road."

"She's losing us," her father said, his voice catching. "It's getting worse all the time. We try our best. She takes notes, keeps lists. We walk a lot, down to the bay. And the old photographs," he smiled sadly. "Those help."

"How long has she been like this?"

Celia's mother had been diagnosed with Parkinson's years before, but her parents had coped so well that her condition seemed barely noticeable. Until this visit, when her shakiness and disorientation were obvious.

"A couple of months, I guess. There was a doctor up here a few weeks ago running a clinic. I took her in for tests: blood, urine, the whole nine yards. Dr. Kesler was supposed to call back with results. Nothing yet." His forehead creased as he fought to hold back tears.

"What did she say about Mom's symptoms?"

"She said she wanted to see her results first. She should have called by now. It worries me that she hasn't."

"Now, Dad, no news is usually good news," said Celia. But as it turned out, she was wrong.

"Would you like some tea, dear?" Emma Jones said kindly. She held the kettle in the air. It was the third time she'd asked. Each time the kettle boiled empty when she forgot to unplug it.

"Thanks, Mom." Celia followed her mother into the kitchen.

A burning pot, a frying pan left unattended, could burn down the entire house. Celia was starting to understand what her father had been dealing with.

She felt guilty; she hadn't known. She and Alex had been caught up in their own affairs, getting Beatriz ready for surgery, trying to navigate a tangled bureaucratic maze.

Emma looked puzzled. "I don't understand why you're home so early this year, Celia. Have you finished school already?"

Celia sighed. She gave her mother a hug. She'd got her law degree over a decade before. She'd been a lawyer with the Rideau Regional Police Force in Ottawa for more than six years.

5

Inspector Ramirez stood inside the lobby of the museum while Detective Espinoza briefed him. His stomach growled; he hadn't eaten all day. "How long was the vandal inside the museum, Fernando?"

"Less than ten minutes. Just long enough to spray paint all over the Italian masterpieces. Señor Testa says the ones that were damaged were the most valuable in the collection."

"Who is Señor Testa?"

"Lorenzo Testa. He's the curator of the Italian exhibition. He's here from Rome." Espinoza checked his notes. "He demanded to speak to the senior officer in charge." Espinoza lowered his voice. "I'd like to get him out of here, frankly. He's in the way."

"Are the paintings ruined?"

Espinoza shrugged. "They're up there now, analyzing the damage. The museum director, Romero Garza, says the exhibit will have to be closed down. Señor Testa wants the paintings sent back to Italy for restoration work immediately. This is a huge loss of revenue to the museum, not to mention a loss of face. Another thing, Inspector. Assuming the vandal wasn't a real policeman, someone had to steal a uniform to pull this off. But no one has reported any missing."

"What else is on the fifth floor?" Ramirez asked.

"The European rooms. Señor Garza says they contain some extremely valuable art as well. The Dutch masterpieces alone are worth millions. But it doesn't look like anything was taken."

Ramirez shook his head. "It makes no sense. The building was empty. A thief could have stolen anything in the confusion. Why take such a risk just to damage some art?"

Espinoza shrugged. "He was making a point. It looks like a political protest."

Ramirez nodded slowly. Espinoza had already told him about the large "75" sprayed on the wall above the paintings. That number had significance: It represented what dissidents called the Black Spring of 2003, when seventy-five political dissidents were rounded up and sent to jail.

"A protest without an audience," said Ramirez. "The people in the museum never saw it, and the media will never report it."

Granma reported only Communist Party propaganda, and the television stations were government-run. They carried Brazilian soap operas, old Hollywood movies, and Chinese game shows— nothing that might frighten tourists.

Ramirez looked up at the balconies overlooking the atrium and the wide staircase that wound to the top level. The vandal was athletic, he thought. Five flights of steep marble stairs, and he'd scaled them in minutes.

"He pulled the fire alarm before he ran out the emergency exit," said Espinoza. "That triggered the second alarm. He probably mingled with the police on the sidewalk before he melted into the crowd. The technicians are upstairs dusting for prints."

"Is Apiro here?"

Espinoza shook his head. "No. He's been called to the industrial section. Some children playing on the beach found a man's body about an hour ago. It's going to be busy, Inspector. It's a full moon this weekend."

"Yes," said Ramirez wearily. "I know."

———

Inspector Ramirez and Detective Espinoza stood in front of the black-and-white monitor at the museum security desk as Carlos Hernandez played a surveillance tape for them. The head of security's neck was bright red. Ramirez guessed he was angry as well as embarrassed at being duped.

The three men watched the blurred image of the vandal running up the massive marble stairs.

"That's from one of the cameras above the reception desk," said Hernandez. "I'm afraid it's not very clear."

Ramirez stood as close to the screen as he could, hoping the grainy resolution would improve, but it didn't. "What about witnesses? Do we have a description?"

"About the only thing they agree on is that it was a man," said Espinoza. "After that, he was tall, he was short, he had a moustache, he was clean-shaven. A dozen witnesses, a dozen different opinions. No one paid attention to details. As soon as they heard the word *bomb*, they panicked. Even the security guards ran."

"Of course they did," said Ramirez. "No one quarrels with a bomb."

Hernandez rewound the tape. "He pulled the fire alarm just before four. The emergency exit alarm went off three minutes later. I was standing in the street by then. I thought it was another fire alarm."

Espinoza turned to Ramirez. "I wonder why he didn't take the elevator instead of the stairs. It would have been faster."

"Elevators aren't supposed to be used during an evacuation," said Hernandez.

Espinoza nodded. "It also means he didn't have to push any buttons. No fingerprints. That's probably why he left by the fifth floor exit. That door has a push bar. He could open it without using his hands."

"Are there any security cameras on that floor, Carlos?" asked Ramirez.

"Yes," said Hernandez, "but he sprayed them with paint. The only one he seems to have missed is an outside surveillance camera. We can look at that tape as soon as you're finished with this one."

"Are you sure there's nothing missing?"

Hernandez shook his head. "It will take days, maybe months, to inventory everything. We have almost fifty thousand pieces of art here. But so far, it doesn't look like it. There are no obviously empty spaces on the walls. And none of the display cases are broken."

"Well, let's watch this tape again to see if we missed anything."

Hernandez pushed Play.

"Hmmm," said Ramirez, leaning forward as something caught his eye. "Can you rewind that a few frames?"

Hernandez pushed another button. The policeman on the tape ran backwards down the steps and raced up them again. "Stop there, will you?" said Ramirez, pointing.

Hernandez pressed Pause. Ramirez pointed to the holster hanging from the policeman's belt. "Look, Fernando. No gun."

Espinoza leaned in to look as well. "You're right, Inspector. He wasn't armed. Definitely not a policeman."

"That flashlight on the other side of his belt? I'm guessing that's an aerosol can. People see what they expect to see. I'll bet if you ask those witnesses, they'll all say he had a gun."

Espinoza frowned. "I wonder where he got it."

It was virtually impossible to buy spray paint in Cuba. Or almost any paint for that matter. It was the reason that most buildings in Havana were a mishmash of peeling colours.

"Smuggled in, no doubt," Ramirez said. "Maybe someone going to the hip-hop festival."

Once the festival started each year, foreign graffiti artists sprayed slogans like "*¡Cuba sí!*" and pictures of Che Guevara throughout the city. The festival was underway in Alamar. The city was full of *raperos* enjoying government support: Fidel Castro had decided that rap music was the authentic voice of the revolution. "You say there's another tape as well, Carlos?"

"Yes." Hernandez took out the first tape. He replaced it and fast-forwarded the new one to the appropriate time frame.

"*Coño*," said Ramirez, impressed despite himself. "It explains how he got away so quickly. Can you replay that in slow motion?"

Hernandez nodded. They watched the policeman push through the exit, then swing by one hand from the iron railing at the top of the landing. He pirouetted gracefully through the air, the camera catching only the blur of his back before he dropped out of sight.

"You know," said Espinoza hesitantly, "that looks like Parkour."

"You know this man?" said Ramirez, surprised.

"Oh no," Espinoza said, and laughed awkwardly. "It's not a person, it's an activity. It started in France. A way for young people to show their skill at getting around the urban landscape. They climb walls with only their fingers and jump over cars, like Bruce Lee or Jackie Chan."

Ramirez tried not to smile at the reference to "young people." Espinoza was barely twenty-one.

The young detective continued. "It's part of street culture. They're called *traceurs* in France. Because they don't leave a trace."

"Then it sounds like they're aptly named." Ramirez's cell phone rang. He walked out of earshot to take the call.

"Good evening, Ricardo," said Hector Apiro. "You may have heard about the body that washed up on shore? I'm at the scene now. It looks like a drowning, but there are some things about it that are troubling. For one thing, the man was in his underwear and all the labels were cut out." Ramirez looked at the dead man, who had followed them around the museum, admiring the art on the walls. The ghost nodded and pointed to his briefs.

"For another," Apiro continued, "there is severe bruising to the face and abdomen. It could be from the rocks, but I want to do an autopsy tomorrow morning to be sure. Will you be able to attend, say at nine?"

"I may be a little late." Ramirez summarized the events at the museum. "I have to brief the minister. I tried to reach him, but he's at a government function tonight. I'm having trouble understanding the motivation for this crime, Hector. Why not steal something while he was in here all alone? Why ruin paintings?"

"It does seem strange," said Apiro. "But wasn't it Picasso who said the art world is full of criminals?"

6

A man wearing an elegant tailored suit pounced on the two detectives as soon as the elevator doors creaked open.

"Is this him?" he asked in heavily accented English, gesturing towards Ramirez, his face scored with indignation. "Are you the officer in charge? I demand to see your identification. Why would I trust any of you after what happened here this afternoon?"

Ramirez reached in his pocket and produced his badge. "My name is Inspector Ramirez. I am in charge of the Havana Major Crimes Unit of the Cuban National Revolutionary Police. And you are?"

"This is Señor Testa, Inspector," said Espinoza. "The man I mentioned. The woman over there is his assistant, Dominique Gatti. Señor Testa wanted her to be present while the technicians check for prints. He wants to make sure no further damage is done to the paintings."

"That idiot," Testa said, pointing to one of the white-overalled technicians. "He was going to put black dust on them. *Che coglione*."

Ramirez assumed it wasn't a compliment. "Fingerprint dust can be removed with a damp cloth, Señor."

"*Me ne frego*, are you crazy? Nothing can touch the surface of those paintings. They're centuries old. Extremely fragile. You're not the Havana police chief, then? Why is he not here?"

"Our unit investigates all crimes that could be considered a threat to Cuban security," said Ramirez.

Technically, Ramirez's unit was supposed to report to the police chief, General de Soto, but since Ramirez's return from Canada a few months earlier, the chain of command had been rerouted. Ramirez now reported directly to the Minister of the Interior.

The minister considered Ramirez to be not fully corrupted and therefore untrustworthy. Falsifying reports, accepting bribes, these were the pathways into the politician's inner circle. Ramirez still hoped to secure the politician's full confidence.

"I can assure you that this incident threatens *your* security," said Testa angrily. "If even one of these masterpieces can't be fully restored, the Italian government will demand an explanation. As well as full compensation."

"We trusted this gallery to safeguard our national treasures," said Testa's assistant as she joined the three men. She had a surprisingly deep voice, Ramirez noted, and muscular legs. "It will take months of painstaking work to restore them. Even then, they may never be the same. That animal sprayed enamel paint on them."

Testa put his face directly in front of Ramirez's. He waved his arms in the air and pulled back his lips. "It was hard enough to arrange to loan a collection here, given the political situation. Years of work down the drain. Whose fault, I want to know. Yours? Why weren't police guarding the exhibition? Those security guards were useless. They ran away like little girls."

"This gentleman offered to give money to the firemen to put out the fire. A hundred CUCs to each of them," Espinoza said quietly. "Shall I charge him, Inspector?"

"Charge me? What for?" Testa sputtered.

"Bribery is a crime in Cuba, Señor Testa," Ramirez responded calmly. "Regardless of the circumstances, we can't have firemen deciding which fires to put out based on who offers them money. I can appreciate how angry you are, but I'm sure you understand that a bomb threat has to be taken seriously. The good news, I suppose, is that there was no bomb. It could have been much worse."

"I doubt that our insurers, or my government, will be reassured by that fact," said Dominique Gatti. She tossed her hair. Ramirez caught a glimpse of thick gold around her neck. The dead man, who stood beside him, peered at the necklace.

"The paintings are insured?"

"Of course," said Testa. "But insurance won't begin to cover our losses if these paintings can't be restored. The premiums to fully insure such works are astronomical. And they'll be even higher after I file a copy of the police report with our insurers. You will provide us with one, of course?"

"Of course." Ramirez inclined his head, although he doubted that the Ministry of the Interior would agree to release a copy of an internal police report to a foreigner already threatening legal action. The last time they did, a tourist advisory was issued by Denmark. But even if they agreed to do so, the report would be edited to the point of being nonsensical. As a matter of official policy, red spray paint would probably no longer exist. "What are the paintings worth?"

"Who knows?" said Testa. "They're not on the market. But the Caravaggio alone, millions. Dominique can give you the details. I can't bear to look at what this monster has done."

The Italian curator stomped down the stairs.

"Nice shoes," said Espinoza.

The dead man frowned.

Five portraits of varying sizes had been sprayed with drifts of bright red paint, creating what looked like a fish with spiny fins. Although it could be a spider, Ramirez thought, turning his head sideways. Perhaps the vandal was an impressionist. The dead man shook his head sadly.

Above the paintings, as Espinoza had said, the intruder had sprayed the number 75.

In the Black Spring of 2003, on the same day that the United States invaded Iraq, Fidel Castro ordered the arrest of the seventy-five dissidents. They were accused of receiving money from the head of the U.S. Special Interests Section in Cuba as paid agents. Most were still in jail. Their wives had formed a group called the Ladies in White, and every Sunday they marched in protest. The Americans had displayed a huge billboard with the number 75 in the parking lot of the Swiss embassy, where their Special Interests Section was located. Castro responded with billboards depicting George Bush as a vampire and a Nazi. It could well be political, thought Ramirez.

"This whole thing reminds me of *Guernica*," said Gatti.

"Guernica?" said Ramirez.

"It's a painting by Picasso. The most famous anti-war painting in the world. It depicts the bombing of a village in the Basque region of Spain by German warplanes during the Spanish Civil War. It was in the Museum of Modern Art in New York in the 1970s when someone sprayed it with red paint. He was protesting President Nixon's decision to pardon a soldier involved in a Vietnam War massacre."

"Why would someone opposed to war damage an anti-war painting?" asked Ramirez.

"Who knows? It was a controversial work, as Picasso intended. During World War II, a Gestapo officer saw it and asked Picasso if he was responsible. Picasso answered, 'No, you are.' I used to think it was ironic that, after the painting was damaged, it was guarded by armed soldiers. Now I understand why they were necessary." Gatti looked at Ramirez, her brown eyes level with his. "We could have used a few of those today."

"Did the protestor paint an image like this on Picasso's mural too?" said Espinoza.

"No. But there's something like it in the mural itself. Picasso called it a *bombilla*."

"A light bulb?" said Espinoza, puzzled.

"One can interpret it in different ways. A light bulb, a bomb, an eye. It may have been Picasso's way of saying the world was watching Germany."

"Interesting." Ramirez looked more closely at the spray-painted image, but he had a hard time imagining it as any of those things. "Tell me more about these paintings, Señora. Why target them? They appear to be nothing more than portraits."

"They are extremely important works. The Tintoretto, Botticelli, and Titian in particular. Then the Caravaggio. The Sirani is not as well-regarded as the others, but that's because she was a woman. Women's art has never been valued as highly as that of men, but Sirani was the first commercial female artist in Italy. Her work is historically and culturally important. Its value is expected to go up significantly over time. This painting is priceless. It is believed to be a portrait of the woman who poisoned her. Her maid."

The dead man pointed to his throat and clutched his stomach. Ramirez found the performance a bit melodramatic, although being critical of a ghost's acting ability was like arguing with the content of a speech delivered by a dog. He turned his eyes back to Gatti.

"How much are they insured for, Señora Gatti?"

"The Titian alone for ten million U.S. dollars. Don't look so surprised, Inspector. Botticelli's *Madonna and Child* sold for seven and a half million dollars at auction last December. It was a world record.

These paintings are collectively insured for over twenty million dollars." She pointed to the four large canvases. "The Sirani, for two. But Lorenzo is right; the paintings are priceless."

Ramirez whistled. "I can understand why Señor Testa is so upset."

"Paint cures the longer it dries. We need to get these back to Rome, where we have the resources to restore them properly, as soon as possible. As you can imagine, we are now concerned for the safety of the entire collection. Next time it very well could be a bomb."

"We'll make sure the paintings are guarded until they can be returned to Italy. By soldiers with machine guns, if that makes you more comfortable." Ramirez smiled. "I promise you, no one will enter this room except my men and our technicians. How long will you be in Havana?"

"Only until we can arrange to have the paintings shipped back to Italy. We'd like to put them on a flight tomorrow."

"We'll need a little more time than that, Señora. It will take us at least a few days to conduct our investigation. Where are you and Señor Testa staying?"

"At the Hotel Nacional."

"I suggest you return there and try to relax. The hotel is a pleasant place to pass the time. I understand it has an interesting tour of the rooms where the gangsters Al Capone and Meyer Lansky slept. Although not together, of course. There is also a very nice terrace bar."

Ramirez had never been to the bar himself, although it was said to have a panoramic view of the ocean. Cubans weren't permitted on the grounds unless they worked there. "It will go more quickly if the technicians are left alone. The sooner we complete our investigation, the sooner we can release the paintings to you."

"I understand," she said, relieved. "I apologize for Lorenzo. These oil paintings are as important to him as his own children. Maybe more."

Ramirez nodded. "No need to apologize. You can assure him that we will move things forward as quickly as we can."

"We're grateful, Inspector. Caravaggio may have been a murderer, but his oils are extremely popular. There are only a hundred of them left. The international art community will be devastated if even one is lost because of this"—she searched for a word—". . . terrorist."

7

It was almost ten o'clock when Inspector Ramirez finally made his way home. He parked the blue mini-car across the street from his apartment and wandered over to the food stall on the corner. He looked up at the charcoal sky as he crossed the street. It was filled with dazzling pinpoint stars. The moon was lush, streaked with violet, rimmed with gold. It hung heavily in the night sky.

Ramirez bought a slice of pizza and a sugar-coated *churro*. He hoped the rumours that street vendors were melting condoms to look like cheese were no more than that. He chewed slowly on the hot pizza as he walked home, ignoring the dank smell of urine that rose from the gutter.

He climbed carefully up the rickety stairs of his apartment building to the second floor, demolishing the pastry and wiping the sugar from his lips with his fingers. Once inside, he threw his jacket on a wooden chair.

He picked up the phone in the kitchen and dialed his in-laws' number. He almost dreaded his wife's reaction to him calling so late.

"Ricardo, it's good to hear your voice," exclaimed Francesca. She sounded happy; he was surprised. "The telephone lines have been down all day. We were hoping you'd eventually get through."

Ramirez sighed with relief. "I tried a few times," he lied. "But no luck."

"How are you? Do you miss us yet?"

"Of course. I can't wait for you to come home. How was the journey?"

"Well, you know the trains. They were hot and slow, and needless to say we were late. But we got here."

With the exception of the *Trens Francés*, most Cuban trains had been built to transport sugar, although there were some newer ones from Russia that were only thirty or forty years old. Even those lacked air conditioning and washrooms. Even so, tickets were expensive. Cubans called the trains *casas de guano*, houses made of money.

"How was the game? Did Edel play well?"

"His team won," said Francesca. "Edel stole base three times. My father was so proud of him. It was fun, but then they always are, with all the music and the cowbells. There was a band and conga drummers this evening. People were dancing and singing in the stands. And how are things at home? Did you have to work again tonight?"

"It was quiet today, *cariño*," he lied again, having heard the note of exasperation in her question. "Nothing much going on." It was best she not know about the bomb scare or the man's body that had washed up on the beach. If all went well, the paintings would be back in Rome and the murder investigation over by the time she returned. "You're still coming home on Monday?"

"God willing. And of course, the trains. Here, Estella wants to say hello. I'll go get Edel; he's outside with his grandfather playing catch. I let the children stay up late; we were hoping you'd call."

"*Papi*," his little girl said moments later. "I miss you. Grandpa scares me a little. He keeps pinching my face and laughing."

Ramirez smiled broadly, careful not to laugh. "I miss you too, sweetheart."

"When can we come home?"

8

After a lengthy search for a bed suitable for a tall woman and a short man, Maria Vasquez had finally moved into Hector Apiro's apartment. They quickly eased into old routines: Apiro did the cooking, Maria cleaned.

Unlike in other Cuban homes, the green-tinged black-and-white television was rarely on. Instead, most evenings, before Maria went out to meet clients, Apiro retaught her chess moves she'd almost forgotten in the nine years that had passed since she'd lived with him during her treatment.

Sometimes they read to each other from Russian literature, so that Apiro could tutor Maria in the language he'd learned in Moscow and still loved. But after they shared their precious time together, Maria always went off to work, and Apiro tried not to think too much about what she was doing or who she was with. "I've discovered that sex relieves tension," Apiro told Ramirez after Maria moved in. "But love causes it."

"Now look at this," Apiro said to Maria, placing the worn chess pieces on the board carefully. "Although it's more often used as a defence, the King's Indian can also be an attack."

Apiro arranged the pieces until he was satisfied. "The Sämisch variation involves players attacking each other's kings," he explained. "What do you think?"

Maria wrinkled her forehead as she concentrated on the sequence. "It's hard to imagine that you can defeat your opponent with only a pawn, and without even a rook, until you see it."

"Rooks are powerful, but so are pawns," Apiro smiled. "You know, a rook means a crow in English. That's the only bird I know of that has learned how to use tools. Imagine!"

After that evening's chess lesson, Maria brought out a surprise. It was a chunk of dark chocolate and a bowl of thick cream she had whipped into peaks and tucked into the small refrigerator before Apiro got home.

"Maria, this is incredible," Apiro exclaimed. He hadn't tasted chocolate in years. It was as uncommon in Havana as a cell phone, a thing so rare that Cubans had nicknamed them "chocolates." There was no chocolate to be found on the black market, but even if there had been, he couldn't afford it on his monthly salary of twenty pesos.

And as for milk, except for the frozen cones at the Coppolia and other *kioskos*, it was nearly impossible to find any. Only very young children and the elderly were entitled to a few ounces in their monthly rations.

Apiro pushed away any thought of how Maria had acquired the money to purchase these delicacies. He was all too aware that, if not for Maria's earnings, they wouldn't have been able to afford the used queen-size bed that had replaced Apiro's small one.

"Please, Maria, sit. I'll get the bowls and the cutlery."

Apiro began to get up, but she pushed him back on the sofa. Her eyes sparkled with mischief. "You misunderstand how we will eat this, Hector," Maria grinned. "No bowls. No spoons. Trust me, after this, you will never want dessert any other way."

He looked at her, confused. As she unbuttoned his shirt, he was still trying to imagine what she meant. It wasn't long, however, before he figured it out.

Later on, the metal tub in the bathroom turned out to be just big enough for two people to wash each other off. Or perhaps one and a half, given his size and the contortions required.

———

While they snuggled in bed, Apiro told Maria about the vandalism at the museum. "Ricardo says there are political slogans popping up on buildings throughout the city. I have to say, Maria, that I've never really paid much attention to such things."

"No, you wouldn't," said Maria fondly. Apiro usually kept his eyes on the ground when he walked, alert for obstacles that a normal-size person might not notice, like high curbs and steep steps. She stroked his damp hair. "I've seen them too. But it's festival week; there are *raperos* everywhere. And he's right; there's a lot more graffiti."

Apiro turned his head to look at her. He marvelled at her face, at how well she'd healed after the surgery. "Are *raperos* involved with graffiti?"

"Rap and graffiti are part of the same culture, Hector," said Maria. "And 'bombing' is what graffiti artists call it when they go out tagging."

"Tagging?" Apiro suddenly felt old and out of touch.

"That's what they call the signatures they leave behind on walls and underpasses. Maybe the image the vandal left on the wall at the museum was his tag."

Apiro nodded thoughtfully. He didn't really understand rap music. He loved classical music and the opera—the original basis of his friendship with Ramirez.

The two men had been seated next to each other a decade before in the Gran Teatro during an afternoon performance of Meyerbeer's *L'Africaine*. Although strangers, they chatted at the end of the opera about whether Selika could really commit suicide by lying under a *manzanilla* tree and breathing in the toxic perfume of its leaves as she sang her operatic farewell.

"Highly unlikely," Apiro scoffed. "She might get blisters from the sap, but only if it was raining. I wouldn't recommend eating the fruit, but I doubt very much that someone could die simply by inhaling near it."

"I always thought it was the *failure* to inhale that caused death," said Ramirez. "With the possible exception of tobacco."

Apiro laughed like a creaky door. "Have you heard? Castro has quit smoking. He's decided that tobacco is a poison. One can't blame him, really, after all the times his Montecristos were poisoned by the CIA. And yet he signed hundreds of humidors full of cigars to sell at the *Habanos* festival this week."

Every year, Castro autographed humidors filled with cigars for sale at a fundraising auction attended by foreigners with deep pockets.

Ramirez smiled. "I've heard that he's hoping our enemies will bid on them."

Apiro roared with laughter. "He's said the proceeds will go to cancer research. Perhaps that will be our next major industry." The smile left his face. "These days, with the lack of supplies, we can only research the disease, but not treat it. And now we're running short of medical specialists too. Castro has exported thousands of doctors all over the world in exchange for oil." He lowered his voice. "He won't let them take their children with them, though. To make sure they'll come back."

"You're a physician?"

"A plastic surgeon. I was trained to deal primarily with those who are deformed because of congenital defect or injury. I did my post-doctoral studies in Russia. El Comandante asked me to cut my studies short, to help develop a tourist industry in cosmetic surgery."

"You know Fidel Castro personally?"

Apiro smiled. "We've met a few times, yes."

It was only when the two stood up to shake hands and say goodbye that Ramirez realized his seatmate was a dwarf. But after that, the only size that mattered was heart, and Apiro had a big one.

Apiro turned his head to look at Maria. From what Ramirez had said, the vandalism was well thought out. But then, with so much security in the museum, it had to be. "What I don't understand is how a political protest can be effective if no one sees it."

"But people did see it, Hector," said Maria. "Museum officials, the police, the Italian curator and his staff, the firemen who went to the scene. And of course, the vandal himself. Word will get around quickly."

"Poor Ricardo. It's the last thing he needs right now. He's under a lot of pressure at work."

Apiro hadn't told Maria that with his help Ramirez had blackmailed the Minister of the Interior in order to get charges laid against a priest for child abuse without political interference. From the moment Apiro and Ramirez had hatched the plot, Apiro was afraid the minister would retaliate against his friend. He hoped nothing would happen, but he could see how Ramirez's stress levels had gone up.

"I think he may be having problems at home as well," Apiro said. "Francesca packed up the children and left for a week without any warning. He says Edel has some kind of baseball tournament, but I know it caught him off-guard."

"Is there anything you can do to help?"

"I've thought about suggesting he talk to someone, perhaps a family counsellor, but I don't really know how to approach it."

Maria nodded thoughtfully. "I've only met him that one time," she said. "In your office. But I thought he seemed preoccupied. He kept looking behind me as if there was someone else in the room. He seemed almost haunted."

9

Inspector Ramirez opened his eyes slowly, letting his eyes adjust to the darkness. The phone rang again. Groaning at how much *añejo* he'd consumed, Ramirez kicked off the worn sheet and crawled out of bed. As he passed by the tiny bathroom, he reached for a thin towel and wrapped it around his waist.

After hearing the joy in his son's voice about a baseball game he couldn't attend, Ramirez had felt unbearably lonely. He'd tucked a bottle of rum from the exhibit room under his arm and driven his small car to la Moña, the site of the hip-hop festival.

The festival was one of the few public venues open to ordinary *habaneros*. The *raperos* and their followers, *moñeros*, were mostly black. Young women swayed their bodies to the sexually suggestive lyrics, holding their arms high above their heads. Ramirez enjoyed their energy more than the music, and drank too much rum. It reminded him of what life was like when he was single. He joined in the clapping and cheering at the end of the last performance. It was exhilarating and fun, but more exhausting than he'd remembered. He'd walked back to his car reluctantly, not looking forward to sleeping alone.

He stumbled to the kitchen to answer the insistent phone. He was careful to step around scattered children's shoes, and in doing so almost collided with a dead woman. The ghost leaned lazily against the wall, a black scarf tied around her neck.

Ramirez grabbed for the telephone and knocked it from its cradle. As he scrambled to pick it up, his towel fell to the ground. He retrieved the receiver and shook it gently. Luckily, nothing rattled. Relieved, he tucked the receiver between his shoulder and ear and re-wrapped the faded towel tightly around his waist. A towel he could replace, but not a telephone. The dead woman's eyes crinkled with amusement.

"Good morning, Inspector Ramirez," said Sophia, the night dispatcher. "I am sorry to wake you up, but there is a woman's body."

"I thought there might be," said Ramirez. His mouth was dry and full of grit. He swallowed and took a closer look at the apparition.

She wore high heels and an extremely low-cut top. Her short white skirt was embellished with yellow flowers. One bare-skinned leg was braced against the wall. She held a cigarette loosely in her fingers.

Ramirez tried to concentrate on the call, but it wasn't easy. He wondered where his pants were and how long it would be before he could comfortably zip them up. He pulled the towel even more tightly around his waist.

"Dr. Apiro is already at the crime scene," said Sophia. "He said to tell you it looks like the Verrier murder. From last year."

Ramirez nodded slowly. If Apiro thought the two cases looked similar, they were undoubtedly related. A serial killer in Havana? The only serial murderers Ramirez knew of worked for the government.

The dead woman held the cigarette to her lips and waited for him to light it. She'll be waiting forever, he thought. It was one of the implicit rules of the spirit world, from what he'd gleaned through his experience—no physical contact. She ran her tongue around her lips, removing bits of loose tobacco that clung to her bright red lipstick.

"Where was she found?"

"In the woods beside the Calzada de Bejucal," said Sophia. "Three kilometres north of the airport."

"I'm on my way. Get hold of Detective Espinoza, will you? Tell him I'll pick him up in half an hour."

Ramirez walked around the small apartment looking for his pants. He found them hanging on the wrought iron balcony where Francesca had left them to dry. Seeing how carefully she'd arranged them made him feel ashamed of himself for looking at another woman, even a dead one. He glanced at the ghost to let her know things would go faster if he dressed alone. She shrugged and swayed languidly back to the kitchen.

Ramirez buttoned up his shirt and snapped on his belt and shoulder holster. He unlocked the drawer to the side table that held his gun. He picked up his hat and tucked his notebook in his shirt pocket, then opened the door to the hallway.

The dead woman swiveled her hips as she meandered down the sagging stairs. Ramirez put on his hat and straightened the brim. He followed her down towards the morning light, admiring her ass.

10

Keeping track of time wasn't something Charlie Pike considered all that important. But from what he could see through the cracks in the curtains, it was still pitch black outside.

Miles O'Malley's Irish brogue boomed on the other end of the line. "I hope I didn't wake you up, Charlie."

Pike pulled the sheets aside, shaking the dream from his head. Snarling dogs fought while a fox quietly watched. He envisaged his *mishomis* frowning at the bad omens. His grandfather, a trapper, had relied on signs like these to get him through winter safely. It worked pretty well, until the waters of Manomin Bay dragged him back to the Creator.

"I'm sorry, lad," said O'Malley, "but there's another victim. She was dumped on an Indian reserve this time, way up in Northern Ontario. It's created a helluva mess."

Pike had a pretty good idea of the kind of complications that could cause. "Let me guess. The OPP won't go in to investigate."

"Ah, now, Charlie, that's why I called you," said O'Malley. "You understand these things, whereas they simply bedevil me. I'm told they can't. Not without a native police officer to accompany them."

Most Canadian police forces introduced that policy after the 1990 Oka crisis, when a Sureté du Québec officer was shot to death at a Mohawk blockade, even though ballistics later established it was police fire that killed him.

"The APF can escort them in." Pike sat up, tucking the phone between his neck and ear as he reached for a rubber band on the bedside table. "It should be their lead anyway." He pulled his long hair into a ponytail.

In 2003, the Anishnabeg Peacekeeping Force, or APF, was created. After that, the Ontario Provincial Police wouldn't enter any First Nation reserve covered by the APF funding agreement unless an APF member was with them. They were afraid of another Oka crisis, thought Pike. The First Nations wouldn't let the OPP in their territories without one either, but that was because they were afraid of the police.

"Normally, yes," O'Malley said. He sounded exasperated. "But the funding agreement expired last Friday. And now the province and the feds are fighting over who's going to pay the tab. Until they sort it out, the APF can't do anything."

Pike wasn't surprised at the political paralysis. The two levels of government—federal and provincial—always pointed fingers at each other when it came to Aboriginal peoples. Whatever the obligation, each said the other government was responsible for it. Ontario probably wanted Canada to pay up because Indians and lands reserved for them fell under federal jurisdiction. Canada would want Ontario to foot the bill because policing was supposed to be provincial.

Until things were worked out, no police officer from any federal or provincial force would enter the reserve. The government lawyers would claim that if they did, they'd be admitting liability.

"The horsemen are staying out of it," O'Malley confirmed,

referring to the Royal Canadian Mounted Police. "But the feds and Ontario are at the negotiating table. They hope to get this settled quickly."

Pike snorted. "With their track record on land claims, I guess they might be able to resolve a simple funding dispute. In a couple of decades."

O'Malley chuckled. "Well, Charlie, the long and the short of it is that we've been asked to step in for a few days to help out. Since we're a regional police force, they're hoping that will get around the political sensitivities. I want you to go up there and handle things. Adam Neville is on his way from Winnipeg."

"You said the body was found up north? Whereabouts?"

"Not far from the blockade."

Pike shifted uneasily. The only blockade he knew about in Northern Ontario was at the pulp mill near Manomin Bay. "That's a long way outside our jurisdiction."

"I know that, Charlie. But the minister thinks it could be hard to explain to the voting public why he can have dozens of OPP officers standing by twenty minutes from a crime scene without sending a single one of them onto an Indian reserve to investigate a woman's death."

"How is the First Nation going to feel about an outsider coming in?"

"Well, that's the thing, Charlie. You won't be an outsider. I spoke to the chief up there a few minutes ago. It's a man named Bill Wabigoon. He says you two know each other. That should help move this along."

Pike wasn't so sure. He looked at the tattoos on his knuckles and between his thumb and index finger. Billy Wabigoon had scratched them in with a pin and blue ink when they were in jail.

11

Celia Jones picked up the phone, keeping a wary eye on her mother. There was no door in this house an elderly woman couldn't open, no dead-bolt she couldn't turn. It was like babysitting an adult-size toddler.

"Celia, it's Miles O'Malley. How's the weather up there?"

"Hey, Miles. It's a balmy minus ten. But there's another storm on its way. How are things in Ottawa?"

"Heating up in our little corner of the world. Listen, Celia, Charlie Pike's heading to White Harbour to handle an investigation on the Manomin Bay First Nation. The OPP won't touch this one, and the RCMP won't have anything to do with it either. I'm worried about him trying to stickhandle this alone. I'm hoping you can lend a hand." He described what was going on.

"I don't know, Miles. I have some family issues to deal with. My mother isn't well." Jones lowered her voice while she explained.

"Ah, Celia, I'm so sorry. My God, you've had a lot on your plate lately. Which reminds me, Dr. Mann still wants to see you."

Jones had promised O'Malley for months that she'd speak to the departmental psychiatrist. She'd been involved in a hostage-taking in Cuba, and only a week later was threatened by a knife-wielding man in Ottawa. But she kept cancelling the appointments.

She wondered if she was afraid of what Dr. Mann would tell her. She didn't have time to deal with post-traumatic stress, not with a young child to look after. She looked at her mother, still fixated on the television. *Make that two of them.*

She grimaced. "I'll call him when I get back, I promise. I'm only here until Sunday. Alex took a week off to stay with Beatriz so I could come. But sure, tell Charlie to get hold of me if he needs anything."

"How's she doing, that little girl of yours?"

"Her colour is a lot better. The good news is they don't need to do a heart transplant. Alex says they can replace her mitral valve. But we're running into all kinds of problems with the bureaucracy. We'll work it out."

"When it comes to bureaucrats, nothing surprises me anymore. Let me know if I can do anything to help. Well, listen, Charlie won't be up there much longer than that himself, Celia. The deputy minister has assured us that, one way or the other, the OPP will take the investigation over this weekend."

"That sounds ominous," said Jones. "Have they already forgotten what happened at Ipperwash?"

The police had moved in during the dead of night during a protest at Ipperwash Provincial Park. An unarmed Aboriginal man, Dudley George, was shot by a policeman and later died. The policeman was convicted of criminal negligence.

"They're treading lightly this time, but the media is probably going to get hold of the story soon," said O'Malley. "Someone has to tell them to fuck off so Charlie can do his job. Nicely, of course."

"And you thought of me?" Jones smiled. "That would make it my favourite assignment to date."

Before she went to law school, Celia Jones was a hostage

negotiator with the RCMP. Negotiations required a certain measure of diplomacy. She'd learned the controlled aggression of lawyers as an articling student. She recalled her principal's written correspondence with another solicitor that said simply, "Fuck you. Strong letter to follow."

"You said Charlie's on his way up here now?" she asked.

"He's probably still at the airport waiting for the flight. Those planes stop at every little whistle stop on the way. It could be dinner before he gets there."

"My parents' place is less than a kilometre from the Manomin Bay First Nation. I drive by OPP vans at the blockade every time I go into town. They're parked at the side of the highway, monitoring the traffic."

"I knew you were close; that's why I called. Keep an eye on things, will you? There are a lot of politicians at Queens Park hoping like hell this doesn't blow up."

"Why the sudden interest?" Jones asked. "They didn't care much about these victims before."

Oh sure, she thought, the Ministry of Public Safety had created a cross-jurisdictional task force, but the Highway Strangler Task Force was grossly under-resourced. Charlie Pike didn't even get all the case files he needed until a group of national Aboriginal organizations held a press conference accusing the task force of racism. First Nations were quickly discovering that reporters trumped lawyers and were a whole lot less expensive.

"Ah, Celia. I forgot to tell you. This victim is white."

Oh crap, thought Jones, as she hung up the phone. It was going to be a political nightmare. If the Ontario government provided more investigative resources to the task force than it had in the past, First Nations would say it was because of the victim's race. If it didn't, the government would be criticized for being indifferent to a serial killer who targeted Aboriginal women. The Ministry of Public Safety wanted a scapegoat, not an investigator.

BFI, she thought, as she walked back to the living room to make sure her mother was all right. That's what the RCMP used to call them whenever a call came in involving an Aboriginal person: Big Fucking Indian.

But the racial slur could just as easily be turned into Blame the Fucking Indian. And that would be Charlie Pike.

12

The air was already muggy outside as the morning sun began its slow creep over the ruins of Vedado. Inspector Ramirez passed a tractor-trailer hauling a container, with barred windows, stuffed full of tired passengers on their way to work.

He pulled his car in front of the three-storey stone building where Fernando Espinoza lived with his parents. He was careful to avoid parking too close to the sidewalk in case any chunks of stone fell from the crumbling exterior.

Espinoza bounded out the front door, oblivious to danger. Despite the time of day, he was as alert as a ground squirrel. Almost too chipper, thought Ramirez, stifling a yawn. There was a reason why ground squirrels were extinct on the island.

The young detective handed Ramirez a battered metal thermos as he climbed into the passenger side. "*Hola*, Inspector. Here, fresh coffee. My mother made enough for both of us."

"That was kind of her." Ramirez balanced the thermos on his knee as he pulled away from the curb. A yawn finally escaped him. "Thank her for me, will you?"

"She values our work. She says she feels safer at night knowing we're here."

"I wish she felt a little safer during the day. My wife finally ran out of patience with me working so many late hours. She took the children home to her parents."

"She left you?" Espinoza sounded shocked.

"Only for a few days." Ramirez said. "There's a boys' baseball tournament in Santa Clara. Edel is playing shortstop. They'll be back on Monday, around dinnertime, if the trains run on time."

All Cubans were entitled by law to one government-paid holiday. Since they couldn't easily leave the country legally, that meant visiting another part of it. It was like getting new underwear, thought Ramirez, and discovering you had received your neighbour's used ones.

"You never know," said Espinoza. "Miracles can happen. At least you *have* a wife." Espinoza was looking for one himself. "Sleeping in the same room as my mother and father doesn't make romance easy, trust me."

"It probably doesn't do much for theirs either." Ramirez chuckled. He turned the small car down Airport Road. Several new billboards had appeared overnight, including one that announced, TO DIE FOR MY COUNTRY IS TO LIVE! The dead woman shook her head in the side-view mirror as if to disagree.

President George Bush grinned maniacally on another poster. Trails of blood ran from the corners of his lips. EL ASESINO was the caption, the letter L formed by a black gun.

The angry words would never be seen by most Americans. It was illegal for *americanos* to travel to Cuba from the United States without a special licence. The war against capitalism had become a childish one, thought Ramirez.

"Don't be too anxious, Fernando. You have to make sure you find the right person. You don't want to take chances, believe me. Otherwise, you could end up living with someone you don't like. At least you get along well with your parents."

Seventy percent of Cuban marriages ended in divorce, but half of all divorced couples were forced to live together anyway because of the housing shortages.

They drove past a *camello*. It was on its way in from the countryside, spewing clouds of black exhaust. The buses were made of old bus parts, wagons, and recycled train compartments welded together, the centre portion raised in a hump. They were hot and uncomfortable, and crammed with hundreds of passengers.

Ramirez looked in his side-view mirror at the dead woman. The glass was stained with rust, discoloured from salt air. His cracked rearview mirror had disappeared a week or two earlier, no doubt recycled by the same thief who had discovered that Ramirez's car doors no longer locked. It was almost easier to travel to China than to find a replacement part for a Chinese car.

Degrees of impossibility, thought Ramirez. Like the dead woman sitting in the back seat, looking out the window, and the dead man he'd found in the washroom admiring himself. They were impossible too. And yet they seemed so real.

The dead woman tapped a cigarette on a gold-coloured compact and put it in her mouth. She opened the compact and rubbed her fingers in the pressed powder. When she noticed Ramirez watching, she turned her hand slowly from front to back, making sure he saw the chalky smudges on her fingertips. She snapped the compact shut and winked at him. She pointed to the interior light and shook her head, holding her index finger to her full red lips.

"I was at a concert last night at Revolution Square," said Espinoza. "The statue of José Martí had a piece of grass stuck on its head like one of those bristle haircuts."

"Really?" Ramirez chuckled. "Someone was brave. Or very

drunk." The statue was at least seventeen metres high, and the square was always packed with tourists.

"There are rumours that a famous graffiti artist has come to Havana for the hip-hop festival. His name is Banksy. That's the kind of thing Banksy would do."

Ramirez raised his eyebrows. "There are famous graffiti artists?"

"Celebrities all over the world collect his work, Inspector. Actors, like Brad Pitt. They pay millions of dollars for it. When he paints something on the side of a building, people will pull down the walls to get at it."

"No need for that here," said Ramirez, and snorted. "A little patience and they'll come down all by themselves. What does he do that's so special?"

"Well, for one thing, he gets his art into places that no one else can. He once spray-painted graffiti inside the Vatican—an image of the Pope being patted down by riot police. Even his private parts. The Pope's, that is. And he went into the Louvre in broad daylight and hung up one of his own paintings. It was a conquistador being burned at the stake while a group of Indians watched."

"So he's a subversive," Ramirez said. "Are the rumours true? That he's in Havana?"

Espinoza shrugged. "There's no way of knowing. No one knows his real name or what he looks like."

They drove past the largest of the anti-Bush billboards. It towered over the exit leading to the Palacio de Convenciones. It was erected the previous year, in 2006, just before the convention centre hosted an international conference on terrorism that focused almost entirely on Castro's obsession, Luis Posada Carriles. A simple mathematic formula linked the caricatures of the three men it vilified: "Bush + Hitler = Posada."

The U.S. Special Interests Section had retaliated by putting up an electronic ticker tape that displayed continuous human rights messages. Over a hundred thousand pro-Castro demonstrators had been bused to the Plaza Anti-Imperialista at the end of January to protest, but the electronic ticker display continued. This week's message attacked Fidel Castro's dictatorship: "The people best suited to running the country are those driving taxis and cutting hair."

Given the number of doctors, architects, and engineers driving cabs, Ramirez thought it was probably a fair comment.

13

The same youngster who stowed Charlie Pike's baggage clambered into the pilot's seat. It made Pike uncomfortable knowing that the tiny plane would be flown by someone not much older than his battered luggage. But he was uncomfortable flying at the best of times. His father's clan—the Pikes—came from the water, not the air. Pike was Wolf Clan by his Mohawk mother. Wolves weren't supposed to fly either.

Pike had forgotten just how small the northern bush planes were. When he sat down, the top of his head brushed the ceiling, and he wasn't all that tall. He could see all the way through to the cockpit and out the front windshield to the overcast sky. There was no security door to separate the pilot and his co-pilot from the passengers. The co-pilot handed out packages of small white foam earplugs; once they got going, he explained, the engines would be noisy.

They'd land in White Harbour around six o'clock Eastern

Standard Time, five o'clock in the north. But even gaining an hour, it would be dark in Manomin Bay when Pike got there, and there were no streetlights where he was going. White Harbour was at least a half hour from the airport, and the Manomin Bay First Nation was another half hour's drive, forty-five minutes if the roads were bad.

As the small plane gained altitude, Pike looked out the narrow window beside his cramped seat. He watched a solitary Canada goose glide below them, its wings extended. It was a good thing it wasn't flying in front of them, he thought. A goose could easily take down a plane this size. Caught in the engine, it could sink a jet. Pike wondered if the bird had lost its flock, if that was why it hadn't migrated. He liked the fact that it was escorting them. The old man would consider that a good omen.

The old man wasn't Pike's real grandfather—Pike's Ojibway grandfather was dead—but Pike called him *mishomis* as a term of respect. The old man was Ojibway too, and homeless. He was dying of hepatitis but refused to go to a shelter. Most often Pike found him wrapped in thick blankets near the police station, where he shot up in the mornings. The heroin helped him deal with the pain. Pike hoped he'd be all right while he was away. O'Malley had promised to look out for him.

It was the old man who told Pike that humans had descended from animals, that each clan was a link back to creation. He told Pike stories about Nanabush, the trickster—or, as he called him, Nanabozho—and others, like Muskrat and Crow. He exchanged stories and Anishnabe legends with Pike for coffee, a sandwich, a bowl of hot soup.

Pike pulled a beaded cuff from his pocket. It was a wide bracelet woven of black, white, yellow, and red beads.

"Keep this, son," the old man said softly and pressed the bracelet into Pike's hands. "It's all I have left."

"*Miigwetch*," said Pike, accepting the gift and the responsibility that accompanied it, as the old man knew he would.

Before he left for the airport, he tracked the old man down and told him where he was going. The old man leaned back on the park bench and pulled his blankets around him. Pike knew he was tired, that even talking these days was an effort. His breath froze, suspended in the air.

"Your people are *Ginoozheg*. Fish Clan. Mine are *Anaandeg*, on my mother's side. We have big families." He laughed and patted Pike's hand. "Go back to your people, that's where you belong. Don't worry about me. It's not my time to cross the river."

As Pike stood to leave, the old man reached out and gripped his hand. "Our people think Nanabozho is a trickster. They don't like to talk about the bad things he did. Once, he tricked his daughters into marrying him. When people found out, he was so ashamed that he crawled into the mouth of a fish." The old man looked at Pike, his face creased with concern. "Some people think Nanabozho is still hiding in the water."

Charlie Pike balanced his file on his knees and reread the preliminary conclusions of the Highway Strangler Task Force. Formally, it was the Coordinated Joint Operations Task Force for Dead and Missing Aboriginal Women.

O'Malley sometimes called it the Highway "Straggler" Task Force, because it got so little done. Pike winced when he overheard one of the other members joke it was too bad it wasn't the Task Force for Dead Indian Madams, in which case they could call it TEDIUM. Pike didn't find it funny, not the joke or the attitude behind it.

The task force's mandate was to review cold files, closed files, and unsolved cases to see if there were links between the victims' deaths. But so far they'd only managed to cobble together a report on four that looked related. Five, if the latest body fit the profile. There were too many different police forces involved to reach consensus on much of anything. Pike wondered how many victims there really were. Aboriginal women had been disappearing his entire life.

Part of the problem was that few police forces had initially responded seriously to complaints from worried families that their daughters, mothers, and sisters were missing.

"These women are transients," one police spokesman said to the media. "Sex trade workers don't stay in one place for long. They move away, change their names, cut their family ties. We don't have any reason to think these women are dead. They'll turn up."

But most didn't. There were over fifty posters of missing Aboriginal women on the bulletin board in the corridor of the Rideau Regional Police Force Homicide section, more than five hundred across all of Canada that Pike knew of.

Things changed in 2002, after pig farmer Willy Pickton was charged with killing twenty-six women in British Columbia, mostly prostitutes. He told an undercover officer that he'd planned to kill fifty but got caught at forty-nine.

As public outrage mounted, police forces finally started talking about coordinating their investigations. But it was difficult. Murderers didn't stay within provincial boundaries; criminals roamed. In Ontario and Manitoba, the missing and murdered women not only fell under different jurisdictions, but in different sections of the various police forces involved. Pike found himself liaising with investigators in Unsolved Homicides, Criminal Investigations, Major Crimes, and Missing Persons, as well as with the OPP and RCMP.

It took more than five years before the various authorities could even agree on the structure of a Manitoba-Ontario Joint Operations Force. When they did, O'Malley argued it should at least have "one bejesus Indian" on it. Pike thought that the fact that *he* was the token Indian was pretty funny.

When he became police chief, O'Malley insisted that Pike apply. He said he didn't care about Charlie's past. "That's all behind you now, lad. Old history."

But it isn't, thought Pike. Not if he's making me go back.

14

Blue lights twinkled in the dawn like a string of Christmas lights. A dead body attracted swarms of bored policemen almost as quickly as it summoned flies.

At least twenty white *fianas* lined the sides of the highway. The Peugeots had been tourist rental cars before the government appropriated them to the Cuban National Revolutionary Police in the late nineties. A half dozen *caballitos* leaned sideways on rusted kickstands.

Inspector Ramirez pulled his car onto the shoulder. He and Espinoza got out, slamming the doors hard to secure them. The dead woman teetered behind the two men as they walked towards the roped-off area. She hobbled a little in the dirt, her high heels catching in the ruts.

Just inside the trees, Ramirez observed several plastic numbers stuck upright in the forest floor. Each one indicated that Hector Apiro and his technicians had found something of interest, not to mention a supply of plastic markers.

Apiro kneeled on the ground beside the body, which rested on a tarp. Ramirez and Espinoza approached the small pathologist. The ghost followed close behind. She peeked over Espinoza's shoulder and covered her eyes with her fingers.

Ramirez leaned over the rope to look at the corpse. He winced at the exposed bones, the holes that had once been eyes, a nose. The clothing was badly stained by heat and rain.

"Good morning, Ricardo," said Apiro. He stood up to greet them, brushing the dirt from his pants. "It looks like she was asphyxiated, but it isn't always possible to identify the exact cause of death in such cases. I should know more after the autopsy. I'm assuming that this case is the priority now and not the man who washed up on the beach?"

"Yes," said Ramirez. "We have no reports of missing foreigners." Until they did, or until Hector Apiro decided the man had been murdered, the dead man was technically outside the jurisdiction of Major Crimes.

Looking at the woman's ruined body, Ramirez was glad Francesca was out of town. His workload had just increased exponentially. He glanced up, half expecting to see the full moon glow in the morning sky.

"Was she raped, Dr. Apiro?" asked Espinoza.

The Cuban Penal Code had recharacterized sexual assault as "lascivious abuse." But outside the courtroom, the police called it what it was. "*Llamar al pan, pan y al vino, vino,*" was the saying. Bread is bread and wine is wine. Rape was rape.

Apiro shook his large head. "We may never know. We use a stain to look for spermatozoa, but the acid phosphate test is only presumptive. Semen degrades quickly even without all this heat; the maximum detection time is only about fourteen hours. The prostate specific antigen test is far more accurate. If we had one." Due to the heightened embargo, the shortage of equipment and forensic supplies was even worse than usual.

"The good news," said Apiro, "is that her histology card was in her purse. Not all that helpful now, is it? A bit late for organ donation. Patrol ran the name for me. Antifona Conejo. Well-known to the police, as you would say."

"Prostitution?" asked Ramirez.

"I'm afraid so."

All Cubans were legally required to carry biomedical information under the "voluntary" organ donation program. Looking at what was left of the body, Ramirez had to agree with Apiro. This woman was long past being a contributor.

Apiro handed Ramirez a plastic exhibit bag with the victim's card in it. Ramirez pulled out his cell phone and called the police switchboard. He asked to be patched through to Natasha Delgado, the only female detective on his squad. Reading from the histology card, he gave Delgado the woman's date of birth and her address.

"Pull all the files we have on her, Natasha, will you? Have Patrol take you over to her address to inform the family of her death. Make sure to ask when they last saw her and who she was with. But approach it delicately. They may not know what she did for a living."

***

"There was a cigarette butt near the remains with smudges of what appears to be red lipstick," said Apiro. "A Chinese brand. Shuang Xi. It means Double Happiness. There was a purse beside the body too. It had the usual items in it. Lipstick and a powder compact. A package of condoms. A thin wooden stick. I'm not sure what she used it for. Perhaps for manicures. I would guess she was mulata, from her complexion and hair."

Ramirez wondered how Apiro could determine the colour of her skin. The woman's head was almost black from bloating. The scarf around her neck was tied so tightly it had cut into the flesh, or what was left of it. A cloud of flies buzzed around the corpse. Apiro waved them away.

Ramirez looked at the ghost again. Her complexion seemed darker than that of a mulata, but it was difficult to see her properly in the shadows cast by the morning sun. The flowers on the blue mahoe trees were already changing from primrose to orange. By evening they'd be red, almost the same shade as the ghost's lipstick.

Prostitutes were usually black. Maria Vasquez, the woman Apiro lived with, was an exception. With her streaked blonde hair and pale complexion, she could pass for white. But she was hardly typical.

"And then there is this." The pathologist carefully untied the scarf and dangled it from his gloved hand. "Another stocking."

Ramirez looked more carefully at the ghost peering over Espinoza's shoulder. What he had first thought was a black scarf tied in a bow around her neck was a sheer nylon stocking. "Prima Verrier's killer tied a stocking around her throat too," he explained to Espinoza.

"There is another similarity, Ricardo," said Apiro. "These small round impressions in the dirt."

Ramirez stepped closer to the cordoned-off area. He squatted to look at the marks beside the plastic numbers. They were evenly spaced, about five feet apart.

Espinoza crouched beside him. "What are they?" he asked.

"I'm not sure," said Ramirez. "What do you think, Hector?"

Apiro shrugged. "At first, I thought they might be from the victim's shoes, but the heel on her shoes is wider."

"There were marks like this at the first crime scene," said Ramirez.

"Prima," said Espinoza, raising his eyebrows. "That's ironic, isn't it, if this turns out to be the second victim?"

"Yes, I suppose it is," said Ramirez, nodding slowly. *Prima*, in Latin, meant "the first."

"Is that what he used to choke her with, the nylon?"

"No." Ramirez shook his head. "He used his hands."

Ramirez glanced at the *jinetera* again. Her hand went to the stocking around her neck. She straightened the bow. "She was a beautiful woman, Señora Verrier. But not so pretty after a month in the bush, I can tell you that."

The dead *jinetera* shivered. She rubbed her arms as if she were cold.

15

While her mother napped, Celia Jones dialed the number on the medical appointment card she'd found behind a magnet on the fridge. A university switchboard operator answered. Jones asked for Maylene Kesler and was surprised to be put through to the Department of Environmental Genetics.

The receptionist managed to sound both weary and impatient at the same time. "I'm sorry, Dr. Kesler is out of town. Can I help you?"

"My name is Celia Jones. Dr. Kesler was at a clinic in White Harbour a few weeks ago. She tested my mother. She was supposed to call her back with the results. I was wondering if they're ready. Emma Jones?"

"Dr. Kesler has been in White Harbour for several days, Ms. Jones. She'll be meeting all the patients she examined in person to talk about her findings. I'm sure she'll call your mother to arrange a time to see her. She has dozens of appointments to line up."

"Is there a number where I can reach her?"

"She has a private cell phone but I'm not supposed to give out the number. She's been very busy. You're not the first person who's called here looking for her."

"Thanks," said Jones, disappointed. She was about to hang up when a thought crossed her mind. "Does Dr. Kesler specialize in Parkinson's or Alzheimer's?"

"Dr. Kesler? No. She's an expert in envirogenomics."

"Envirogenomics?"

"The effects of the environment on genes."

Jones thought for a moment. "Is there someone I can speak to about her research?"

———

Dr. Martin Strasser took the call. "I'm sorry to hear about your mother's symptoms," he said. "I'm afraid your husband's right; it doesn't sound like Parkinson's. I've been doing research into Alzheimer's for years. It's a terrible, devastating illness. But it doesn't usually affect Aboriginal people. We think there may be a protective effect of a gene or genes in the Native American population that the rest of us don't have."

"My mother isn't Aboriginal, Dr. Strasser."

"Oh, I'm sorry. I thought she was. That's the focus of Dr. Kesler's work. Indigenous populations."

"I'm confused," said Jones. "If that's the case, why test my mother?"

"I have no idea," said Strasser. "I know that she's looking into the environmental components of a number of cluster illnesses in that area, but I'm not completely familiar with the details of her research. Maybe she was testing non-Aboriginal people as a control population. But I'm afraid you'd have to ask her that yourself." There was an undertone to his words. Celia Jones got the sense that Dr. Kesler wasn't particularly well liked.

"Okay. Well, thanks for your time, Dr. Strasser. Oh, before I let you go . . ." Jones lowered her voice so her mother wouldn't overhear. "Are there any new treatments for Alzheimer's? Anything that can reverse it, or at least slow it down?"

"Not yet, I'm afraid. Although there is some new research in the United States that's quite exciting. There's a drug that balances the transport of heavy metals across cell membranes. It seems to reverse the effects of Alzheimer's in mice within days. I'm hopeful the manufacturers can get it to market eventually. And of course, that it will work as well in people as it does in rodents."

"There's nothing we can do, then, if that's what she has?"

"We find that social interaction helps. Computer games, painting. Even jigsaw puzzles. And exercise. Some studies suggest that caffeine can delay the onset of symptoms. Make sure she drinks lots of tea and coffee."

"Believe me," said Jones, frowning, "she's trying."

16

Inspector Ramirez remembered the first crime scene all too well. Prima Verrier's skeletonized remains had been discovered almost exactly a year earlier. Her killer left her body in the woods beside the Avenida San Francisco, north of the nearly abandoned Parque Lenin, not far from its Chinese-built amusement park.

The late Detective Rodriguez Sanchez was dispatched to the wrong address. He wasn't remotely amused when Patrol mistakenly delivered him to Lennon Park downtown. A bronze statue of the dead Beatle sat on a wooden park bench even though John Lennon had never visited Cuba. A distressed security guard kept replacing and removing the statue's wire eyeglasses, insisting he knew nothing about a woman's body. Sanchez, of course, being Sanchez, didn't believe him. Luckily, by the time the error was discovered, the man wasn't badly injured.

Señora Verrier was only twenty-three when she was murdered. She was studying to be an engineer at the University of Havana and worked as a prostitute to help feed her family. She'd gone out after class to meet a client and never came home. Her body was found by a cyclist riding a heavy Chinese-made bicycle, as he looked for a shortcut through the woods.

Ramirez had stood beside Apiro, horrified, while Detective Sanchez searched the tall grass for evidence.

"Are you sure it's a woman?" Ramirez asked. "I thought the skull would be smaller."

"It's a myth that men have big heads, despite their egos," the small surgeon laughed. "But the skull is actually not considered all that useful these days when it comes to determining gender. There are far too many subjective traits. The innominate bone of the pelvis is far more reliable. Of course, the fact that she's wearing a skirt, or at least what's left of one, helps."

Apiro's technicians had used shovels and trowels to excavate the site—there was no fuel for backhoes. The digging was time-consuming, perhaps the reason the killer had left his victim lying on the ground.

"When a body isn't buried, decomposition takes place quickly," Apiro explained. "There are two hundred and six bones in the adult skeleton. Many are quite small. Fingers, toes, even teeth, eventually loosen and sink into the ground. Sometimes birds and animals carry them off. That's why we need to look under the topsoil."

Along with a few small body parts, the technicians found a cigarette butt buried in the dirt. It was Sanchez who discovered the woman's purse in nearby vegetation, where it had been carried off by feral dogs. There were chew marks in the leather.

"If leather purses are good enough for dogs to eat, maybe we should start boiling them for soup," Sanchez joked. "Purses, I mean. The dogs are too thin. They would have to taste better than whatever that meat substitute is in our rations. Remember in the Special Period, when they started calling it population meat?"

"I always wondered what part of the population it came from," said Ramirez.

From the ground where he was kneeling, Apiro snorted.

Despite a meticulous ground search, that was all they'd uncovered. No blood, no hair, no fibres, no fingerprints on anything, not even the victim's. The fact that the skeleton had pink teeth pointed to strangulation, Apiro explained at the autopsy: erythrocytes, or red blood cells, had been released into Prima Verrier's dentin.

But without a forensic trail to follow, there was nowhere to go. It was Ramirez's only cold case since taking over the Major Crimes Unit.

But now there was another victim. Ramirez's adrenaline surged— he might have a second chance.

———

"How long has she been dead?" Ramirez asked Apiro.

"Given the degree of decomposition, I'd say at least two weeks. I found arthropods in the remains, which may help narrow down that time frame. There's a visiting forensic entomologist at the Centre for Legal Medicine. Dr. Yeung. I'm sure she can help us identify them."

"Arthropods?" said Ramirez.

"Blow flies," said Apiro. He brushed one from his forehead. "I found what might be beetle larvae as well, but I'm not an expert."

"What is a forensic entomologist?" Espinoza asked.

"They study the insects that colonize bodies," Apiro explained. "They work back generationally to determine a time of death based on their life cycles."

The ghost stepped away from Espinoza. She bent her index fingers, mimicking a camera. She pretended to snap several shots of the body. She stopped and shook her head sadly.

Ramirez turned to look up and down Airport Road. Traffic

was getting heavier as the sun rose. A steady stream of taxis and air-conditioned tourist buses transported *turistas* to the José Martí International Airport. Every truck that drove by had passengers squeezed in the back, some holding bicycles.

"He took a chance, didn't he?" said Espinoza. "Leaving her this close to the highway. It's busy no matter what time of day."

Ramirez nodded.

"I have one question for both of you," the small pathologist said, straightening one of his short legs painfully as he stood up. "Where did he get the nylons?"

It was a good question, thought Ramirez, one so obvious he hadn't thought of it. But Hector Apiro lived with a prostitute. He was probably more conscious of the shortage of women's hosiery than any detective.

If Francesca was right, there were no nylons to be found in Havana, except in shops that catered to tourists at prices few Cubans could afford.

Ramirez looked at the dead woman. She bent her leg and posed for him, displaying her bare skin again. She wasn't wearing nylons when she was murdered, he thought. Apiro was right. They needed to know where the hosiery came from.

Apiro pulled the stocking over his gloved hand to reveal a narrow black seam at the back. "I don't think these are all that common anymore, are they?"

"I haven't seen one in years," Ramirez said. He remembered stockings like this in old pin-up pictures and calendars. Shapely women wearing garter belts, leaning against the hoods of Chevrolets, back when the Chevys were new. The cars were still being driven, fifty years later, but the pin-up girls were in their seventies.

"Where's the other one?" asked Espinoza.

"Let's hope it's not tied around another victim's throat," said Ramirez. "Fernando, when we get back to town, I want you to sign out a police car. Check the stores in the tourist hotels and malls and see if any of them sell stockings like these. It shouldn't take long. There aren't many places left that carry women's clothing."

Espinoza nodded. "I'll try the Avenida. And the Plaza de Carlos Tercero and the Galerías de Paseo in Vedado." The Avenida de Italia on San Lázaro had once been a centre for fine apparel. But the stores no longer carried much stock.

"Good idea," said Ramirez. "This woman is in the system. Get a copy of her photograph to take with you." He hoped the photocopier hadn't run out of toner. "The sales clerks may remember seeing her with a client. We need to question the *jineteras* who work in the areas where she was arrested before. They may know something. This nylon had to come from somewhere. Let's hope it wasn't a gift from her elderly grandmother."

17

Inspector Ramirez dropped Fernando Espinoza off at police head-quarters and drove to the Plaza de la Revolución to brief the Minister of the Interior.

The dead man sat in the back seat looking out the window. Every now and then he turned his head to follow an attractive woman with his eyes, rounding his lips, making a soundless whistle.

Ramirez had to agree. As much as he loved his wife, he was acutely aware of how many beautiful women there were in Havana. The young ones were dressed in tight, skimpy clothes and low-cut tops, but even the older ones showed off their legs. He could see them laughing and flirting and gesturing with their hands as they gossiped and haggled with street vendors. There was no doubt about it, as even the ghost in the back seat of his car could see, they were full of life.

Ramirez pulled into the plaza and parked his small blue car beside a row of ministry sedans, easily identified by their olive-green licence plates. He walked up the wide concrete path into the imposing complex that housed the Ministry of the Interior. Its exterior had a huge steel outline of Che Guevara's head, a gift from the French government.

A stray dog, head down, its skin ravaged with mange, panted lightly on the sidewalk. It was completely indifferent to passersby, even one who stopped to place the remnants of a sandwich beside it on the ground.

Followed closely by the dead man, Ramirez walked down the hallway to the minister's office, past the familiar black-and-white photograph of Padre Rey Callendes in the Sierra Mountains ministering to the doomed supporters of President Batista. Callendes had collected and distributed child pornography. His crimes had provided Ramirez with a political advantage, one he planned to use as long as he could get away with it.

"I need to see the minister," he told the minister's clerk. "It's important."

"Do you have an appointment?" she said crisply, knowing he didn't. "The Major Crimes Unit is supposed to report to General de Soto."

She emphasized the word *General*. It was one thing for the minister to contact Ramirez whenever he chose; another for the inspector to appear at his door uninvited.

Ramirez smiled. "I'll wait."

He sat in a worn chair and picked up a copy of *Granma*. He rarely read it; the contents of the Communist Party newspaper were always the same. It focused on Cuba's great progress despite the embargo and bemoaned the moral depravity of the rest of the world. Today, however, two stories caught his eye.

Twenty-six American CIA agents were about to be tried in Italy for kidnapping and torturing a Muslim cleric in 2003. The ringleader, Seldon Lady, was Honduran-born and linked to Luis Posada. The trial was proceeding *in absentia*. Lady was believed to be somewhere in Central America, working with the CIA on files involving Cuba.

The second article described the use of waterboarding as an interrogation technique at Guantánamo Bay. The American vice-president, Dick Cheney, was quoted as saying its use on prisoners was a "no-brainer." The story repeated Fidel Castro's protests that the American detention camp at Guantánamo Bay was illegal and that the Americans had no right to torture enemy combatants on Cuban soil in violation of international law.

Guantánamo Bay was a constant source of friction to Castro. It had been leased to the Americans in 1903, but after the revolution Castro refused to cash the rent cheques; he claimed the lease was obtained under duress. The Americans insisted Guantánamo Bay was their sovereign territory and American soil. The uncashed cheques were said to be stuffed in Castro's desk drawer.

Before Ramirez had a chance to finish reading the article, the clerk waved him into the minister's office. She looked surprised, wary of his new-found power.

"Come in, come in, Inspector Ramirez," said the minister. He seemed nervous. Ramirez wondered if the politician was like that normally or whether Ramirez was having that effect on him.

After Detective Rodriguez Sanchez's death, Ramirez had recovered an encrypted distribution list for child pornography from his laptop computer. Natasha Delgado was working her way through the aliases. But Ramirez believed that at least one of the names belonged to the man seated behind the polished mahogany desk.

The minister couldn't be sure exactly how much Ramirez knew, and that uncertainty had introduced new vigour into their relationship. The politician no longer saw Ramirez as a mere vegetable in the political food chain, but as a top-line predator.

Blackmail had its privileges, thought Ramirez. It equalized relationships in a way Marxism had never quite achieved.

"You're lucky I could see you," the minister said. "I'm extremely busy. Our delegates are in Geneva this week, attacking the Americans for the immunity they've given Luis Posada and all the other anti-Cuba terrorists they shelter."

It was widely believed that Posada, a CIA operative, was behind the 1976 bombing of a Cuban plane. He was charged in Venezuela but acquitted after intense pressure by the United States. A new trial was ordered, but before it could be held Posada escaped to El Salvador, where he allegedly built another network as well as more deadly bombs. He really shouldn't have gone to all the trouble, thought Ramirez. These days Cuba's buildings collapsed by themselves. No bombs required.

"This won't take long," said Ramirez. He described the incident at the museum.

The minister frowned. "I'm surprised I haven't heard screams from the Italian embassy. Is there anything to link this to Luis Posada?"

"I don't think so."

"That's a relief," said the minister. "I think Castro would shut down tourism altogether if he thought Posada's men were on the island."

The previous November, one of Posada's supporters in Miami was found with machine guns and explosives. Rumours had quickly spread that there could be another Bay of Pigs invasion, supported by CIA agents operating out of Guantánamo Bay.

The minister removed a cigar from the humidor on the large polished desk. "Too bad the vandal didn't spray the abstracts; perhaps no one would have noticed. Have you made any progress in finding out who's responsible?"

"Not yet. But we're extremely shorthanded at the moment with Detective Sanchez gone. Detective Espinoza is good but lacks experience." Ramirez told the politician about the woman's body and his certainty that it was related to the Prima Verrier murder.

"How can there be a serial killer murdering prostitutes?" said the minister, wrinkling his forehead. "We haven't had prostitution for years, not since the crackdown."

Ramirez raised his eyebrows.

"Don't be so literal, Ramirez," said the minister. "You know what I mean. El Comandante will never acknowledge a problem that doesn't exist. It's like AIDS. We don't have any here either. He's very proud of that fact."

"Yes," said Ramirez, "but I hope he realizes that's why so many tourists come to Cuba in the first place."

The minister frowned again, tapping his fingers on the top of his desk.

Fidel Castro had initially encouraged prostitution. He even invited Hugh Hefner to the island for a *Playboy* photo shoot called "The Girls of Cuba." But when the Special Period turned out to be the normal course of affairs, Castro decided that *jineteras* posed a capitalist threat. He called them *peligrosas*—dangerous—and said they were too aggressive towards foreigners.

Thousands of women were loaded onto buses and sent to rehabilitation camps where the Federation of Cuban Women attempted to deter them from further sexual misconduct by making them muck out barns and pluck chickens. Ramirez sometimes wondered how *turistas* would react if they knew how much of the meat in tourist restaurants was prepared by prostitutes.

The minister narrowed his eyes. He sat down heavily in his worn leather chair. "What do you want?"

"I need at least one more person to help me investigate these crimes properly."

The minister chewed on the end of his cigar. He was back in his comfort zone, wheeling and dealing.

"I can't give you another detective, Ramirez. There's no money left in your budget. Besides, we have other priorities at the moment. Luis Posada's trial is about to begin in the United States. The last thing on Castro's mind right now are *jineteras*." The politician snorted. "The Americans insist on sticking a fork in his eye with that stupid ticker display at the Swiss embassy. Billboards. That's where El Comandante's mind is these days. He wants Posada convicted."

The minister waved his cigar in the air. "And now the Americans have the *cojones* to insult Castro's leadership. With all this going on, do you really think he cares about a few dead *jineteras*?"

"The *turistas* will notice if their girlfriends start disappearing," said Ramirez. "They'll ask questions. This could hit the foreign media." Although the complication for the minister wasn't when *jineteras* disappeared, Ramirez realized. It was when they showed up.

The minister looked at Ramirez for a moment. Then he smiled. That unexpected smile made Ramirez extremely uncomfortable.

"I'll give you Manuel Flores for a few days. He's working at the Centre for Legal Medicine this month, advising us on issues related to the Posada charges."

"Manuel Flores?" said Ramirez. "I thought he was dead."

18

The **jinetera's remains were laid out** on the metal gurney that Hector Apiro used for autopsies. *Remains* was the only word that accurately described what was left of Antifona Conejo.

Apiro and his technicians had removed the woman's clothing. There was no sign of her ghost inside the morgue. Like the other apparitions who visited Ramirez from time to time, it seemed she wanted nothing to do with her further dismantling.

Ramirez slipped into the white overalls visitors were required to wear in Apiro's work space. Opera music played quietly in the background, Carmen taunting Don José, saying if he really loved her, he would go with her to the mountains.

Ramirez looked up quizzically at the fluorescent lights overhead. "¿*Alumbrón?*"

Alumbrón was slang for the unexpected: light. Although the shortages had improved since the "energy revolution," when Cuban youth were sent by the government throughout the country to replace light bulbs with energy-efficient ones, Cubans still expected that on most days they would lose power.

"Yes," said Apiro, grinning. "Not just the lights but the refrigeration units too. They've been running all day. I have to keep pinching myself."

Ramirez told his friend about his meeting with the minister.

"Interesting that he's loaned you Dr. Flores," Apiro said thoughtfully. "Do you trust him?"

"I'm not sure," said Ramirez. "When I worked with him, I sometimes wondered if he was simply very good at predisposing people to believe whatever he told them. He told me he'd studied with an American psychiatrist who developed a profile of the Mad Bomber of New York, right down to his double-breasted suit. I was impressed until I realized it was like predicting a man having a beard during the revolution."

Apiro chuckled. "I think he probably looks for things so obvious that others don't pay much attention to them. Personally, I have a problem with psychiatry in general. I spent far too many years in the Soviet Union watching dissidents diagnosed as 'sluggish' schizophrenics and sent off to rehabilitation camps. The psychiatrists deemed that anyone who didn't support Communism was mentally ill."

"Why did they call them 'sluggish' schizophrenics?"

Apiro shrugged his shoulders. "Because there was nothing wrong with them. They said they suffered from 'delusions of reform.' It's all too easy to characterize someone as mentally ill for political reasons." Apiro looked at his friend sadly. "It's apparently the definition of insanity now to hang a flag the wrong way."

One of Apiro's medical colleagues, Oscar Biscet, had been sentenced to three years in jail for hanging the Cuban flag upside down. A month after his release, he was rearrested and accused of being a CIA operative, one of the seventy-five dissidents jailed in the crackdown. Then Fidel Castro called him a "crazy little man." That designation earned the physician an additional twenty-five years in isolation.

Apiro shook his head, disgusted. "The irony is that Oscar would be better off in a mental institution like Mazorra. They play music in the garden whenever foreign doctors visit. At least he'd be able to interact with other people occasionally."

At Mazorra, there was a ward set up for foreign visitors. It was like the washrooms constructed at the Terezin concentration camp outside Prague for the International Red Cross to view during World War II, thought Ramirez. They held rows of gleaming sinks and showers but had no plumbing.

"Maybe so," said Ramirez. "But they'd all be crazy."

"I doubt it," Apiro said. "The government only puts the sane ones in institutions." He shook his head. "I'd be careful around Dr. Flores, Ricardo. He has friends in high places."

Manuel Flores had fought beside Che Guevara at Sierra Maestra. After the revolution, he headed the Centre for Legal Medicine. That's where Ramirez first met him, in 1997, during the investigation that year into the Havana hotel bombings. The first bomb had exploded in Havana in April at the Hotel Ambos Mundos. Others went off minutes later at the Sevilla and the Plaza. A second attack struck the Meliá Cohiba four months later. In the third wave of explosions in September, an Italian tourist was blown to pieces at the Copacabana; three others were badly injured.

The last Ramirez had heard, Flores had returned to the United States to seek medical care for an aggressive form of cancer. His wife had died years before. Ramirez recalled him mentioning a daughter who had left Havana to find work. He wondered what it was that brought Flores back.

Hector Apiro began, as always, by moving his three-rung stepladder around the body as he performed a visual examination. He stopped occasionally to take pictures. "I would take more," he apologized, "but I'm almost out of film."

"There's none in the exhibit room?"

"Not at the moment."

Ramirez shook his head. When supplies ran low, the police exhibit room acted as an unofficial warehouse for the Major Crimes Unit. But thanks to the Internet, tourists were becoming more aware of the installations they weren't permitted to photograph. Fewer took pictures of the airport or the police station, and with Fidel Castro hospitalized while recovering from a mysterious illness, there were no opportunities to confiscate cameras from tourists trying to capture his image either. The fact that more tourists were using digital cameras made pilfering film even harder.

Ramirez wished Sanchez were still alive. Remembering his friend, he felt a sharp pang of loss. Sanchez would have decided that something innocuous was illegal, like snapping pictures of mariposas, the national flower, and the shortage would have been temporarily resolved.

"Put this on the counter for me, will you?" Apiro handed Ramirez the camera. "Well, let's see what we have here." He positioned himself on the top rung of his stepladder and leaned over the body. "She appears to be a normally developed female."

She was actually rather well-developed, thought Ramirez, thinking of the dead woman who waited for him in the hallway. Although the corpse no longer looked much like her, or any other woman for that matter.

Apiro pulled off his latex gloves, climbed down, and moved the stepladder to the front of the gurney. He climbed up again, put the gloves back on, and lifted the corpse's head. He turned it towards him, examining it carefully.

"Look how symmetrical her cheekbones are, her ears," Apiro said. "That's extremely rare. Most of us are somewhat lopsided. Me more than anyone." He let out his staccato laugh, making the sound of a small jackhammer.

Ramirez couldn't see exactly what appealed to his small colleague about the dead woman's features. But he had to admit, her ghost was striking.

"She had pierced ears. Silver earrings." Apiro removed them. "Gloves, Ricardo?"

"Sorry." Ramirez retrieved a pair of thin latex gloves and a plastic exhibit bag from the steel counter. He slipped on the gloves and Apiro passed him the earrings. Ramirez looked at them before he placed them in the bag. He initialled and dated the bag and returned it to the counter.

"You know, the way she was lying there in the woods, with her arms folded across her chest, she reminded me of the woman in the Russian children's story," said Apiro. "The one poisoned with a *manzana*." An apple. "The dead princess. You know the one I mean. Pushkin wrote a poem about it. He stole the idea from the Grimm brothers, but it came from a Russian folktale."

Ramirez nodded. Estella had the storybook, a gift from Ramirez's mother to help his little girl learn English. "Of course. *Blancanieves*." *Snow White.*

"It has a peculiar plot, doesn't it?" Apiro reached up to adjust the gooseneck lamp. It had a longer than usual neck to compensate for his size. "Snow White was already dead when she was kissed by her prince. Most cultures would consider that necrophilia." Apiro laughed. He looked closely at the woman's neck. "The mark from the ligature runs horizontally, crossing the anterior midline of the neck just below the laryngeal prominence. The skin of the anterior neck shows petechial hemorrhaging."

He pulled the corpse's mouth open and ran his gloved finger around the teeth. He lowered the lamp, shining its light into the cavity. "Petechiae are present also in the mucosa of the lips and mouth.

No injuries to her teeth or gums. Nothing obstructing her throat. She didn't choke on any apples."

"Then I guess her prince won't be coming."

"I don't think he'd want to kiss her this time." The pathologist pretended to shudder. He stepped down and picked up a small electric saw from the counter. He plugged in the cord and clambered up the stepladder again. "Isn't she the one who lives with all those dwarves? They aren't in the Russian version."

"Yes," said Ramirez. "Seven of them. Grumpy, Bashful, Dopey . . . I can't remember all their names."

Apiro raised a thick eyebrow. "Hardly flattering."

He carved a line around the top of the skull. As he did, the lights in the room went out. He climbed down again and walked across the room, exchanged the saw for a scalpel, and returned to his original position.

"If you could turn on your cell phone, Ricardo, and hold it up over the body, I'll be able to see what I'm doing. You'd be surprised how many times we have to do this during operations on live patients."

Apiro had worked full-time as a plastic surgeon before he started doing autopsies for the Major Crimes Unit. For a while, he gave up surgery for a living altogether. But now that Maria Vasquez had moved in with him, Apiro was seeing private patients again. His salary without doing so was not enough to support himself, much less a live-in girlfriend, and a large one at that, thought Ramirez.

Ramirez held up his phone. As the faint blue light illuminated the woman's body, Apiro removed the top and back of the skull and then the brain.

"The Grimms' story that always terrified me was Rumpelstiltskin," Apiro said. Ramirez knew the pathologist was trying to distract him. Ramirez always found it hard to keep his stomach contents down when Apiro was examining a brain. "He offered to pay a woman gold to have his child and ended up robbed of his money *and* his progeny. He jumped out a window and was burned to death in a frying pan. I used to toss and turn at night at the orphanage, worried I'd end up deep-fried if I even thought about having children."

Ramirez wondered if Apiro wanted a family. They had never talked about it. As far as Ramirez knew there was no biological reason to prevent it.

Apiro had soldiered through life stoically, despite the enormous obstacles he faced daily. But he might not want to take the chance on having a child like himself, exposing a child to the ridicule, the taunts. And, of course, Maria Vasquez could never have children.

The lights flickered on again. Ramirez put his cell phone away, swallowing hard as Apiro held the brain gently and turned it towards the fluorescent glare.

"It was Rapunzel for me," said Ramirez. "My mother told me she was really Santa Barbara and that it wasn't her hair they cut off, but her head. Every time I went to church with my father, I was afraid I'd be decapitated for being Catholic."

"Rapunzel was pregnant in the original Grimms' story, you know, although you won't see that in the children's edition." Apiro stepped off his ladder and put the brain on a scale on the counter to weigh it. "Frankly, it's the idea of heaven that I find offensive. The chief of the Taino Indians told the Spaniards when they first arrived here that he'd rather burn at the stake than go to heaven if it was full of Christians. I don't blame him. The whole notion that the dead might be wandering around above us in the clouds somewhere watching us, is silly."

But Ramirez could easily imagine the dead woman wandering around his apartment, watching him. Disrobing. Lying down. Parting her legs for him. He would enter her smoothly, the way a silk scarf slipped to the floor.

The deadly sin of lust would only be exceeded by that of murder, if Francesca found out he had strayed, even if only in his thoughts.

––––––––

Hector Apiro walked back to his stepladder, holding his scalpel. He leveraged himself against the side of the gurney and grimaced with effort as he sliced a straight line down the woman's chest.

"See here, Ricardo, these are the strap muscles." Apiro pointed a gloved finger. "Just above them is a little bone in the throat that's shaped like a horseshoe. That's the hyoid bone; it's superior to the thyroid cartilage. It appears to be fractured. That suggests manual compression. The cricoid cartilage is fractured as well, and there is froth in the trachea and bronchi. She was strangled."

"How much force does that take?"

"Surprisingly little. Ten pounds of pressure is sufficient to obstruct the carotid arteries. A woman could do it. For that matter, so could a child."

Ramirez removed a cigar from his jacket pocket. The pungent smell of the badly decomposed body was getting worse.

"Good idea." Apiro smiled. Smoke helped mask the odour.

The lights flickered again as Apiro climbed down and walked to the counter, the autopsy completed. He removed his gloves and set them aside for resterilization, then returned to his stepladder and sat on the second rung. Ramirez pulled over a wooden stool. It was his way of accommodating Apiro's small stature. It allowed the two men to speak face-to-face, as equals.

Apiro rooted around in his pockets for his pipe. When he found it, Ramirez lit a match. The pathologist leaned forward, holding the bowl of the pipe in his slender fingers. He drew on the pipe until the embers glowed.

"This man is callous," Ramirez said to Apiro. "He treats these women as disposable. He left them lying on the side of the road, like trash."

"I would guess he doesn't see them as people anymore," said Apiro. "He probably sees them as a means to a particular end. And by 'end,' I mean whatever it is that he thinks he needs. You just have to look at the atrocities of the past to know how easy it is to dehumanize any group of people. Look at the Jews in World War II. It's always bothered me how quickly the Germans went along with the notion of Aryan superiority. I just have to think of all the dwarves Josef Mengele had killed and boiled so he could put their bones in their museum."

"Mengele did that?" Ramirez said.

Apiro smiled sadly. "He collected dwarves for his medical experiments too. There was a family of seven dwarves at Auschwitz: the Ovitzes. They were lucky, I suppose. They survived. Dr. Mengele poured boiling water in their ears, even the toddler's, to see how they'd react. He did terrible things to them, then humiliated them by making them parade nude in front of his colleagues."

Ramirez shook his head. "I'm not sure I could ever get inside the head of a man who could do something like that to people who were so vulnerable."

"Be grateful that you can't," said Apiro. "If you ever do, you'll have lost something of your humanity."

19

Charlie Pike took his time looking through the case files. The airline didn't have any movies or magazines or snacks, but that was okay with Pike—he didn't want any distractions.

The photographs of the victims sickened him. Rita Desjardins. Gloria TwoQuill. Miriam Tobias. Sally Cardinal. Each woman had a stocking knotted tightly around her neck. The bodies were posed on their backs, arms crossed in front, eyelids closed. The killer left all their belongings behind: clothing, makeup, even their purses and ID.

The only difference this time, if the body on the reserve was another victim of the Highway Strangler, was race. Maybe the strangler was changing his MO, expanding his pool of victims. That would make it harder to find him, although it was proving pretty hard already.

There was something that caught his eye when he examined the photographs of exhibits. The nylon stocking tied around Gloria

TwoQuill's neck had a square seam at the back of the heel that he hadn't noticed before. Pike made a mental note to find out if that was unusual.

He put the photographs back and rested the folder on his knees. He looked out the window and went over what O'Malley had told him about the most recent victim.

A band member—a boy playing in the woods—had discovered the woman's body that morning beside the gravel road, just off the exit from secondary highway 562, on the Manomin Bay First Nation Indian Reserve.

Pauley Oshig was fourteen years old. Pike shook his head. Not even born when Charlie Pike ran away from home.

The lab techs would be on the reserve now, processing the scene. They might have flown in from Winnipeg or Toronto, although Winnipeg was closer. Maybe they drove. Billy Wabigoon wouldn't care whether they came from Manitoba or Ontario. He wouldn't recognize either province as having authority on his reserve.

Adam Neville should be there by now. That was good. Adam would know what to look for; he'd autopsied three of the other victims.

According to O'Malley, the Manomin Bay First Nation had a bylaw officer guarding the crime scene until Pike released it. Bylaw officers were appointed by the band, but they weren't trained policemen. They handled whatever bylaws the Federal Indian Affairs Minister let the band enact under the Indian Act. Those were pretty limited. Beekeeping, garbage disposal, wild dogs.

Pike wondered if it was someone he knew. He hoped, whoever it was, that they knew enough to stay out of his way.

———

The small plane bounced once or twice on the runway. Charlie Pike unfolded himself to stand up and made his way unsteadily down the metal stairs to the tarmac, legs stiff from sitting for such a long time. He retrieved his bag from the young pilot who apparently doubled as the baggage handler.

Pike had arranged for a rental car before he left Ottawa. He was assured by the person he spoke to that an SUV would be left in the parking lot, keys tucked in the wheel well. But when he walked outside, the lot was almost empty—only two pickup trucks and a giant yellow snowplow. He checked the wheel wells of both trucks: no keys.

It was already dark out, and charcoal grey clouds were moving across the sky. Pike walked back inside the airport building. "Do you know where my rental car is?" he asked the woman behind the counter. "I don't see any SUVs out there."

"No idea, hon," she said. "We're closing up now. Maybe someone forgot? The roads are real icy today from the storm and there's another big one coming. Lots of delays. Even the plows got stuck yesterday."

Pike reached for his cell phone.

"That might not work here. No towers for miles. Sometimes they do, sometimes they don't. But there's a phone over there. Help yourself." She pointed to a wall-mounted telephone.

"Thanks," Pike said. This was going to be an old-fashioned investigation. No cell phones, no gun, maybe no car. The kind O'Malley liked.

"Geez, I'm sorry about that," the Esso station owner apologized. "I've been trying to track down a rental that didn't come back. Give me a half hour: I'll be right out with another one."

"Thanks," said Pike. He wondered if he should wait outside. The airport staff were packing up, anxious to get home before the heavy snow began to fall.

"You stay right there," the clerk said, reading his mind. "Just pull the door closed when you go. We're finished for the day. Shut off the lights when you leave, though, will you?"

Northern Ontario wasn't too worried about terrorists sneaking across the American border, thought Pike. Unlike down south, where he'd been ordered by the security guards at the Ottawa International Airport to remove his shoes. He was patted down in front of Tim Hortons by a guard who snapped on his gloves with a little too much enthusiasm for Pike's liking. Pike guessed he met the profile: long-haired, tattooed, visible minority. Even without a gun.

He'd left his Glock in his locker at the Rideau Regional Police station. He figured otherwise he'd spend so long explaining to the airport security guards why he had one that he'd miss his flight. If they didn't shoot him first. As it was, he could see the surprise on the guards' faces that someone like him—a rough-looking Indian—was a detective.

But Pike didn't blame them. He was still kind of surprised by that himself.

20

Inspector Ramirez *drove back to his* office and looked for a shady place to park. The temperature had to be over thirty, the air thick and sticky with humidity.

He walked through the iron gates and up the cracked path to the front door of the beautiful stone building that served as Havana's police headquarters. The wisteria climbing up the walls was in glorious bloom.

The dead woman stopped to admire the purple flowers. Ramirez wondered if she could smell their perfume; if she could smell his sweat.

He looked around and saw no sign of her male counterpart, but that wasn't uncommon. Ramirez's ghosts usually appeared one at a time. They were courteous and well-mannered, almost eager to please. They communicated mostly through gestures, nods, raised eyebrows, occasionally a frown. Ramirez often found their silent messages hard to decipher, with the exception of a street mime beaten to death on Calle Obispo a few weeks earlier. The busker had been a pleasure to deal with; his murderer quickly identified.

Ramirez nodded to the guard at the front reception. He strode up the stairs to the second floor and made his way down the narrow, dingy hall to the Major Crimes Unit. As soon as he sat behind his desk, Natasha Delgado knocked on his office door.

"*Hola*, Inspector," said the detective. "I went to that address on Antifona Conejo's card with Patrol, like you said. It's in Cayo Hueso. At least it used to be. But the building doesn't exist anymore. It was demolished last October. No one knows where the families went."

Cayo Hueso was an inner-city neighborhood in Central Havana. A giant slum, or *llega y pon*, it had the highest population density in the country. But after decades of neglect much of the housing in Havana was considered uninhabitable.

On a hot day like this, usually followed by thunderstorms, it wasn't unusual for several buildings to disintegrate. Most occupants were evacuated in time, with surprisingly few fatalities. Perhaps because Cubans were so cautious in old buildings, thought Ramirez. They picked their paths carefully, the way the superstitious walked around ladders and avoided touching baby's heads.

"Rita Vargas is the local block captain of the Committee for the Defence of the Revolution," Delgado said. "She says the former resident was a *yerbera* named Mama Loa." A *yerbero* was a traditional healer, a herbalist. "Señora Vargas says the police were called to the apartment a few times last fall for noise complaints. They must have been domestic arguments; I couldn't find anything in our records. There are hundreds of calls like that each month from out that way. No one wastes any paper on them.

"The only incident report I could find for Antifona Conejo," she continued, "was filed by a foot patrolman on February 14. Señora Conejo was standing in front of the Hotel Nacional at 4:15 p.m. She was joined by a foreign woman. The patrolman asked her to produce her identity card and she did. The patrolman had no way of knowing the address on it wasn't valid. Because she hadn't actually entered the premises, he let her go with a warning."

Three warnings for talking to foreigners too often and Antifona Conejo would be sent to a rehabilitation camp or deported to another province. "That's interesting," said Ramirez. "Did she register a new address?"

"I found nothing."

Ramirez nodded slowly. There probably were no official records for any of the residents forced to leave their homes. They could be anywhere.

Demand exceeded available housing. People lived wherever they could find space. Shantytowns had sprung up at the edge of the city like puffballs after heavy rains. They lacked running water and electricity, and proper sewage drains.

The last time the government had confiscated vacant spaces to assign as housing, it received over a hundred and fifty thousand applications for seven thousand units. These were eventually distributed by trade unions based on need, job performance, and bribes. A *jinetera* would never have qualified, thought Ramirez. Prostitutes and escorts weren't unionized.

"See if you can track down Mama Loa. She's our only lead."

"I'm on it, Inspector."

"Good work, Natasha. Keep me posted."

———

The dead woman leaned out the open window while Inspector Ramirez began to piece together a police report about her death. The late afternoon breeze caught her hair. For the third time in less than an hour, Ramirez adjusted his seating position, painfully conscious of her sexuality.

Hector Apiro poked his head through the doorway. "I have some preliminary results for you, Ricardo, from this morning's autopsy?"

"Please, come in, Hector, sit down."

Ramirez reached for a cigar. Apiro patted his pockets and retrieved his wooden pipe. Ramirez struck a match. He stood up and leaned over, holding it to Apiro's pipe until it caught. The ghost held her cigarette to her lips, waiting. She looked disappointed when Ramirez sat down again and lit his cigar.

The pathologist seated himself in a wooden chair on the other side of Ramirez's desk. His feet dangled above the floor like those of a child. He reached forward and handed Ramirez a piece of paper. As always, his autopsy report was neatly typed and precise. Apiro was meticulous about his work.

"The bad news first," said Apiro. "The histological card we found in the victim's purse wasn't the victim's. I checked the tissue and blood samples against the information on the card. Nothing matches."

"The card is someone else's?"

"Apparently." Apiro smiled. "Someone named Antifona Conejo."

Ramirez frowned. "Well that's a *galleta*." A slap in the face. "So we don't know our victim's real name?"

Apiro nodded. "Because of the marked decomposition of the body, I was unable to get fingerprints. But there is something the lab technicians found that's unusual. Ironic, really, given our discussion this morning. The victim's stomach contents contained the remnants of an apple. My technicians hadn't seen one in so long, it took them a while to identify. It was largely undigested, which means she died within an hour or two of eating it."

The ghost turned her head to look at Ramirez. She parted her lips, and ran her tongue around them.

"An apple?" Ramirez hadn't tasted an apple in almost five years, although he certainly remembered them. The flesh was crisp and non-acidic, the flavour more subtle than that of tropical fruit. "Where would she get one?"

"I haven't seen one on the black market for months. But the fact they're so rare might help you to trace it."

During the Special Period, the government had imposed strict rationing. Castro called it the *"opción cero,"* or zero option. Cubans called it *"nada de nada, nananina,"* meaning "zero everything." Hot dogs became "chicken dogs," then "chicken-less" dogs. Mangoes and pineapples disappeared altogether. Guava bars were made from oranges. Things had got better in the past several years. But even the black market rarely carried apples.

Nylons, apples, spray paint. Ramirez was starting to wonder if there was another black market he didn't know about. The dead woman caught Ramirez's eye and shook her head.

"I'll have Espinoza check the tourist restaurants and hotels," said Ramirez. "If the killer gave it to her, it could be a very good lead."

"Perhaps your young detective can track down the real Señora Conejo and ask her who she gave her histology card to as well."

"That could be difficult," said Ramirez. He glanced at the dead woman. She inclined her head slightly. "It seems the address on the card is no longer valid."

But Ramirez also knew they would never find Antifona Conejo alive. Whatever the identity of the corpse, the picture on the histology card matched the face of the woman who was leaning against his windowsill.

He told Apiro about the demolition of the building in Cayo Hueso. "Natasha found out that Señora Conejo was at the Hotel Nacional two weeks ago. But that doesn't help us much now that we know she isn't actually our victim."

"It's almost as if we're chasing a ghost," said Apiro, frowning. "By the way, I spoke to Dr. Yeung before I came here. She's confirmed that some of the larvae in the remains were from dermestid—skin beetles—as well as blowflies. The beetles show up in a body after most of the blowflies have abandoned it. Until this morning, I had only seen their work in museums."

"Museums?"

"Taxidermists once used blowflies to clean their carcasses."

"I hope you mean the animals they stuffed." Ramirez chuckled.

Apiro smiled, and then his expression changed to one more serious. "Once again, there was no foreign material on this woman's body. No tissue, no blood, not a single hair. I should have found something." He held the stem of his pipe thoughtfully. "Locard's theory is that every encounter results in trace evidence. A person always leaves something of themselves behind and takes something else away."

Ramirez shook his head. He was tired of dead ends. "Did Dr. Yeung say when she'll have a time of death for us?"

"She suggested you call her later today. She's fluent in English, by the way. Her Spanish isn't very good, but then my Mandarin is a little rusty. A cautionary note, Ricardo. She's an excellent scientist, highly regarded. She studied at the Guangdong Entomological Institute in Guangzhou. She works with the Centre for Forensic Studies in Shanghai. But she can be rather eccentric. I've heard she carries vials of maggots around with her so she won't miss any stages of their development."

Ramirez raised his eyebrows.

"Well, remember," the pathologist laughed, "almost every great tree starts out as some kind of nut. Oh, before I forget. The nylon stocking around our victim's neck was applied post-mortem, as it was with Prima Verrier. There was deep bruising in the soft tissues. In each case, the stocking was tied directly over those marks."

"Why would he do that?" Ramirez mused.

"They were beautiful women," said Apiro. "Perhaps he didn't want to spoil their appearance."

"But he leaves them in the open to decompose."

"Yes," the pathologist grinned. "That does tend to ruin their looks."

Ramirez smiled. The black humour helped them cope. Then he

remembered how the dead woman pretended to snap photographs at the crime scene. The killer *did* keep souvenirs, he realized. He took pictures.

The dead prostitute shook her head sadly. She retied the stocking like a bandana, covering her nose and mouth.

21

Charlie Pike sat on a red vinyl bench in the deserted airport as he waited for the rental car to arrive. A hand-lettered sign over the drinking fountain read: DON'T DRINK THE WATER. Another poster tacked on a bulletin board said: LEGION DINNER, FRIDAY NIGHT. WE'LL SUPPLY THE HOT DOGS—BRING YOUR OWN GUNS.

Pike smiled. This far north, there was no way of knowing if that was a typo or not.

A red SUV followed by a truck pulled into the parking lot and flashed its headlights. Pike shut off the light switches as the counter clerk had instructed and pulled the exit door closed. It didn't lock, but there wasn't much he could do about it. No one seemed to think there was anything thieves might want to steal from a small northern airport. If Pike had known that fifteen years ago, he and Sheldon would have cleaned the place out.

Pike settled the paperwork with the gas station owner and

accepted the keys to the car. He offered to drop the man off at the Esso station, but the man pointed to the truck and said his wife would drive him home.

Pike started up the SUV and drove away slowly, the way years on patrol had conditioned him. Speed was out of the question. The airport clerk was right: The roads were slick with black ice. You didn't know it was there until you applied your brakes and discovered there was nothing to grab on to.

On the way, he stopped at the old Tops Motel, glad he'd thought to call ahead and book a room. It was the only motel for probably a hundred miles around. It looked like the local OPP had brought in reinforcements to handle the blockade at the pulp mill. A dozen black-and-white police vehicles were parked in the lot, mostly SUVs and vans.

Polka music played in the cavernous Polynesian-themed restaurant as he walked up to the reception desk. He filled out the forms. He bought a pack of Players cigarettes and a pouch of tobacco for the elders he would likely run into.

The clerk asked him if he had a status card and Pike shook his head. Funny how he'd forgotten all about that down south. But the north was Indian Country. Whether you were a status Indian or not determined whether you paid taxes on your purchases, at least the ones you planned to use on reserve.

He climbed back into the rental car and headed west down the highway. A lot of homes along the 562 were for sale. There wasn't much industry anymore, not since the price of pulp dropped and the mills closed down. According to the news reports, the only one left was at the Wabigoon River, and now it was blocked by protesters.

Two black-and-white OPP vans were stationed near the exit from the 562. Pike was sure they were making note of every vehicle that travelled to or from the barricades.

Pike turned left at the sign to the Manomin Bay First Nation. His heart jumped a little when he pulled onto the gravel road.

———

A few hundred yards inside the reserve, a white truck was parked on the shoulder. BYLAWS was written in large letters on the driver's side door.

Charlie Pike swung his SUV around. As he pulled in behind the truck, his vehicle skidded. The all-season tires might as well be hockey skates, he thought, except it was easier to stop on those. Pike recognized the driver as soon as he climbed out of the truck. They grinned at each other.

"Good to see you, Charlie," Sheldon Waubasking said. He clasped Pike's shoulder as he pumped his hand. "Wow, been a long time. Wasn't sure they could get someone up here today, with the storm coming. Chief asked me to stay till you got here. Thought I might have to sit here all night too."

Pike wondered how Chief O'Malley had managed to get hold of Sheldon Waubasking. Then he realized Sheldon meant Bill Wabigoon.

The years hadn't changed Sheldon much. He was heavier. The thin moustache he'd tried to coax through puberty had finally filled in. But he had the same big smile as always.

A rifle leaned casually against the window on the passenger side of his truck. It surprised Pike that Sheldon had a rifle, given his youth record. But then it probably wasn't registered. First Nations peoples pretty much ignored the federal gun registry. Besides, the people up north all used rifles, not guns. The church in White Harbour wouldn't have to worry too much about anyone taking that typo too seriously.

"You here all by yourself?" Pike looked around. No vans, no cars, no technicians.

Sheldon shook his head. "Everyone was slowing down to look,

but after those guys left, no one stopped except my wife. She brought me lunch. You remember Jenny Akiwenzie? We lived together for a long time. We got married a few months ago. Went to Cuba for our honeymoon. Only place I've ever been where the housing was worse than ours." Sheldon grinned.

Pike did remember. Jenny was the slim, shy woman who used to work at the tobacco stand every summer when the tourist season began.

"So I've heard," Pike said. Ricardo Ramirez and he had turned out to have a surprising amount in common when the Cuban police inspector visited Ottawa in January and Pike escorted him around. "Congratulations, Sheldon. Any kids?"

"A boy and a girl. Seven and three. You?"

"None that I know about."

"Must be a few around," said Sheldon. "You used to be a handsome devil, you. What the heck happened?"

They both laughed. Pike's nose had been flattened a few times. Rugged, one of his kinder girlfriends had said. Definitely not handsome, although "devil" might still fit.

Pike shook his head. He pulled out the cigarettes, shook one from the pack. He offered the pack to Sheldon, who shook out another and handed it back.

"You should buy your smokes on-reserve, Charlie. It's cheaper. No taxes."

Sheldon lit a match and cupped it in his fingers. He drew on the cigarette until it caught, then held his hands out with the match inside. Pike leaned over, lit his. They stood for a moment, backs to the wind, remembering.

"How long you been working bylaws?" Pike asked.

"About a month. Not much work up this way. Doesn't pay a whole lot, but it's tax-free, that helps. I think the chief just wanted to have someone to keep an eye on things, once he heard the APF funding was going under. What with the protest and all."

"Funny seeing you in law enforcement," said Pike. But then, Sheldon was Bear Clan. Bears were meant to be warriors.

"Didn't expect you to be the cop they sent here either," said Sheldon. Pike had broken his clan's rules by joining the police. Northern Pikes were supposed to be peacekeepers and teachers, not carry guns, although Pike rarely carried his.

"You can blame O'Malley for that. He's the chief of the Rideau Regional Police Force now."

"Still bald as a peeled egg?"

Pike nodded.

"So he talked you into joining the cops, eh?" Sheldon said. "Probably the last thing in the world I thought you'd end up doing."

They looked at their feet, respectfully avoiding eye contact. Pike was sure Sheldon was remembering the alternative when they first met O'Malley. The Indian Posse.

"Where was she?" Pike asked.

"In there." Sheldon inclined his head towards the woods. "*Niiwana'w ningwa.' Onaabanad wadikwan.*" He killed her first, then buried her.

"Guess that's better than the other way around," said Pike.

"No kidding," said Sheldon, chuckling. "That's good that you still speak the language."

"Not that fluent anymore. Don't hear it much in Ottawa."

"It'll come back. You know that *vegetarian* is an Ojibway word, eh? Means 'can't hunt.'"

Pike chuckled. "O'Malley said it was a boy who found the body. Pauley Oshig?"

"Molly Oshig's son. You remember Molly, eh? Oshig's her married name. Kept it after the divorce, I guess. They split up a long time ago. She disappeared a few weeks back. Hitchhiking to Winnipeg, looking for work." Sheldon threw his cigarette on the ground and tramped it into the snow. The humour in his voice was gone.

Sheldon's high school girlfriend was the most recent of the

missing women who stared at Pike from the posters in the corridor outside his office. Their eyes pleaded with him to find their bodies. Pike hadn't known that Molly had a son. He didn't ask for details. Sheldon would tell him whatever he thought Pike should know.

"He's fourteen, but he's kind of slow," said Sheldon. "He has FAS, eh? *Aanimendam*." He suffers in the mind.

Pike nodded slowly. Children with fetal alcohol syndrome often had learning problems. "Can he write out a statement if I ask him to?"

"I don't know. Have to ask him that yourself."

"Did you caution him before you talked to him?"

Sheldon raised his eyebrows. "I didn't think he was a suspect."

Pike didn't answer. Until he knew more, everyone was a suspect. Sheldon was a bylaw officer; his jacket had shoulder flashes. A defence lawyer would say that was a uniform. He could be considered by the courts to be a person in authority if it turned out that Pauley Oshig was involved in the woman's death. If so, nothing the boy said to Sheldon could be used as evidence.

"Any chance he did this?" asked Pike.

Fetal alcohol syndrome could make kids behave aggressively, even violently. A fourteen-year-old boy was almost full grown. At fourteen, Sheldon had almost killed a man himself. Billy Wabigoon probably still had the scars.

Sheldon shook his head. "I don't think so. But he gets bullied sometimes. I seen bruises on him." He exhaled. His breath floated above them.

"He must have been scared, finding a dead body."

"I think he was more scared about getting punished by Bill for skipping school. He's a funny one, him. He told me the crows showed him where she was." Sheldon frowned. "You know, Charlie, it was the strangest thing I ever seen. There must have been a hundred of them, sitting in those big pine trees, not making a sound. Like they all got together for some kind of funeral."

22

Inspector Ramirez walked Hector Apiro out to the hallway. He returned to his office and checked with the switchboard for messages. Dominique Gatti had called; she told the operator it was important. He phoned the Hotel Nacional at once, but Señora Gatti was out. So was her boss, Lorenzo Testa. He left messages for both of them.

He riffled through Hector Apiro's report looking for clues. Nothing jumped out. The dead woman sat on one of Ramirez's wooden chairs, her long legs crossed at the ankles. She opened her compact and removed her lipstick from her purse. She looked in the tiny mirror and reapplied it carefully. She rubbed her red lips together. She snapped the compact shut and winked at him.

Where were you killed, Antifona? How can I find your killer if I don't know where your body is?

It's as if they're all invisible, thought Ramirez, as he walked to the exhibit room to get a bottle of rum. No fingerprints at the museum. No forensic evidence at any of the crime scenes, and Antifona

Conejo's corpse was still at some unknown location, waiting to be discovered. Random events, linked only by the complete lack of evidence.

He shook his head, frustrated. On his way back to his office, he found Detective Espinoza in the corridor chatting up an attractive night clerk. She excused herself when Ramirez approached them. Ramirez told the young detective about Apiro's revelation that the murdered woman wasn't Antifona Conejo after all.

"*Coño*," Espinoza swore. "What a waste of time. I wasn't getting anywhere anyway. People say they recognize her, but no one has seen her for a while. There's a rumour she was taken away to a rehabilitation camp. And now you say she's not even our victim?"

"Apparently not. And Natasha hasn't made any progress finding out where the real Antifona Conejo lived either," said Ramirez. "The occupants of the address on the histological card were evicted; there's no new address on record."

Espinoza exhaled. "All right. I'll start going through missing person reports."

"Any progress on the stockings?"

"Nothing yet," said Espinoza. "Not even the hotels carry them. Too hot, the managers say. The tourists come here to wear shorts and sandals, not to dress up."

Ramirez nodded. "Keep at it, Fernando. Something will turn up. By the way, I want to meet with Dr. Flores first thing in the morning to ask his opinion. Can you meet me out front, say at eight? Maybe you can sign out the exhibit boxes from the Prima Verrier murder. We'll need them, as well as the exhibits from this one."

"Sure. Who's Dr. Flores, Inspector?"

Ramirez realized that Espinoza was probably in elementary school when Ramirez last worked with Manuel Flores.

"A criminal profiler. The ministry is loaning him to us to help us identify our killer's characteristics, his personal traits."

Ramirez left Espinoza and returned to his office. He immersed himself in routine paperwork—mostly requisitions for supplies that might as well be ghosts themselves.

The nine o'clock cannon fired at the Fuerte de la Cabaña, closing the harbour to boat traffic, even though the American cruise ships no longer came. Ramirez looked out the window and realized he'd lost all track of time. The sun had almost set. The azure sky rippled with orange, burgundy, and pink streaks. He dialed Dr. Yeung's number and hoped he hadn't missed her. He was relieved when she answered.

"It's Inspector Ramirez, Dr. Yeung. I apologize for calling you so late."

"I was sent here to work, Inspector," said Dr. Yeung. "I am only here for a few days."

"I was calling about the insects Dr. Apiro found in our victim's remains. Do you know when your tests will be finished?"

"I should have results tomorrow, yes. The body's proximity to the airport has been helpful. Because daily temperatures are measured there, I can use meteorological data to calculate ambient temperatures."

"That's excellent," said Ramirez. "You know, Dr. Yeung, I don't know anything about forensic entomology. Can you enlighten me?"

"Don't worry, Inspector," Yeung said. "It is very reliable. It dates back to AD 1235 in China, when a farmer was hacked to death with a sickle. A lawyer named Sung Tz'u told the suspects to put all their farm tools in the sun. The one that attracted flies had blood residue on it. All our provinces and municipalities have committees of experts in entomology to assist the police in their investigations."

"How does it work?"

"There are three stages of decomposition. The first is when eggs are laid and the body is colonized by sarcosaprophagous insects. These are called *necrophages*. Dr. Apiro found blowfly larvae in the remains as well as skin beetles, which show up in the second period. The third stage is skeletonization. There are very few insects in the third stage because there is nothing left for them to feed on."

Ramirez winced.

"But in this case, decomposition was still active. The stages of colonization can be calculated quite precisely. I should be able to tell you when death occurred almost to the hour."

Ramirez could sense her excitement.

"I will call you when the time gets closer," Dr. Yeung said. "We can see the last stage together."

23

Charlie Pike looked up and down the empty road. "When did the medical examiner and the technical team leave?"

"Maybe an hour ago," said Sheldon Waubasking. "They took the body into town. There's a morgue at the new health clinic on Main Street. Well, I guess 'new' means around ten years old. Wasn't built when you lived here." He fell silent for a moment, embarrassed.

"It's okay, Sheldon. Things worked out fine."

Sheldon nodded. "I think they wanted to get out of here before the storm hits. Supposed to be a big one. That doctor, he said to tell you they don't have a tent strong enough to handle that kind of load. Said he'll meet up with you in town tomorrow at the autopsy."

"He say when that's going to be?"

"Tomorrow at two. Wanted to give you some time to get there, because of the snow."

Pike frowned. The last thing he needed was bad weather. It

would take hours for the plows to clear the roads and the SUV wouldn't drive well in drifts.

"You been here all day?"

"Day's not over yet," Sheldon said. "Since around eight thirty this morning, anyway."

Pike noticed that Sheldon wasn't wearing a watch either. That was a long time to sit around waiting, but then Sheldon had always been patient. That was why he always "stood six" at break-and-enters while Charlie went inside.

"What time did Adam Neville get here?"

"That's the doctor? Around eleven, I guess. CBC News came on the radio just after he pulled in." Sheldon anticipated Pike's next question. "Pauley went running to get Bill as soon as he found her. Bill called me right away. Took me a few minutes to get dressed, get the truck warmed up."

"Why did he go looking for Bill?" asked Pike.

"Pauley lives there," Sheldon said. He looked at the ground, uneasy. "Ever since Molly went missing. Bill's his uncle, remember? Molly's brother."

Pike nodded. "So Bill's the chief now, eh?"

"Yeah." Sheldon shifted from foot to foot, as uncomfortable, it seemed, as Pike was at the idea.

"Did he come here to take a look too?"

"No. Said he was going to phone the RCMP and Indian Affairs. He don't even talk to Ontario anymore. Says they don't have any business on our lands; all our treaties were with the Queen. He told me he'd let them send someone up as long as it wasn't the OPP. Doesn't want to screw up the APF funding negotiations by letting them think they can come into our territory whenever they like."

Indian politics. Pike shook his head. "Techs say if they're coming back?"

"No," Sheldon said. "As far as I know, they're headed for

Winnipeg. Heard them complaining when they were packing up about getting paid."

Pike wondered why they'd left so quickly. Was the evidence Adam Neville found that strong? Or was it the fear of being caught in a storm? Maybe they were afraid of being alone in the woods on an Indian reserve in the dark. If so, he couldn't blame them.

"Well, I guess I better look around." Pike walked the crime scene whenever he could. Not to get inside the killer's head; he was better at getting inside the victim's.

"I got a couple of flashlights in the truck if you need them," said Sheldon. "They ran some of that yellow tape in there, around the trees. Hard to see it now. Gets dark early these days."

"How far in the woods was she?" Pike asked.

"Just enough to be out of sight. I put down some red pylons to show what I found after they left. *Edawayi'ii.*" On both sides.

"The technicians missed something?" Pike was surprised. Neville and his team were usually pretty good.

Sheldon shrugged. "There were some footprints on the road, in the crust. You could only see them after some of the snow blew away. I took measurements when it was still light out. In case the storm got here before you did."

"You didn't tell them?"

"They told me to stay out of the way, so I waited in the truck. I walked around a little after they left. Needed to stretch out my legs."

Pike shook his head. Sheldon Waubasking had been trained as a tracker by his *mishomis*. His grandfather had been one of the best hunters and trappers in the Manomin Bay First Nation traditional territory until he died from cancer. Besides, Sheldon had been charged enough times to know the rules of evidence inside out.

Even so, Pike was impressed. This was textbook containment—

pylons, measurements. He looked at the sky. He sniffed the crisp air, smelled the cold front moving in.

———————

They walked back to the truck. Sheldon pulled two heavy black flashlights out of the glove box and handed one to Pike.

"Before we go in there, did the technicians take casts of your boots?" asked Pike. He hoped so. Otherwise, he'd have to keep his old friend well back from the yellow tape; he didn't have anything with him to make casts.

"You kidding? That guy Adam Neville, he even took my fingerprints," Sheldon said. "I told him I didn't go nowhere near that body. Said he needed them anyway. About the only thing he didn't take was my blood."

"Wanted them for elimination, I guess," Pike said. "Nothing personal."

Sheldon nodded. He'd been in and out of jail enough times that he didn't need an explanation. "Who would have thought we'd end up on this side of the law, Charlie?"

"I guess fate has a sense of humour."

———————

"All right," Pike said, looking at the dark sky, the heavy night clouds. He felt the weight of what Adam Neville was going to do to the woman's body descend over him. His grandfather would have been horrified at the idea that a dead woman would be cut into pieces, her soul permanently severed from her bones.

Wiyo was the Anishnabe word for the physical body. That was the part that slowly disappeared and returned to the earth. But *atisken*, the word for bones, meant "the souls."

Charlie Pike's people on his father's side were Ojibway, part of the Anishnabe linguistic family. Ojibway were supposed to be buried intact, in the land where they'd been born, unless they were Hare Clan. Bones of the Hare Clan had to be burned and the ashes scattered so their souls could go back to the sky where they belonged. If these things weren't done, the *udjibbom*, the second soul, would be lost, left to wander near the grave forever.

It was why the women on the posters pleaded with him, Pike thought. They wanted him to find them and bury them properly.

"Now, remember this, Charlie, animals are people too. And that goes for fish as well," his grandfather had explained when Charlie was little, as they tugged their heavy nets into the boat. Dying fish flopped helplessly inside. "You have to bury their blood and guts on shore, away from the water. You always burn a little tobacco to thank them for giving up their lives so we can eat them. If you put fish blood in the water, the fish won't come back, because you don't respect them. It's like the Hare Clan. If you bury someone from the Hare Clan in the ground, the snow comes to punish you."

Pike lifted his nose, smelled the punishment of snow. "We better get started, Sheldon," he said, "before this storm buries all of us."

Sheldon Waubasking walked in front of the truck. He pointed to tire tread marks in the snow at the side of the road.

"*Biijidaabii'iwe, ezhhishin.*" He drives here, leaves a mark. "See?" he said, taking a few steps and pointing. "There's a woman's footprint. She walked up to the driver's door and then went into the woods."

Pike took a ruler out of his satchel as well as his camera. He bent down on one knee and set the camera flash. He put the ruler next to the shoe print and snapped a few shots.

It was the best he could do. He had no sulfur prill to make a cast in the snow. Even if the techs agreed to come back, by the time they did, the shoe prints would be covered by drifting snow.

They should have asked for Sheldon's help, Pike thought. The tire marks were barely visible now, as the wind began to whip ice pellets across the road. He squatted to take a closer look.

"They must have drove here in one vehicle," said Sheldon. "There's only one set of tracks on this side of the road. Tread's not that deep. Could be all-season tires. You can see where they slipped sideways."

Only rental cars had all-season tires; everyone else used winters. Something nagged at Pike, something he should remember. "Looks like a pretty wide base. Truck or SUV? What do you think, Sheldon?"

"The only people who come into the territory driving SUVs are lawyers. Well, except for you, I guess." He smiled. "They rent them. You can't tell much from the width. Frames are pretty much the same size. But most people up this way drive trucks."

Pike agreed. You could throw a moose or deer in the back of a truck during hunting season. Couldn't do that with a car or an SUV, and not with a rental.

"By the way, do cell phones work anywhere around here?" asked Pike. "I couldn't get a signal at the airport."

"Depends where you are. Should work some of the time, anyway. Nearest tower is about fifty miles away. I have a BlackBerry if you need it. They work pretty good for emails."

Pike smiled. Manomin Bay might not have clean water, but it was the most connected hub in the world when it came to information sharing. What others called gossip.

"She was *iwidi*," said Sheldon, pointing. Over there.

They walked into the woods until Pike saw the cordoned-off area. A stack of brush was piled beside a fairly deep trench in the ground.

"I guess the killer put that over the body to hide it," said Sheldon. "Pauley said he moved it so he could get a better look at her."

Pike frowned. The technicians should have taken all the branches with them to check for fibre, hair. Lots of things snagged on twigs. That's how you tracked animals, looking for fur, not just their tracks. Depressions in the ground where they lay down. Moults.

Pike pulled a pair of latex gloves out of his satchel. He handed a second pair to Sheldon. He stood back to see if anything caught his eye. He tried to imagine how the body had been posed, what it was like before the technicians carried it away.

He looked out to the road. Sheldon was right; it would have been hard to see the body in the woods if you were driving by. The killer had dug a pretty deep hole in frozen ground. That took time.

"I think maybe he used some of those branches to sweep away his footprints. Cut them down over there." Sheldon motioned towards some pines.

Pike shone the flashlight at them. A couple of wounded trees bled sap where their limbs had been cut. He bent over to examine the grave. The edges of the hole were straight, sloped inwards.

"He stopped here for a smoke," Sheldon said. "*Nandokawe*." While he looked for his tracks. "There's a little pile of burned to-bacco and paper. They missed that too."

Pike took a pair of metal tweezers from his satchel. He squatted down and carefully picked up the tobacco and the scorched piece of cigarette paper. He put them in a plastic exhibit bag, dated and initialled it, and put it in his satchel.

The killer was relaxed enough to stop for a roll-your-own smoke, thought Pike. Maybe Sheldon was right. Maybe he was taking a break before he checked to make sure he didn't leave any evidence behind. Pike's mind flashed back to the cigarette butts at the other scenes, the loose tobacco at this one. Why the difference?

Stupid, the techs not asking for Sheldon's help. Sheldon had learned from his elders how to be quiet, how to move without mak-ing a sound. He knew how to disguise his smell, his presence, and then, when he was done, how to remove any trace that he'd been there.

It wasn't Sheldon's fault that they'd been arrested. Pike hadn't got out the window fast enough. Sheldon knew enough to back away, to not draw attention to himself. If O'Malley hadn't been walking a beat with another cop that day, Sheldon would have got away clean.

———

Pike looked at the grave carefully. That kind of planning was probably beyond an FAS kid. But it was pretty strange that in a forest filled with deadfall, Pauley had found the woman's body that easily. If he hadn't, she would have been buried in the storm, her body hidden until spring thaw.

"People still trap in these woods?" Pike asked.

"Just the old women. Nothing much in here these days except rabbits. Maybe a fox. Every now and then a big old black bear. We leave her alone, she leaves us alone."

"Find anything else, Sheldon?"

"I think maybe something happened over here." Sheldon pointed his flashlight beam at an area about six feet outside the yellow tape, where he'd set another red pylon.

No wonder the technicians missed it, Pike thought, as he shone his flashlight on the ground. He stared at the small disturbance in the ice-crusted leaves, moved the snow and leaves out of the way with his pen. There was a small groove in the snow crust. A narrow indent, the shape of a wedge.

"Not sure I would have caught that. Good eye."

Pike took more photographs, more measurements. He stood up, swept his flashlight back and forth across the ground. "Don't see much else around here except some old bear scat."

"See what's in it? Little bits of metal from those bells the white people wear to keep the bears away." Sheldon laughed.

"It's like those warning signs on the highway for moose," said Pike. "If they really want to keep moose off the road, they should put up a sign with a picture of a great big semi on it."

They both chuckled as they walked out of the forest. Sheldon picked up the red pylons along the way. He stopped to show Pike a series of small round impressions in the snow. They looked like someone had driven a tent peg into the ground repeatedly.

"That guy, Neville, he took lots of pictures of these."

"There were marks like that at one of the other crime scenes too," said Pike. "We think maybe they're stiletto heels."

The heels were sharp enough to damage hardwood floors. They would leave an indentation even on frozen ground. But they weren't the kind of shoes women would wear outside in the winter, not even a hooker.

"Funny, I didn't see any shoe prints around here from a man," Pike said. The techs had been careful to map out a corridor around the evidence.

"Snow must have covered them up. You call them shoe prints, eh?"

"Footprints means bare feet in my line of work."

"Yeah? What if you're wearing moccasins?"

Pike smiled. A few snowflakes swirled in the air as the wind started to pick up. The storm was coming, no doubt about it.

"You think the Highway Strangler killed her?" Sheldon asked.

"*Endogwen.*" I'm not sure.

Sheldon shrugged. "*Awenen gaye?*" Who else?

———

Sheldon loaded the plastic pylons in the back of his truck. Pike wiped the snow off his latex gloves and pulled them off. He put them in his satchel along with the camera and the exhibits. He leaned against the truck and tried to imagine what happened.

The woman, almost paralyzed with fear, stumbling into the woods on her impractical shoes. The killer probably walked behind, prodding her with something. What was he holding? A rifle? A knife? A gun?

He had something that scared her enough so she'd do what he wanted instead of running away. But where could she run, in the deep snow, on an Indian reserve? It was only a short distance to the nearest house on the highway, but a white woman probably wouldn't know that, unless she lived or worked nearby. Was she local? The two communities, First Nation and white, maintained an uneasy distance.

"The victim, did Pauley recognize her?"

Sheldon shook his head. "Said he never seen her before. And me, I never saw her face. They had her all zippered up in a black bag when they carried her out of there."

"Killer took his time covering things up," said Pike. "Hard to see the ground in the dark, even with a flashlight. I don't think he could do that at night."

"You think he killed her in the daytime?" said Sheldon.

Most people were surprised to learn that it was easier to hide what you were doing if you committed your crimes in broad daylight. People saw someone carrying a widescreen television down the street in the afternoon, they assumed it was the owner. It was only at night that people thought *thief*. Pike knew; he'd stolen almost everything that wasn't nailed down.

Pike nodded. "Unless he dug that pit before he killed her. The edges are pretty clean. He could have used an axe."

The thought had never occurred to him until the words came out of his mouth. An axe gave the killer a weapon *and* a tool. It explained how he cut down branches. That wedge-shaped mark on the forest floor, that was where he dropped it. Freeing his hands so he could choke her.

Just how organized was this killer? Digging a hole beforehand gave him what he needed most: time. He could have prepared the burial ground days, even weeks, earlier.

This killer was no Willy Pickton, thought Pike. This one was smart.

24

Inspector Ramirez stopped to visit his parents on his way home. He tried to drop by every few days to see how they were doing. They were getting old. He worried what would happen to his mother if his father died.

His mother, although still an American citizen, was more Cuban than most Cubans. Even so, the government might cut off her rations and kick her out of her own home. It had happened to other American-born widows. His sister, Conchita, and her husband and teenaged children lived with them. If that happened, they would all be forced to find somewhere else to live.

Ramirez tried not to think about it. There wasn't enough room in his apartment to take his family in, and yet he might have to. Francesca would not be happy, but she would accept they had no choice. This was the reality of living in Havana. Overcrowding, terrible living conditions, people struggling to get by.

"Ricky," said Conchita, opening the door. She smiled as she

peered around him. "You're alone. Is Francesca back yet? I'm guessing not. You look like you've lost weight. Come in, come in, we're
watching television. An American movie, with Tom Cruise."

"It's a silly movie," said his mother, shaking her head. She sat on
the old sofa, crocheting. "The clues are all Bible verses."

"It's good!" said Ramirez's father. "I like Tom Cruise."

"The Bible is as crazy as that Tom Cruise's Church of Scien-
tology," his mother said. "After fifty years, you'd think your father
would listen to me, Ricky. What kind of man believes in such nonsense?"

"The Bible isn't crazy," said his father.

"No, it's stupid. You know how I know it's stupid? There isn't a
single part that was written by women."

Ramirez smiled. Like Fidel Castro, his mother was raised a Catholic, but she had enthusiastically converted to atheism when official
government policy required it.

His father still believed in the church. His mother, Ramirez's
Yoruba grandmother, had followed Santería, a melding of Catholic
beliefs with the animist religion brought to Cuba by Nigerian slaves.
The Yoruba believed the dead returned, the Catholics in the resur-
rection. Ramirez's mother, a former university professor, dismissed
it all as nonsense. She said the invisible looked just the same to her
as the non-existent.

"I won't stay long," Ramirez said. He walked over to the couch
and kissed his mother on the cheek, patted his father on his shoulder. "I brought this for you." He handed his father the bottle of Havana Club he had retrieved from the exhibit room.

His father's face creased into a smile. "*Gracias*, Ricardo. We had
only a few ounces in our rations this month and those are already
gone. Imagine, living in Cuba and not having enough rum." He
shook his head sadly.

"It's the Bacardis' fault," said his mother. "If they hadn't taken
their yeast with them, we'd still have good rum."

"I think it's the quantity that's the issue, not the quality," said Conchita. "It's not really their fault their factory was nationalized."

"They could have stayed," his mother said. She was a fierce defender of Communism. "Lots of people gave up everything they owned. It was the price of freedom."

Ramirez wasn't sure he agreed, but he knew better than to take on his mother.

Change would eventually come; after all, Fidel Castro wasn't supernatural. At least Ramirez hoped he wasn't. He was afraid Castro's ghost would find a way to speak to him from the grave, and his long-winded speeches were legendary.

Conchita rolled her eyes at this family debate that had lasted for decades and would never be settled. "Sit down, Ricky. Tell us what you've been doing. Have some *picadillo*. I had to make it with ground soy. That's all we had."

"I'm sure it will be delicious." Ramirez pulled over a chair. His father poured him a glass of rum; his sister brought him a plate of the dish traditionally made with tomatoes, olives, raisins, and ground beef instead of texturized protein. They chatted for a while, until the flickering images on the television lured them in.

Mission Impossible was the movie. Tom Cruise played Ethan Hunt, an agent framed for the murders of his team by a mole within the CIA.

His mother was right, thought Ramirez, yawning with fatigue despite the fast action. It really was a silly plot.

25

When Inspector Ramirez pulled in front of police headquarters the next morning, Fernando Espinoza was waiting out front, two large exhibit boxes stacked beside him on the sidewalk. He leaned into the open passenger-side window. "I started looking through missing person reports this morning. Nothing yet. But it's a very big pile."

Hundreds of Cubans tried to leave the island every year by any means they could find: pieces of wood, tires, inner tubes, small boats, even the shells of old cars, anything that could be made to float. Most of what they used didn't.

If they could get as far as Florida, they could apply for permanent residency, but only if they first touched American soil. Those who survived the dangerous journey across the Straits of Florida were usually intercepted by the American Coast Guard. Sometimes, the Americans used pepper spray to stop them from landing. Once returned to Cuba, they were jailed for the treasonous act of trying to leave the island without the proper paperwork.

Many families said nothing for fear of retribution. As a result, missing person reports were incomplete. Even so, there were thousands.

Ramirez got out and helped Espinoza put the boxes in the back seat. They drove to the Instituto de Medicina Legal, the Centre for Legal Medicine.

On the way, they passed another billboard: VOTE FOR SOBRIETY! But Cuba was a country where no one could really vote for anything, thought Ramirez. And how many drunks would vote for sobriety even if they could? Part of being drunk was not always knowing when one was drunk, or being too drunk to care. It was one of those government slogans that preached, as religion so often did, to the converted.

Ramirez leaned on the horn, startling a coco-taxi driver who had broken down in the middle of the road. The man pushed the small vehicle, which looked like a bright yellow tennis ball, out of the way.

"Why all the interest in Luis Posada this week?" asked Espinoza, looking out the window. "Half the billboards in Havana have his picture on them."

"He will be appearing soon in an American court to face charges. That's why Dr. Flores is here. He's been working on Posada's file for decades."

"You know him?"

"Dr. Flores? We investigated the hotel bombings in the late nineties together. He developed a profile of the men involved. It was very accurate; both men confessed."

Two Salvadorans, Otto René Rodriguez Llerena and Raul Ernesto Cruz Leon, had been arrested. Cruz Leon was interviewed on Cuban television. He said he needed the money. He had a few ex-wives and too many children.

Ramirez pulled his thoughts away from the smell of burned

flesh, the rubble, the mangled body of the young Italian tourist whose only crime was vacationing in Cuba.

———————

"We're here to see Manuel Flores," Inspector Ramirez explained to the security guard, as he and Detective Espinoza signed in at the front desk.

The dead man walked over to the photographs that lined the wall. He waved at Ramirez to get his attention. He pointed to one of Manuel Flores posing beside Fidel Castro in the Sierra Mountains, both men grinning and cradling rifles. Ramirez glanced at the ghost briefly and gave him a look to indicate he should go away. He was too busy to deal with distractions. The ghost shrugged apologetically and walked out the main door.

"What is this place, Inspector?" asked Espinoza. "I've never been here before."

"It's a centre for forensic medicine. It has resources that far outstrip anything we have, and Dr. Flores is one of them. Or at least he was, before he left for the United States a few years ago."

"Do they do autopsies here too?"

"Not many," said Ramirez. "They used to handle all suspicious deaths in Havana, but now they work more closely with Cuban Intelligence than with us."

"Why the change?"

Ramirez lowered his voice. "There was an incident a few years ago. A Danish tourist was shot dead by security forces. He was walking down the sidewalk on the Avenida Territorial behind the Ministry of Defence. He was on his way back to his hotel, a little drunk after a night out in the bars."

"Why did they shoot him?"

"The guards said he was in a restricted military area, but there were no signs prohibiting access. The family's lawyer managed to obtain a videotape of the autopsy. Their medical experts said it looked like he was executed. Our government finally admitted that a volley of shots was fired inappropriately. Denmark issued a travel advisory warning its citizens that they could be shot and killed here without warning. The Major Crimes Unit was established not long after. Dr. Apiro was contracted to do all our autopsies."

"Why? Because there are no videotape cameras in his morgue?"

Ramirez smiled. Espinoza was smart. "Now listen, Fernando. We only show Dr. Flores the physical evidence we've gathered. We don't tell him our theories. We don't want to influence his thinking by pointing him in any particular direction."

———

Ramirez knocked on the psychiatrist's office door.

"It's open," Flores called out. "Good morning, Inspector Ramirez. My goodness, it's been a long time. And who is this young man with you?" The elderly psychiatrist stood up from behind his desk to greet them, beaming.

"Detective Espinoza. He's new to my section, but learning fast."

"*Hola*," said Espinoza. He shifted his box awkwardly onto one knee so he could shake hands.

"You can put those down over there." The profiler tilted his head towards a scratched coffee table in front of a worn sofa. Espinoza and Ramirez complied.

"Did the inspector tell you that he and I worked together over a decade ago on the hotel bombings? He's the one who discovered that the explosives were smuggled into Cuba in a shampoo bottle and in the soles of Cruz Leon's shoes. It was excellent police work."

Ramirez smiled. "I wonder sometimes why shampoo and Salvadorans are still allowed in the country."

The unexploded bombs were now on display in a museum. If Castro could have, thought Ramirez, he would have stuffed the Salvadorans and displayed them there as well.

In response to the bombings, Castro had recruited seven thousand new *policías* from the countryside. The policemen were poorly trained, bored, and trigger-happy. One shot the young Danish tourist.

"Ramirez and I were assigned to the same team, although he was only a detective then. Well, I shouldn't say 'only.' Ramirez has always been very good. But here we are again," said Flores, grinning. "Imagine. It's as if I've come back from the dead. Glorious day, don't you think?" He nodded vigorously, rubbing his gnarled fingers together. "A sunny day makes me feel connected to the universe. There's nothing like death to trigger thoughts of one's mortality. El Comandante discovered this recently himself. He has reached the conclusion, a little late perhaps, that speeches should be short."

Ramirez laughed. He had forgotten how charming Manuel Flores was. And how tall. Even stooped with age and illness, Flores towered over the two detectives. They shook hands; Flores clapped Ramirez on the back.

"Forget the universe," said Ramirez. "Profile this for me. Why are dead bodies always discovered so early in the morning?"

"Wait until you're my age before you complain. It's the worst part of getting old, being robbed of sleep. But that gives us more waking hours, yes? Not a bad compromise, given the alternative. In fact, at my age, I'm happy to wake up at all. Not that there's much I can do with my free time. These days I'm softer than a man swimming in the Atlantic." Flores chuckled. "So, Ramirez, I understand you need some assistance navigating the terrain?"

Ramirez nodded. He knew what terrain Flores meant. Not the physical crime scene but the psychological landscape of their killer.

"Please, gentlemen," said Flores. "Sit down. Open your boxes and show me what you have." He motioned to the sagging, lumpy couch.

Ramirez and Espinoza seated themselves, careful to avoid the broken springs that strained the upholstery. Flores sat across from them on an equally lumpy chair.

"Let's start with the physical evidence first," Flores said. He removed a pair of eyeglasses from his shirt pocket. "Then the photographs."

Ramirez opened the larger of the boxes. He handed Flores a clear plastic bag that held a cigarette butt. "This was found near the second body this week. It's a Chinese brand. The name means Double Happiness."

Flores looked at it closely before he handed the bag back.

"There was a cigarette butt found at the first crime scene too," Ramirez said. "A British brand. Silk Cut." Ramirez opened the second box. He riffled through it until he found the exhibit bag and handed it to the profiler.

"Do you think the cigarettes mean anything, Dr. Flores?" asked Espinoza.

The profiler shrugged. "It's too soon to say. Everyone in Cuba smokes. The tobacco companies may be seeing their profits decline everywhere else, but never in the Third World. But still, it's interesting that both are foreign brands."

"The women's purses were left behind at each crime scene," said Ramirez. "Their belongings were inside. Nothing obvious missing."

He supplied the pathologist with a pair of latex gloves, then put on a pair himself before bringing out the bright fuchsia bag that Sanchez had found at the Prima Verrier crime scene. He handed it to the profiler along with the plastic exhibit bags that held the items found inside. When Flores finished examining them, Ramirez passed over the remaining exhibit bags, including the remnants of the women's clothing and their shoes.

"May I see the photographs?" said Flores, after he had worked his way slowly through each item.

Ramirez turned them over. Flores shuffled through the pile slowly. He laid a few of them on the table, like playing cards. He chose one shot of Prima Verrier's body and placed a similar picture of the unidentified female victim beside it.

"He poses them to look like they're sleeping. I think this means he doesn't want to accept the consequences of his actions. At some level, he feels deeply ashamed of what he's done. Profiling," Flores explained to Espinoza, "is built on a careful examination of the crime scene as well a close review of witness statements and expert reports." He smiled. "Then a good profiler ignores all of that and relies on intuition."

"Not to be rude, but I thought you had retired," said Ramirez. He didn't mention that he thought Flores had succumbed to his illness.

"I've been asked to prepare material for the American CIA. Luis Posada's trial will be held in Texas in a few weeks."

"We work with the CIA now?" said Espinoza, surprised.

Flores shrugged. "When it's in our interest, yes. Believe it or not, the Americans shredded all their evidence against Posada. They asked for our help to reconstruct it. I've had to go over all my notes from three decades. It brings back memories, I can tell you. But I've discovered nostalgia isn't what it used to be."

"Is the trial in Texas related to the hotel bombings?" Espinoza asked.

"No," said Flores. "Immigration charges. Posada asked the Americans for political asylum when he entered their country. He told immigration officials that he took the bus; they allege he came by boat. It's like the gangster, Al Capone, being charged with tax evasion.

"Posada lives very comfortably in Miami from what I understand. He tells everyone he sleeps like a baby. But most babies don't sleep all that well. I sleep like a baby too. I wake up every few hours to piss." The profiler grinned. "You've done well, gentlemen." He leaned back in his chair, forming his long fingers into a tent. "You've learned a lot about this killer already. Technically, I should point out that he's a multiple murderer, not a serial killer—we need at least three victims before we can call him that. But I'm quite sure it's the same man."

He sat forward and tapped on a photograph. "In both cases, the cigarette butts were in almost exactly the same spot beside the body. The women were left fully clothed. Skirts were down, not hiked up. There was no apparent attempt to undress either of them. Was there any sexual interference?"

"Not as far as we know," said Ramirez.

Flores nodded thoughtfully. "I've been reading the most recent studies by the American FBI on serial killers. The *yumas* have so many that they've produced quite a comprehensive review. Although, in fairness, the Russians had Pichushkin and Chikatilo, and Colombia is still dealing with La Bestia. But those were men of low intelligence. What I see in these"—he tapped the photographs again—"is the stamp of someone organized. Although there are aspects of the murders that are disorganized too."

"What's the difference between an organized killer and a disorganized one?" asked Espinoza.

"The organized killer is intelligent," said Flores, looking up. "He prepares carefully, sometimes for months. The thrill for him is the planning, not the execution." He chuckled. "No pun intended. This man is socially competent. High-functioning. He's a perfectionist, constantly finessing his craft. If you find him, Ramirez, try appealing to his ego. He may boast about his crimes."

"And what about the disorganized killer?" asked Espinoza. He held his pen expectantly.

The young detective seemed fascinated with every statement that left Flores's mouth, as if one of the marble statues in the Plaza Vieja had suddenly started speaking. Whenever the profiler spoke, Espinoza scrambled through the pages of his notebook, writing furiously.

"He's opportunistic. He takes his victims where he finds them. The disorganized killer often keeps souvenirs, even though this puts him at risk of being caught. Huang Yong in China kept his victim's belts, for example. The organized killer is too smart for that. He takes pleasure from planning; the disorganized one from remembering.

This one may be a mixture of both. He's taken his victims to areas he can't completely control. The organized killer would never take that chance. He would use an abandoned building as his killing ground. There are certainly enough of them around."

"I'm confused, Dr. Flores," said Espinoza. "If he's so smart, why do you think he might boast about his actions?"

"He doesn't see what he does as a crime," Flores explained. "He believes his acts serve a social purpose. Huang Yong was similar. He argued he was doing China a service by removing males from the population. He considered it more heroic than killing women."

"That's just fucked up," Espinoza blurted out. He blushed.

"He's bold," said Ramirez. "But that's part of it, isn't it?"

Flores nodded enthusiastically, a teacher admiring his student's intuitive grasp of a difficult subject. "A man like this thrives on adrenaline. He may need more stimulation as time goes on. He'll take more risks. I think he wants the bodies found before too much time passes, so that others can admire his craft."

"According to Dr. Apiro, Prima Verrier's body was there for a while," said Espinoza. "That doesn't seem to fit the profile of someone who wants his victims found quickly."

"Perhaps the killer hasn't read the most recent studies," said Ramirez.

Flores smiled. "If he's a hybrid, he'll be unpredictable. You know what to expect with an organized murderer. The disorganized killer will alter his approach if the right opportunity presents itself."

"Are you sure the second one isn't a copycat?" asked Espinoza.

"It can't be, Fernando," said Ramirez. "*Granma* never reports murders. Only the murderer could have known about the stocking tied around Prima Verrier's neck."

"Except for those of you involved in the investigation," said Flores. "I wouldn't rule out someone in law enforcement."

"We can't rule out anyone," Ramirez agreed. "But we kept the police and the *guarapitos* well back."

The *guarapitos* were a level below *patrulleros*. They wore green uniforms instead of blue. They dealt with traffic mostly. When Prima Verrier's body was discovered, they were put to work rerouting buses and taxis away from the crime scene.

"I hate to say this, Ramirez," said the profiler, "but it would be helpful if we had a third victim so that we could establish a pattern. If I'm right, we won't have long to wait."

"You think he'll do it again?" said Ramirez.

The older man nodded. "I'm sure of it."

"Why does he do it at all, Dr. Flores?" asked Espinoza.

"Why does a dog lick his balls?" The profiler smiled. "For the same reason men climb mountains. Because they can."

26

After a restless sleep, Charlie Pike finally pulled himself out of bed, showered, and dressed. He took a seat on one of the vinyl banquettes next to the window in the motel's restaurant and waited for the waitress to take his order. According to the people eating breakfast at the next table, almost thirty centimetres of snow had fallen overnight.

Pike scanned the local paper's headlines. They were a day old because of the storm. "Mohawk Warriors Join the Lines: Mayor Calls for Federal Government to Get Involved."

He'll be calling that number for a long time, thought Pike. He looked carefully at the photographs of the protestors and the OPP officers, but he didn't see anyone he knew from either side of the conflict.

Outside, all the police SUVs and vans were gone. Pike ordered kolbassa sausage, eggs over easy, and brown toast. The waitress refilled his coffee cup.

After he finished breakfast, he went back to his room and retrieved his satchel before walking out to the parking lot. The snow was up to the wheel wells on one side of the SUV; on the other, the car was almost buried in a drift. He brushed off the windshield with his sleeve, scraped the ice off the door handles, and opened the back door. He reached inside for the plastic brush and scraper.

Once he'd cleared away the worst of it, Pike climbed in. He let the SUV idle, giving the heaters time to take the frost off the windows, then blew on his fingers to warm them up. He looked at the clock on the dashboard beside the radio. It was just after eleven. Three hours until the autopsy.

He sat for a moment, thinking how to best use his limited time.

Pauley Oshig, he decided. He pulled the SUV out of the lot, rocking it across the snow ridges left by the plow, and headed to the Manomin Bay First Nation. He was behind a salt truck most of the way. The salt pinged off the rental car like hailstones.

The gravel road into the reserve had been plowed. Pike slowed down to avoid striking two stray dogs that were wandering along the shoulder, but they stayed clear of his car. One lifted its head when Pike drove by, its yellow eyes meeting his, curious. Great, thought Pike. He probably saw the killer driving on this road too, but he can't tell me what he saw.

The parking lot beside the Manomin Bay First Nation Band Administration building was jammed full with trucks. The clouds had parted, leaving a glimpse of indigo sky.

Pike stepped out of the SUV. He didn't bother locking the doors. No one locked doors on the reserve. No one had anything worth stealing. Besides, if someone needed something, they helped themselves and returned it or replaced it later.

Pike thought it was funny that it was only off-reserve, where doors were locked, that people stole from each other. He'd first learned to steal in the Catholic day school. He started off small, taking food.

He walked up to the wooden building. It looked new, with sharp rooflines. The front of the building was angled towards the bay.

He steeled himself and pulled open the wide glass door, wiping his feet on the bristled mat. He didn't recognize the young woman sitting behind the reception desk. She was probably a toddler when Charlie Pike's mother and brother were thrown off the reserve by Chesley Wabigoon, Billy's dad.

Chief Wabigoon was on the phone, she explained, when he told her he was here to see Bill. "He's speaking to the media about the blockade. I'll let him know you're here. He'll be with you right away. Can I get you a coffee?"

"*Miigwetch.*"

A few minutes later she brought him the coffee in a paper cup. "Don't worry," she said. "The water's bottled."

Pike settled in for a long wait. Nothing happened quickly in Indian country. Whatever you were doing at the moment was the priority until the next crisis came up. That's how things were. Pike was fine with it. He worked the same way.

After a half hour or so, he stood up and stretched. He read the notices on the band council bulletin board. *Rummage Sale.* "Get rid of those things not worth keeping around the house. Bring Your Husbands!" "Electric girdles needed for the pancake breakfast March 6!"

A few minutes later, Bill Wabigoon stepped into the reception area.

"*Anii*, Charlie," he said, smiling. "Geez, it's good to see you. Come on in."

Pike followed the chief down the hall to his office. "*Anii*, Bill. Wanted to let you know I was in the territory."

It was protocol for anyone who lived off-reserve to stop by the band office, let the chief and council know they were in the territory. Had been like that all the way back to the 1700s, maybe even before. That's when the Ojibway tribes at war with the Mohawks and the other Haudenosaunee nations met with the French Governor de Callières in Montreal and agreed to turn over the war kettle. "The Dish with One Spoon," they all called it. Both Pike's Ojibway and Mohawk relatives recited it as law, and it was a ritual every First Nation person knew to follow.

If the Ojibway and Mohawks hadn't reached that agreement, Pike doubted he'd even exist. His mother's and father's nations had been determined to wipe each other out in the wars over who would supply the Europeans with beaver pelts. But the chiefs and principal men made a verbal treaty with the French and each other, and they kept their word despite the centuries that passed. They couldn't write back then, but they could remember.

Bill Wabigoon's office was bright with a glorious view of Manomin Bay. An elaborately beaded eagle feather rested high on a shelf alongside First Nation carvings and quill boxes. "You have to keep an eagle feather off the ground," Pike remembered his *mishomis* saying. "Never let it touch the dirt." The feather shared space with carved butternut birds from Georgian Bay, a tamarack twig goose from James Bay, a woven ash splint basket. On the walls, prints by Norval Morriseau, Daphne Odjig, Roy Henry Vickers.

"Nice office, Bill."

"*Miigwetch.* Sit down, sit down. Geez, you look good, Charlie. Man, it's been a long time, eh? Too bad it took a murder to bring you here. You think it's that guy, that Highway Strangler? So you think he used an axe, eh? Maybe he's *ateshkodawewinini.*" A fireman. "Or could be an ice fisherman, I guess. Doesn't narrow it down too much, eh? Almost everyone around here is a volunteer fireman. And probably every man around here ice-fishes. Women too."

Pike smiled. Sheldon's BlackBerry had been busy. "I can't really talk to you too much about the investigation, Bill. Not until I know more."

Wabigoon shook his head. "Those girls, hitchhiking. No choice, eh? The buses don't run up north anymore. You hear that old joke about the Anishnabe woman hitchhiking? She gets into a truck and there's a big bottle of booze in the passenger seat. 'Got that for my old man,' the driver says. And the Anishnabe woman says, 'Yeah? Good trade.'"

Pike laughed. He'd forgotten how funny Bill Wabigoon could be. But that was how Billy recruited gang members. Made them laugh, made them feel good. Made each of them feel like he was the only person in the world Billy was interested in. Until they were hooked on drugs, booze, violence, and his approval. Then he moved on to someone else.

"I need to talk to Pauley Oshig. I hear he's living at your place."

"Yeah, ever since Molly . . ." Wabigoon didn't finish his sentence. There was no need. He ran his hands through his hair. It had touches of grey in it. He was only four years older than Pike but looked like he had a decade on him.

"Freda kept Pauley home from school today in case you wanted to see him. He's not like other boys, eh? He has a hard time concentrating. Doctor said his brain didn't develop right. It's like he started drinking before he was born. Most of the time he's okay, but sometimes he hits himself. Makes it hard for Freda to look after him. He has lots of problems at school."

Freda Nadjiwon. A second, maybe third, cousin of Bill's. "The priests said it was okay to marry our cousins," Pike's *nokomis*—his Ojibway grandmother—had told him. "Before that, we never married our own family. The elders always picked out who married who. They knew who was related. But they lost the old ways because of those residential schools."

Pike pulled his thoughts back to the investigation. "Did you keep Pauley home yesterday too?"

"Yeah, I told him to come straight here after he showed Sheldon where the body was. I wanted to keep an eye on him. Found out he's been skipping school for months. I let him play computer for a while, then I sent him home for lunch."

"Okay if I go over to your place to talk to him?"

"Sure. But I can't go with you. I have a band council meeting that's already late getting started, and it's going to run late too. There's so much going on up here now, Charlie. Our new water treatment plant isn't finished. Indian Affairs, they send in truckloads of bottled water, but the shipment couldn't get through this week because of the storm. Our land claims are going nowhere fast. And then there's the blockade. Sometimes I feel like I'm one broken-down truck and a dead dog away from being a country-and-western song." Wabigoon chuckled. "Yeah, go on over. Freda's at home. We live in my dad's old place. You know Chesley passed away, eh? Cancer took him. You probably haven't had any lunch yet. Tell her I said to set you a plate."

"*Miigwetch.*" Pike remembered he had an autopsy to go to. He hoped he'd be able to keep down whatever he ate.

"We should get together when you have more time, Charlie. We have lots to catch up on, you and me. We lost three elders this winter. A baby too, from that bird flu. And we had a couple of suicides. Two young kids." Wabigoon shook his head. "Sometimes I think the government's just waiting us out. You know what our land claims researcher found out? Ontario gets our land back if we go extinct. It's in the agreement they signed with Canada when they set aside our reserves. Can you believe that? *Extinct.* That was the word they used too." Wabigoon sighed. "You been out to see your auntie yet? I'm sure she knows you're around."

"Not yet," said Pike. He had hoped to get away without seeing anyone, but that wasn't going to be possible. Everyone would know he was back. Gossip passed for recreation in Manomin Bay.

Wabigoon frowned. "She lives in the elders' lodge. We built it a few years ago. Got a half million from the feds, paid for the rest from our share of casino proceeds from Rama. We have a nurse who makes sure they take their medication. And there's a traditional healer comes by too. She's doing pretty well, for a woman her age, your auntie. You know she's in a wheelchair now, eh? Diabetes took one of her legs but her eyes are still good."

"I'll get over to see her later." Pike shifted in his seat. He hadn't known about the diabetes. He hadn't kept in touch with anyone. "I need to do some door-knocking while I'm here, Bill. Ask some questions. Hope that's all right."

"Yeah, sure, go ahead, Charlie. But most people won't want to talk to you. They don't like police coming here from outside. Me and a bunch of chiefs are hoping to set up our own police force, if the APF funding don't work out. Maybe even if it does. Exercise our inherent right to self-government. Maybe I can talk to you sometime, pick your brain. We need people who know what they're doing."

"*Miigwetch*, Bill. Sure, I'll see you before I head back."

"What are you looking for?"

"There was a vehicle parked on the road right beside where the body was found. I need to find out if anyone saw it. I also need to find out when the snow stopped falling yesterday so I can figure out the timeline. I've been meaning to call the airport but my cell phone isn't always working up here."

"No one's there until just before a flight comes in anyway. Should open up around four, four thirty." Wabigoon thought for a moment. "I can find out for you now, though." He picked up a phone and dialed a number. He spoke in Ojibway to someone, asked when they started work. He thanked the person and hung up.

"Patrick Akiwenzie drives our snow plow. Says he started clearing the roads just after four on Thursday. Nothing much moving before then except snowmobiles. He doesn't plow till the snow stops. There's no point; he'd just have to do it again, and we don't have a big budget for snow-clearing. You'd be surprised what our education budget ends up paying for—snow removal as well as land claims. If we could get our lawyers to pick up a snow shovel, we could save ourselves a whole lot of money."

"Four in the afternoon?"

Wabigoon nodded.

"When did you find out about the body, Bill?" Pike pulled out his notebook, leaned it on his crossed knee, rooted around in his pocket for his pen. It was more for show than anything else. He almost never took notes.

"Yesterday morning. Pauley was supposed to be on the 8:00 a.m. school bus but he ran home to tell me what he found."

"What time did he leave for school?"

"About thirty minutes before that, I guess. Bus stops on the corner, where the gravel road meets the highway. Boy doesn't wear a watch. He can't make out numbers too good. I don't own one either. Because it don't matter what time it is, I'm always late."

"Know what you mean," said Pike. He hadn't worn a watch in years either.

If it was 4:00 p.m. when the snow stopped falling, he thought, then the woman had to have been killed after that or her body would have been buried in the snow. It was 7:30, maybe 8:00 a.m. the next day when Pauley Oshig found her. That was a reasonable window of time to investigate—around sixteen hours.

"You should drop by the blockade too," said Bill. "They're having a sweat tonight. Starts at sunset. You look like you could use one. You been drinking?"

"Me? Not for years."

"Then you're good to go."

Pike nodded. A sweat sounded like a good idea. "What's going on with the blockade, Bill? We don't get much news about it down south."

Wabigoon shook his head. "Federal government promised my dad that pulp mill would never open again, not after what happened. But they started her up a few months ago. We tried to get Indian Affairs to close it down and they ignored us. They said the province issued the licence, deal with them. Ontario said it was legal;

if we had a problem in our traditional territory, deal with the feds. 'Never' don't mean much to the white man."

"What do you mean, after what happened?"

"Back in the seventies, when my dad was chief, that mill dumped twenty thousand pounds of mercury in the Wabigoon River. Used it to bleach the paper. My dad told me the levels of mercury were three times higher than Health Canada's guidelines. Federal government told everyone to stop eating fish." Wabigoon snorted. "The province shut down our guiding operations up here about ten years later, then the commercial fishery. Put everyone out of work. Even though they said we couldn't prove we were poisoned. Ontario said if there was mercury in the water, it got there by itself. Feds finally settled up with us a few years ago after we sued them, but they never did anything to clean up the water."

Pike could feel his anger rise. The Wabigoon River was where the Manomin Bay First Nation got its water, its food. "Don't eat the big fish," his *mishomis* had always warned. Now he knew why. "What about the mill? What do they say about it?"

"Mill says they don't dump mercury in the water anymore, so it's not their problem. But our biologists say it's still there. Soon as they start logging timber, the erosion's going to cause it to leach back into the bay. More of our people are going to end up sick again. Or dead."

Pike shook his head, disgusted. It seemed like First Nation land was always a dumping ground for other people's garbage. "Aren't the feds going to do anything?"

"You kidding? We had to pay to get our own medical experts to come up here and check us out. We took the money out of our trust funds. They force us to go to court, but they don't give us money for lawyers either. The doctor we used to get everyone tested, that came out of this year's education money too."

Pike exhaled. "What did the experts say?"

"Still waiting on the results. Brought a professor up from the

University of Manitoba. Maylene Kesler. She ran a clinic in town; tested everyone, even some of the white people that live nearby, but I still haven't heard what she found. We had a doctor come all the way from Japan a few months ago too. That's where they first got this disease, eh? Minamata disease, they call it. They had two thousand victims over there. They got a settlement too—eighty-six million dollars. Doctor said he was shocked. He was here before. He tested everybody back when Chesley was still chief. Every single person he saw the first time round is dead, even the children. He says that most everyone has symptoms now, or will.

"It's exposure, Charlie. The more you're around mercury, the sicker you get. But Health Canada don't even test us anymore. They say our mercury levels are below their safety guidelines. I think maybe the problem is those guidelines. They're made for people who eat fish once in a while, not people like us who eat it every day."

"Jesus," said Pike. "No wonder you're trying to shut the mill down."

"Funny thing, eh? If we hadn't left, you and me, we'd probably be sick too." Wabigoon nodded. "Once the weather clears, we plan to rent a couple of buses and head south to march on Queens Park. Two hundred and fifty dollars, Charlie. It's enough to make you cry."

"What's that, Bill?" asked Pike. He closed his notebook and put it in his pocket as he got to his feet.

"That's how much the feds paid to settle the lawsuit. Two hundred and fifty dollars for each one of our people that died."

27

As he drove up the long driveway, Charlie Pike remembered the first time he'd been sent to knock on Chesley Wabigoon's door. Chesley was chief then: a tall man with a big paunch and a bigger temper.

Charlie's mother had given him a gift to take over to Billy's mom, who had just come home from the south with another baby. The Wabigoons were a large family with six or seven children. Billy was the oldest, but he'd been forced to go to residential school over Chesley's objections. Billy's mother cried when they put her son in the back of the police car. Billy came back the summer he turned fifteen, angry, his father's son.

As the young Charlie approached the Wabigoons' front door, Billy and another boy that Pike didn't know blocked his way. "You got any smokes?" Billy said. He was older than Charlie and heavier. Stronger. Charlie was twelve, and still pretty small. "Got some money?"

Charlie shook his head, confused. Where would he get money or cigarettes?

"What's in the bag?"

"Scones. For your mother. Because of the baby."

"Yeah? Well, give them to me."

Charlie weighed the odds of getting the shit kicked out of him if he didn't turn them over. He reluctantly handed Billy the bag. His mother would be mad at him, but she wasn't likely to bloody his nose.

"You're the baby, asshole," Billy Wabigoon said.

"Fucking Mohawk." The other boy spat on the dirt.

Charlie walked down the road slowly, not wanting to look like he was running away. He expected to hear the bigger boys pounding down the gravel behind him. When he was far enough away to feel safe, he looked back. The boys were sitting on the step, pushing the warm pastries into their mouths.

———

Charlie Pike knocked on the door a couple of times before he opened it. "Freda?"

"Well, hello, Charlie," said Freda Wabigoon as she walked into the front room. "It's been a long time, eh?"

Pike remembered her as a young woman in her early teens. A strong woman from a family of fishermen, she often went out on the boats in the spring and ice-fished in winter. She had put on a lot of weight over the years, had the bloating that usually accompanied diabetes or alcoholism, or both.

"I have some baloney and a pot of macaroni and cheese on the stove. You want some lunch, Charlie? Got some whitefish we pulled up this morning. I'd make bannock, but we can't get to the stores today, everything's closed. But even then, it's expensive, eh? Twelve bucks for a bag of flour."

Processed food was killing First Nations people everywhere. When Pike ran away, the people of Manomin Bay were still hunters, trappers. They sold their fish, too, despite the laws against it. They were quiet about it. They didn't take them door to door in White Harbour, peddling their fish, brooms, and baskets the way they did when his *mishomis* was a young boy. But Pike hadn't seen many skins hanging to dry on the sides of the houses.

Not that hunting and trapping were any easier than fishing. Pike's grandfather had to wade waist-deep into ice-cold waters to set his muskrat traps. And even this far north, white men sometimes shot at him and lifted his traps.

"I'll get your lunch ready," said Freda. "I'll make some tea. You take sugar?"

"*Miigwetch.*"

"Pauley?" she called out. "Someone's here to see you. He must be on the computer in his bedroom," she explained to Pike when no one responded. "Our other boys are at school today. Imagine, three teenage boys in one little room. We have a daughter too. Doris. She wants to be a nurse. She's at college. At Lakehead."

"You must be proud of her."

Freda smiled. "I'm proud of Bill too. He's done good, Charlie. There's lots of people who want him to run for regional chief of the Assembly of First Nations."

Like O'Malley, Charlie Pike thought all politicians were crooks, whether they were white or Aboriginal. But Indian politics was as fast as lacrosse and required just as much skill. Bill was good at lacrosse, and he knew how to skate too.

"Sounds like politics is where he belongs, Freda. Are you Pauley's legal guardian?" He got out his notebook. "I should maybe talk to him before we have lunch."

"Yes, I'm his guardian, but only because Molly's gone."

"He's fourteen, right? I need his birth date for my report."

"August 11, 1992. You go ahead, I'll get things ready."

Pike thought for a moment. Pauley Oshig was a youth under the

Youth Criminal Justice Act. He wasn't supposed to be questioned at all without an adult present. He was a witness, not a suspect, but even so Pike didn't like the idea of questioning the boy without an adult.

"You can come in if you want, Freda. You have that right. Might be a good idea."

Freda Wabigoon shook her head sadly. "No, I have things to do in the kitchen. I don't want to hear about that poor dead woman anymore, anyway. I said another little prayer for her today."

28

Manuel Flores stood up. He looked tired and weak. It was clear that their session was over. Inspector Ramirez and Detective Espinoza got to their feet. They gathered the exhibits and put them back in the cardboard boxes.

"How do you do it, Dr. Flores?" asked Espinoza. "How do you get inside their heads?"

"I wish I could say I found it harder, Detective, but I've seen a lot of men die. An eye for an eye, a hanging for a shooting. That's what it was like in 1961, after the Bay of Pigs. They lined them up against the wall at La Cabaña. The firing squads always shot them at night when the cannon was being fired, to mask the noise. For years, I used to wake up my wife, shouting. I still see those men sometimes in my dreams."

Flores smiled. He placed a hand on Espinoza's back, steering him towards the door.

"You think that the killer brought those stockings with him, don't you?" said Espinoza.

Flores nodded. "I told you, he's organized. He's a hunter, this one. These murders are his expeditions. Like the photographs of Hemingway in the Hotel Floridita, standing over a dead tiger. The killer uses nylons tied like a ribbon to show off his prize. I think this week's victim was his second kill. Remember the brand of cigarette? Double Happiness."

————————

Inspector Ramirez drove Espinoza back to police headquarters. He and Espinoza carried the boxes up to the exhibit room and logged them in, then Espinoza returned to his desk to check missing person reports. As soon as Ramirez entered his office, the phone on his desk trilled.

"I have a call for you from Celia Jones, the Canadian lawyer," the switchboard operator said. "Shall I put her through?"

"Yes, of course."

The line buzzed for a moment as the operator made the connection.

"*Hola*, Celia," said Ramirez. "How are things in Canada?"

"Honestly? Really freaking cold. I'm at my parents' place in Northern Ontario for a few days. It's been almost thirty below zero, if you can imagine. I'd like to know why the hell my Scottish ancestors picked this country to move to instead of somewhere warm like California."

Ramirez smiled. He looked out the window. Hundreds of tourists jammed the sidewalks, snapping photographs, dropping coins at the feet of street musicians. A sixty-degree difference in temperature between the two countries was astonishing, but he could imagine it all too well. When he visited Ottawa on police business, he thought his brain would seize when he stepped out of the plane into the cold.

"How is Beatriz adjusting to her new home?" Ramirez had helped clear the way for the child's adoption, although he bent a few rules along the way.

"Already improving, thanks. And the really good news is that she won't need a heart transplant, just a new valve. That's still major surgery, but not *as* major—she won't have the rejection issues. She may need to be on blood thinners, but Alex says she'll be running around in no time at all."

"I'm very happy to hear it," Ramirez said. "And Hector will be too." Apiro had accompanied the child from Havana on the medical transport in January.

"I'm sorry to bother you with this, Ricardo, but Beatriz is the reason I called. We're in a bit of a predicament." Jones explained the problems with the Canadian adoption process.

"Why would they send her back here?" said Ramirez, surprised. "There's no one to care for her."

"I know. I can't bear the idea of her being in an orphanage again." Jones was on the verge of tears. "And Alex is dead set against it. But if we can't stop it from happening—worst-case scenario—can you help us to find her a good home?"

"Don't worry, Celia. I'll make sure of it." Although Ramirez wasn't sure how. No family he knew could easily afford another mouth to feed.

"Oh, thank you. That means the world to me." Jones paused for a moment, composing herself. "I'm sorry; I didn't even ask how you were," she said, her voice hoarse with emotion. "How are things? Are you busy?"

"Very," said Ramirez. He told her about the two deaths. "A third woman," he added, looking at the dead woman's ghost, "seems to be missing. Another prostitute."

"That's terrible," Jones said. "We've had murders like that in Canada too. There's a trial going on right now in British Columbia. A pig farmer named Willie Pickton murdered dozens of women. They think he fed his victims to his pigs. I never thought of it as something you'd have to worry about in Cuba, not with all the police you have around."

Ramirez shook his head. "Such women are always vulnerable."

"I'm sure racism is a big factor up here. It's not like no one noticed—all these women were reported missing by their families. But the police put their heads in the sand because they were Aboriginal and quite a few were drug addicts or hookers. Charlie Pike's on a task force that's looking into some of the murders in Ontario and Manitoba, where it looks like it could be the same killer. In fact, he's not far from here right now, investigating another one. We call him the Highway Strangler. The killer, I mean. He leaves his victims by the side of the road and then vanishes into thin air."

"As does ours. It's very sad to know that there are such vicious men in this world." Ramirez glanced at his watch. "I'm sorry, I should get back to work, Celia. Things are very busy. Please keep me posted about Beatriz, will you?"

"Absolutely, Ricardo. And thanks again."

29

Pauley Oshig's bedroom was dark, the lopsided curtains pulled tight. Where there should have been an overhead light fixture, wires dangled from the ceiling. The walls were speckled like a killdeer's egg with black mould. The room was the size of a jail cell. It was so small that Charlie Pike was surprised the boys didn't sleep standing up.

Bill Wabigoon was right, thought Pike. There was never enough money in a band council's budget for repairs, much less new housing, particularly with the long waiting lists of C-31s who wanted to live on the reserve. These were band members who'd either lost their official Indian status because they'd married a white man or were born to a woman who had, then applied to get it back when Bill C-31 changed the law. Pike knew all about it.

He let his eyes adjust to the dark.

There were some drawings tacked up on the walls, but he saw none of the posters of girls that boys this age liked. No hockey sticks, no skates. There was a bunk bed against one wall. Both bunks were messy, with faded, tangled sheets. A twin bed was pushed against the other wall.

The only light in the room came from the flickering monitor of an old computer on a small table jammed beside the twin bed, the resolution so low the screen moved in waves. Pauley Oshig sat on a rickety chair, his fingers moving rapidly on the keyboard. He was small for his age and thin. Pike glanced at the computer game he was playing—Grand Theft Auto.

"How do you like that?" Pike asked, sitting on the edge of the twin bed.

The boy shrugged. "It's okay, I guess. A bunch of Loonies took over the city. I'm being chased by a cophead."

Pike smiled. "I guess I'm a cophead too. My name is Charlie. I work with a police force down south. I need to ask you some questions about that woman's body you found yesterday. Is that okay with you?"

The boy turned to look at Pike. His face reflected the blue light from the monitor. It made him look like something in an aquarium. "Where's your gun?"

"I didn't think I needed it."

A long silence before the boy spoke. "Bet you're glad you have one, though. Easier than running people over with cars."

"Pardon?"

"In this game"—the boy nodded towards the screen—"I have to kill people by running over them. It's a lot harder than shooting them. They keep running away."

Sheldon was right, thought Pike. The boy was different. Pike looked at the drawings on the walls. Pencil drawings of crows, finely detailed. "Did you do those?" he asked.

The boy nodded.

"They're pretty good," said Pike.

"Do you like crows?"

"Smart birds."

"I have to chase them off the road sometimes to make sure they don't get hit by cars," said Pauley. "If they're so smart, why do they walk everywhere? Why don't they fly away when a car comes? They're going to get run over."

"I don't know," said Pike. "But I'm sure they have their reasons." He took a deep breath. He wasn't quite sure where to start with this boy. "Pauley, like I said, I need to ask you some questions. You can have your auntie in here if you want. And you don't have to talk to me at all, if you don't want to. It's up to you."

"It's okay," the boy said. He suddenly sounded weary. Pike decided to ease the boy into the interview.

"Just tell me what you saw."

Pike let the silence run until the boy finally spoke. That was the Anishnabe way, giving someone time to think, not pressing them with questions. That was the hardest thing about the south for Pike, the way people interrupted each other constantly. He was already starting to feel the rhythm of the reserve, the way silence filled empty space. Although it wasn't completely quiet. In the background, the computer chirped as more Loonies escaped.

"She was lying down, under some branches," the boy said. "I moved them so I could see if she was all right. I thought maybe she was sleeping at first. But she wasn't breathing. So I ran home to get my uncle and tell him."

"That was a good idea, Pauley. How long after you found her did you do that?"

"I dunno. A few minutes, I guess."

"Did you see anybody around, any cars or anything?"

The boy shook his head, avoiding Pike's eyes. "No."

"Did you touch anything?"

"Just the branches."

"Did you have a smoke while you were in the woods?" Pike asked. "Maybe a roll-your-own?"

The boy shook his head. Pike looked at the boy's fingers. There were no nicotine stains, no smell of smoke.

"We found one near the body," Pike said. "Did you see it when you were there?"

The boy frowned, twisting his hands repeatedly. "I didn't see anything on the ground except some footprints. I think they were the lady's."

"How did you know she was there, Pauley? How did you find her, under all those branches?"

The boy shrugged. "The crows told me where to look. They thought she was my mother." He shifted in his seat, his fingers fluttering. "They can tell our faces apart, but they can't describe us very good."

"I see," Pike said slowly, trying not to smile. "So they'd have trouble picking someone out of a police lineup."

"No," the boy said, seriously. "They can't do that. They felt bad she was the wrong colour. They can't see colours like we do. We're all just 'not-crow' to them."

"You mean because she was white?"

The boy looked puzzled. "No. Because she was blue."

Pike shook his head. "What do you mean, blue, Pauley? Blue like when your fingers get really cold, that kind of blue?"

"No. Blue like this." The boy motioned to the computer screen, his hand-fluttering more agitated.

A knock on the door and Freda Wabigoon came in holding a cracked mug of steaming hot tea. "Your plate is in the kitchen, Charlie. Pauley, you ready for some lunch?"

The boy shook his head.

"I'll be there in a minute," said Pike. "*Miigwetch*."

Freda closed the door.

"Can you tell me what you saw again?"

But the boy didn't answer. It was like he had gone away in his head somewhere, thought Pike. Maybe he was scared of something. Of him? Of Freda? Pike waited for several minutes before he finally gave up.

"Well, thanks for talking to me, Pauley. If you think of anything else, you let me know, okay? I'm going to give you a card with my number on it. My cell phone doesn't work all that great up here, but I should be able to get emails. You know how to do that, right? My email address is on that card."

Pike stood up and put his card next to the computer. The only sound in the room when he left was the whirr of the computer, and the small *bips* of copheads and Loonies as Pauley ran them over.

Charlie Pike drove up the road to Manomin Bay First Nation Seniors Centre. He put the old man's beaded cuff on his wrist where he might have worn a watch, and turned it nervously. He inhaled deeply and forced himself to get out of the SUV. He walked to the front of the building and opened the heavy door.

"I'm here to see my auntie," he said to the woman at the desk. "Alma Wagamese."

"She's in the craft room, down the hall."

The old woman was sitting in a wheelchair, knitting. "Well, now, is that my little Charlie?" she said, grinning widely. She took his hand and patted it. "It is you, isn't it? My, my, I'm glad to see you. I heard you were visiting the reserve. I thought I might die without ever seeing you again. Look at you! How tall you are."

Pike pulled over a chair. "You look good too."

She patted his hand again, smiling. "See here? I've been knitting. Making little socks for the babies." She showed him a pile of tiny wool socks. "In the old days, I'd make them moccasins, but my fingers are too stiff and my eyes are too old. Don't need to see well to knit, anyway. Your hands do it all by themselves, you just point them in the right direction, and they know what to do."

She held up the knitting. Precise rows of stitches, fine detailed work.

He remembered when she made quill boxes. She'd wait until the spring, when the bark peeled in sheets from the birch trees, then cut out the round circles that formed the bottoms and tops of the boxes. She'd skin a porcupine and remove the quills and dye them, making stew from the carcass, using the fur for hats and mitts. Then she'd line the quills up, piercing the shell of each box with intricate designs, and weave sweetgrass around the tops so the boxes smelled fresh and pure and clean.

It took her a whole week to make a single quill box. When he was a child, she was lucky to get a few dollars for one.

"They're really nice."

"*Miigwetch*. You been to see your dad yet? He'd have liked it where they buried him, looking out over the water. We missed you at the service all those years ago."

Pike shook his head. When his father died, he was still in Winnipeg, stuck in remand with Sheldon Waubasking. Then he heard his family had been evicted. Kicked out of the only home Charlie had ever known.

"I didn't think I was allowed to come here anymore."

"Oh Charlie. I'm sorry about what happened. It wasn't your mother's fault, you know. Back then, if an Indian woman married a white man, she lost her Indian status and so did her children."

"She divorced him before we were born."

"I know that, Charlie, but he was white, so the law said she was white too. My brother—your dad—wanted to marry her, but he was Catholic and she was divorced. Under our laws, they *were* married, though, your mom and Ralph. They had a traditional ceremony with elders, and a big feast. I remember, I was there. But Indian Affairs never did recognize our customs. That's why they took her off the list, and you boys too. As far as the government was concerned, all of you were white. If it wasn't in a church, it wasn't a wedding."

"Chesley had a choice," said Pike. "It wasn't fair, throwing us off the reserve."

"Chesley had a lot of people waiting for housing. Once your dad died, he had the Indian agent to deal with. And don't forget your mom is a Mohawk. Lot of people up here have never forgotten the old wars." She sighed. "I'm sorry, Charlie. But now they have Bill C-31, you can apply to be an Indian again, get your status back. Your mother can too. How is she doing?"

"She died two years ago."

"Oh, my," said Alma. "I'm sorry, Charlie. I didn't know."

Pike took a deep breath. "I tried to get her buried at Six Nations, because that's where she was from, and the Mohawk band council said I couldn't if she wasn't an Indian anymore. She had no legal right to be buried in their cemetery."

Now his mother wandered, Pike believed, severed from everything important to her. But her soul had been stripped from her bones long before the cancer took her, when Canadian bureaucrats had decided a full-blooded Mohawk woman was white because of the race of a man she'd once married.

"I talked to the clan mothers at Oka. That's where her mother was born. They said the band councils don't represent the Haudenosaunee, only white man's laws. They told me I could put her ashes in The Pines, where the Haudenosaunee used to bury their dead. That's where she is now."

"Your mom deserved better, Charlie. But then, we all did," Alma said, shaking her head. "I still don't have a will and I'm eighty-four years old. Because I'd have to give a copy to Indian Affairs for the minister to approve, and I don't think it's the minister's business what I do with my few little things. And what about you, Charlie? Are you going to apply to get your status back?"

"Where I work, it doesn't matter," said Pike stiffly. "They all think I'm an apple anyway. Red on the outside. White on the inside."

"I'm so sorry, Charlie."

Pike nodded uncomfortably. He toyed with the beaded bracelet on his wrist and changed the subject. "I wanted to ask you, did you ever know a family named Manajiwin up this way? There were three brothers. The oldest one is in his late sixties, maybe early seventies. He's in Ottawa, and he's pretty sick. One of his brothers drowned at residential school. I want to see if I can find the other one, while there's still time."

"Now, I don't know of any Manajiwin—that's not a name I've heard before—but there's a woman who lives here at the lodge who might. She's even older than I am. She used to work in the kitchen at the residential school in Kenora. She's from Sandy Bay, but she married a Nahwegahbow. She's got a good memory, Mabel. She always beats me at cards."

30

Inspector Ramirez drove to the medical tower for his second autopsy in as many days. He parked on a side street and glanced at his watch—he was late.

He jogged down the stairs to the morgue and pushed through the swinging doors. The dead man's body lay stretched out on the metal gurney. After being submerged in the ocean, it was almost unrecognizable as human. The skin was as shrivelled as old fruit. The smell of kerosene wafted through the room. There was always a thin layer of it on the waves; it left rainbows on the rocks.

Hector Apiro stood at the counter, organizing his scalpels and bone saws. "Overalls, Ricardo," the pathologist reminded him.

Ramirez pulled a pair off the hook by the door and slipped them on over his clothing. "I'm sorry I'm late, Hector. Detective Espinoza and I met with Manuel Flores this morning to discuss the murders. It took longer than I expected."

"No need to apologize. I did the visual examination before you got here and took photographs."

"You found film?"

Apiro smiled. "There were some seizures last night at the hip-hop festival. It seems the exhibit room has been restocked. You know, I wasn't even aware until this week that there *was* a hip-hop festival. I feel like I'm learning a whole new language." He laughed.

Apiro walked over from the counter holding a razor-sharp scalpel. "I looked around for graffiti this morning when I walked to work. There was one that impressed me. An image of a toddler strapped with a belt of what looked like explosives. On closer examination, they were cell phones. Subversive, of course, but clever."

Apiro climbed to the top rung of his stepladder. He leaned over the body and made a cut down the cadaver's chest. Gas escaped. Ramirez turned his head.

"Ah, yes," said Apiro. "The body returns to an elemental state quickly, doesn't it? Carbon dioxide, ammonia, methane gas—a veritable primordial stew. When I hear of scientists trying to come up with the right conditions to re-create life in their test tubes, I often think they choose the wrong media. A decomposing corpse has all the essentials. Imagine bringing one of *these* back to life."

Ramirez nodded uncomfortably. He could all too easily imagine it. "Is it safe to light a cigar in here, Hector?"

"Not only safe, but essential." Apiro grinned. "But stand well back; the body could ignite. Let's not create a real bomb this time, shall we?"

"After what happened at the museum, I'm not sure the fire department would rescue us unless we paid them." Ramirez stepped away. He reached beneath his overalls and removed a cigar from his jacket pocket. He lit it, cupping his hand around the match. "Initial thoughts?"

"He was in the water for at least two or three days. The skin on his hands and feet has slipped off; that's one indication."

Ramirez coughed lightly. He tried not to look. When he was in Patrol, he had attended autopsies of drowning victims where their skin could be removed as easily as socks or gloves. Sometimes entire fingers and toes were missing, nibbled away by fish. And in a badly decomposed corpse, the feet were often entirely gone. They sometimes washed up on the beach still wearing their shoes.

"The nice thing about finding a body in the Atlantic," said Apiro, "is that the salt and the cold water retard bacterial growth. Even so, his stomach is swollen as much with gas as with water. It's the putrefaction that caused the body to float. One thing that's surprising is that his corneas are filmy. Drowning victims usually float with their heads down. The water protects their eyes from the air. Quite startling, really, to see a corpse look at you with bright, clear eyes."

So I've learned, thought Ramirez. He pulled over a wooden stool and sat down, smoking quietly while Apiro went about his business.

Apiro removed the man's brain. He stepped down again and took the organ to the counter. He measured and weighed it before he placed it in a large glass jar full of formaldehyde. He peeled off his gloves and made a note on a pad of paper. The lights flickered, went out, then came on again.

"Nothing remarkable," said Apiro. He looked at the ceiling warily, but the lights stayed on. "The brain, I mean. The power being on is always remarkable. An interesting fact about the brain: It's one of the few things where size makes no difference. Marilyn Monroe's was actually larger than Albert Einstein's." He chortled.

He put his gloves back on and clambered up his stepladder again. He made another incision, carving the body neatly all the way down to the pubic bone. He pulled the skin back to reveal the rib cage. He removed the man's stomach. It looked like a wrinkled pink sack. He sliced it open.

"I don't see anything markedly unusual, Ricardo. Perhaps my

intuition was wrong. It could have been a drowning. Maybe he took off his clothes to go for a swim and was caught by the current. Although we didn't find any men's clothing on the beach."

But we wouldn't, thought Ramirez. Clothing abandoned on the rocks would be quickly recycled by anyone who came across it. If it hadn't washed out to sea with the body.

"We could probably close this file, then," said Ramirez, "if it wasn't for the ligature marks."

"Ligature marks?" asked Apiro. He lifted his head and raised his thick eyebrows.

Coño, thought Ramirez, realizing his mistake. The marks he had seen on the ghost had slipped away with the corpse's skin. He tried to think how to explain away the comment.

"Hmm," said Apiro, peering closely at the body again. "There *is* bruising in the soft tissue of the wrists and ankles." He looked at Ramirez quizzically. "I would have missed it, most likely. It does look as if it was caused by restraints."

"Handcuffs, or rope?"

"Impossible to tell. I'll examine samples of the tissue under a microscope and let you know what I find."

"Was he wearing any jewellery?"

"No, nothing."

Ramirez thought about the wide gold chain around the ghost's neck. Was it a robbery after all, then, a snatch-and-run that went terribly wrong?

"I hope we find out soon who he is," said Apiro. "We can't keep him in the morgue indefinitely. It's very sad. He has a family somewhere. He deserves a proper burial."

Ramirez nodded. Where possible, the dead were buried within eight hours. The tropical heat was not kind to corpses, not even in morgues with refrigeration units, because of the constant power outages.

For the first time, it crossed Ramirez's mind that Apiro would die someday. Ramirez always thought of his small friend as larger than life, as immortal. "Do you ever think of what you want people to say at your funeral, Hector?"

Apiro paused for a minute, cocking a bright eye. Then he cackled with delight. "I'd like someone to lean over my casket and shout, 'Oh my God, he's alive!'"

31

Charlie Pike almost hoped the autopsy had been cancelled due to the lousy weather. Dead people didn't frighten him, but seeing them cut open always unsettled him. He left his rental car in the parking lot by the nursing station. The SUV he parked beside looked like a creamsicle, almost completely covered under thick layers of ice and snow.

He approached a woman standing behind the reception desk and asked for Adam Neville.

"Dr. Neville is probably in the morgue," the nurse practitioner said. "That's down the stairs to your left, beside the vending machines. If he's not, there's a temporary office for visiting physicians on the lower level, too. He could be there."

When Charlie Pike walked through the swinging doors to the morgue, he found Neville wiping down a metal gurney with bleach. A woman's body lay on a stretcher beside it, resting on top of what looked like a black plastic sheet.

"Hello, Charlie," said Neville. He appeared tanned and healthy. "Hell of a way to get back to work."

"*Anii*, Adam. You were on holiday?"

"We were travelling down south for a few weeks. Denise is still in Pinar del Río. The president of the Columbian Mountain Climbing Federation is teaching a course she's always wanted to take. She says it's been wonderful. Pristine mountains, but not too challenging. She wanted me to stay, but I really had to get back to work. It's her first time hiking and climbing in quite a while. She'll be back at work as soon as they can find a place for her."

"I'm glad to hear she's better," Pike said. He liked Denise Labelle. She'd worked in the Winnipeg crime lab before she went on disability a couple of years earlier after suffering a minor stroke. "I didn't know you were a mountain climber."

Neville smiled. "Oh, yes. Denise and I met on Everest, actually. We were in the same climbing group. Contrary to popular belief, Everest isn't all that challenging if you acclimatize yourself and have a decent sherpa. The biggest risk, to be honest, are the lineups. We passed our share of dead bodies on the slopes; people who'd run out of oxygen because they were stuck in the queue trying to go up or down. Several had been there for years, frozen solid. Believe me, that was a shock."

"You couldn't bring them back down with you?"

"Oh, Lord, no. If someone dies on the mountain, that's it. The porters can only carry so much. Sad, really. But that's one of the risks of climbing. You'd be surprised how much trash gets left behind on that mountain. Abandoned equipment, axes, oxygen tanks."

Pike didn't much like the idea of dead climbers being left behind like garbage.

"By the way, Charlie, I have some photographs for you from the crime scene. They're on my laptop. It's over there on the counter. Go ahead, take a look. I'll get you hard copies when I get back to

Winnipeg. The file is on the desktop; it's named 'Jane Doe.' The exhibits are on the counter too. I've already processed the victim's clothing. Everything except the ligature."

"Any ID on the body?" asked Pike.

"No, nothing this time."

Pike walked to the counter. The screen saver on the laptop was a photograph of Adam and Denise Neville, tanned and smiling, hanging from harnesses on the side of a mountain.

Pike clicked on the file icon labelled "Jane Doe" and scrolled through the crime scene photographs, cringing as he saw the woman's body. She wasn't blue, he thought. Definitely white.

He and Sheldon had done well in the dark, he realized. Nothing looked different from what they'd found. He thought of telling Neville about the roll-your-own that the technicians missed, but he didn't want to embarrass the pathologist. Besides, Pauley Oshig could have been lying—he might have gone into the woods to have a smoke himself.

Still, it was sloppy. Pike decided he'd maybe talk to Chief O'Malley about the way the technical team had rushed through the investigation without thinking how that might come off to the First Nation. Then again, Bill Wabigoon probably wouldn't give a shit. He just wanted the body out of there—one less problem to deal with.

Pike riffled through the exhibits. He held up a bag containing a cigarette butt and raised his eyebrows. Neville nodded. "Yes, it was placed in almost exactly the same position as the others. But it's a Lucky Strike."

Pike wondered about that. None of the other crime scenes had two cigarette butts left behind.

"Put these on, will you, Charlie?" Neville handed Pike a pair of overalls, as well as a white mask and latex gloves. He pulled on his own.

"Can you give me a hand moving her off the body bag and onto the gurney? These body bags are terrific. Absolutely sterile. The nurse practitioner upstairs told me that Health Canada sent them here last fall after Chief Wabigoon asked for some help with the flu season. He wanted doctors; they sent body bags. Needless to say, he was furious."

Pike grunted as he helped Neville lift the body from the stretcher. Bodies weighed more when they were dead, he was sure. It was a mean trick that gravity played.

"I guess he drove over here and dumped them on the doorstep," Neville added. "After he called the CBC, of course. They've turned out to be surprisingly useful. The bags, I mean. Not the CBC, although God knows this place is crawling with reporters. They're all staying at Tops Motel. I had the pleasure of hearing them discuss sound bites last night at the bar. Are you staying there too? I suppose it's the only motel around here."

Pike nodded. "I think that's why they call it 'Tops.'"

Once the body was in place, Neville walked around it slowly, first pointing out the obvious. "A female, approximately five foot seven inches. Thirties, I'd guess. Caucasian. There is a ligature knotted around the neck. It appears to be a nylon stocking. Skin colour. I suppose my wife would call it nude. There are petechial hemorrhages in the eyes and a protruding tongue. Those suggest asphyxiation. By the way, Charlie, I've fingerprinted the body already. I should know if she's in the system before the end of the day. The OPP are going to run the prints for me."

Neville removed the stocking from around the woman's neck. Pike didn't see anything unusual about the knot as the pathologist untied it.

"It's not a full stocking, but a knee-high." Neville peered at the woman's skin beneath the stocking. "Almost no decomposition. That's the upside of these cases. The cold is a damn good preservative. I'd guess she was killed less than twenty-four hours ago. Can't tell you for sure until I examine her stomach contents. Hmm, Charlie. See the swelling on the neck? That means that pressure was transferred to the left side. It suggests that the perpetrator was right-handed. I think he used his right forearm to strangle her."

"His forearm?"

Neville glanced at Pike. "Looks like it could have been a chokehold. Maximal pressure, minimum effort. If he'd let go, she would have had a headache, but at least she would have survived. He kept the pressure on long after she lost consciousness."

Pike nodded. That by itself was enough for first-degree murder. "How long did he have to do that before she died?"

"At least a few minutes. But she was probably unconscious within seconds. And to answer the question you haven't asked yet: Yes, it looks the same as the others."

"When you first saw the body, was she blue?"

"You mean, other than her lips and tongue?"

"I'm not sure what I mean. The boy who found the body said she was blue. Said she glowed like a computer screen."

Neville frowned. "I can't imagine what he was talking about. The body has the purplish mottling you'd expect once circulation stops, but nothing you'd describe as blue, except perhaps the cyanosis from deoxygenation on her lips and fingertips. You can see it for yourself." He pointed. "Perhaps he meant that?"

Pike nodded doubtfully. "Maybe. Was she raped?"

"I won't know until I do a rape kit. There's nothing obvious. But the physical evidence of sexual assault can be very minor, Charlie."

Neville lifted up her hands, examining each finger. "See here? An expensive manicure, ruined. She must have tried to pry off his arm when he was choking her. But she was wearing leather gloves, so there's no tissue under her nails. Pity."

Pike looked at the woman's hands. The victim had struggled hard enough to break the tips of two fingernails. "Was she wearing any other clothing?"

"It's all bagged there on the counter. Down parka, black slacks, turtleneck, toque. Everything except footwear and her socks or stockings. I'm assuming, although I don't know, of course, that the nylon around her neck was hers. But her pants were done up; nothing to suggest he tried to remove them. Same as the others."

"Her boots were gone?"

"Well, we know she was wearing shoes or boots when she walked into those woods; we made casts of the prints. But she didn't have anything on her feet when I arrived. No socks, no stockings, nothing."

"There were tire tracks from the vehicle that parked on the shoulder. Did you see the shoe prints by them? Are they the same?"

Neville raised his eyebrows. "The only shoe prints we found were inside the woods. Did we miss something?"

"Sheldon pointed some out. They look like they were on the driver's side of the vehicle that was parked on the shoulder. They were hard to see. I took pictures and measurements."

"Good catch. Get me copies, will you? I'll compare them to the casts." He frowned. "Now don't tell anyone, Charlie, but the techs left as soon as they found out about the funding dispute. They called their union rep; he told them to get the hell out. No one was sure who was going to pay them. He was worried about liability too. I'm embarrassed, but there was nothing I could do. They drove back to Winnipeg as soon as they dropped the body off here. I certainly hope that's all they missed."

Pike nodded, uneasy. "First time he's done that. Taken away a woman's shoes, I mean. All the others had their boots or shoes on."

Neville shrugged. "Hard to say what a man like this might keep as a souvenir."

"When will you have results from the rape kit?"

"I have specimens from the posterior fornix and the endocervical canal to examine, as well as the vagina and rectum. There's a fairly well equipped lab here that I can use. I'll see what I can do before I head back to Winnipeg. Flights are all backed up because of the storm. I had planned to leave later today, but the earliest I can get out now is the day after tomorrow at noon. You around tomorrow, Charlie?"

Pike nodded. "Call me as soon as you have something, will you?" Then he remembered his cell phone problems. "Reception's not that great around here. If you can't reach me, call Celia Jones. You know Celia, don't you? Our departmental lawyer? She's up at her parents' place, visiting. It's not far from Manomin Bay."

"Sure. Just write down the number for me, will you?" The pathologist gestured to the counter.

Pike walked over and picked up a pen. He scrawled the number on a piece of paper. "So you think it's him?"

Neville looked at Pike. "Except for the missing footwear, everything else looks consistent. And the nylon tied around the neck; that's never hit the press."

"True," said Pike. "But you have to ask what the Highway Strangler would be doing all the way up here. All his other victims were a lot further south."

"I've heard people on the task force speculate he's a long-distance trucker."

"The only trucks going up the 562 are media vans and police SUVs right now, because of the blockade."

"Now, don't forget about the protestors," said Neville. "There must be a few dozen Mohawk Warriors at those barricades. No offence, but there are probably quite a few who have criminal records. You can't rule them out, Charlie."

"An Aboriginal serial killer?"

Neville smiled. "We don't want the task force to be accused of being racist again, do we? These are the days of equal opportunity. We can't rule out someone from the Manomin Bay First Nation either."

"People there don't generally hurt outsiders," said Pike. "They hurt themselves."

32

When Inspector Ramirez got back to his office, there was a message waiting for him from the entomologist, Dr. Yeung. He picked up the phone and returned her call.

"I was afraid you would be gone for the rest of the day," said Yeung. "It is almost time. Can you meet me at a Chinese restaurant in half an hour?"

Ramirez frowned. "Cubans can't go into tourist restaurants," he said. "Those are for foreigners only." He realized as soon as he said it that Dr. Yeung *was* a foreigner.

"Except in Chinatown."

She was right, thought Ramirez. The sole restrictions on Chinese restaurants related to their ownership, not who could dine in them. Only *chinos naturales* and their direct descendants could operate restaurants and food stands in Chinatown. They alone among Cubans had special licences permitting them to keep their profits.

The Chinese embassy supplied them with cutlery and linens. Los Tres Chinitos—The Three Chinese—was the best known, for its pizza.

"Besides, we won't be eating. There's someone I want to see. Can you meet me in front of the Seniors Centre in Chinatown in twenty minutes? Once the metamorphosis starts, it won't take long."

Ramirez looked at his watch. He could get there if he hurried. "I'm on my way."

He ran down the stairs to the parking lot and started his car. He quickly drove to the Capitolio and parked beside a line of old Chevys and horse-drawn carts. The horses shook their heavy heads in the late afternoon heat. Cigar ladies sat on the massive stairs, hiding their faces coyly behind their fans until camera-toting tourists dropped pesos at their feet.

Ramirez strode down Dragones. Children in the Parque de la Fraternidad played catch with empty plastic bottles and kicked around deflated soccer balls. An instructor led a group of foreigners in tai chi moves: The *extranjeros* grasped birds' tails, repulsed monkeys, lost their sequences, and started over, their faces rigid with concentration.

A rectangular *paifang* defined the entry into Chinatown. The wide concrete archway was funded by the People's Republic of China in a show of solidarity and friendship.

Ramirez strode past a century-old pharmacy. Like most in Havana, its shelves were mostly bare. A sign for traditional Chinese medicine, acupuncture, and traditional tuina massage announced that these would be provided by Drs. Romero, Santiago, and Lao.

Bodegas, laundries, and fruit stands lined the pedestrian walkway of Calle Cuchillo. Red paper dragons and lanterns hung from storefronts and restaurants.

Old men sat at plastic tables in front of the Seniors Centre arranging mah-jong tiles. Dr. Yeung was waiting by the front door.

She was plain, with oversized glasses. She shook Ramirez's hand lightly and dropped it. Ramirez sensed she was displeased that he was late. "I'm sorry. I came as quickly as I could."

She nodded without speaking and escorted him into a nearby restaurant. It was dark and cool inside. Waiters clad in silk jackets served tables. One sported a fake ponytail. Yeung pointed to a Formica table at the back. The dead woman wandered out of the shadows. She leaned against the table, amused.

Yeung motioned to a waitress, a *habanera* in a red silk dress with a Mandarin collar. She spoke rapid Chinese but the waitress shook her head, clearly not understanding.

The Barrio Chino was the largest Chinatown in Latin America, but there were few real Chinese left anymore. Of four Chinese language dailies, only the *Kwong Wah Po* remained in print. The paper was handset with Chinese characters by a man in his nineties. When he died, the newspaper would close, thought Ramirez. No one else knew how to do the printing, and no one cared to learn.

"She doesn't speak Mandarin or Cantonese, only Spanish," said Yeung, frowning. "Can you ask her to bring us some green tea? We need one bowl of steamed rice, and one set of chopsticks. While we wait."

Ramirez conveyed the instructions to the server in Spanish. When the waitress returned with the tea and the rice, Yeung turned the place setting to face the door. She stuck the chopsticks upright in the bowl.

"I thought we wouldn't be eating," said Ramirez.

"We won't be." Yeung smiled for the first time and looked almost pretty. "The rice is for the Yuān Guǐ. When we place the chopsticks in the rice bowl this way, we invite her to join us."

A smile tugged at the side of the dead woman's lips. She looked quizzically at the rice bowl. She finally sat down in the chair in front of the place setting, crossing her long legs. She pulled out her cigarette and tapped it on the surface of the table, swinging her foot, while Yeung poured the tea into small white porcelain cups.

"And just who is this person we are waiting for?" said Ramirez.

Yeung smiled. "It's not a person, Inspector. The Yuān Guǐ is the hungry ghost. But you need an 'ask rice' woman to speak to one."

———————

"An 'ask rice' woman communicates with ghosts," Dr. Yeung explained. Ramirez glanced at the dead *jinetera*; she shrugged her shoulders, amused. "Each vowel in Mandarin has four tones. With a slight change in tone, *mun mai poh*—ask rice—becomes 'spirit medium.'"

Ramirez sat back in his chair. He picked up the faded menu. It listed roughly eighty different choices, including chow mein, fried rice, and Hatuey beer. No spirit mediums were listed on the menu. There was no mention of fortune-telling, no reading of tea leaves. He put the menu down and raised his eyebrows.

"I am a Taoist, Inspector Ramirez," said Yeung. "We believe animals have souls. And we believe there are three kinds of ghosts. There are orphan ghosts, who have no children to honour them properly. There are the ghosts of those who die violently, who sometimes come back for revenge. And then there are the hungry ghosts, the ones who can't feed themselves enough no matter how hard they try. Most murdered women are hungry ghosts."

The dead woman tilted her head sideways. She looked at Ramirez and winked.

"Why is that?" Ramirez asked.

"Because they are more likely to be abused," said Yeung. "And far too often their needs are not met. An 'ask rice' woman can find out what is important to them. We can burn paper effigies to provide whatever it is they need. This stops them from wandering, and in return the hungry ghosts will give us clues about how they died."

Ramirez's ghosts provided him with clues whether he burned paper effigies or not. His face showed his skepticism.

"You don't have to believe in ghosts, Inspector Ramirez," said Yeung. "What's important is whether they believe in you."

"So this bowl of rice is supposed to summon a ghost?" said Ramirez, gesturing to the bowl.

"No," said Yeung. She sipped from her cup. "The chopsticks provide the invitation. When they are put in the rice upright, it signifies 'death.'"

A wizened Chinese woman entered the restaurant through curtains at the back. She nodded to Yeung and smiled. She wore a cluster of gold coins on a chain around her neck. She bowed to each of them. She sat in the chair next to the place setting, across from Yeung and Ramirez. Yeung poured her a cup of green tea.

"Normally," said Yeung, "we would use rice from the dead person's family. In this case, we don't know who she is, so this bowl of rice won't be enough. But we have these. They look like rice, and they were living in her body. It's the best we can do."

Yeung looked at her watch again. She opened her purse and removed a vial of squirming maggots.

Yeung handed the vial to the medium, who gripped it in both hands. The medium motioned towards Inspector Ramirez and spoke rapidly in Chinese. Yeung shook her head and shrugged her shoulders. The exchange lasted for several minutes before the old woman finally nodded and put the vial down on the table, then stood up and bowed to Ramirez. Yeung opened her purse and placed several tourist pesos on the table. The old woman picked them up and folded the bills inside her sleeve. She bowed to Yeung and Ramirez a final time and scuttled into the shadows.

"What did she say?" asked Ramirez.

Yeung looked at him cautiously. "We talked about Zhuangzi. He was a Chinese philosopher who dreamed he was a butterfly. When he woke up, he wasn't sure if he was a man who dreamed he was a butterfly, or a butterfly that dreamed it was Zhuangzi."

"I'm not sure I understand."

Yeung shrugged. "Taoists take the idea of opposites literally. Think of water. It is the opposite of hard. But it can break concrete."

"That's what she said?"

"It is not possible to translate exactly from Mandarin into English. The concepts are different between languages. But your investigation will be about opposites. Good and bad; hot and cold. You must be watchful for the *sei gweilo*."

"What is that?"

"Literally? It means the 'dead white ghost.' That's what the Chinese called the first white people they saw, because their skin was so pale. But it also means 'foreign devil.' Easily confused with *sei chai lo*."

"And what is a *sei chai lo*?"

"A bad policeman."

"It is time," said Dr. Yeung. She picked up the vial, pulled the stopper from the top, and emptied the glass tube into her palms, cupping her fingers together so that nothing spilled out.

As she slowly opened her fingers, Inspector Ramirez recoiled, expecting to see white larvae writhing on her palms. Instead, a dozen or more iridescent green flies crawled up to her fingertips. One by one, they cleaned their wings delicately, elegantly. Then they flew towards the door, drawn to the outside lights.

"Sheep blowflies. *Lucilia cuprina*," said Yeung. She removed a calculator from her purse and began entering numbers. "Some larvae were still in the woman's body when the dermestids moved in. They are beautiful, aren't they? You should see them under the magnifying glass. Silver heads, purple legs, red eyes, green metallic backs. The female blowfly mates only once; she lays nine batches of eggs during her lifetime. Pre-oviposition ranges from three to thirty-five days. The mean generation time is nineteen days, sixteen hours."

She turned the calculator towards him so he could see the numbers. "Your victim died on February 14, between 6:00 and 8:00 p.m."

She returned the empty vial and the calculator to her purse. "What are you, Inspector Ramirez?"

"I'm sorry?"

"I tell you a hungry ghost will join us and you express no surprise. You don't watch a bowl of rice, you watch an empty chair. The old woman asked me if you were *mingbairen*. I told her I think so."

"What is that?" asked Ramirez.

"One who sees ghosts."

33

Charlie Pike knocked on doors for several hours, but as Bill Wabigoon had warned, few band members wanted to talk to him about the murder. They were polite and invited him in, offered him cups of tea, asked him how things were in Ottawa, but changed the subject when he brought up the woman's death. A few who recognized him from the old days were a little more forthcoming.

"Yeah, come to think of it, I seen Freda Wabigoon's truck at the side of the road that day when I was heading out for gas, after the plow went by," Greg Keeshig said. "Hood was up, she had the pylons out. But Freda's truck is always in the ditch. Her winter tires are practically worn through. She wasn't in it, anyway. I left a message at the band council office for Bill to let him know. Saw her driving around later, so I wasn't too worried."

Darlene Big George remembered driving by an elderly white woman walking along the gravel road just after the storm ended. She was going to stop and see if the woman was okay, but then a man in an SUV pulled over and picked her up. He made a U-turn and drove back to the highway. She thought they were the white people who lived around the corner, but she didn't know their names. She'd never met them in person.

That was typical, thought Pike. The people she'd seen probably didn't know anyone from the reserve either. The two cultures might as well be living on different planets.

Nothing else came up in his round of canvassing. He clambered back into his rented SUV and turned on the ignition. He sat, idly tapping his pen on his notebook while the vehicle warmed up, trying to decide what to do next.

Sheldon Waubasking pulled beside Pike's car and rolled down his window. Pike rolled his down too.

"Want to come by for dinner?" Sheldon said. "Wife's a good cook. Venison. Fish right out of the bay. Bet you don't get that too often in Ottawa."

"Thanks," Pike said, "but I should get going. I need to get introduced to the local OPP watch commander."

"Pete Bissonnette? He's not a bad guy, once you get past all the swearing."

———————

The OPP station was in White Harbour. It was a flat brown building located across from the liquor store. Pike parked his car in the almost empty parking lot. He walked inside, identified himself to the officer behind the counter, and asked for the sergeant in charge.

"He's on the phone," the constable said. "He'll be with you in a minute."

A burly man with reddened skin and short red hair sat behind a desk in the open part of the office. Pike couldn't help but overhear.

"Well, we're really fucking busy. More Mohawks on the blockade. Crazy fuckers, coming here from fucking everywhere—Six Nations, Wahta, Oka, Cornwall, even New York. Who blockades a logging road in fucking minus-thirty weather? They're going to kill somebody, all the fucking rifles they've probably smuggled in behind the barricade. And we can't do fuck all about it until the company gets an injunction, which the local Crown says they may not be able to get, because the blockade's in the middle of a fucking land claim. Yeah, I know. Well, they've got till Friday, and then the AG wants us to do something. Tell you what, though, if we have to move in, all hell's going to break loose. Yeah, there's media all over the fucking place."

He put down the phone, and the constable approached him, motioned to Pike, and whispered something Pike couldn't hear.

"So you're Charlie Pike," the sergeant said, as he walked from his office to the counter, his hand extended. "I'm Pete Bissonnette. O'Malley called me. Said to expect you. He's a good man; known him for years. He didn't tell me you were an Indian."

"My mother was Mohawk." Pike didn't mention his father or his connection to Manomin Bay.

"Ah, fuck," said Bissonnette. He wiped his lips with the back of his hand. "I have a big mouth sometimes. What do you need, Pike?"

"Call me Charlie. I know you're monitoring traffic going up to the blockade. I'd like to see your daily logs for who drove on or off the Manomin Bay reserve between 4:00 p.m. on March first and 8:00 a.m. on the second. I'm going to want to run some motor vehicle and criminal record checks on anything that looks interesting."

Bissonnette reached below the counter and pulled out a log-book.

"Yeah, we're keeping an eye on things. At least trying to. The Quebec police never did that at Oka. Made it a fucking nightmare later on, trying to figure out how many people were inside the community centre when the army went in. We need to control this blockade, Pike, I mean Charlie. No violence. No Dudley Georges. Those are instructions straight from the AG."

He flipped through the lined pages and ran a nicotine-stained finger down the entries for the first and second of March. "All right. There was nothing moving on the 562 on March first until the plows went through. Then, starting at 1712 hours, there was a whole caravan of trucks and buses filled with . . . fuck, sorry . . . filled with Mohawk Warriors. My men stopped them. Found some rifles, shotguns; nothing registered. They seized the weapons and issued a few firearms charges, but let them go through."

"Did you run the plates?"

Bissonnette reached beneath the counter for a sheaf of papers. "I'm not a complete fucking idiot." He grinned and handed them to Pike. "Here, take a look. We can make copies of anything you need. Are you planning on going up there yourself?"

"Right after I leave here. I'd appreciate it if you let your men know I'm coming. I'm not armed. I'd rather not get shot, if things start to go south."

"You want to take a shotgun with you?"

Pike shook his head. "Then someone would shoot me for sure."

Charlie Pike scanned through the entries. A beige truck left the reserve at 1623 hours, Ontario plate 209LDA, registered owner William Wabigoon. That was 4:23 p.m. The same vehicle returned thirty-two minutes later. Must have been Freda's truck, Pike thought. The one Greg Keeshig saw broken down at the side of the road.

Pete Bissonnette had already pulled a copy of Bill Wabigoon's record off CPIC. A couple of common assaults. Nothing for more than ten years.

Nineteen other vans, trucks, and SUVs had been observed heading up to the blockade. Three of the registered owners had records, including everything from traffic violations to possession of drugs and firearms offences.

Sheldon Waubasking's bylaw truck had gone back and forth to the blockade twice. But Sheldon had no adult criminal record, only his youth convictions, and that record was sealed: O'Malley had made sure of that.

Nothing else stood out. The OPP hadn't checked any of the tires or tire widths on the vehicles that passed them. They were looking for armed protesters, not the Highway Strangler. They had no idea at the time that a woman had been murdered and left in the woods.

"Thanks," Pike said to Bissonnette. He looked out the window. The sun was low in the sky. "I think maybe I'll head up to the blockade now."

"Yeah, well, keep your fucking head down. It's a full moon tonight."

34

The air was thick with grey exhaust from dozens of idling police cars, media vans, trucks, and SUVs, as well as clouds of soot and ash. Oil cans burned with refuse and pine branches. A couple of blue portable toilets stood at the side of the road. Four Ojibway men sat around a large hide drum with a cloth skirt and elaborately beaded tabs, pounding it with their drumsticks.

Pike parked the SUV and walked the gauntlet of OPP officers, his hands open wide, showing them he was unarmed. He approached the one who appeared to be in charge.

"Did Sergeant Bissonnette call you to say I was coming?" He reached for his wallet with his police ID. "Just getting my badge out. I'm Charlie Pike. Rideau Regional Police. Ottawa."

"Yeah," the man said. He looked at the ID and handed Pike back his wallet. "He said it's okay to let you behind the lines. What's an Ottawa detective doing up here? Is it that murder on the reserve?"

Pike nodded. "Some of the people back there may know something. Might have seen something on their way here."

"Go ahead. But anything happens to you, it's not our responsibility, understand? You're on your own."

"Don't worry," Pike said and grinned. "I'll blame the feds."

The protestors had constructed a sweat lodge a few hundred yards back of the two overturned school buses. A bear skull sat on top of a two-by-four stuck in the ground. A small pile of offerings rested at its base—tobacco, sweetgrass, sage. A fire burned behind a barrier of plastic garbage cans set up to keep people from falling in the flames after they left the sweat.

Pike walked over to the firekeeper—the man tending the fire—and introduced himself.

"Where you from, Charlie?" the man said. "I knew a Henry Pike a long time ago. His Indian name was Assinack, same as his father."

"Manomin Bay. Henry Pike was my grandfather."

"He drowned, didn't he? He was a good man."

"Yes, he was."

"You go on in," the firekeeper said. "I'll look after your jacket and your shoes for you. You can strip down when you get inside. It's going to get real hot in there." He put another rock in the fire. The rocks were already red-hot, turning to grey ash.

The sweat lodges that Pike remembered from his youth had been covered with deer hide and moose skins. This one was made with canvas, plastic tarps, and carpet remnants. Pike was careful to approach the opening from the left. Eyeglasses, watches, and rings rested in a tin can outside the door. Pike removed the beaded cuff and dropped it in the can.

Once he entered, Pike moved around clockwise until he found an empty space and seated himself cross-legged against the tent wall. Another man, an elder, then sat beside Pike. He was Midewiwin,

Pike guessed, from the medicine bag he placed at his feet, a small deerskin pouch holding traditional medicines. The Midewiwin were healers, members of a secretive medicine society. He called to the firekeeper to close the flap.

Inside, it was pitch black. There was complete silence except for the sound of men breathing shallowly as they took off their socks and shirts. Then the elder spoke.

"If it gets too uncomfortable for you and you need to go, just call out 'all my relations' before you leave. We'll begin with a prayer once the stones are hot enough. But first, we'll have a smudge."

All my relations. The old phrase affirmed the equality of peoples. Pike recalled one of the old man's lessons: "Everyone, and everything, is connected." But for years Pike had felt disconnected. He sat back on his tailbone, thinking about his family. His dead father and mother, his *mishomis*. The little brother he hadn't seen for years. The elderly auntie he'd barely summoned the courage to visit.

The elder lit a braid of sweetgrass in a clamshell. He made his way around the circle clockwise, crawling on his knees as he moved in front of each man. He swept the smoke towards Pike with an eagle feather. Pike waved the sweet smoke over his chest, his face, cleansing himself, purifying his thoughts. The elder moved slowly, smudging each man until he returned to his original position.

The only light came from the tip of the burning grass. It could have been minutes or hours that passed before the elder called for the firekeeper to bring in the hot stones.

The firekeeper opened the flap and carried in the red-hot rocks with a shovel. When he was done and the flap was closed again, the rocks glowed red like the end of a campfire in the deep of a summer night. The cleansing smell of cedar boughs was soon replaced with the pungent scent of men.

"So now we'll begin. We'll dedicate our prayers tonight to the Grandfathers, and pray to the Sky Father," said the elder. "To honour the four directions, we'll have four rounds tonight. The fourth is going to be the hardest. It always is."

Grandfathers was what the Anishnabe called rocks. The bones of Mother Earth. His grandfather's bones. Pike felt tears prick his eyes at the thought of his *mishomis* being pulled down in the water, his bones resting like stones at the bottom of Manomin Bay.

The elder threw cedar water on the firepit with a dipper and the sweat lodge filled with steam. He picked up a small hand drum and thumped it methodically, calling out to the spirits in Ojibway.

"Thank you for making this world," he said. "Thank you for the air and the water, the animals, the plants. Make us strong enough to lead our children out of the darkness, to heal our bodies and our minds."

But in Pike's ears, it wasn't the elder who spoke, it was the old man. Pike recognized his voice, the soft lisp of missing teeth. "You'll need courage, son. Courage to find out where you belong, courage to see the truth. White, red, yellow, black—in the womb of Mother Earth, we're all equal."

The elder spoke again in his own voice. "We're going to go around the circle, so you can tell the Creator your clan and why you're here, so the spirits can guide you."

A talking stick was passed from hand to hand. No one interrupted another man's story. The familiar voice to Pike's right surprised him. He hadn't seen Sheldon come in. Pike leaned forward slightly, listening attentively.

"I'm Bear Clan. I'm here because I feel guilty. A white woman was murdered in our territory." Sheldon hesitated. "I don't know the right thing to do, if I should talk about it or not."

The elder splashed water on the rocks; the steam hissed. "We honour the Bear Clan tonight because it's a full moon," he said. "The Bear Moon is the time when we can see beyond the curtain and share our deepest thoughts. You don't have to say anything out loud if you don't want to; the Creator will hear you. That goes for everyone."

The talking stick made its way around the circle. Pike was the last man to hold it. "I'm here because of an old man," he said. "He's the only man alive who still calls me son, and he's dying. I guess I'm afraid of losing him too."

Pike recalled the old man's last story, the burden he'd transferred to Pike when he gave him the beaded cuff, the weight he'd carried too long. The old man had already told Pike that he was sexually abused by a visiting priest at residential school when he was nine, the same day his little brother drowned. But this time, he'd provided details.

"You know, it's been sixty years, and I can still smell his breath. I knew it was wrong, but I was scared. If you didn't do what they told you, you'd get the strap. I felt as low as a snake after that. The only thing that made me feel better was alcohol and sometimes women, but the women never stayed, and the bottles were always empty the next morning.

"I have a lot of children, but they all have different mothers. I have grandchildren, but I don't know where they are anymore, so when you call me *mishomis*, that means a lot to me. I learned about Indian medicine when I served time for manslaughter. That's where I found my language again. That's funny, isn't it, that I learned to be an Indian in prison."

I've lost every man I cared about, thought Pike. My father. My grandfather. And I'm going to lose the old man soon too. *All my relations*. He blinked back smoke from his eyes.

When no one else spoke, Pike realized he hadn't named his clan. "I'm Northern Pike by my father, but my mother was *Kahniakehake*. Mohawk. She was Wolf Clan. I'm Wolf Clan, too, I guess, by her people's laws."

"The Creator gave you two clans for a reason," said the elder. "He gave you two ways to deal with the world. That's your strength."

The elder picked up his little drum again and began to sing. Thunder crashed in Pike's head. He saw his father weighed down with furs, eaten away by cancer. He saw his grandfather drowning in the bay, his brown hand disappearing beneath the ice. He saw the old man, wrapped in his blankets, seated on a bench, the snow falling on his soft cheeks like frozen tears.

A woman's body lay in the forest, covered with branches. Black crows anxiously cawed overhead. Pauley Oshig leaned over to touch her, then ran off to tell his uncle what he'd seen, a man who, according to Sheldon Waubasking, the boy feared even more than a dead body. What was it that Pauley saw?

He heard the sound of thunder. Rain rolled down Pike's cheeks before he realized it was tears.

———

"That was something, eh?" Sheldon Waubasking said to Charlie Pike afterwards. They sat in the snow, cooling off. "Makes you think. Might be the longest I've ever gone without talking."

The sky winked with millions of stars. Spirits of the dead, his grandfather called them. The moon was the lady in white. *Ohmahauuk Namakshi.* She who never dies. The moon was full but partially obscured by clouds. A Bear Moon, like the elder said.

"What do you mean, Sheldon?" said Pike. "You talked about the dead woman. I talked about my family."

Or did he? For a moment Pike wasn't sure if the words had escaped his mouth or he had simply thought them.

Sheldon looked at his friend. "You feeling okay, Charlie? No one said a word after the elder told us it was a Bear Moon, that we were going to slip through the curtain. He told us we could speak through our thoughts."

35

As soon as Inspector Ramirez hung his jacket on the back of his chair, Detective Fernando Espinoza walked through his doorway.

"Good. You're back." Espinoza held a piece of paper, grinning. "I wasn't sure if you'd be working again this evening. I think I found something." The young detective's eyes were rimmed with red from reading through stacks of missing person reports. "There was a woman who disappeared two weeks ago. She was reported missing by her husband on February 16. She's twenty-one. Brown hair, brown eyes. She was wearing silver earrings. Her name is LaNeva Otero."

Espinoza handed Ramirez the report. "The husband, Juan Otero, gave an address on Pedro Perez, but it's not in the system. And Inspector, I checked our records. Señora Otero received two *cartas de advertencia* last year." The warning letters were given to prostitutes to tell them they could be fined or sent to rehabilitation camps if they didn't reform. "She was deported to Santiago in January after she was stopped a third time for prostitution."

"It looks like she came back," said Ramirez, and reached for his jacket.

Pedro Perez was a well-treed boulevard in Carraguao, not far from the baseball stadium. The Great Stadium del Cerro was known for its grass turf. All the major baseball games in Havana were held there, as well as concerts, soccer matches, even a bullfight once. But its roof was falling apart and the floodlights no longer worked.

Cerro, the neighbourhood around the stadium, was a busy spot for the police, the centre of the local crack cocaine trade as well as prostitution.

Ramirez steered skillfully around huge potholes that threatened to engulf his small car while Espinoza watched for the address. The dead woman sat in the back seat, gripping her cigarette nervously. When they found it, Ramirez parked beside the cracked curb. He and Espinoza climbed out. The dead woman followed.

No laundry hung from the building's windows. No televisions flickered on the balconies. Doors and shutters hung askew. The building looked abandoned.

"Maybe it's been condemned," said Espinoza, looking up. "If it hasn't, it should be."

"It and every other building around here," said Ramirez. "Let's start on the top floor and work our way down. But be careful. We want to come down the stairs, not through them."

Ramirez, Espinoza, and the ghost walked up the rotted staircase to the third floor. They rapped on each of the scarred doors, making their way down the hallway. No one responded. They moved carefully, avoiding loose floorboards, stepping around gaps. Finally they knocked on a door that creaked open. A young man peered around the door frame. He was black, perhaps in his twenties, with a flat stomach and strong arms.

"Señor Otero?" said Ramirez. "You filed a missing person report?" He produced his badge.

"Are you here about LaNeva?" the man asked, trembling.

"May we come in?"

Otero nodded, and Ramirez and Espinoza entered the apartment. All the windows were cracked. Ramirez looked around the unit as his eyes adjusted to the light.

There was a stained mattress and pillow lying on the floor. The kitchen was a tiny space with two rickety wooden chairs and a small table on which an ancient television rested. It wasn't plugged in; it was obvious that there was no electricity. A shelf held a battered metal bowl. There were no signs of children, no small clothes, no toys. For that, Ramirez was grateful.

The apartment bore signs of a man unaccustomed to living alone. Dirty clothes littered the floor. A broken mirror hung crookedly on the wall. A framed photograph of a woman lay on the ground, its glass shattered. Ramirez made a mental note of the hole in the wall where he guessed the photograph had hung, about three feet from the mirror.

"May I see your *carnet*?" he asked.

Otero produced his identity card. Ramirez turned it over. The address on the back was for Holguín province instead of Havana. Ramirez didn't comment on this illegality and handed it back. "When was the last time you saw your wife, Señor?"

"On February 15. She left around seven that night to go to work. I reported her missing the following afternoon."

"Why wait until then?" said Espinoza, pulling his notebook out of his pocket.

"She often stayed out late." Otero hesitated. "She was sometimes gone overnight."

"What did she do for a living?" asked Ramirez. He wasn't sure if Otero would answer truthfully. Prostitution within their own families was something Cuban men didn't like to acknowledge. Most were uncomfortable with the idea of women as primary breadwinners, although mothers urged their young daughters to grow up pretty so they could meet foreigners. He thought of his little daughter, Estella, and hoped the day wouldn't come where she'd have to sell her body to strangers to get by. He looked at the ghost; she shrugged her shoulders as if to say it hadn't been her first choice either.

"Is LaNeva all right?" Otero asked. He twisted the bottom of his T-shirt in his fingers.

"Señor, answer the inspector's question," said Espinoza. "Where did she work?"

Otero took a deep breath. "She was a waitress at El Bosquecito. She didn't tell me much about it. She said she didn't want to get me in trouble if she was arrested."

"Arrested for what?" said Espinoza.

"This apartment wasn't assigned to anyone. Will you report me? They'll send me back to Holguín. There's no work there."

The young man had abruptly changed the subject. This caught Ramirez's attention; it was often a sign of guilt.

"We're not concerned with your housing arrangements, Señor," said Ramirez. "We're here about your wife. Did she have another address in Havana? Somewhere else she might stay?"

Otero shook his head. "No. After we got married, we lived with one of her relatives, but her building was declared dangerous to public health; it was built on top of a garbage dump. We have to be processed to work in Havana, but neither of us can work without a residency card. We heard this building was empty and moved in. We had nowhere else to go; we had no money."

Ramirez nodded. Regulations required that each resident have a permanent home, but living in a building declared uninhabitable didn't qualify. The fee for a residency card was one hundred convertible pesos, more for the bribe. That was six months' salary for most Cubans—impossible to obtain if one couldn't work legally.

They must have been desperate, thought Ramirez. Without residency cards, they couldn't get food legally either. The *libreta*, the coupon book that allowed Cubans to purchase rations, could only be used at the bodega that served one's official residence.

The rules were intended to prevent overcrowding, but instead tens of thousands of Cubans who came to Havana looking for work were declared illegal immigrants and deported from their own capital. Otero was clearly afraid of becoming one of them.

"How could her employer pay her if she didn't have a card?" said Espinoza.

Good question, thought Ramirez. And probably the reason LaNeva Otero feared arrest. She would be in more trouble for working illegally than for being a *jinetera*. Working without a residency card was a serious crime.

Otero hesitated. "They didn't give her money. They let her keep the food the tourists left on their plates. That's how we got by."

"Did she ever bring home fruit?" Ramirez asked.

"Sometimes. Overripe bananas mostly. Once, a pineapple."

"What about apples?"

Otero shook his head. "I would have remembered that. Why do you ask?"

Ramirez didn't respond. If LaNeva Otero was dead, her husband could be responsible. As an investigator, it was best to keep one's cards close to one's chest in these situations. "Do you have a photograph of your wife, Señor?"

Otero gestured to the picture on the floor. Ramirez bent down and picked it up. He held it in front of him, squinting to see the photograph in the dim light. The dead woman stood beside him. She wiped tears away with her fingers.

From her complexion in the picture, LaNeva Otero appeared

to be *javao*. She was leaning against an old Chevy with raised fins, holding a bouquet of white flowers. She wore a white wedding dress.

The ghost smiled through her tears and shook her head slightly. Ramirez understood: LaNeva was no virgin.

"Can we take this for our investigation?" Ramirez asked. "I promise to return it."

Otero nodded. "Where is LaNeva? Have you found her?"

"Maybe," said Ramirez. "But if it is her, Señor Otero, I am afraid we have very bad news."

———

The excitement in Detective Espinoza's voice mounted as they drove back to police headquarters. Ramirez kept casting his eyes to the back seat, but there was no sign of the female ghost, and the male ghost had disappeared once Ramirez had banished him at the ministry.

"If she worked at El Bosquecito, she could have met her clients there," said Espinoza. "It's a popular tourist hangout."

The Little Forest Bar. It was like the Grimms' fairy tales, thought Ramirez. Everything bad happened in the forest. "We need to be sure it's her this time," said Ramirez. "Talk to the employees as well as the manager. They're more likely to tell the truth if they find out she's missing. Tell them we're not interested in charging them, only in finding LaNeva alive. If she was there on the fifteenth, we need to know what time she left and if she left alone. And let's make sure she wasn't arrested in a sweep."

Jineteras could be jailed for months before anyone knew they were there. Even the police could have a hard time tracking them through the rehabilitation camps.

"I'll check to see if Juan Otero has a criminal record as well," said Espinoza.

"Good idea," Ramirez agreed. Most murders were domestic.

People who cared for each other were the most likely to kill each other.

"Shall I have Patrol bring Señor Otero to the morgue to identify the body?"

"I'm not sure anyone can," said Ramirez, recalling the condition of the remains. "But he might recognize the purse."

Ramirez dropped Espinoza off at police headquarters and drove home. He parked his car down the street from his apartment and stopped at a food stall for a *cucurucho*. It was a treat made from coconut, orange, papaya, and honey; the first thing he'd eaten all day.

Ramirez wished Francesca was home to cook him a late dinner. She could make rice and beans taste special. She could make even plantains delicious, sometimes thinly slicing the green ones and frying them into wafers, or mashing the black, ripe ones and serving them with crispy pork rinds.

She prepared punched plantains—*plátanos a puñetazos*—by smashing them hard with the side of her fist before she returned them to the stove. The thought of his wife's unbridled aggression towards harmless vegetables made Ramirez smile.

But he would have to fend for himself.

Ramirez's cell phone rang as he passed a handful of domestic pesos to the vendor. He held the phone to his ear, his voice muffled by the sweet stuffed in his mouth. "*Hola.*"

"Señor Otero is at headquarters now," said Espinoza. "Patrol took him to the morgue, but he couldn't identify the body because of its condition. I had them bring him here to look at the victim's clothing. He recognizes the silver earrings. He says they were his mother's, a wedding gift to his wife. But he's never seen the purse before."

"Most men wouldn't pay much attention to a purse," said

Ramirez. "It might not mean anything one way or the other. I think we can safely assume, now, that our victim is LaNeva Otero, unless Dr. Apiro tells us otherwise."

He gave Espinoza further instructions and put the cell phone back in his jacket pocket, troubled.

36

There was a rap on the back door. Surprised, Celia Jones got up from the couch to answer it. Her parents didn't often have visitors this late at night.

Charlie Pike poked his head through the doorway. "Hey Celia. I know it's getting late, but I thought you might have the kettle on."

"Are you kidding? It's always on these days," she said. "Good to see you, Charlie. Come on in. I'm glad you dropped by. Adam Neville called a few hours ago and left a message for you; he said your cell wasn't picking up. He wanted me to tell you the OPP couldn't match the fingerprints he took from the victim. She's never been printed before."

"I gave him your number. Hope you don't mind. My cell phone doesn't always work up here."

"Of course I don't mind. Quick now, close the door, get in out of the cold."

Pike brushed some snowflakes from his long hair and stamped his feet to shake off the snow. As he pulled off his jacket, Jones once again noticed the blue tattoos on the back of his knuckles. "I was expecting you," she said. "Miles called. He said you might need a hand."

Jones introduced Charlie Pike to her mother. Emma Jones was watching television, seemingly mesmerized by the flickering images of camouflaged Mohawk Warriors at the blockade, bandanas wrapped around the lower half of their faces. The same breathless reporter announced that the standoff was getting worse.

"That's such an odd choice of words, isn't it, dear?" Emma Jones said. "A standoff is a stalemate. If it got worse, or better, it wouldn't be a standoff anymore. It's quite the situation, isn't it?"

"Frankly," said Pike, "I'm surprised there haven't been more." He caught Jones's eye and gave a quick nod towards the doorway. He wanted to speak to her in private. They walked into the utility room and out of earshot.

"I need to bounce something off you. I have a witness I don't know how to deal with. A boy with fetal alcohol syndrome. He found the body. I think he maybe saw something, but he's not easy to figure out. You free to go somewhere where we can discuss this? I could use some advice."

"Sure. Why don't we go into town and grab a coffee at the A&W? They're open till eleven. My dad's here, so I can leave for a while." She lowered her voice. "I wouldn't mind a break from babysitting anyway."

"Sounds good," Pike said.

Jones told her father she was going out and kissed her mother on the cheek. She pulled on her parka and boots and they walked out to Pike's car.

The A&W restaurant looked deserted. As Pike turned into the parking lot, the SUV skidded sidewise and almost rammed a truck.

Jones gripped her door handle tightly until he got it straightened out. "Christ," she said. "That was a little scary."

———

Over coffee, Pike told Celia Jones about Pauley Oshig and how he'd described seeing the blue lady.

"That's weird, isn't it?" Jones said, wrinkling her forehead.

"I don't know what to make of him," Pike agreed. "He's not like any FAS kid I've ever heard of. For one thing, he can use the computer to play video games. And he draws. He's pretty good at it too. But he doesn't always make a lot of sense. He was talking to me fine until his auntie walked in. Then he clammed up. I think he's scared."

"Of what?" When Pike didn't answer, she guessed. "Do you think he's been abused?"

Pike looked out the window at the falling snow, avoiding Jones's eyes, not sure how much information to share. "The bylaw officer on the reserve is an old friend of mine. He's seen bruises on the boy. He thought Pauley was being picked on at school. Pauley's uncle, Bill Wabigoon, is the chief now. He says that Pauley hits himself sometimes, but I know what Bill was like when he was a kid. He was a bully. I don't know how much he's changed. Pauley's staying at Bill's place. It worries me."

"Shouldn't you do something? Tell Children's Aid?"

"Tell them what? They'd probably come in, take one look at the living conditions, and scoop him up, and then we'd have a riot at the blockade for sure. He's the chief's nephew."

"I don't know, Charlie. You can't ignore child abuse when you see it."

He shook his head again. "That's the problem. You never see it. People hide it. Look at all the things that happened at the residential schools around here. It's complicated, me being here. I know things about the people that someone from outside wouldn't know."

"That's good, isn't it? Having an insider's view?"

"Makes it harder to be objective."

Jones nodded and drank from her coffee. "You said the chief was a bully. Was he violent?"

"You ever hear of the Indian Posse?"

"The street gang? Sure. Gang members were all over the reserves in Saskatchewan when I was stationed there with the RCMP."

Pike looked out the window again, remembering. A car skidded in the snow. It almost hit another. Horns blared. The drivers gave each other the finger. Tensions were running high, with the bad weather and the blockade.

"Richard Wolfe started it up in Winnipeg. Members used to wear red bandanas. Richard wanted Indians to respect themselves. He used to say, when you see red, you see a proud Indian. Billy Wabigoon was Posse too. My best friend, Sheldon, and me, we were strikers."

"What does that mean, being a striker?" asked Jones.

"We were prospects. Billy did just about everything he could think of to get us to join."

Until Sheldon Waubasking beat the shit out of him, thought Pike, and almost killed him. "Then O'Malley found us pulling a B & E, and that was the end of that."

"O'Malley caught you breaking into a house?"

"Well, actually," Pike said, "it was an apartment."

37

Charlie Pike had been wriggling out of the window when someone grabbed him by the scruff of the neck and pulled him the rest of the way out. *Fuck*, thought Charlie. He had a small plastic radio in his hands. It dropped. He heard it crack on the sidewalk.

The sky fell as he was rolled face down on the ground; his arms were yanked behind his back, he heard the metal click of handcuffs. Then he was pulled up into a sitting position and propped against the wall of the building. A cop with a neck like a bull and a shiny bald head was holding him by his shirt collar. The bull-man had a patch on his shoulder that said, "One, With the Strength of Many." *No shit*, Charlie thought. His biceps were as thick as Charlie's thighs.

"How old are you?" the cop asked.

"Twelve," Charlie lied. He was small for his age; maybe the bull-man would let him go. Twelve was too young to be charged under the Young Offenders Act.

"What's your date of birth?"

Charlie hesitated while he tried to figure it out. Math wasn't his strongest subject. He calculated wrong.

"So now you're fourteen? Make up your mind, son. Where are you from?"

"White Harbour." It was close enough, and he didn't want the cop calling the school.

"Where's that?

"I dunno. A couple of hours from Kenora."

"What are you doing in Winnipeg? Besides stealing other people's property?"

Charlie shrugged.

"Don't be a smartass, son. You're in a deep pile of shit at the moment."

He said "shite" not shit, Charlie noticed. He had a thick accent. But he didn't seem angry. More amused. "I came here with my buddy," he answered.

"The one who melted away like the last bit of snow when he saw us walking towards you? Good friend, that one. How long have you been in Winnipeg?"

Charlie looked around. The cop was right. Sheldon had fled. "I dunno. A couple of months."

Another policeman, just as beefy but a foot shorter, walked towards them dragging Sheldon beside him. Sheldon's hands were cuffed in front of him. The other cop sat Sheldon on the ground beside Charlie. "He's got an Indian Posse tattoo, Sarge," he said.

"Yes, so does this one. What's your name?" the big bald cop asked Sheldon.

Charlie relaxed a bit. He and Sheldon had agreed that if they got busted again, they'd make up fake names. He was still thinking about what name to invent when the other cop shook Sheldon by the shoulder. "You heard him. What's your name?"

"Charlie Pike," Sheldon said.

Charlie twisted around to glare at his friend. "I told you to *make up* a name. Not give him *my* name, asshole."

The bald cop laughed; a deep sound that rumbled from his stomach all the way up to his massive chest. "So this is organized crime? Pretty disorganized, I'd say. Now, give me your real names. And if you lie to me again, I'll have to charge you with obstruction."

They gave their names, although reluctantly.

"Go call these in, Albert, and let's see just what kind of delinquents we have here."

The other cop walked up the street to a patrol car. He came back a few minutes later, smiling smugly. "Supposed to be in kiddy court next week to enter pleas. Six counts of break and enter, possession of stolen property under."

"No convictions?"

"Not yet. Won't take long."

"You boys are lucky. Even if you're convicted, in a couple of years those records will disappear, if you keep your noses clean." The bull-man sat on the ground beside the two boys. "So, you're supposed to be Posse, are you?"

Sheldon wasn't saying anything, leaving it to Charlie to navigate their way out of trouble.

"Well, I don't think you're Posse at all. I think you just pretend to be." Charlie shook his head in wonder. Maybe the bull-man was some kind of shaman. "I think you put those tattoos on yourselves. Or someone else did it for you. For one thing, the *IP* is upside down. It says *dI*."

It was Billy Wabigoon's idea. "Here," he had whispered to them. "You do this and they'll leave you alone. You got to be careful in here. Those big boys, they get their hands on you, they're going to hurt you. They'll fuck you in the ass. You understand? You let me put these on you, they'll think you're Posse."

Charlie looked at the tattoos. It stung to have the ink rubbed in, but it worked like a talisman. They had been left alone. Maybe the other Indian Posse members couldn't read so well upside-down either.

"Who's supposed to be looking after you? They don't let you out of custody in that court unless there's an adult who can keep an eye on you."

Neither boy spoke.

"Do you want to go back to jail?"

Sheldon caught Charlie's eye. No, neither of them wanted that.

"Sheldon's sister," Charlie said.

O'Malley pulled out his notebook. "And so why isn't she keeping tabs on you?"

"Sophie? I dunno. She goes out a lot."

"Sophie Waubasking?" The big cop sighed. He pulled himself to his feet, walked over to the other cop. Charlie could hear them talking, even though the bald cop kept his voice low.

"The sister's gone missing. She's a hooker, an addict. A sad case. I've dealt with her before. These boys are homeless."

"What do you want to do with them, Sarge?"

"If we charge them, they'll go right back into custody. There's something about this pair I like. Maybe their cheekiness. I don't usually see it with Indian kids."

"Jesus, Sarge," the other cop said. "Can't you just give money to the SPCA like anyone else? You still like stray cats, don't you?"

O'Malley roared with laughter. "I never did like stray cats," the big man said. "But stray kids, now that's a different story."

38

"*My God, Charlie, I had no* idea you and O'Malley went back that far," said Celia Jones. "Did he charge you?"

Charlie Pike shook his head. "We were lucky. The apartment we broke into was his. He thought we should have a second chance because we were kids. But so were most of the Posse members. Richard Wolfe was only fourteen when he and his brother Daniel and two others created the Posse. He wasn't what you think of when you think 'gang leader.' He had a kind of charisma, but he was quiet, talked a lot about family. They chose the name Posse because they thought that's what it meant. But then they got into debt collection, drugs, robberies. Things got violent." Pike looked at his knuckles. "The Cripps and the Posse started fighting for control of the drug trade. Going to jail didn't stop them. That's where the Posse was most active."

"And Bill Wabigoon, how was he involved?"

"He was one of the founding four."

Jones raised her eyebrows.

"That's what has me worried," said Pike. "There are Warriors coming here from all over the country to support the blockade. A lot of them are Bill's friends. I'm sure some are Posse members. Adam Neville says we can't rule out one of them as the killer. He may be right."

"I wish I could help, Charlie. I'm way out of my element with this stuff."

Pike shook his head. "I know. I'm just feeling kind of stuck. I still don't know who our victim was. I can't figure out how she ended up in the territory. There aren't any reports of a white woman missing around here, so she must have come from somewhere else, maybe down south. But if she had a car, where is it? There was only one set of tire tracks at the side of the road."

Jones thought for a minute. "Maybe she was hitchhiking and the killer picked her up."

"I don't think so. Adam said she had an expensive manicure. People with money don't hitchhike. Unless her car broke down in the storm and got towed. But then, whoever towed her would have taken her to wherever she was staying." Pike picked up his mug, turned it in his fingers while he thought. "Maybe the killer pretended *his* vehicle broke down. He could have flagged her over and drove her to the reserve so he could kill her. Could be somebody who knew about the funding issues with the APF, how hard it is right now to get a police investigation done on a First Nation reserve. Tell me something, Celia. If you saw a man hitchhiking around here, would you stop?"

She hesitated. "Honestly, I'm not sure. It would depend."

"Depend on what?"

"Charlie, most women are nervous about male hitchhikers. Red, white, black, green—I don't think it makes a difference. An older white man or a kid with a backpack, maybe. A biker with tattoos, probably not. I know it's wrong, but to some extent we all believe in stereotypes, right? Police use them all the time. But you know, just

after a bad storm, I'd like to think I would stop. You'd feel sorry for
the guy. You wouldn't automatically think 'axe murderer.'"

Pike nodded slowly. It hadn't occurred to him that white people
were afraid of anything. He had been trying to see this from the perspective of an Aboriginal victim, but this victim wasn't First Nation.
That made a difference. Pauley Oshig was right. She was the wrong
colour.

"There's something else. I was looking at the photographs of
the Highway Strangler exhibits on the way up here. There's something funny about the stocking that was tied around one of the victim's necks. It had a kind of a square seam at the heel, like this." He
reached for his pen and drew a sketch for her on a paper napkin. "I
don't pay much attention to women's nylons. Are these common?"

Jones looked at it carefully. "No. Definitely not. But I've seen
stockings with seams like that before somewhere." She tried to remember. "I think it was in a photograph in one of my mom's photo
albums. I'll look for it tomorrow morning and ask her. Are you
heading back to your motel?"

"Yeah, it's pretty late. You can call me there in the morning if
you come up with something. Your mom can remember that kind
of detail?"

"It's mostly the present she's losing, Charlie. Not the past."

39

When Inspector Ramirez entered the Major Crimes Unit the next morning, Natasha Delgado was grinning. "I found Mama Loa, that *yerbera* whose address was on Antifona Conejo's ID card," she said. "The block captain was right. Everyone in Cayo Hueyso knows her. Her last name is Adivino, but she's not in any of our records. I think maybe she made it up. She lives on the Isla del Polvo."

"Adivino?" The word meant fortune-teller. "I thought she was supposed to be an herbalist."

Delgado shrugged her shoulders. "The people I talked to say she's a psychic, that she can tell the future."

"Where's Detective Espinoza?" asked Ramirez, glancing around the office. Espinoza's desk was empty.

"Out looking for women's nylons. I told him, if he finds some, to get me a pair."

Ramirez smiled. "You want to come along and help me interview

Señora Adivino? We still need to find out why LaNeva had Antifona Conejo's identification in her purse. Maybe she knows."

The Isla del Polvo—the Isle of Dust—was in the Marianao district. It was a kind of makeshift refugee camp. There were similar shantytowns all over Havana, housing the thousands of migrants who streamed in from the countryside in search of jobs that didn't exist.

They built homes out of corrugated steel and bits of wood. Some looked like they were constructed by mud wasps. Thirty thousand people lived in roughly five square kilometres. But here, as in Cayo Hueso, everyone seemed to know Mama Loa. Ramirez and Delgado were directed to her shanty.

They found her sitting on a mildewed rocking chair in front of a lopsided shack on the edge of the shantytown.

Ramirez couldn't tell the old woman's age; she could have been sixty or eighty. She had long brown hair streaked with grey that wound down below her shoulders in coils. She wore a white bandana and a long red skirt. Somehow, she had managed to keep them clean.

A Taino tobacco idol with shell eyes sat on a wooden crate beside her chair, next to a metal can that held plastic flowers. Beside it rested a *guano*, a large green leaf blessed by a Catholic priest. Ramirez noticed the crucifix that hung around Mama Loa's neck. Whatever religion she believed in, thought Ramirez, she wasn't taking any chances.

"Señora Adivino?"

"Some call me that, yes." The old woman opened her eyes slowly. They were clear, the irises and pupils as dark as her ebony skin. Her rocking chair slowly creaked back and forth. "But most call me Mama Loa."

She spoke with a Creole accent, her *s*'s soft and prolonged. She was probably from Haiti, thought Ramirez. One of the waves of immigrants who came to Cuba in the thirties and forties.

"Señora, we're here about Antifona Conejo," said Ramirez. "She listed your address in Cayo Hueso on her official papers."

"I know that's why you're here. That police lady with you, I know why she's here too." The old woman nodded her head towards Detective Delgado. "Because you think Antifona's dead."

"We don't know that, Señora," said Delgado. "We only know that, at the moment, we can't find her."

"Oh, she's not dead *yet*." The old woman sat in her chair, rocking silently, her eyes pressed shut. Finally, she nodded, resigned. "But she's going to be. Nothing you can do about it, neither. Nothing nobody can do."

"Why do you say that?" said Delgado. "Did someone threaten her?"

The old woman shook her head. "I see the future. Just like his grandmother." She nodded towards Ramirez. "I knew you was coming today before you got here."

"You knew my grandmother?" said Ramirez.

The old woman smiled. "She's been dead for what, thirty years? She told me you'd come to see me someday when someone in my family goes missing. She say you be a big, tall policeman with a pretty lady. She give me this to give you. I've been keeping it all this time."

She reached down, taking her time to find a smooth, round rock in the dirt. She handed it to him. "It's from when she made *santo*."

"Making *santo*" was the process of converting to Santería. The initiate was bathed in water and shaved. Sacrificial blood was poured over sacred objects and stones. The stones were said to hold the *santos*, the gods, summoned during the ceremony.

Delgado rolled her eyes. The ground was dotted with almost identical stones.

Ramirez nodded slowly. Perhaps Mama Loa was crazy. But his grandmother had believed in the supernatural, a belief this old woman apparently shared. Whatever gift Mama Loa might have, though, it didn't seem to include seeing the ghost of Antifona Conejo. The dead woman stood off to the side, watching an airplane leave a clean white line in the blue sky. She looked completely bereft.

"My grandmother died when I was ten," Ramirez explained to Delgado. He rolled the stone in his fingers. It was cool to the touch. "Are you sure you have the right person?"

The old woman smiled, her teeth flashing white. "Oh, I got the right boy all right. I see you running around the squares, playing pirate with your little brother. You got something red tied around your head. My memory, she's pretty good for ninety-one."

Ramirez *did* remember playing with his younger brother in Old Havana. They had scrambled through the alleys around the Plaza de Armas, near the Castillo de la Real Fuerza. He wore a bright red handkerchief as a bandana, pretending to be Jacques de Sore, setting fire to the city, while his brother limped around on a pretend wooden leg as Peg Leg Leclerc. They would have murdered forty priests and thrown them in the ocean the way that Sores did—his grandmother said there were Jesuit crosses buried deep in the ocean floor—but none of the other boys felt like diving that day.

"That's very interesting, Señora," said Delgado, "but we need to ask you some questions for our investigation." She glanced at Ramirez, afraid she might have overstepped. He nodded, encouraging her to continue. "May I ask what your relationship is with Antifona Conejo?"

"She lives with me when she wants to get off the streets. And me, I know the pain of selling my body to feed my children, from when my own husband walked out on me. I tell her what to do. Make peace with the spirits, I say, or they be angry. Bring you bad luck."

"She's not your daughter?" asked Ramirez.

"No. My goddaughter. I adopt her, but no papers."

Delgado frowned. "How exactly did you tell her to make peace with the spirits, Mama Loa?"

"I tell her, you say goodbye to men, turn your soul over to your *lwa*. I say you try it; maybe it works. She say she needs the money. I tell her, you trust your *lwa*. Your *lwa* brings you what you need, not the same as what you want. When money comes too easy, you say no. Don't never sell your soul."

"What is a *lwa*?" asked Delgado.

"Your *lwa* guides you when you get lost, helps you find your way home."

"It's a spirit guide," said Ramirez. "In Haitian Voudou. Did Antifona have a boyfriend, Mama Loa?"

The old woman nodded. "She say some foreign man wants to marry her, take her away. He got no children. He wants to get him some."

"She wanted to leave Cuba?" said Ramirez, not really surprised. Most prostitutes hoped to find a foreign boyfriend. Few could afford to leave Cuba without one. It was six months' wages for an exit permit, and fifty convertible pesos—more than three months' wages—for the passport, more for the bribe.

The old woman nodded. "She say she's not going out with other men no more, only him. And I want to believe her, yes. But she looks sad when she say that. Like someone who wants to tell the truth but knows they can't."

"Does she live with you here?" asked Delgado, motioning to the shack.

"No. Back in Cayo Hueso. The city say we got to move. No room here for either of my girls. No roof either."

"When was the last time you saw her?" Ramirez asked.

"Maybe a week ago. She come to see me. She say, 'Mama Loa, my heart's broke. My belly hurts, my boyfriend don't come.' I give her some pine oil and honey to make her feel better."

"The boyfriend, what's his name?" asked Ramirez.

"I don't know. I only seen him once. He got an accent, I remember that. And lots of money." She pointed to her neck. "You can tell by the gold chain."

"You said 'girls.' Do you have another daughter, or goddaughter?" asked Ramirez.

The woman nodded. "She gone now too. She got married last year, on February 14. Lovers' Day. She used to live with me in Cayo Hueso, but she's with her husband now. He's a strong boy, you know? From lifting rocks."

40

The first time Maria Vasquez had lived with Hector Apiro, she was fifteen and trapped in a body as foreign and uncomfortable to her as Apiro's was to him. Apiro had transformed her, and in doing so had changed her life. And now that she was back, his was changed too.

Apiro was happy for the first time that he could remember. He no longer felt like the ugly little dwarf that people stared at and whispered about. In Maria's eyes, he was a man.

And yet every day, he worried about losing her. Not to another man—it wasn't jealousy Apiro struggled with, but fear.

Maria could be arrested for prostitution and taken away to a rehabilitation camp, and even Ricardo might not be able to find out where she was. That kept Apiro on edge, as much as he tried not to think about it. And now, because of the cruel killer who hunted *jineteras* and strangled them to death in the woods, he worried even more.

Maria sat in Apiro's cramped office in the medical tower, sipping a cup of his freshly brewed coffee. Apiro had decided to tell her about the murders. He didn't wish to frighten her, but she needed to know so she could protect herself, take precautions.

"I have something I need to tell you, Maria, and I'm afraid I'm not quite sure where to start."

"You're not breaking up with me, are you?" she said, furrowing her smooth brow.

"No, of course not," Apiro said. "Never be afraid of that." He reached for her hand and held it tightly as he told her about the murders. "He seems to be targeting *jineteras*."

"My God." Maria gasped. She pulled her hand away and crossed herself. "Killing my sisters? But why?" Tears welled in her eyes.

"I don't know," said Apiro. "There is no accounting for evil." He reached into one of his pockets and handed her a clean handkerchief.

She accepted it and dabbed at her eyes. "The two girls that died, what are their names? Oh, my God, I hope I didn't know them."

"Prima Verrier was the first victim, a year ago. Ricardo is reasonably sure that the second victim was named LaNeva Otero. Once I can get her health records, I can confirm if this is so. There's a third woman he can't find. Antifona Conejo. Her histological card was in LaNeva's purse when her body was found, but Antifona seems to have vanished."

Maria widened her eyes. "But I saw Antifona a week ago. She was excited. She said she was leaving the country. She was involved with an *extranjero* she'd met online. He came to Havana once before to meet her in person, and he was returning on business. She was sure they were going to get married. He told her he wanted to have a family. Maybe she went somewhere with him?"

Apiro felt enormously relieved that one potential victim might have been accounted for. "Perhaps. I'll let Ricardo know. Did you know either of the other girls?"

Maria shook her head. "Prima Verrier, no. But LaNeva, I often saw her. She worked on the Malecón at night. Sometimes I saw her walking to the highway to hitchhike. If we had time, we always chatted. I can't believe that she's dead." She wiped her eyes again, streaking mascara across her lovely face.

"Did she ever mention receiving gifts from a client?" asked Apiro. "Perhaps nylons? Stockings seem to be this killer's trademark."

"No," said Maria. "But we're given such things all the time. I have a Canadian friend who gave me condoms yesterday. Good ones too." She pointed to her tote bag resting on the floor. "A woman," she smiled. She and Hector never talked about her clients, but she knew he worried for her safety. "The girls don't often talk about the things they receive; it can be embarrassing. After all, most of them would go out with a man for a bottle of aspirin or nail polish. The younger ones—boys and girls—are even worse. They'll settle for a few cigarettes or a bottle of pop."

She paused for a moment. "There is one girl who mentioned something to me about nylons recently, though. Nevara. The last time I saw her, she told me a client promised to bring her some the next time he comes here. She told him not to worry about it; it's too hot to wear them anyway. I remember it because she said it was just like a man to think she wanted stockings when what she really would have liked was a steak."

"What is her last name?"

"I'm sorry, Hector. I don't know."

"Well, she needs to be careful," said Apiro. "Her client could be extremely dangerous. Do you think she would be willing to talk to Ricardo about him?"

"I doubt it," said Maria, shaking her head. "Forget the sex, she could be sent to a rehabilitation camp just for admitting she talked to a foreigner. And they don't give them new clothes when they go to those camps, not even overalls. They have to go into the barns with whatever they have on when they are arrested. It's horrible." She shuddered.

Apiro thought for a moment. Maria had a point. In such

circumstances, none of the *jineteras* were likely to be forthcoming to the police. They would consider the police a far greater threat than any client.

"Maybe you can ask her more about him when you see her? Any information she could provide would be extremely helpful."

"Yes, of course," Maria nodded. "I'll do whatever I can." She wiped her eyes again before folding the handkerchief neatly and handing it back to him.

Apiro smiled. "I appreciate it, Maria. Ricardo needs to narrow down the search before more women are killed."

He thought for a minute. Part of his inability to help Ricardo was that he had so little knowledge of Maria's world. In part, his ignorance was deliberate. But he could hardly protect Maria if he knew nothing about her business. He took a deep breath. "Forgive me for asking, Maria, but how do these girls meet their clients?"

"Since the crackdown? Mostly online. Some hitchhike, but it's dangerous. It's too easy for the police to spot them on the Malecón or the Autopista. The ones who do that are younger, more desperate for money. They take chances. LaNeva is one of those." Another tear rolled down her face. "Or was. We call girls like that *chupa-chupas*."

"Lollipops?" said Apiro, raising his bushy eyebrows.

"Oh, Hector. I keep forgetting how new all this is to you. It's slang for someone who provides oral sex."

41

"How are you making out with your investigation?" said Manuel Flores. He had caught up to Fernando Espinoza in the lineup for lunch in the basement cafeteria of police headquarters.

"Dr. Flores," said Espinoza, surprised. " I didn't expect to see you here. Doesn't your centre have its own cafeteria?" Cubans got a subsidized lunch at work, mainly to deter absenteeism.

"I'm working on another file for the ministry as well as yours. How are things going?"

"We're making good progress." Espinoza said. "We know the name of the victim now. LaNeva Otero. Another *jinetera*."

"Prostitution is so common these days." Flores shook his head. He looked at Espinoza's ring finger. "I see you're single. My daughter tells me that the girls here think Cuban men should pay for sex too. It must make it hard to find a wife."

Espinoza nodded sadly. "Most of the girls I've gone out with would leave the island in a minute if they could find a foreigner to marry. How old is your daughter?"

"In her thirties. A little old for you, I'm afraid." Flores smiled. "Although she's in very good shape. She was a gymnast on the national team when she was twelve. She competed in the World Rhythmic Gymnastics."

"Is she in Havana?" asked Espinoza. He liked strong women. He might be willing to compromise on age.

"No." Flores smiled. "She lives in Guantánamo City, not far from the American base. She teaches foreign languages."

The server on the other side of the counter handed Espinoza a plate of food and passed another to Flores. "I see they've changed the menu." Espinoza frowned. "It's beans and rice today. Yesterday it was rice and beans."

Flores chuckled. "I can't wait to taste the new menu."

They walked to a table. Espinoza pulled out a plastic chair and Flores sat across from him.

"How do you like working with Inspector Ramirez, Detective?" asked Flores.

"It's better than standing on street corners watching out for purse snatchers and street hustlers," said Espinoza. He smiled. "I'm learning a lot. It was hard at first. I just started at Major Crimes in January. Inspector Ramirez had to leave for Canada a day or two after I was transferred from Patrol. I had to find my way around by myself, although Dr. Apiro was very helpful."

"Ramirez went to Canada?" Flores raised his eyebrows.

"To help the Canadian authorities with an investigation. There was a Catholic priest charged with possessing child pornography at an airport in Canada. Padre Rey Callendes. We linked him to child abuse at an orphanage in Cuba. But he died of a heart attack on his flight back to Rome. He was never charged. I think the inspector feels robbed."

"Yes, I'm sure he does," said Flores, nodding. "That's the kind of thing that would affect Ramirez deeply. He has a strong sense of fairness. Which isn't always the same as justice."

"What was it like, living in the United States?" asked Espinoza. He shovelled a forkful of beans into his mouth.

"When I was first there, back in the sixties, New York wasn't a good place to be," said Flores, picking at his food. "There were rental strikes and street riots that started over a lack of affordable housing for blacks. The Black Panthers were involved in the strikes, but the Latinos were behind the riots. The Young Lords, they called themselves. Detroit went up in flames. Dozens died; thousands were arrested." He shook his head. "Our government is lucky that Cubans are so passive. It's the heat, I think. It makes us lazy."

"It doesn't seem to affect Inspector Ramirez," said Espinoza. "He's always working." He lowered his voice. "I think his wife is angry at him because of all his long hours. She went away for a few days with the children this week."

"Really," said Flores, leaning forward. He smiled. "Tell me more."

42

Celia Jones flipped through the photograph album until she found the picture. It was a faded black-and-white shot of her grandmother in front of a house in London during World War II. Her grandmother leaned against a car, one leg bent, posing in her kitten-heeled shoes. Jones could see the narrow rectangle that extended about six inches above the heel of her seamed stocking.

"Do you know anything about these kinds of nylons, Mom?"

"My goodness, Celia," her mother said, walking over to the couch and sitting beside her. "I haven't seen stockings like that since I was a little girl. I remember my mother said they were expensive because they were made out of separate parts, sewed together, and joined at the seam. They were hard to get hold of during the war; they needed all the silk to make parachutes and all the nylon for tires. My mother used to draw a line up the backs of her legs so she looked like she was wearing them. But the ones in that photo were real. She was so proud of them; she used to take very good care of them so they wouldn't snag."

"How did she get them, if they were so hard to find?"

"How do women get anything, Celia?" Emma Jones said, laughing. "From men. The American GIs were the only ones who had them. Well, those and chocolates. Although I seem to remember her telling me the Wrens used stockings to recruit women into their ranks as well. I suppose you could say the GIs used stockings to recruit women too. They were a pain in the ass, if I may say so. The stockings, I mean. Not the men, although she said those American soldiers could be persistent. We still had stockings like that when I was young, before pantyhose were invented. You had to attach them to a garter belt, and they were awkward to wear, but my goodness they made you feel sexy." She winked at her daughter.

Celia Jones kissed her mother's lined cheek.

She spent the next hour on the Internet looking up factories that made seamed stockings. Then she called Charlie Pike.

"Listen, I may have found something," she said, when he answered. "That stocking with the square seam, the one you drew the picture of for me? There are only two factories in the entire world that produce them, and they're both in England. Oh, and Charlie? I don't know if this means anything or not, but they call it a Havana heel in the trade."

———

Charlie Pike sat on the bed in his motel room, going over his files, thinking about Celia's call. He finally remembered what had been nagging at him—a rental SUV that wasn't returned on time. There might be only two factories in the world that made that kind of stocking, but there was only one place in White Harbour that rented cars.

"Funny you should call me about that one," said the Esso station owner. "A woman from Winnipeg leased it last week for a couple of days, but she never did bring it back. The OPP called me this morning to let me know it was sitting in the parking lot behind the health clinic. Been there all week, I guess. I was just about to send the tow truck out to pick it up. Battery's probably as dead as a doornail."

"Who rented it?" Pike asked.

He heard the sound of paper rustling.

"Her name was Maylene Kesler," said the station owner.

"Got a copy of her driver's license there in your paperwork?"

"Sure do. We always keep a photocopy for insurance."

"Maybe you can make a copy for me. I'm on my way over. And maybe wait till I get there before you send out that tow truck."

Behind the counter at the gas station were magazines, potato chips, bottles of pop, and rows of cigarettes. Players, Export A, Lucky Strike, Kools.

"You sell a pack of Lucky Strikes to anyone recently?" Pike asked the Esso station manager.

"Probably did," the manager said, "but I'd never be able to tell you who."

"Got video surveillance?"

"Whatever for?" The manager looked surprised.

Pike nodded, disappointed. He examined the photograph of Maylene Kesler from her driver's license. No question, it was the woman in the morgue. He tried his cell phone but, as usual, there was no signal. "Okay if I borrow your phone for a local call?"

"Sure. Go ahead."

Pike called the OPP and explained to Bissonnette what he'd found.

"Shit. I had no idea that the person who rented that car was your Jane Doe. I'll check with Winnipeg City Police, see what they can find out. Meanwhile, we'll get the SUV towed to our station. Could take us a few days before we can get any techs up here, though. They may want to transport it to Thunder Bay. That could take a while. Fucking snow."

"Adam Neville, our pathologist, is still in town. He can maybe process the vehicle, look for prints. I know he has his kit here. He took prints at the crime scene." Pike gave Bissonnette Neville's phone number.

"I'll get hold of him, see if he can help us out. Where are you going to be?"

"I'm going to see our lawyer, Celia Jones, to let her know what we've got. Media will be all over this as soon as they find out. My cell phone doesn't always work that close to the rez. If you want to reach me, here's her number." Pike recited it from memory. "Adam's got it too. Keep me in the loop, will you?"

43

"*Maylene Kesler? That's the Jane Doe?*" Celia Jones said to Pike as she made them a pot of tea. "Shit, she's the doctor who was supposed to get hold of my mom. She was up here running some kind of clinic a month or two ago. The university told me she was back doing the follow-up. No wonder she never called. I still don't know what kind of tests she was running. They told me she specialized in indigenous people's health. Environmental genetics."

"She was testing people from the reserve for mercury poisoning," said Pike. He told her about his conversation with Bill Wabigoon.

"Mercury? I've been watching the news reports, Charlie. They said the mill had closed down before, but not why. There must be millions of dollars tied up in that operation—government grants, jobs. What if she found out something that could close it down? What if her murder wasn't random at all? You know, it could be entirely unrelated to the Highway Strangler."

"Maybe," said Pike. "There are a few things about this one that are different from the others. But there's an awful lot about it that looks the same." He shook his head. "I don't know, Celia. I don't much like coincidences."

"We need to find out," said Jones. She stood up and paced around the kitchen table. "You need to get hold of her research. Maybe she kept copies at the health clinic. She was using it to run her tests. She must have had an office there. Was there anything in the SUV?"

"No idea yet. Adam or the OPP will call me once they have a chance to go over it. But the nurse at the clinic told me they have a temporary office for visiting doctors. It's the one Adam's been using."

"Well, let's find out." Jones picked up the phone and called the health clinic.

"My name is Celia Jones," she said to the woman who answered. "I'm with the Rideau Regional Police. I'm working on an investigation." She made a face at Charlie, knowing she was stretching the truth, letting the woman at reception think she was a police officer too. "I need to know if Dr. Maylene Kesler has an office in your building."

"Well," the receptionist said, hesitantly. "Dr. Kesler does use an office here sometimes. May I ask what this is about?"

Jones ignored her question. "Does she keep her patient files there?"

"She has a filing cabinet, but it's locked. She's the only one with a key."

"We need to see those files in relation to a homicide investigation."

"I wouldn't be able to let you into it even if I had a key. You could ask her, I suppose, although I doubt very much Dr. Kesler would share that information with you. She's very careful about doctor-patient privilege."

"Unfortunately, I can't do that," said Jones. "I'm sorry to be the one to tell you this, but Dr. Kesler is dead."

"Dead? How can she be dead? I just saw her a few days ago."

Jones looked at Pike and raised her eyebrows. "When?"

"On Thursday. She called me from the airport. She wanted to know if she could use the office to set up some appointments. She asked me to leave her a key; said she wanted to get to work right away. She'd made arrangements to see one of her patients."

"What time was that?" asked Jones. "Do you know which patient?"

"She didn't say. The Thursday afternoon flights always come in at the same time. It was four thirty, maybe five, when she phoned. I know it wasn't after five; I didn't stay late, because of the storm that was coming. Funny, though, now that you mention it, I didn't see her on Friday, but she'd left her rental car in the lot. I assumed she'd gone to visit one of the First Nation communities she was working with and got a ride up with one of the band members rather than drive alone on the bad roads. My God. She's dead? How? What happened? Some kind of car accident?"

"She was murdered," said Jones. "You may have been one of the last people to see her alive."

———

Jones sat down at the kitchen table. "She's right about one thing, Charlie. You can't get into that office without a warrant. Doctor-patient privilege applies to those files. There's no court that's going to let you go on a fishing expedition, not even in a murder investigation. Damn it. Those files could be the key."

"Don't worry about it, Celia. I'll figure something out."

The phone rang and Jones got up to get it. She listened for a moment, then covered the receiver with her hands. "Maybe you won't need to," she said. "It's Adam. He says he's found fingerprints in the SUV that aren't Maylene Kesler's or the Esso station owner's. And he's got a match." She handed the phone to Pike.

"Hey, Adam, what do you have?"

"Bad news. I'm sorry to tell you this, Charlie, but the prints I found are your friend's. The thumbprint is nice and clear. No doubt about it."

"Bill Wabigoon?"

"No," said Neville. "Sheldon Waubasking. I pulled a match off the elimination prints I took from him at the crime scene. I'm sorry, Charlie."

"You're sure about this?"

"Positive. There was an index finger and a thumbprint on the dash. Ten-point match. This is going to be messy, isn't it, with him being from the reserve and the blockade going on."

"I'll sort it out with Bill," said Pike. He hung up the phone, stunned. Sheldon? Why would Sheldon kill Maylene Kesler? He relayed to Jones what Adam Neville had said.

"But that's so hard to believe," said Jones.

Pike nodded, although the more he thought about it, the less he felt like he should be surprised.

He thought back to the way the nuns used to beat him and Sheldon at day school. The worst part was the food, they'd agreed later. Cabbage soup, hamburger pie with rotten meat, sour milk. It disgusted them, but even if they threw up in their bowls, they had to eat it. Sheldon could handle the beatings, but after he had to eat a bowl of his own puke for the third time, he told Charlie he'd had enough.

Pike didn't want to think how many times he and Sheldon got kicked in the butt or slapped around the ears for kidding around.

"I don't know, Celia. Maybe it's just been a matter of time."

The first time he and Sheldon ran away from the school, they'd headed for the railway tracks. The principal found them and dragged them back. He made them strip naked and whipped them with a big leather belt until they cried. Then he tied their long grey wool socks around their necks and pulled them back to the classroom as if they were dogs.

"It could be him, Celia. O'Malley found us a foster home in

Winnipeg. He was worried about us getting beaten up, with all the gangs after us. He took us to his gym and taught us to box."

"Now, Charlie, you're a counterpuncher," O'Malley had said. "You know how to spot your opponent's mistakes. A good counterpuncher never lets anyone know exactly where he's going, and he never telegraphs a punch. He dekes people out. That's you. You're smart. Accurate with your hands, and fast. You see, Sheldon? Someone like Charlie could take you down and you'd never quite know what hit you."

Charlie had brightened. "And what about Sheldon? What's he good at?

"Sheldon?" O'Malley smiled. "He slips out of the way so the other guys miss him. That keeps them off-balance. He likes to keep his hands free so he can use them. He's more defensive than you are, Charlie, but that's a good strategy. He's cautious. Flies under the radar."

Charlie had nodded. That was Sheldon to a tee.

Pike shook his head. He pushed the teacup away and got to his feet.

"Two nights a week, we took martial arts at O'Malley's gym. He made sure we learned all the basic moves in kickboxing and Wendo. And how to do chokeholds."

44

Shortly after Inspector Ramirez entered his office, Manuel Flores knocked on his door. "I hope you don't mind me dropping by, Ramirez. I thought I'd check on your welfare. I know these are particularly difficult cases. Detective Espinoza mentioned your family is out of town. I thought it might help if you had someone to talk to." Flores put his hand on the door frame to steady himself. "If that's what you want, of course. Are you going to invite me to sit down?"

"I'm sorry, Dr. Flores," Ramirez said, taking to his feet until the older man had lowered himself onto one of the hard wooden chairs. Ramirez thought he looked even more tired and drawn, his breathing laboured. "It's nice of you to be concerned about my welfare when you're . . ."

"When I'm what, Inspector? Dying?" Flores smiled. "I'm not dead yet. The Americans have some amazing new treatments for cancer, ways of targeting tumours without killing the healthy cells around them. Once my work is done here, I'll be heading right back to New York to start an experimental therapy. But let's talk about you. I thought you seemed stressed the other day. How can I help?"

Ramirez sat back in his chair. He did feel burdened by his secrets. He had never found a way to tell Francesca about his ghosts; he was afraid she would think he was losing his mind. And he had never been able to broach the topic with Apiro either. He didn't want it to affect their friendship.

Adding to his unease was the fact that the attractive female ghost who had showed up this week had him thinking about what it would be like to sleep with another woman. After twelve years, his relationship with Francesca was not as passionate as it once was, although she was always responsive. He loved his wife, but his marriage was showing cracks. Francesca knew something was wrong, but not what, and he didn't know how to tell her. The ghosts were bad enough, but that he had blackmailed the Minister of the Interior? She'd be frightened that he'd put their family at risk. And he worried that he had.

"Things are a little complicated at home," Ramirez said.

Flores nodded. "They often are for policemen. Divorce rates have always been high in our business. With the shift work and the terrible things we see, it's amazing that any of us manage to have healthy relationships. I worry about you in particular, because I know you try to see things from the perspective of the murderers you're investigating. That makes you vulnerable to all kinds of psychological reactions. Post-traumatic stress is one, but there are others. Are you managing?"

Ramirez took a deep breath and exhaled. He had to tell someone; his secrets were making him crazy. "Sometimes I think I can see the murder victims from my investigations. My grandmother was Yoruba. She believed the dead come to life in our dreams."

"Ah, yes, the Yoruba. Fascinating, their belief systems. *Okan*, they call it. *Okan re ti lo.* Buried in thought." The psychiatrist shrugged.

"I've become far more tolerant of other people's beliefs as I deal with my own mortality. The world is far too complex to ever fully comprehend. I still find it incredible that light travels faster than sound. How vivid are these visions?"

"Very vivid," Ramirez said. "I see them when I'm awake and sometimes when I'm falling asleep. Or waking up."

"Ah," said Flores. "We call those lucid dreams. They're quite common. So, what is it that you see, exactly?"

Ramirez sighed. "It's as if I can see their ghosts. But they're not transparent; they're solid and real. They never speak; they just gesture. And I feel helpless, because I can't understand what it is they're trying to tell me."

"Interesting," said Flores. "It sounds as if you're having what psychiatrists call an apparitional experience. It's not a mental illness. It simply refers to a situation where someone who's perfectly sane sees someone who isn't really there, and most often a stranger."

"That's what it's like with me," Ramirez exclaimed.

"Well, it's not paranormal or even supernatural, if that makes you feel better, unless of course you believe in ghosts." Flores smiled.

"I'm not even sure I believe in God, Dr. Flores."

"Well, I don't think you have to believe in God to believe in ghosts, or in ghosts to believe in God, but this condition, for lack of a better word, is nothing to be worried about. In the 1970s, two American scientists—I think one was named McCreery—examined hundreds of reported cases. They weren't able to determine a cause, but they did find certain commonalities. The people who saw the apparitions weren't frightened by them but usually found them reassuring and supportive. They tended to see the visions at rather ordinary places, as opposed to somewhere that might typically be considered haunted, like a graveyard. And the visions could often be so real, so substantial, that patients realized only later that they weren't."

"Did they ever speak to them? The ghosts?"

"The researchers don't like to call them ghosts, because that implies something paranormal, and that's not what this is. No, the patients rarely communicated with these visions; verbal interaction would be considered unusual. And scientifically, the researchers couldn't find any difference between their perceptions and normal ones. The people who had an apparitional experience were lucid and not drugged. They were completely, utterly, sane."

"Why does it happen?" Ramirez asked.

"I think probably some portion of your brain is processing symbolic information, subconsciously trying to help you with your investigations. It's a way we have of adapting to stressful conditions, making it easier to cope without being overwhelmed."

"So I'm not crazy?"

"Not at all." Manuel Flores smiled. He took to his feet. "It's been a long day; I need to get back to work. I wish my problems were as easy to solve as yours. But I hope that helps you feel better."

"It does," Ramirez said gratefully. He felt an enormous weight lift from his shoulders. "*Gracias.* It really does."

———

As soon as Manuel Flores left Ramirez's office, the inspector's telephone rang. His sense of being unburdened was short-lived. "I've been trying to reach you all day," said Dominique Gatti, the Italian curator's assistant, impatiently. "Our government intends to file a formal complaint if our paintings are not released tomorrow. We have a small window of opportunity to make the necessary repairs, and we're running out of time. We are far more concerned with that than with you making an arrest. I sincerely hope you are close to completing your investigation."

"We're making progress," Ramirez lied.

"I'm glad to hear it," Gatti said. "Because if we don't have those paintings back tomorrow, this will become an international incident. I'm sure you don't want that."

"I'll call you as soon as I have some information. Please be patient, Señora."

As soon as Ramirez hung up, the phone rang again. He picked it up and immediately recognized the voice of the minister's clerk.

"The minister is being harassed by an Italian curator named Lorenzo Testa," she said crisply. She sounded confident, her authority restored. "He said to tell you, he wants no more calls. The paintings will be released to the Italians tomorrow. You have until tomorrow noon to close this file, or else."

Ramirez wasn't sure what the "or else" might be. But the fact that it was the minister's clerk and not the minister issuing the threat was not a good sign.

"Tell him I'm working on it," he said.

He sighed, not knowing where to start, and put the phone down.

45

Ramirez found Detective Espinoza seated at his desk, flipping through a sheaf of papers. He told Espinoza about the impending deadline.

"I've been working on it," said Espinoza. "I checked with Customs yesterday. They said they stopped several *extranjeros* with aerosol paint cans in their suitcases, as well as microphones. But they didn't seize them."

In Cuba, a microphone was a dangerous weapon, capable of inciting dissent. The penalties for possessing one were harsh. But rules were relaxed during the hip-hop festival. Fidel Castro had even ordered that microphones and sound systems be supplied to the rappers. It allowed the security forces to shut down any performer whose message was counter-revolutionary simply by shutting down the feed.

Castro's approach to capitalist technology reminded Ramirez of the Ayatollah Khomeini. He too had used a microphone to denounce Western science on television.

"I really have no idea how to track down a political dissident," said Ramirez. Most of them were in jail already. "But I'm going to head over to la Moña. I know someone who might."

———————

La Moña, the site of the hip-hop festival, was east of Alamar. The roads in the area were choked with parked taxis, coco-taxis, scooters, bicycles, and tourist buses, but Ramirez finally found a spot for his small car.

He got out and slammed the door. His shirt was wet and sticky because of the humidity. When he reached the venue, he could see thousands of people clustered around a dozen or more plywood stages. A reggae band played on one. The sound of *guaguancó*—Afro-Cuban percussion music—drifted from another.

Ramirez pushed his way through the throngs, looking for Nassara Nobiko. Another policeman might call her his *chivato*—his snitch—but she preferred to think of herself as an elder states-woman. She had brought the first African-American rappers to the island, and it was mostly because of her that the government created the Agencia Cubana de Rap, as well as a rap record label.

Thousands of young foreigners and Cubans were enjoying the music. The occasional whiff of marijuana hung in the air. Men and women held their arms high, waving pieces of cloth to the music.

Young Cubans were intrigued by rap and hip-hop. In the begin-ning, they had used the music to send political and social messages, even if the lyrics were less politically charged than those in the United States. But all that had changed. The sound of *reggaeton* drifted from another stage. Ramirez walked up to the intelligence officer who was monitoring the music and asked if he'd seen Nassara.

"She's at the main stage," the officer said, pointing. After search-ing through the crowd for a few minutes, Ramirez finally saw her standing at the side of the platform.

She frowned as he walked over. "*Reggaeton* is crap, Ramirez.

Rappers used to be the voice of protest," she said. "Now they just sing about getting drunk and getting laid. They don't want to get put in jail because they sang something nasty about some badass politician."

"All legitimate desires, Nassara," said Ramirez. He took her soft dark hands and kissed her on the cheek. "Getting laid, getting drunk, *and* avoiding arrest. Those are not so easy to accomplish these days."

She smiled. "I hear you're working with Manual Flores."

"He called you?"

"He dropped by for tea. I have to tell you; the man looks like hell. So Fidel is going to let him go back to New York for medical treatment? No idea how he worked that one out; that stuff is expensive. I knew him in the sixties, you know, back home in the U.S. Even then, he was the only shrink I ever met who wasn't completely crazy."

Ramirez laughed. "You're looking well, Nassara."

"I'm getting older and I don't like it. Youth is wasted on these kids." She smiled at him warmly. "You know, Ramirez, I'm the only one left. Rationing, the embargo, all that shit drove the others out. They'd rather spend time in an American jail than live here and starve."

Nassara Nobiko had been a Black Panther—an American revolutionary—charged with shooting a policeman in the 1960s. She hijacked a plane to Cuba, where she was granted asylum, along with other leaders of the movement. The rest fled back to the United States, appalled by the poor living conditions.

"Hard to blame them," said Ramirez. He looked around at the crowd. "How many rappers do you think are here today?"

"Oh, I don't know. Five hundred? There are going to be dozens of street kids performing tonight as well as the established artists—Las Krudas, Amenaza, Primera Base. Must be a few thousand followers here already. It gets bigger every year."

"Have rappers really stopped protesting?"

"Of course not. Only the smart ones. They don't want to lose their government funding."

Ramirez smiled. He took Nassara by the arm and led her to a quiet spot behind the stage. "Nassara, I could use your help in an investigation."

"Now that's funny," the black woman said, laughing. "In my day, you were The Man. You want me to help you arrest someone? My, how the world does turn. Here, buy me an ice cream cone and tell me all about it." She slid her arm through his. "It's hot today, Ramirez. You'd think by now I'd be used to it."

They walked together to an ice cream stand and joined a long line of *habaneros*. It was the one thing that even the embargo couldn't destroy: the fresh taste of vanilla bean mixed with milk and ice.

Ramirez paid for two cones, handing one to Nassara. He described the damage to the paintings in the museum. Nassara doubled over and laughed until she cried.

"Oh, man, that's a good one. Spitting in the face of rich white people. No money in it, but lots of street cred. Oh, my, I wish I'd thought of it, back in the day. We used to take down banks, but any fool can do that. This is *creative*."

"Who would do this, Nassara? You say the *raperos* are the voice of protest. Do you think it might have been one of them?"

"One of those deadbeats? I doubt it." The corners of her eyes wrinkled with humour. "They wouldn't know how to get hold of a police uniform. You need to know someone on the inside for that. They'd probably be looking for one that had a crotch hanging down around their knees. So they be cool." She laughed.

"No, this is *big*, Ramirez. The only thing I don't get is who'd do all that work to pull off a stunt like that. No newspapers to fuss over it; no media attention. That's the main reason why you do this kind of shit—publicity. Usually, when you want to make a political statement, you want people to know about it. Like Eldridge used to say: use the right gun, you can hear a shot around the world. Have you spoken to Cuban Intelligence about this? Hell, I talk to them even when I don't want to." She grinned at him and made a face. "They bug the hell out of me."

Ramirez finished eating his cone and wiped his hands. "What do you mean when you say this was probably done to spit in the face of rich white people? The protester used the number 75. That has to be a reference to the Black Spring."

"But he could have painted that number on the wall without ruining all those paintings. Why hit a visiting exhibition? It wasn't Cuban art that was destroyed, was it? Just whitey's. You know, Lenin was right when he said that the good thing about capitalists was that communists could buy their ropes from them before they hanged them. We used to hit banks because they represented what we hated. And because we needed the cash. What do those paintings represent, and to who? Way I see it, somebody just lost a fortune. Maybe you should follow the money, my friend. Find that out, maybe you can answer your questions."

46

Ramirez was pulling up in front of his apartment building when his cell phone rang. It was Natasha Delgado. She sounded excited.

"Inspector, I got a call from the manager of the mine where Juan Otero used to work. Señor Otero was fired because he assaulted another employee. Apparently, he has a very bad temper. There were rumours he beat his girlfriends. And Fernando just spoke to the bartender at El Bosquecito. He says LaNeva Otero never worked there. He's never heard of her. Fernando says he believes him."

"So Otero lied to us." Ramirez turned the small car around in a U-turn, ignoring the blasts of angry horns. "Get Patrol to pick him up at Pedro Perez. If he's not there, tell them to keep the building under surveillance until he returns. I'm heading back to headquarters now. When they bring him in, put him in the interview room. Tell him I have a few follow-up questions for him about his wife. Don't let him know he's a suspect. Meanwhile, check with Holguín

Province to see if there have been any reports of murdered women with nylons tied around their necks."

"I've already called them. They're going through their records."

"Good. See if you can get hold of Dr. Flores to join us to observe the interrogation. At the moment, Señor Otero is our best suspect."

And our only suspect, thought Ramirez. He put his foot firmly down on the gas pedal.

Inspector Ramirez stood in the anteroom, watching Juan Otero through the mirrored glass, assessing him, trying to decide how best to proceed. The suspect sat behind the Formica table on a red plastic chair, fiddling with a small gold cross around his neck. The fluorescent light flickered against the cracked grey walls.

"He didn't give Patrol any trouble," Detective Espinoza said to Ramirez.

Natasha Delgado nodded. "He thinks he's here because of the investigation into his wife's murder."

"He's right about that," said Ramirez.

Manuel Flores knocked on the metal door to the anteroom before he entered. Ramirez thought he looked even more tired than before.

"Thank you for joining us on such short notice, Dr. Flores," Ramirez said. "I'd like you to watch while I question the suspect. I'd appreciate your input as to whether he fits the profile. Let's run a tape recorder on this side, Natasha. If I take one in with me, he'll be suspicious."

Delgado nodded. "I'm sure it's him, Inspector. Good luck."

"Señor Otero, I appreciate you coming here today. I'd like to ask you a few more questions," said Ramirez as he entered the interview room. He closed the metal door behind him. He sat beside Otero, pulling his chair close to the suspect's. It was one of Ramirez's favourite tactics: letting him think they were about to engage in joint problem-solving, catching him off-guard. "I hope you don't mind that I sent a patrol car to pick you up. I doubted you had transportation."

"Have you found out something about my wife's death?"

Death, Ramirez noted. Not *murder*. But Flores had said that the killer might not want to admit what he'd done, not even to himself.

"Not yet. That's why I wanted to talk to you, to get a better sense of what LaNeva was like, and what she was doing in the hours before her death. I'm sorry; I know this is difficult. I also wanted to personally thank you for coming in last night to identify your wife's body. Believe me, I know how hard that is."

Otero's eyes welled up.

Death was something most people denied, pushed aside, pretended happened only to other people. But there was nothing like a decomposing corpse to change all of that, thought Ramirez. Even someone who killed another person often didn't fully imagine what happened to the body until confronted with it.

"I won't keep you long," Ramirez lied.

He would keep the suspect for days if he had to, but he always thought it best to let a suspect think otherwise. Later, as the suspect tired, Ramirez could imply that he might never leave police custody. That usually wore them down. Interrogation, he'd learned over the years, was a delicate balance between hope and despair.

"I forgot to ask you when we met, Señor—how long have you been in Havana?"

"I moved here last summer."

"The date?" Ramirez opened his notebook and reached for a pen in his pocket.

"Early June. I don't remember the exact day."

"Did you come to Havana with your wife?"

"No. We weren't married then." Otero paused, and Ramirez

picked up the hesitation. "I couldn't stay in Holguín with my family any longer. They couldn't afford it."

No mention of being fired, thought Ramirez. Juan Otero had a selective memory. "You said you came here to find work. Had you been working before then?"

"Yes. In a mine. But it was shut down."

"That must have been very hard for you," Ramirez said, ignoring for the moment that he was lying. As a matter of pride, many men would lie about being fired. "The same thing happened to me before I joined the police force. I had a job in a factory that closed. I was in my twenties. My wife was pregnant with our first child. I had no idea how we could survive without any income." He leaned closer to Otero. "I had to pretend to be strong. *No es fácil.*" The common refrain among Cubans: It isn't easy.

"Completely untrue," Flores whispered to Espinoza. "Ramirez's first job was with the police. He's never worked in a factory. This is good. He's empathizing with the suspect, trying to find common ground."

Otero swallowed. "I thought I'd be able to get work quickly and send money home. I didn't know all the rules about housing. We don't hear much about that in the country."

"Our bureaucracy." Ramirez shook his head slowly. "It's incredible how badly they treat our own citizens. How did you get here from Holguín? Did you hitchhike?"

"I drove with a friend," said Otero. "In his car."

"What's your friend's name?" Ramirez asked casually.

"Rider Aguilera."

Ramirez nodded slowly. He made a mental note but didn't write down the name. It was time to change the subject before Otero wondered why Ramirez was asking questions unrelated to his wife's death.

"Now, tell me about LaNeva. Was she from Holguín too? Is that where you met?"

"No, she's from Santiago. We met in Havana, actually. Not long after I arrived. I went out with her sister first." Otero smiled slightly. "But I knew right away that LaNeva was the one for me. She was easy to get along with."

"And the sister wasn't?"

The man shrugged.

Time to tighten the screws, thought Ramirez. "But not *always* so easy, correct, Señor?" He pulled a report from his jacket pocket and put it firmly down on the table. "We have a citizen's complaint, reported by the Committee for the Defence of the Revolution. People heard loud arguments in the building on Pedro Perez, the sounds of things breaking. You're the only people living there. What did you fight about?"

"What's he doing?" said Espinoza. "There are no CDR reports."

"The only reports I found were from Cayo Hueso," said Delgado. "Do you think he's confused?"

"That's one of Ramirez's tactics," Flores smiled. "There are no reports. Note that he hasn't mentioned a date. He's guessing. He likes to let the suspects think he has evidence when he doesn't. That piece of paper could be anything. I've seen him use office supply forms."

"The usual things. Nothing serious," said Otero.

Ramirez let this second lie pass without comment. It was another tactic, letting the suspect back himself into a corner before Ramirez pounced. "What did you argue about the night she disappeared?"

"What makes you think we argued?"

Ramirez shook his head. "I saw the broken mirror in your apartment, Señor. Your wedding photograph was on the floor, the glass smashed. Someone threw it down in the heat of an argument, I'm guessing. Was it you or was it her?"

Otero sat silently, jiggling his foot.

"If my wife broke something that important," said Ramirez, "she would pick it up later, however angry she was. She would never leave it lying on the floor in pieces. That makes me think that LaNeva ran out of the apartment and didn't come back."

"I saw those things too," said Espinoza. "But I didn't connect them. He's good, isn't he?"

Flores grinned. "He's one of the best interrogators I've ever known. Watch closely and learn."

Juan Otero got up. He pushed the chair out of the way and paced around the room, running both hands through his short wiry hair. "All right, I admit, we argued the day before she disappeared. It was Lovers' Day. I wanted her to stay home with me. She said she had to go to work. She said that it was one of the best nights of the year to make money."

She was right, thought Ramirez. Lovers' Day was a national holiday, a major celebration not just for spouses and intimates, but for friends and family. He suddenly remembered Mama Loa's comment about her goddaughter and the strong young man she'd married on Lovers' Day.

"And you knew what she meant, didn't you?" he said. "You knew she wasn't talking about earning tips at the bar."

Ramirez waited. Silence made most suspects uncomfortable. They often volunteered information to fill the vacuum.

"No," Otero finally said. "I didn't know what she was doing. Not at first. Maybe I didn't want to know."

"And when you *did* find out, it made you angry?"

Otero rearranged the chain around his neck, saying nothing.

"It's nothing to be ashamed of. I can understand your feelings," said Ramirez. "Knowing your wife was with other men, that they paid her to do things to them. That would make any man furious."

"He's getting him to imagine it," said Flores. "To visualize what she did. It will anger him all over again and give Ramirez a glimpse into how enraged he might have been the night she disappeared."

"How did the mirror get broken?" Ramirez asked. "Did you push her against the wall and knock it down?"

"No," Otero said, shaking his head. He clenched his fists. "I never struck her. The photograph fell on its own."

"Señor," said Ramirez, shaking his head. "I asked about the mirror, not the photograph. I saw where that photograph used to hang, the nail hole in the wall. It was at least three feet away from the mirror. If it wasn't thrown on the ground, then something must have hit the wall hard enough to knock them both down."

"It was a shoe. She threw her shoe at me after . . ." Otero paused.

"After what?"

"After I called her a *puta*."

"I see," said Ramirez. He didn't fully believe him. One shoe couldn't bring down both the mirror and the photograph. He kept his expression neutral and leaned back in his chair. "If she was sleeping with other men, I don't blame you for losing your temper." He lowered his voice again. "Sometimes my wife hints at having an affair when she's angry at me. She's angry with me now, so I know exactly how you feel. Just the thought of it makes me crazy. We promise to be faithful when we marry." He watched Otero fiddle with the cross around his neck again. "Adultery is a sin."

Otero hung his head. "I couldn't believe it," he whispered. His eyes spilled tears. "That she was fucking other men. That she wanted to do it with a stranger on Lovers' Day."

"And not just Lovers' Day, but your wedding anniversary."

Otero nodded. Tears rolled down his cheeks. He pinched his nose with his fingers.

"I know you hit her, Juan. Please, don't forget, we've done an autopsy on the remains. Our pathologist is very good. I already know the answer; I simply want to hear it from you."

"Was there any bruising on the body?" Flores asked Espinoza.

"Nothing," said Espinoza. Natasha Delgado grinned.

"I admit I pushed her," Otero said.

"I think maybe you pushed her twice," said Ramirez. "Once against the mirror and once against the wall. That's why your wedding picture fell down. And who could blame you? It's not like you hit her with your fist. Our pathologist says it barely left a mark."

"This is very good," said Flores. "It diminishes the nature of the assault. It lets the suspect admit to it without feeling guilty. Notice how Ramirez says 'it' instead of 'you,' so he's not accusatory."

Otero brightened a little. "It was more like a slap."

Flores turned to the two detectives. "Excellent! He's established motive *and* opportunity."

"But how did Otero get her to the killing ground?" said Espinoza.

"Inspector Ramirez isn't done yet," said Flores. He smiled. "Give him a few minutes."

———

"So you honestly didn't know that your wife was a *jinetera* before you had this terrible argument?" Ramirez asked. He chose the word *argument* instead of *fight* to minimize the extent of the violence. He lit a cigar, then reached in his pocket for another and offered it to Otero. "Sit down again, please, Señor Otero. Relax."

"Of course not." Juan Otero bristled, but he sat on the plastic chair again and accepted the cigar.

Ramirez leaned over and lit it for him. "How did you find out about the other men?"

Otero sighed and blinked back tears. "She brought home stockings."

"Ah," said Ramirez. "A gift from a client?"

Otero nodded. He drew on the cigar and coughed.

"That would drive any man insane," said Ramirez. "You've lost your job; you have no money. It's Lovers' Day. You want to give your wife a gift and can't afford to. And then she comes home with something like that. I suppose she waved them in your face."

"It was my fault, she said, that she had to fuck strangers on our anniversary."

"And before this, you had no idea?"

"None."

Ramirez quickly changed the subject so the suspect would have no time to think. "This car your friend Rider Aguilera owns. Does he let you borrow it?"

"Yes, sometimes," Otero said. "Why?"

Ramirez ignored the question. "We know LaNeva was in Santiago in January. Why did she go home?"

"To see her parents."

"Are you sure of that?"

"That's what she told me"

"According to our records, LaNeva was deported to Santiago after she received her third warning for prostitution," said Ramirez. "But she didn't stay there for long. Only a few days. I think you borrowed your friend Rider's car and drove her back."

The man began to shake. "I didn't know where she was going, okay? She disappeared. Then she called me from Santiago and said she wanted to come home."

"Called you how? You have no phone."

"She . . ." Otero hesitated, trapped. "I . . . she had a cell phone."

"Which she left with you because she couldn't take it to Santiago. Having one is illegal. You're not stupid, Señor. You know how rare 'chocolates' are, and how expensive. How do you think she paid for such a phone?"

"I don't know. I didn't ask."

"Really? You and your wife really didn't communicate very well, did you? Tell me, how did you pay for the gas to get all the way from Havana to Santiago and back?"

Otero's face blanched.

"You've already told me you had no work. You didn't even have enough money to live with your own family. I think your wife paid for the fuel, by selling herself in Santiago."

"Pardon me?" said Otero. "Can you repeat that?" The cigar in his hand was shaking uncontrollably.

"I think you knew that your wife was a *jinetera*, Señor. You admit, it made you furious that she preferred to be with foreign men on Lovers' Day. Is that why you choked her?"

"I didn't choke her," said Otero. "I swear to God."

Invoking God was another way guilty men tried to emphasize their innocence. Ramirez slammed his hand on the table.

"Stop lying to me. You fought. You wanted her to stop talking about the men who gave her things you couldn't afford. You put your hands around her throat to make her stop. I'm sure you didn't mean to kill her; it was an accident. And then you used her cell phone to call Rider, to borrow his car. You told us she went missing on February 15, but she was already dead by then. She died on February 14, Señor. That's the day you admit the two of you argued. The day you strangled her to death with your bare hands."

"But I never did that," Otero shouted. "I only hit her once, I swear. Maybe twice. Okay, I lied about when she went missing. I knew people might have heard us fighting the night she disappeared. I knew I would be blamed if something bad had happened to her, so I said she left for work the next day. She ran out of the building, crying, and I never saw her again." He broke down and wept. "And now she's dead. How do you think I feel, knowing that the last words I said to my wife were angry ones, that I called her a whore?"

"Ramirez has him now," said Flores. "The lies, the denial, the admission he hit her more than once. That's more than enough for the arrest."

"He still maintains he didn't kill her," said Ramirez to Manuel Flores after Espinoza and Delgado left to take Juan Otero down to Booking. "And he denies borrowing his friend's car that night. We'll track this Aguilera down, but what do you think?"

"Clearly, he felt cuckolded. It was an explosive situation. I'm still working on my profile, but I can always change it."

"You would rewrite a profile to fit the criminal?"

Flores smiled. "If that's what you need, Ramirez. We want to get a vicious killer off the streets, don't we?"

"Only if we can be sure that's what we've done."

"It's more than possible. Hold him for a few days while you fill in the gaps. It was smart of you not to ask him questions about Prima Verrier's death. Best not to ask a question unless you know the answer."

"I don't know," said Ramirez, shaking his head. "I can only keep him in custody for three days. Then I have to turn the case file over to the Attorney General's office to proceed with the indictment."

"All you need to prove is that he's likely to have committed this murder on the balance of probabilities. You're close to that now with the circumstantial evidence. Once he's indicted, you'll have a year or more to tighten up the charges. It will take that long to get him before a juridical panel. That's if he survives prison, of course." Flores patted him on the shoulder and smiled. "Good work, Ramirez. I'm proud of you. Well done."

47

Before he arrested his old friend for murder, Charlie Pike needed to know what was in those medical records. Breaking into the health clinic was a whole lot easier than he expected. The door didn't even have a deadbolt, just a lock.

Pike pushed his ID card between the door and the jam, and slid it up and down. The door popped open right away. No alarm beeped, nothing went off. That was good; it gave him more time. His heart was pounding the way it had when he was fourteen. But this time, he was on the side of the law. Heck, he *was* the law.

If Pete Bissonnette or one of the OPP saw him inside, he'd say he was driving by, found the door open, and was checking in case there was a break and enter in progress. If they asked why he hadn't called for backup, that was easy. His cell phone didn't work, and once he was inside the building, it was too late to worry about backup anyway. He turned on the lights. There was no need to work in the dark, not with his cover story.

Pike wasn't really sure what he was looking for. He searched through the reception desk until he found a set of keys.

He decided to start in the morgue. He walked downstairs and unlocked the door.

The woman's body was still in a metal drawer in the refrigeration unit. He pulled it out, winced at the ragged scar running down her chest, the large staples. She was purple, though, not blue. What's black and white and red all over? he thought. Angry nuns.

He closed the refrigerator drawer, locked the morgue door, and backed out instinctively, the way Sheldon had taught him, to cover his tracks.

He let himself into the visiting doctor's office, the one Maylene Kesler had been assigned before she died. The one Adam Neville was using. Maybe the filing cabinet still held her files.

Pike took a paper clip from a container on the desk and jiggled it in the filing cabinet lock until it popped open. A series of files hung in coloured folders. He riffled through them until he found what he was looking for.

Maylene Kesler's report on the Manomin Bay First Nation was in a thick green folder. From the looks of it, she'd co-authored a couple of draft articles on mercury contamination and the Northern Ojibway too. The file contained an article from a medical journal published on Minamata disease and its effects. He read through it quickly, taking note of the symptoms.

Sensory disturbance and constriction are typical among patients: dysarthria, tremors, walking problems, hearing, and coordination disturbances. Symptoms can range from mild to serious. Some mild cases of coordination disturbance are difficult to identify.

There was another medical study on the purported link between autism and thimerosal, the mercury used in vaccination. A newspaper story was folded between its pages. One paragraph had been underlined:

> Between 1962 and 1970, natives in several northern Ontario communities discovered their main food source had record-high levels of mercury from a paper mill up the river. The finding resulted in the mill being closed down along with northern fishing lodges. While physicians debate the extent of their health, with their food supply destroyed as well as their local economy, natives have endured decades of alcoholism, poverty, and abuse.

Got that right, Pike thought. He went back to the filing cabinet and searched through its contents until he found Maylene Kesler's test results. They were lined up neatly in a red folder. To preserve confidentiality, there were no names, only number-letter combinations. Another folder held a stack of consent forms.

He shuffled through the reports. Forty-two band members had submitted to blood tests, including all of Bill Wabigoon's family. Even Molly Oshig and her son, Pauley, participated. Another twenty non-Aboriginal people from White Harbour and Manomin Bay provided blood.

He scanned through the individual results. It was scientific mumbo-jumbo, until he found an entry that caught his eye:

> Tests on P-1 and P-A3 indicate consanguineous relationship with resulting autosomal recessive disorder in PO. Mean excess mortality of 4.5% for first cousins likely to be exceeded. Consult with departmental lawyer regarding Section 155 of the Criminal Code and obligation of disclosure. Also suggest complete evaluation of P-A3 by appropriate professionals. Subject manifests marked impairment in social interaction, qualitative impairment in communication, preoccupation

with abnormal and restricted pattern of interest (birds), hand- and finger-flapping. Possible trigger mercury?

Pike tried to remember what was in that section of the Criminal Code. Sexual offences. Touching. Sex with minors. But he'd left his pocket Code on his desk back in Ottawa.

He looked around for a medical dictionary and found one on a shelf. He looked up *recessive*: "*Genetics*. Of or pertaining to a recessive." Great, he thought. A dictionary meaning that relied on itself.

He thumbed through the pages until he found *autosomal*: "a chromosome that is not a sex chromosome." Then, *consanguineous*: "relationship by blood or common ancestor." And *dysarthria*: "trouble speaking, difficulty forming words."

He could spend an hour or more trying to decipher what all that meant, and it was getting pretty late. He slid the contents of the reports under the photocopier in the corner and pushed Copy. The room lit up with a bright blue light like Pauley Oshig's computer screen.

Pike sat down behind the desk. Adam Neville's laptop was on, the screen saver still displaying the photograph of Neville and his wife on the mountain.

Pike used the paper clip he'd used to open the filing cabinet to jimmy the desk drawer. Inside, he found a pack of cigarettes—Lucky Strike. One was missing. Well, that explained the cigarette butt at the scene, he thought. It was probably the victim's.

There was a black medical bag in the corner. He stood up and walked over to it. He opened it up and rummaged through the contents of what appeared to be a standard pathology kit.

It was Neville's, he realized, not Maylene Kesler's. It included latex gloves, tweezers, a plastic bottle of Luminol, a bottle of peroxide, and a disposable container of ninhydrin. There was a flashlight. He turned it on and realized it had an ultraviolet light bulb; it was used for picking up bloodstains after a surface was sprayed with Luminol. He looked at the plastic bottle of Luminol and was surprised to see it was almost empty.

The bottle of ninhydrin had been opened as well. He walked back to the desk and examined the screensaver on the laptop more carefully.

Then he put everything back where it belonged and locked the filing cabinet. He slipped the pack of Lucky Strikes into a plastic exhibit bag, initialled and dated it. He put it in his jacket pocket, then closed the desk drawer. He couldn't lock it up again, but hoped no one would notice.

He walked upstairs and turned off the lights. There was no way to secure the front door either, but maybe the nurse practitioner would think she'd forgotten to do it on her way out. She'd been upset; she'd just found out that Maylene Kesler had been murdered. That's what she'd tell herself when she showed up in the morning and found everything open but nothing missing. At least, nothing obvious.

The old man had told him, Pike thought, as he drove slowly to the Tops Motel, finally putting the pieces together. Nanabozho was hiding in the water.

———

When Charlie Pike got back to his motel room, there was a pink message slip left by reception under the door. Miles O'Malley had called. Pike was to phone him at home.

It was well after midnight. Pike thought about calling the police chief the next day. But then, it was Pike's turn to wake O'Malley up—after all, fair was fair.

As it turned out, O'Malley was still awake. Pike told him about Sheldon Waubasking and the fingerprints on the dashboard of the victim's car, as well as what he'd found at the health clinic and what he thought all of it meant.

"Ah, shit, Charlie. I can't believe it. You really think he's responsible for this? Did he do it himself or was he covering up for someone else?"

Pike sighed. "Covering up, I think. It's the only explanation that makes sense. I'll see what I find out tomorrow when I question him."

"You're not going to arrest him tonight?"

"It's late. There's no rush. He doesn't even know he's a suspect. He's not going anywhere. I don't want to bust in on him; I don't have a weapon. It can wait until morning. I should have the OPP on hand for backup anyway."

"If you think so. But for God's sake, be careful. He could be armed. By the way, I almost forgot. I've got some news for you too. That was the reason I called you in the first place. The OPP found one of the missing women on that list of yours today. Molly Oshig."

Pike's heart dropped. "She's dead?"

"No. She's working in Kenora as a waitress, at a diner on Lakeview. But she's changed her name to Pauline Johnson. That's good news, isn't it? That she's alive?"

"I hope so," said Pike. "I'll go see her first thing in the morning, make sure she's all right. Before I let you go, Chief, have you got a copy of your Criminal Code handy? I need to know what's in section 155."

"Give me a minute, lad."

A minute later, O'Malley read out the section. Pike nodded slowly, fitting that piece of information with the rest.

"Keep me posted, Charlie. I'm going to get hold of Pete Bissonnette for you now and ask for OPP assistance. He won't be happy when I tell him about the arrest. It complicates things, believe me."

"He'll probably swear at you." Pike smiled. "Don't take it personally. Tell him to meet me at the health clinic at ten a.m. I'll set things up there."

The last thing Pike did before his head hit the pillow was call the night clerk at the motel reception desk and ask to be put through to Adam Neville.

"Sorry if I woke you up, Adam."

"It's late, Charlie. It's after midnight." The medical examiner sounded annoyed.

"You still plan on leaving tomorrow?"

"Noon flight to Winnipeg, yes. I think my work here is done."

"I need to go over some evidence with you before you leave. I'll have to explain all of this to Chief Wabigoon as soon as I make the arrest. Can you free up some time for me before you head out?"

"Of course," said Neville, yawning. "Where do you want to meet?"

"At the health clinic. I'll try to be there for nine thirty. I may be a little late—I've got to meet someone in Kenora first."

Pike hung up. He tried to remember what his *mishomis* had taught him about the best way to set a trap.

48

Although it was very late when he got home, Inspector Ramirez called his in-laws' number anyway. His adrenaline had subsided, leaving him empty with fatigue.

"It's after midnight, Ricardo," said Francesca. "The children are in bed."

She sounded irritated and it deflated him. He wanted to talk over his uncertainties but decided it was best not to discuss his investigation and risk annoying her even more. "I'm sorry, *cariño*," he said. "The day got away from me. How are the little ones?"

"Edel is disappointed. His team lost. Estella has a loose tooth. I think they are both ready to come home."

"I can't wait to see them. I miss you all so much. You know, Francesca, I met an old woman today who knew my grandmother. She remembers when José and I were little boys not much older than Edel is now."

"Really? She must be ancient," said Francesca, but her voice was a little warmer. She was fond of Ramirez's younger brother.

Ramirez laughed. "I'm not *that* old."

"Tell me about her, Ricky."

Ramirez boiled water in a dented saucepan on the stove in the small kitchen as he described the old woman. Francesca's bad mood dissipated as they shared the day's events.

As he spoke, Ramirez carefully measured a handful of rice and poured it into the battered metal pot. He pulled the telephone cord taut so that he could reach the pot while he stirred. His family received only six pounds of white rice each month in their rations. Every grain was precious.

He cradled the receiver between his neck and ear while he stirred the boiling water with a spoon, making sure the rice didn't stick. The dead woman leaned against the door frame, watching him, one bare leg bent. He motioned her away with his free hand.

"I should probably go, Francesca. I don't want to overcook the rice. I've been running around all day. I didn't have time to eat."

"Just rice, Ricardo? No beans? You'll melt away to nothing."

"No fear of that," said Ramirez. He thought of the sweets he'd consumed while his family was away. If Francesca knew how many, she would scold him. They ate badly enough as it was, she would say, without him mainlining sugar.

He missed her terribly when he hung up the phone. When he was still a bachelor, there was no other girlfriend who got as angry at him as she did. That's how he knew how much she loved him.

Juan Otero probably loved LaNeva too, Ramirez thought. Was he angry because she was selling herself, as he claimed? Or because she was indifferent to their wedding anniversary? Were either of these reason enough for him to kill her? Divorce in Cuba was easy; only a few pesos and a notary. There was no property to divide.

The apple in the victim's stomach still nagged at him. Where did LaNeva get it? She had no money to buy things like that on the black market. There was something he was missing. But he was too tired to know what it was.

———————

Ramirez picked up Estella's storybook from the floor. He looked at the picture of Snow White on the cover. Hector Apiro was right. It was peculiar for a woman to want to find true love after she died.

He went into the bedroom. The dead woman lay stretched out on the bed in the same position as Snow White, her hands folded across her ample chest. She opened her eyes and smiled at him.

"What happened to your foreign boyfriend, Antifona? Was he LaNeva's client on Lovers' Day? Did Juan Otero kill him too? Or maybe you did, for sleeping with another woman."

The dead woman shook her head and pointed to the ceiling. He looked up and saw nothing new except another crack in the stained plaster.

"I'm sorry, Antifona," he said. He was tired and had no more time for games. "You really need to leave. I can't have you hanging around my apartment. My wife and children will be back soon, and believe me, Francesca wouldn't appreciate you being here when she's not home. Besides, you're far too attractive. It's distracting."

The dead woman smiled sadly. She put her finger to her full red lips. She got up from the bed and walked through the front door of the apartment. She didn't look back.

49

It was after two in the morning and hot inside the stuffy apartment. Ramirez was too exhausted to sleep, his mind still trying to pinpoint what it was that troubled him about his investigation into LaNeva Otero's murder.

He got out of bed and pulled on a *guayabera* and jeans. He slid on a pair of sandals and walked downstairs to his car.

He drove around aimlessly for a while, keeping an eye on the needle of the gas gauge. He finally parked on a side street in Old Havana and wandered along the Malecón towards Vedado, hoping the long walk there and back would tire him enough to get some sleep. He declined the calls from gay and transgendered men along the seawall to party with them.

He purchased a bottle of Hatuey beer from a *kiosko* and followed the sounds of street music. He stood at the edge of a small crowd, sipping from the bottle, applauding the musicians. As the music got louder, residents poured out of their apartments, smoking, dancing, drinking, laughing.

Foreigners, sunburned and stiff, tried dancing to the music, but they were awkward. Every now and then, locals would show them how it was done. A couple danced salsa to the *clave,* the mixture of African percussion and Spanish music that throbbed through Ramirez's veins like a heartbeat; its rhythm was almost erotic.

The music throbbed. Ramirez ached physically for his wife. He looked at his watch. It was already three thirty. He drained his beer and started the seven kilometre walk back to his car.

Sex workers stood outside the downtown bars, hooting softly to potential clients. One leaned against his car, a bare leg bent against its scratched metal exterior. She wore a tight white skirt with yellow flowers, a blue top, and sheer black nylon stockings. Her face was unmistakeable. She'd haunted him for days.

Ramirez stopped cold. He stared at Antifona Conejo, unbelieving.

"Hey, *cabanero,*" she said softly. "You look lonely. We could go to a nightclub together." The code words for intercourse, the come-on reserved for foreigners. But he was no foreigner. And she was no ghost.

Antifona Conejo was alive? He looked up and down the street. How could that be? He put his hand tentatively on her arm and felt her smooth, warm skin. He felt a jolt of pure longing, the full impact of a week without lovemaking.

"No touching," she said, and winked at him. "Not yet, sweetheart. Not here."

"Do you have a twin?" he asked, bewildered.

"You want two of us? For the right amount, anything is possible."

He was tempted, beyond tempted. "I've been looking for you," he said finally.

"All your life? I hear that all the time." She ran her tongue around her lush red lips. "Believe me, you won't be disappointed."

He considered taking Antifona back to his apartment but decided against it. It was too risky.

"Let's go to my car. We'll get some beer to drink on the way."

She slipped her arm though his. Their hips brushed as they walked down the sidewalk; he felt electric sparks. He stopped at another *kiosko* and bought two more beers, all he could afford. They walked to his car. He opened the passenger door for her.

"Well, aren't you the gentleman." She smiled. "I like a man who treats a woman well."

He walked around to the driver's side. As soon as he was seated she leaned over. She circled his neck with her arm, running her fingers along his stubble. She ran her tongue around his ear. She reached for his fly with her other hand and lowered her head.

"No, not here," he said. He caught her hand in his. "There are too many policemen around."

Her palm was warm, the skin smooth. He felt her heat. His erection strained against his pants. He looked at the nylon stockings she wore, and his heart pounded. "Where did you get those?"

She lifted her face and smiled. "From another woman. Does that make you hot, thinking of two women being together? She was hot too, believe me." She sat back in her seat and hiked up her skirt. She lifted one long leg and put it on the dashboard, wiggling her toes. "They're nice, aren't they? Smooth as silk." Her toenails were painted a deep red. "Do you want me to take them off for you? Or do you want to undress me yourself? I'm all yours tonight." She put her fingers between his legs and squeezed lightly, caressing his balls.

There was a sharp rap on the windshield. A young policeman peered through the dirty glass. Ramirez recognized him, a foot patrolman. The *policía* nodded and walked away quickly, embarrassed.

"I told you, not here." Ramirez turned on the ignition. He decided where he wanted to take her, already knew what he needed to do.

"Where are we going?" she asked, snuggling in to him.

"Somewhere private," Ramirez said. "My apartment has neighbours."

She ran her warm fingers along his thigh, cupping the bulge between his legs. He swallowed hard as they passed the same billboards he and Espinoza had seen on Thursday morning.

On Airport Road, he pulled onto the shoulder and parked the car where it was darkest. The yellow tape was almost invisible in the shadows. He reminded himself to remove it when they were finished. Barrier tape was hard to find.

"Why are you stopping here?" she asked.

"We're going into the forest."

She pulled her hand away and made a little girl pout. "I'd rather take the seat down and do it here, in your car. It's a little small, but that could be fun."

"Look what happened in the city. You don't want to be arrested, do you?"

"But it's dark in the woods. And there are mosquitoes. Maybe snakes too. You're starting to frighten me." She leaned away, pushed back in her seat, straightening herself. She folded her arms across her chest.

"I'll make it worth your while, I promise."

"How worth my while?" she said, smiling, and snuggled close to him again. "You ever see Cuba Gooding Jr. in that movie with Tom Cruise? Show me the *baro*."

That's what's missing, thought Ramirez. There's no money in those purses. But no *jinetera* would be naive enough to go to an isolated spot with a stranger without getting his money up front. "If you show me your *carné* first," he said. He reached into his pant pocket and pulled out his badge.

"Fuck," she said. "I don't have it. I gave it to someone."

"Who?"

"I won't tell you, she'll get in trouble. I'm nineteen," she said, trembling. "I can do whatever I want. And now that she's married, so can she."

He got out of the car and opened the passenger door. He took her firmly by the arm and pointed to the trees. "Come with me."

She walked in front, stumbling a little, catching her high heels in the hard rutted dirt. Déjà vu, thought Ramirez. Except she was alive. How was that possible?

"Are you sure you don't have a twin?" he asked her again.

"Of course not," she said indignantly. "Why do you keep asking? I have a sister, but she's not my twin. Besides, I'm enough woman for anyone."

Headlights of passing cars caught them, but no one stopped. It was just like the young police officer; people averted their eyes. There was nowhere in Havana for unmarried Cubans to have sex; it was the same for married men who wanted to stray. Hotels were for foreigners; apartments were crowded. Ramirez stopped for a moment. He turned his head to look back at the road. A man and a woman walked into the woods. People saw them but looked away. *A profiler sees what's so obvious that no one else notices.*

"Are you going to arrest me or fuck me?" she said, yanking her arm away. "Make up your mind. I suppose this night is going to be free."

Is this how he does it? thought Ramirez. *Bad policeman*, Dr. Yeung said.

Manual Flores had warned that the serial killer could be in law enforcement. Was it one of their own? Or someone pretending to be a policeman, like the vandal from the museum?

"Keep walking." He kept a hand firmly on her back, making sure she knew he was in control. The woods were so dark he couldn't tell what colours the flowers were on the blue mahoe tree. He could barely make out the yellow caution tape strung between the trees.

"Lie down," he said. "On your back." He could barely see her. He might have lost her in the darkness without the white skirt.

"No, I won't," she said. "I'll get my clothes dirty. I have no soap to clean my skirt. It's the only good one I have."

Good, thought Ramirez. She wasn't making it easy. Did LaNeva Otero refuse to cooperate with the killer too? She was proud of her appearance. She wouldn't have wanted to walk into the forest or lie on the debris of the forest floor in her new nylon stockings.

He watched the lights of *chebi*s—official tourist taxis—flicker through the foliage. Antifona could still break and run, despite her high heels. Badge or not, the killer had to have a weapon to keep his victims in line. But then he used his bare hands to kill them. Why?

Because it was personal, Ramirez realized. He wasn't just angry at *jineteras*, he hated them. Juan Otero didn't hate prostitutes, he hated their clients. He was angry at his wife, not at hookers. He had no reason to kill Prima Verrier. Ramirez was suddenly certain that whoever killed those women, it wasn't him.

"What if I pull out a knife? Will you do what I tell you then?"

"Jesus," she said, her voice dropping to a whisper. "Are you going to kill me?"

"I told you to lie down," said Ramirez. He could have this woman all night if he wanted, make her pretend that she liked him, that she enjoyed being violated. But the women weren't raped; Apiro had found nothing. What was the motive?

She pulled off her nylon stockings and stuffed them in her purse so they wouldn't snag. She collapsed on her knees and slowly crumpled on the ground. He could hardly see her, could only hear her stifled sobs and the dry rustling of leaves. He felt sorry for her, but not sorry enough to stop what he'd started.

"I'm going back to the car now. I want you to scream when I walk away. I want to hear you scream all the way from the road."

"You're *loco*," she said. The outrage in her voice was impressive, the fact that it outweighed her fear. "Is this supposed to excite you?

If the police find me alive, I'll tell them that too. You kidnapped me, you left me alone in the woods like some kind of animal. Oh, I'll scream all right. I'll scream until the fucking trees fall down."

He walked back to his car. From the road, he couldn't hear a sound. The white skirt with yellow flowers had vanished in the dark.

Antifona walked out of the woods a few minutes later, picking leaves from her skirt. There were dirty streaks of tears on her cheeks, twigs caught in her thick hair. Ramirez waited, leaning against his car. He held the beer, felt condensation trickle down his wrist.

"What the fuck were you doing? Are you a queer or something?" She got in his car and slammed the door.

He got into the driver's seat. He twisted the top from the second bottle of *cerveza* and gave it to her. Her hand shook as he told her about the murders. She took a deep draught, wiping a drop from her lip as it spilled on her white skirt, concerns about clean clothes forgotten.

"You couldn't tell me that before you scared the shit out of me? Here, light this for me. I'm shaking like a fucking palm tree." She handed him a pack of cigarettes. He pulled one out and put it in his mouth to light it. He handed it back to her. It quivered in her fingers.

"I needed to know what really happened in those woods. You had to be truly frightened for this to work. I needed you to scream as loudly for help as you would in real life. I'm sure now that he uses a weapon. But I'm starting to think that he kills his victims in broad daylight. It's too hard to control women like you at night. You've proved what I've always known. Women are strong. They argue. They fight back."

"Thanks for the fucking compliment," she said, smiling a little. She wiped her eyes. "But how could he do that? We all work nights."

Ramirez pulled on his bottle. "What arrangements would you make to see a client in the daytime?"

"No one hustles during the day, trust me. We're all too tired."

"Tell me about your client. The woman who gave you the nylons."

"What's to tell?" said Antifona. "She was going to be in Havana for a few days. She wanted some companionship."

"What can you remember about her? Anything distinctive?"

"She had a nice back. Well-defined. She said she had to be strong, that they trained them hard. That's all I remember."

"Did she say what that was?"

"No. I didn't ask."

"How did you meet her? Online?"

She thought for a moment. "She must have got my number from someone. I have a cell phone. You're not going to arrest me for that, are you?"

Ramirez shook his head. "Did she tell you her name?"

"We didn't talk much, Señor, believe me. I told her I had a foreign boyfriend. She said she didn't care. She said she swings both ways and then she laughed. Besides, I'm not even sure if I *have* a boyfriend anymore. He was supposed to be here this week, but he never showed up."

"What's his name?"

"What difference does it make? He's long gone."

Ramirez didn't know how to tell her that her boyfriend was probably lying in Apiro's morgue. Besides, if he was right, she would never be able to identify the body anyway; it was no longer recognizable.

"Antifona, you need to be more careful. There could be another government crackdown soon. In fact, I'd count on it."

"It's *la lucha*," she said defiantly. Survival. "They can't stop people from having sex."

"No," Ramirez conceded, "but they can stop you from charging money for it. They can put you in a rehabilitation camp."

Antifona shuddered. "I was in one of those camps. It was awful. I didn't like it."

"It could have been worse. I could have killed you tonight and no one would have heard a thing." He told her about the histology card Apiro had found in the victim's purse. The one bearing her name.

"My card? But I gave it to my sister. She was looking for work. She needed a permanent address."

Not just Mama Loa's goddaughters, Ramirez realized. Antifona Conejo and LaNeva Otero were sisters.

"I'm sorry, Antifona," he said. "There's no easy way to tell you this." He gently removed the bottle from her grasp and took her hands in his. "LaNeva is dead."

50

It **was five in the morning** when Inspector Ramirez got home. His brain felt like cement. In the bedroom, he stepped on something hard, the round stone the old woman had given him. It was lying beside the suit jacket and pants he had dropped on the floor. He picked it up and rolled it in his fingers. He put it down on the small wooden table beside the bed; something amusing to show Francesca. He undressed again.

The bedsprings squeaked as he climbed onto the mattress. If Francesca had been home, he would have made love to her roughly, felt her fingers rake his back, taken pleasure from the pain. But he was alone. He had dropped Antifona Conejo at the Hotel Nacional, as she requested, almost regretting his fidelity.

Ramirez lay on top of the sheets and sank into sleep.

————

He woke up in total darkness, sluggish. He was no longer in bed, he realized groggily, but sitting. Someone pushed him hard. His head cracked against a hard surface.

"The name of anyone who knows you here," said his aggressor. "Come on, Señor. You must have more than one Cuban girlfriend." The man smacked Ramirez so hard that his neck snapped.

It's only a dream, thought Ramirez. But my God, that hurt.

He tried to rouse himself, but he couldn't move. He thrashed around, trying to free himself, aware now that his hands and feet were tightly bound.

His assailant stood back, but it was too dark to make out his features. Outside, waves slapped rhythmically. Warm liquid dripped from Ramirez's nose. He shook his head to clear his nostrils; something trickled down his chin. He licked his lips and tasted blood.

"Careful," said a woman's voice. "We need his clothing for this to work." She stepped forward from the shadows and roughly wiped Ramirez's face with a damp cloth.

"Liar." The man hit him hard again, in the stomach, this time with the flat of his hand. Ramirez grunted with pain. "If you don't tell us who else knows you're here, I promise, she won't live another day."

"Maybe she's the only one," said the woman. "He said he came to Havana to propose to her."

"I do hope you didn't send out any wedding invitations, Señor," said a voice from the shadows, chuckling.

It was gravelly, raspy, a voice Ramirez recognized. But whose? A series of images flashed through his mind—a line of blindfolded men, their hands tied in front of them, the rapid sound of gunshots as they collapsed like dominoes. A tall man in khakis stepped forward and finished each one with a shot to the head. "You picked the wrong side, comrade."

I know you, thought Ramirez. I know that voice. The image vanished when the second man spoke again.

"Hit him again and it won't look like a drowning. Put the blindfold back on before you pour the water. It works better when they can't see."

Ramirez strained against the bonds. The room went black. His eyelashes scraped against harsh fabric.

"Jesus Christ, I hate like hell to kill a man wearing his underwear," the second man said.

"Not to worry," the woman's voice laughed. "You won't need it. No one will get that close to you, believe me. Certainly not me."

They laughed.

Ramirez was suddenly upside down, his mouth and ears full of water. He choked, sputtered. The more he struggled, the more water went down his throat. He gagged. *I'm going to drown.*

Water burned his lungs, came up his nose. He struggled, flailed. The restraints cut into his flesh as he pulled against them with all his strength, gasping for air as his lungs filled with water. He choked, unable to break free, knowing with certainty that he was going to die. His bladder released as darkness overwhelmed him.

Ramirez woke up. He sat quickly upright. Morning sunlight peeked through the curtains. He put his hand to his throat and pulled himself out of his bed. The faded sheets were wet with urine. He looked at them, trembling.

51

Charlie Pike found her in the diner wearing an orange apron and a name tag that said "Pauline." She didn't seem surprised to see him, more like she'd been expecting it. She seemed older than she had appeared in the poster, although only a few weeks had passed. Spent. Maybe tired of hiding her secret.

"It's been a long time, Charlie," she said. "I heard you joined the police. Let me pour you a coffee. You want some breakfast too?"

"A lot of people are worried about you, Molly."

"Not as many as you might think," she said, and she started to cry.

———

They sat across from each other on the plastic banquettes at the back of the café where no one could overhear them. She wiped her eyes with the back of her hand. "I'm not sorry she's dead. She was a monster, you know. She was going to use those blood tests. Publish them in international journals. She didn't care what that did to us. To the community. To my son."

"Her research? Is that what all this is about?"

She nodded, slowly. "I thought you knew. I didn't kill her, although I sure thought about it." She pushed the coffee cup away. "I don't have to talk to you, do I, Charlie? Am I under arrest?"

"No," said Pike. He shook his head. "I'm looking for Molly Oshig. The woman I'm talking to is named Pauline Johnson. Funny, the only Pauline Johnson I ever heard of was a Mohawk poet. She died about a hundred years ago. Hard to arrest a ghost for obstructing justice. I think ghosts are allowed to disappear."

She laughed through her tears.

"English was my best subject, I guess," she said. "'The Song My Paddle Sings.' Her name was the first one I thought of when I applied here."

"Her Mohawk name was *Tekahionwake*. It means 'double life.'"

"Then I guess it fits, doesn't it?"

"Molly, I know something's going on at Manomin Bay. I saw those test results. Talk to me. Why did you leave?"

"You won't tell?"

"I can't promise that. But I'll try not to."

She nodded slowly. "She phoned me. That doctor, Maylene Kesler. She said the genetic tests confused her at first. She thought maybe she mixed them up."

Another long silence. Pike waited. He knew that she'd fill in the space. Molly Oshig could take whatever time she needed to tell her story. Adam Neville could wait.

"She said the good news was that he might not have FAS. Pauley. She said she thought it was more likely a trigger for something different. A condition, she called it, not a disease. She thought I'd be happy that it wasn't my fault. But it was, you know. Because I let him get me pregnant."

The tears spilled down her cheeks. She raised her eyes and

looked at him, then looked away. "She was supposed to be testing us for mercury poisoning. She didn't tell us she was going to look at our DNA too. I think she was one of those vampire doctors, the ones who take people's blood and then claim they own their genes without them knowing. I know she didn't give a shit about us; all she cared about was her research."

She opened a packet of sugar and dropped the contents into her coffee, then another. She stirred the coffee slowly, fiddled with the spoon. "She knew that Pauley's my son, Charlie. Then she found out he's my brother."

It took Pike a moment to comprehend what she was saying. "Chesley?"

She nodded, and then she sobbed. He handed her a paper napkin. She wiped her eyes with it and wept.

"It started when I was thirteen. He'd come into my room at night when he was drunk. They sent me into the city to have the baby when I was fourteen. I stayed in a Catholic home for unwed mothers. I came back when Pauley was three. We told everyone I got married too young and that we split up."

Of course, Pike thought. The real reason Sheldon wanted to run away from school and go to Winnipeg. Not because of the nuns at day school, but because his girlfriend was having his baby. Or at least that's what he thought, until they told him it was someone else's. A husband that didn't exist.

Everyone thought that Oshig was her married name. That's why the police couldn't find her. No driver's licence, no trail. Because Molly Oshig never really existed either. Molly Wabigoon had never been married.

"Dr. Kesler called me to say she was coming back up, that she needed to see me. She said she wanted to publish her results but she needed my consent because Pauley's a minor. She was really persistent about it. Aggressive."

Anishnabe people never asked for something unless they were

certain they could get it, thought Pike. They'd lose face if they asked and the other person said no. Turning down a request was considered disrespectful, because it caused the other person to lose face. So Molly had run. To get away from an ugly secret she thought died with Chesley Wabigoon.

It was what Anishnabe people were taught by their elders—to avoid conflict. To respect others.

"Who else knew about this, Molly?"

"That Pauley was Chesley's son? My mother, I guess. She must have. The walls in that house were thin. She must have heard him, heard us. But any time he was in my room meant he wasn't in hers, beating her up whenever he got drunk. And what was she going to do? Where was she going to go with six kids, if he kicked her out? She had nowhere *to* go."

"What about your brothers?"

"I don't think they knew. Most of them were little. Billy was the oldest, but he was in Winnipeg then. In remand or jail, I don't remember. But I told Sheldon. I had to, Charlie. I loved him. He had to know it wasn't his baby. I couldn't help it. I didn't know how to stop it from happening. Just like I never drank alcohol when I was pregnant. But it didn't matter. Pauley didn't come out right. I should have stopped it, told someone. But I didn't want to break up my family."

Fourteen when she got pregnant. The same age as Sheldon Waubasking when he persuaded Pike to run away from school and head to Winnipeg. The same year that Sheldon almost killed Billy Wabigoon with his bare hands for calling Molly a slut.

Pike wasn't sure what to say. Nothing would make it right. People came out of those schools damaged. Like Pauley, they came out wrong. Most turned their anger inwards, turned themselves, and then their families, inside out. No one wanted to talk about incest. Everyone pretended it didn't happen.

"Did you go to any counselling? Talk to the elders?"

She shook her head and squeezed the napkin. "What was I going to say? And what would that do to Pauley, to find out his grandfather was really his father? Can't you see how fucked up all of this is?"

Pike nodded. He thought for a moment. "There's just one thing I don't understand. Maylene Kesler told you she was going to publish her results. Why did you think leaving Manomin Bay was going to stop her from doing that?"

"Sheldon told me he'd take care of it. He said I should go away for a while. When I heard there was a woman's body on the reserve, I knew right away what happened. I wasn't sure if that made me guilty too. Because I told Sheldon I wished she was dead."

"You think Sheldon killed her?"

She looked up at him, surprised. "Who else would have?"

52

Charlie Pike pulled his SUV into the parking lot at the health clinic. He wiped his feet on the rubber mat and shook the snow from his hair. He nodded to the nurse practitioner at the reception desk. She was rifling through her desk for something, maybe her keys. She looked annoyed.

Pike walked downstairs and knocked on the door to the temporary office.

"Come in, Charlie. Here, have a seat." Adam Neville sat behind his desk, typing on his laptop's small keyboard. His overnight bag was in the corner beside the black satchel.

"Morning, Adam. Sorry I'm a little late. Appreciate you taking the time to see me before you head out." Pike sat down. "I need to go over some things with you. Got to move carefully on this one."

"Of course." The medical examiner folded his hands together on the surface of the desk. "I understand completely, Charlie. Ask away.

But I have to be out of here in an hour to catch my flight. I hope we can wrap this up quickly."

"They're pretty relaxed at the airport. It's not like it is down south. Don't worry. They won't leave without you."

Pike pulled out his notebook and opened it. He fumbled around in his jacket for a pen. Neville handed him one.

"*Miigwetch*. So, Sheldon told me you got to the crime scene around eleven a.m. on Thursday, but he doesn't have a watch. He said it was a little while before the techs arrived. Is that about right?"

"I think it was twelve minutes after eleven, to be precise."

"You told him to stay back. Why was that?"

"Standard procedure, Charlie. I have to keep people out of the way so the crime scene doesn't get contaminated."

"So any evidence that links Sheldon to the crime scene had to be there before you arrived?"

"That's right," Neville said. "He never got near that body once I was there. I made sure of that."

"Were you alone with her for very long before the techs arrived?"

"Maybe twenty minutes. I did a quick walk around. Put up the yellow caution tape, cordoned off the search area."

"And Sheldon had nothing to do with that either? He didn't help you?"

"Absolutely not."

"Good." Pike nodded. He doodled in his notebook. "You told me on the phone that you took his fingerprints?"

"Of course. After all, he had been at that crime scene for at least a couple of hours before I got there; I had no idea what he might have touched. That's how I was able to match his prints to the ones inside the SUV Dr. Kesler rented."

"How did you do that, exactly? Take his prints."

"I used clear plastic tape and put them on a card. I didn't have an inkpad with me. Had to use it to take prints from the body too."

"Didn't you have any ninhydrin with you?" Pike leaned back in the chair, crossed his legs at the ankles.

"Yes," said Neville. "But I only use it to take fingerprints from porous surfaces, so I didn't need it. I've used it to take prints from dead bodies before, but we do it in the morgue, where we can rehydrate the fingers. I had to use lifts on your friend. That's all I had."

Pike made another doodle in his notebook. "I guess that's your kit over there, eh?" Pike inclined his head to the black bag in the corner. "Did you restock it before you left Winnipeg? Make sure everything was full?"

Neville nodded. "In a remote location like this, if I don't have everything I need, I can't get it very easily."

"Understood. I better ask, because the defence lawyers will. Did you have a cigarette while you were at the scene? A roll-your-own?"

"Of course not," said the pathologist, shaking his head. "I'd never contaminate a crime scene. Besides, I don't smoke. I'm a climber. I have to be able to deal with low oxygen levels at high altitudes. Are you suggesting we missed some other evidence?"

Neville closed his email program and Pike caught a glimpse of the screensaver again. "Nice picture of you two," he said, avoiding the question. "We used to climb the bluffs around here, when we were kids, looking for vultures' nests. I see you had one of those little axes—what do they call those ones with the pick on the end?"

"The ice axe? We use it to chop ice and clear away loose rocks. But Charlie, can we move this along please? I'm getting a little concerned about my flight." Neville looked at his watch, making his point.

"Sorry. You know the Ojibway, we run on Indian time." Pike smiled. "All right. When you saw the body for the first time, she had that nylon wrapped around her neck, right?"

"That's why I thought it was the Highway Strangler."

Pike shook his head. "Something's been bothering me. Pauley

Oshig kept saying the woman's body was blue. I didn't understand what he meant at first. But I think I do now."

"I don't understand."

"Luminol," said Pike. He uncrossed his legs and leaned forward. "You spray it on victims to check for blood and DNA, right? It turns blue under a UV light and glows for a few seconds. After Pauley showed Sheldon where the body was, he was supposed to go to the band office, but I don't think he did. He was afraid to see Bill right away, because he knew he was going to get punished for skipping school. I think he hid in the woods for a while and watched what was going on. I think he saw you spray Maylene Kesler's body with Luminol."

"That makes sense. Come to think of it, I did use Luminol on the body, but that's proper procedure, Charlie."

"The defence lawyers are going to ask you about that. The only reason I can think of why you'd use Luminol at the crime scene is if you were checking to make sure you didn't leave anything behind after you pulled off her boots. You didn't know the techs were going to run off like that. One of them might have ended up at the autopsy."

"But she didn't have any boots on. I've already told you that."

Pike stopped doodling. "That's because you took them off so you could get at those nylon knee-highs she was wearing. You needed to tie one around her neck. I think you used the ninhydrin on her boots later on, to make sure you removed your prints before you threw them away. That's why the ninhydrin bottle in your bag is almost empty, even though you said you never used it."

"What?" said Neville, standing up. "Are you accusing me of killing Maylene Kesler? This is insane, Charlie. You already have your Highway Strangler. You just don't want to believe it's your friend."

"You see, now, that's the problem. I know you didn't kill her. Because I know who did, and it wasn't Sheldon. But you tried to make it look like Sheldon. I think you framed him, because he was the only person you *could* frame. That's why you took his prints on plastic tape, so you could transfer them to another surface, even though he told you he didn't touch anything. There's only one reason to frame somebody for a murder you didn't commit, and that's to give yourself an alibi for those other murders. If the Highway Strangler did this one, it couldn't be you all those other times."

"You should have been a fiction writer, Pike. When all this is over, you may want to consider it. Because you have just ended your police career."

"The boots threw me off. But she was frozen pretty good; it would have been hard to remove them, and pretty much impossible to get them back on again. I'm guessing they're in a ditch somewhere along the 562. Or maybe in the garbage behind the motel. Luckily, because of the storm, there's been no pickup. The OPP is checking all those bins for me right now."

"This is bullshit," Neville said, his face flushed. He sat down again, hard.

"Did you throw away the ice axe you used to make those little round holes in the ground or is it in your suitcase? I'd love to know how you got it through airport security. Man, I can't get through security that easy, even without a weapon. I'm guessing you put it in the body bag along with Dr. Kesler's boots and let the techs carry everything out of the woods for you. Like you said, those body bags can be pretty useful."

Charlie Pike reached over and turned the laptop around. In the screen shot, Adam Neville and his wife each held an ice axe.

Pike reached in his jacket pocket and pulled out the plastic exhibit bag containing the pack of Lucky Strikes. He placed it on the desk. "This was in the drawer, right beside where you're sitting. Only one cigarette is missing. The one you left at the crime scene."

"How the hell did you get those," Neville sputtered. "I locked them up."

"Thanks for confirming possession, Adam. From a guy who doesn't smoke, I think that's probably enough to make an arrest."

Neville slumped back in his chair. "It's not what it looks like, Charlie. Believe, me, you've got this all wrong."

"You can come in now, Pete," Pike called out.

Sergeant Bissonnette opened the door. A uniformed policeman stood behind him, holding a pair of women's boots in his gloved hands.

"You were right," said Bissonnette. "We found these in the dumpster outside."

"Charge him with obstruction for now. Make sure you read him his rights. You know, you really shouldn't leave things lying around, Adam," said Pike, standing up. He closed his notebook and put it in his pocket. "People up north are *way* too trusting."

53

Inspector Ramirez jumped when his cell phone rang. His nightmare had left him unnerved and on edge. He steered through the heavy traffic, pressing the small device to his ear, struggling to hear his caller over the rattling exhaust pipes and bleating horns.

"I have a preliminary cause of death for the man from the beach, Ricardo," said Apiro. "He drowned, but not in the ocean. In saltwater drowning, we often find a higher chlorine concentration in the left chamber of the heart than in the right. It's the opposite in freshwater. Freshwater also significantly changes the surface tension of the pulmonary surfactant—that's on the surface of the lungs, Ricardo—seawater doesn't.

"And you were right about the restraints. There were small hemorrhages around the wrists and ankles, and microscopic wood fibres in the skin on one leg, just above the part of the epidermis that detached as he struggled to get loose. It looks like he was tied up and that someone held his head underwater until he died."

"You mean in a swimming pool?"

"Not necessarily. It doesn't take much water to drown. You can drown in a sink or in a toilet, even a bucket."

Ramirez thought about his dream. Maybe the dead man wasn't Antifona Conejo's foreign boyfriend after all. He cast his mind back to the article he'd read in *Granma*.

"He could have been waterboarded. It's something the Americans do to prisoners in Guantánamo Bay. They strap them to boards, lean them back, and pour water over their heads to make them feel like they're drowning. It's supposed to make them talk. He could have been a prisoner in the detention facility. Maybe something went wrong during an interrogation."

"That's certainly one way to dispose of a body, Ricardo. Throw it in the ocean and hope it's never found. But if you're right, it will be almost impossible to prove."

Ramirez shook his head. An Iraqi prisoner from Guantánamo wouldn't be wearing jewellery or expensive clothes. He'd been wrong about Antifona Conejo being dead too. His visions were becoming a problem. They weren't just the product of stress, now they were contributing to it.

He told his small friend about running into Antifona the night before. "I still can't believe I found her alive."

"It sounds to me, no offence, as if she found you," said Apiro. "Since when do *jineteras* pick up Cuban men? I thought you didn't like coincidences. You remember Sherlock Holmes? He used to say, if two highly unusual events happened at the same time, they were usually connected. Be careful, my friend. I have a feeling something's going on."

"Maybe she thought I was handsome," said Ramirez, slightly offended.

"More attractive than a paying client? If I had enough money, even I would look handsome. Not to mention taller."

Ramirez laughed uneasily. He swerved the car to avoid striking another stranded coco-taxi. If he ever hit one, he thought, it would roll down the street like a child's ball.

———

Detective Espinoza called Ramirez on his radio. "Inspector, I'm with Rider Aguilera at his mechanic's. His car broke down weeks ago, it's still here. The mechanic has confirmed that Señor Aguilera had no car to loan."

"I was afraid of that. Whoever did this had to have a vehicle to take those women to the forest. They didn't walk. And they didn't take a taxi. Juan Otero had no money."

As Ramirez said it, he was certain he was right. Even if Otero could have afforded a cab, the driver would have waited by the side of the road, maybe even entered the woods in search of his fare. The killer couldn't take that chance. "It might not be Otero at all. Did you ever find a lead for that apple that Dr. Apiro found in the victim's stomach?"

"I checked with a few hotels, Inspector, but I stopped looking after we took Señor Otero into custody. Of the ones I spoke to, only the Hotel Floridita and the Hotel Nacional had any. They received a shipment on February 11 and put them out in the morning buffet the next day. The manager of the Floridita said they were imported from Quebec. They call the variety a 'snow apple' because of its white flesh."

"Find out how many of their guests ate at the morning buffet on Lovers' Day. Once you have a list, we'll need to cross-reference it to car rentals going back to say, mid-January. Check for the same time period last year. Let's see if we find any names in common."

"There will be thousands of names," Espinoza protested. "The hotel records are computerized, and some of the car rental agencies will be too, but they won't be on the same computers. And many of the car rental agencies have no computers at all."

"I know," said Ramirez. "It's a huge job. Get Natasha to help you." He thought for a moment. "I think Dr. Apiro's technicians should go back to the forest again tomorrow."

"What for, Inspector?"

"To start digging."

54

After he hung up, Ramirez thought more about Hector Apiro's comments. Ramirez didn't like coincidences. If Ramirez hadn't found Antifona, how had she found him?

He recalled the warmth of her lips, her tongue tracing circles around his ear. She was alive, no doubt about that. But she had no twin, and her sister LaNeva was dead. Whose ghost had he seen? And why did that ghost keep putting her finger to her lips? What was it his subconscious wanted him to know?

The dead woman had winked at him and pointed to the interior light in his car. Ramirez swerved across a lane of traffic and pulled to the side of the road, ignoring the blast of angry horns. He got out, leaned inside, and looked carefully around the car interior. He examined the plastic cover over the light above his rearview mirror and saw tiny scratches around the edges. Pry marks.

Embedded inside the light was a small listening device. It wasn't a thief who stole my mirror at all, he realized; it was someone covering up what they did, making sure that if I noticed any damage, I'd blame it on a thief.

He reattached the cover but left the device intact while he considered what to do. If someone had bugged his car, they might have bugged his home as well. Was it Cuban Intelligence, bugging him the way they bugged Nassara Nobiko? But why?

He started the car again and pulled a U-turn. He parked the car outside his apartment building and slammed the door. He ran up the three flights of stairs and tiptoed inside the apartment. He quietly checked every room, not wanting to alert anyone who might be eavesdropping.

The bug was clipped to the electrical junction box for the kitchen light. He removed it and put it in his jacket pocket, then walked slowly back downstairs and climbed into his car. He looked at the interior light while he considered his options. He finally decided to leave the listening device exactly where it was.

After all, he thought, starting the ignition, as Francesca had said during one of their better fights, good communication was always two-way.

55

It *was almost eleven in the* morning and Inspector Ramirez had only an hour before he had to release the paintings to the Italians. He decided to stop by the museum and let the director, Romero Garza, know the artwork could be crated for shipping, that his investigation had run out of time.

He parked his small car in front of the museum and walked up the massive marble stairs to the mezzanine level. He nodded to Carlos Hernandez, who was seated behind the security desk, and asked for directions to Garza's office. He found the museum director shuffling papers.

"*Hola*, Inspector Ramirez, how goes it?" Garza smiled and stood to shake the inspector's hand.

"I'm sorry to say we haven't made much progress. You may have heard. The Italians want their paintings back today. The government has agreed to release them."

"Yes, they've been kicking up quite a fuss. Well, it won't take long to pack up the paintings as soon as you give the go-ahead."

"Before I do, can you answer a few questions for my report?"

"Of course. Please, sit down."

Ramirez removed his hat and seated himself.

"I was wondering. Señor Testa told me that the paintings are insured for quite a lot of money. Could that form any part of the motive for the damage?"

"So that someone could recover the insurance proceeds? I hope you're not suggesting that Señor Testa would be involved in something like that, Inspector. He is a highly regarded curator from one of the top museums in the world."

"Not at all," said Ramirez. "I'm just trying to understand who might profit by damaging the paintings."

"It was a political protest, Inspector, nothing more. Besides, the ownership of these paintings is disputed. It would be very hard to recover on a claim. That's why they can be exhibited in Cuba but not in certain parts of Europe or the United States."

"I'm not sure I understand," said Ramirez.

"If the paintings were ever shown in those places, they could be seized," said Garza. "All of them were once owned by wealthy Cuban families. They were expropriated by the revolutionary government and sold during the Special Period at auction. It's the reason we wanted to display them. They are part of our cultural heritage."

"How could they be seized?"

"Claims have been filed alleging wrongful expropriation. A state can confiscate property from its own citizens; it's perfectly legal. The problem here is that the actual owners of the paintings may not have been the families themselves, but their companies, which were incorporated in the United States. Because of this, there is a legal issue as to whether Cuba had the right to expropriate them at all. American laws allow the original owners to recover a property in such circumstances. The Fanjul family sued Sotheby's auction house following the sale of one such painting in England, the *Castillo de Málaga*. And the De la Torre family recently settled a similar claim for a Mariano. The American courts will claim jurisdiction over any disputed painting as soon as it touches American soil."

"Funny," said Ramirez, "that they will assert jurisdiction over paintings that reach their shores but won't accept any Cubans who manage to get there."

Garza laughed bitterly. "You don't have to feed a painting."

Detective Espinoza stopped Ramirez as soon as he walked into the Major Crimes Unit. "We may have a suspect, Inspector. In the museum investigation. We still have time to make an arrest; it's not noon yet. Patrol picked him up spray-painting a wall in Varadero about thirty minutes ago. He claims he didn't arrive in Cuba until Friday, but he doesn't have his airplane ticket with him. We're checking with Customs. He had these in his backpack, along with a few other very interesting items." Espinoza handed some stencils to Ramirez.

The stencils depicted Fidel Castro urinating on a computer. Despite himself, Ramirez smiled. "What were the other items?"

"Orange coveralls, still in their package. A black hood and plastic handcuffs. And a life-size inflatable doll. A male. Not the type we use here. The handcuffs, I mean." Espinoza blushed. "But no police uniform. He's in the interview room. I thought you might want these too."

Espinoza handed Ramirez an exhibit envelope containing photographs of the damaged paintings at the museum and the image spray-painted above them.

They walked down the narrow hall to the room adjoining the interview room. Ramirez looked through the mirrored glass. A man sat at the Formica table on the red plastic chair. He was short-haired and wore glasses and a hooded jacket. There was nothing remarkable about him.

But that was the problem, thought Ramirez. Most criminals didn't look like criminals.

"Was he carrying identification?"

"A passport. He's English. Robin Gunningham," said Espinoza, handing it over. "He was born in July 1973, which makes him thirty-three."

Ramirez took the passport and stepped into the hall. He walked the few paces to the interrogation room and opened the metal door. When it swung shut, it clanged. The prisoner jumped.

Ramirez recalled Dr. Flores's advice about the organized and disorganized criminal. If this man was responsible for the vandalism in the museum, he was certainly organized. But why would he have an inflatable doll with him? As a diversion of some kind? He remembered the profiler's instructions: appeal to his ego.

"My name is Inspector Ramirez, Señor Gunningham. It appears that you've been gracing our buildings with your art." Ramirez put the photographs on the table. "In Cuba, unfortunately, expressing political sentiments of this type can land you in prison for quite a long time."

Not completely true. A foreigner was more likely to be expelled from the country. But the Englishman had no need to know that. Ramirez pointed to a photograph of the image sprayed on the museum wall. "Is this your work?"

The artist leaned forward and squinted at it, then sat back. "Never seen it before."

"It was sprayed on a wall in our National Museum on Thursday afternoon."

"I didn't even get here until Friday evening. Never even been to any Cuban museums; wouldn't bother. I spend all my free time at the hip-hop festival. Besides, this is clumsy technique. Nothing like mine."

"You sound like you don't think much of museums."

The Englishman snorted. "They're just retirement homes for

old paintings, protected by a bunch of bored punters who don't know anything about art. They can't tell a fake from the real thing."

"And how would you know this?"

"Aren't you supposed to read me my rights or something?"

"I have no interest in whatever crimes you may have committed elsewhere, Señor. The only reason you're here is because of the vandalism in our museum. We're checking out when you arrived; if it's as you say, you'll be released with our apologies."

The man visibly relaxed. "Then I should be out of here in no time. I used to hang my paintings inside museums, right beside the real ones. Takes about two seconds and a dab of glue to hang up a painting. Amazing what a cheap gold frame can do. Most people don't notice for weeks that a painting doesn't belong there. I've had one in the Louvre for years. I go in every now and then with a paintbrush to touch it up."

"You're obviously a perfectionist." Ramirez smiled. He leaned back in his chair. "Do you only enter these museums when they are open to the public?"

"I haven't had to break into one, if that's what you mean. Not that it would be all that hard."

Ramirez fumbled in his pocket for a cigar. "Really? They're heavily guarded."

"You know, you read an art review and the critics talk about how skilfully an artist uses his paint or his palette knife, or about his use of light and colour. But in my kind of work, it's all about access. Besides, it's a whole lot easier to get inside a museum than a bank. Someone broke into one in Dublin last year after some idiot left a ladder leaning on an exterior wall. The IRA pulled off an art heist in Boston a few years ago too. They put on fake police uniforms and tied up the guards. In and out in less than five minutes. They got away with quite a few expensive paintings. Never recovered any of them."

"The IRA? Why would the IRA steal art in the United States?"

"Why does anyone steal art? For money. There are more stolen Picassos in private collections than there are in museums. I'm surprised you didn't hear about that heist, though. It was all over the press. That's the way to do it, you know. You show someone a police uniform, they don't even notice what else you're doing."

"Tell me," Ramirez said, tapping the photograph of the spray-painted museum wall, "what does that look like to you?"

Gunningham slid the photograph towards himself and turned it around. "Honestly?" The Englishman hesitated a moment before he answered. "It looks like a spider."

"You're sure it's not a depiction of the *bombilla* in the *Guernica* mural? You know the Picasso painting, I assume."

"You mean that eye at the top? I've seen the real *Guernica*, and this sure as hell doesn't look like that. There's a copy at the UN Building in New York. Remember the day Colin Powell accused Iraq on television of having weapons of mass destruction? It was hanging right behind him. They put a curtain over it so it wasn't visible as the U.S. made their case for going to war, but even covered up, the horse's arse was directly above his head. I laughed until I cried.

"I put graffiti up at the United Nations Building once myself, in plain view of all the guards. I was wearing a pair of painter's overalls. I walked right up to the building with my paint can and my rags. Walked away with a tour when I was done, tossed the overalls in a bin outside. When you have that many security guards, everyone thinks the other guy's paying attention."

Of course, Ramirez thought. The imposter left the museum still wearing the police uniform. Where was it? Ramirez looked at the mirrored glass and inclined his head. He knew Espinoza would understand.

"You defaced the UN Building? That takes some *cojones*."

The graffiti artist grinned. "Look, it was only a can of spray paint. You can wash latex paint off with water. And even enamel paint can be cleaned off with a little turpentine. I'll bet those paintings in your museum were cleaned and protected with synthetic resin a long time ago. It's pretty easy to remove spray paint from anything that's been heavily varnished. I mean, *Guernica* wasn't damaged at all. Honestly, apart from the shock value, it wasn't much of a crime."

Ramirez leaned back and thought for a moment. He lit his cigar. He pulled another from his pocket and offered it to the man, but he shook his head.

"No thanks. Don't smoke. Bad for you. I'll have a beer if you have one, though." The man was completely at ease now. Which was what Ramirez wanted.

"Maybe later," said Ramirez. He put the cigar back in his pocket. "Now tell me, Señor, why did you have a black hood and handcuffs in your backpack?" He had little interest in the sexual proclivities of others, but he needed to know.

The man almost blushed. "You know the graffiti artist named Banksy? He left one at Disneyworld last fall dressed in orange prisoner overalls and a black hood, with its hands cuffed, like the prisoners at Guantánamo Bay. These days, torture's a form of entertainment. Problem is that Disneyworld's an amusement park. The installation was too successful. People were amused instead of outraged. I thought I'd dress one up and leave it in front of the Swiss embassy where that tickertape display criticizes the Cuban government. Have a little fun."

Ramirez nodded slowly, piecing this information together with what he knew. Then he stood up. "I'll be back shortly," he said. "I'll see about that beer."

He left Gunningham alone with the photographs while he went to the exhibit room to find the man a beer. On his way there, he stopped in the anteroom next door.

Espinoza looked crestfallen. "I'm sorry," said the young detective. "It didn't occur to me to look for the uniform in garbage cans near the museum, Inspector. Anything the vandal left there will be long gone by now. By the way, Customs called while you were interrogating the suspect. He's telling the truth. He didn't arrive in Havana until Friday at 6:35 p.m."

"No need to apologize, Fernando. I didn't think of it either. No, I don't think he's our man, but I'm glad you brought him in. He has me thinking. Listen, I want you to do something for me. Take a police car to the airport and find out exactly when Señor Testa arrived here: the date and the time. Get the tape of his arrival at Customs from the surveillance cameras. But first, get a copy of his passport from the reception desk at the Hotel Nacional."

Espinoza raised his eyebrows but nodded. He inclined his head towards the mirrored glass. "Are you going to let him go?" He sounded disappointed. "I thought maybe he was Banksy."

"He could be, for all I know. But being a famous graffiti artist isn't a crime. I think El Comandante will be amused if he carries out his plans in front of the Swiss embassy. Although perhaps a little less so if he uses those stencils."

Ramirez released the Englishman from custody with a can of warm Cristol beer and a warning about painting graffiti on buildings that could fall down on him at any time.

Then he returned to his office. He checked the light, his desk, and his telephone again but found no more bugs.

56

Inspector Ramirez sighed when he thought about the chase he'd been led on. Rappers, *traceurs*, terrorists, *Guernica*, Basques. He agreed with Picasso—the art world was full of criminals. And when one's only tool was a hammer, everything was a nail. But he blamed himself for missing the obvious, for allowing himself to be distracted. For seeing only what he expected to see.

He glanced at his watch. It was eleven forty-five. He had no reason not to release the paintings now that he knew, or at least thought he knew, what was going on.

He dialed the number for the Hotel Nacional and gave the operator the room number for Dominique Gatti.

The dead man sat across from him, anxiously drumming his fingers on the surface of Ramirez's desk. "I know who you are," Ramirez told the ghost while he waited for the operator to connect him. "Me. Not just my subconscious. And I think I know who killed you."

The dead man raised his eyebrows.

"Patience," said Ramirez. "I could be wrong. After all, I thought Antifona Conejo was dead and she wasn't." The dead man shook his head, his brown eyes sad.

Dominique Gatti answered on the third ring.

"I have good news, Señora Gatti. You can take your paintings back to Italy today. Our investigation is over."

"Oh, thank God," she said, her voice lifting. "The paintings have been crated; there's a flight this afternoon. Did you find the culprit?"

"It looks as if a visiting graffiti artist was responsible," Ramirez lied. "Someone trying to make his mark in the art world. What time does the flight leave?"

"At two thirty."

Ramirez looked at his watch again. If Espinoza moved quickly, they would have just enough time. "Have a good trip back to Italy, Señora. I sincerely hope your paintings can be restored."

Ramirez pushed papers around while he waited, hoping his instincts were right.

Detective Espinoza called him back just after one o'clock. He sounded surprised. "I have the surveillance tapes in my hand, Inspector. Señor Testa isn't the man we met at the museum. In fact, other than his weight and height, he hardly resembles him at all."

"That's what I thought," said Ramirez. "Where are you now?"

"I'm still at the airport."

"Good." Ramirez breathed out. He gave the detective further instructions. "I'll join you there later."

A moment later, the phone on his desk trilled. It was Dispatch.

"Inspector, we have another homicide. Dr. Apiro is at the crime scene. He says it appears to be the real Antifona Conejo this time. She hasn't been dead for long, only hours."

"Where was the body found?" Ramirez asked, his heart sinking.

"A few hundred yards from the one earlier in the week, in the woods beside the highway. Dr. Apiro's technicians were excavating the site, as you had directed when they discovered it. The technicians from the Centre for Legal Medicine are there now. He says they've taken over the investigation."

"Why?" asked Ramirez, but he already knew the answer.

"Dr. Flores wants you to drop by his apartment this afternoon so he can explain." She gave him the address. "He suggested you come around two thirty."

Of course he did, thought Ramirez. That, and Antifona's murder, made Ramirez unspeakably angry. There was no need for it, none at all.

57

The psychiatrist was staying in an apartment in a skyscraper known by locals as the Edificio Coño, the "Oh My Fucking God Building," because of its extraordinary height.

When it was constructed in 1956, the thirty-five-storey structure was considered one of the tallest concrete buildings in the world. It was engineered using what was then brand-new computer technology. But it had been left in shambles when its mostly Russian tenants fled after the collapse of the Soviet Union. For years, turkey vultures nested in its crevices. And in 2000, a cable supporting an elevator snapped, killing everyone inside.

The tower was being renovated. La Torre, the restaurant on the top floor, was supposed to be fantastic. But few Cubans would risk eating there, even if they could, for fear of plunging to their deaths.

Ramirez walked up the stairs to the eighth floor. He knocked on the psychiatrist's door after taking a moment to catch his breath.

Manuel Flores opened the door. He appeared thinner and even more stooped, as if he was wasting away.

"Thank you for coming, Inspector. I gather you've heard that Antifona Conejo's body was found. I thought it would be best to have an essentially unpleasant conversation here instead of at your office, where so many people have ears."

"I am quite sure that applies to all of them," said Ramirez, trying to suppress his anger. "And yes, I heard about Señora Conejo. I've also heard that the Centre is taking over what should be our investigation."

"Ah, yes, Ramirez. Well, I can explain." The psychiatrist walked stiffly to a worn sofa and seated himself. "Please, sit down." He patted the faded cushion beside him.

The profiler had lined up a series of photographs on the wooden coffee table. Next to them rested a typed report and a small tape recorder.

"Is this really necessary?" said Ramirez, sitting down.

The profiler shrugged his shoulders. "We always use a tape recorder in felony investigations, Ramirez. You know that. The pictures are from this morning's crime scene. She was a lovely girl." He leaned forward and picked one up. He handed it to Ramirez. "It certainly looks like the same killer, doesn't it? But of course, it can't be Juan Otero. After all, he's in jail."

Ramirez took the photograph but put it down quickly. There was no mistaking the protruding tongue, the bulging eyes, the nylon stocking tied tightly around Antifona's neck. He thought of her energy and spirit and felt immeasurably sad.

Flores picked up the report. "This is my profile of the serial killer for the Ministry of the Interior. I've concluded that he is highly organized after all. He gives the appearance of being happily married but is having domestic problems. A demanding wife, a difficult job, too little time. Lately, he's strayed, looking for comfort with prostitutes. He has young children, so he feels trapped."

Ramirez raised his eyebrows.

Flores smiled. "He's involved in law enforcement, which is why we never find any forensic evidence. His guilt over his infidelity is what causes him to kill these women. He poses them as if they're sleeping because he can't cope with the knowledge that he's committed such terrible crimes. The cigarette butts, the purses, their identification—he leaves those behind because deep down he wants to be caught." He handed Ramirez the report. "I think you'll find my conclusions interesting."

Ramirez turned to the last page and read aloud: "Subject displays classic symptoms of paranoia and sluggish schizophrenia with visual and auditory hallucinations. The Centre for Legal Medicine confirms that DNA on the cigarette butt found beside the woman's body matches blood samples kept on record. Listening devices installed in his apartment and private vehicle confirm his prior relationship with the victim. Recommend full psychiatric evaluation and isolation at Mazorra while charges are reviewed by the Attorney General. Consider suspect extremely dangerous."

"I think it's a rather good profile, don't you?" said Flores.

"I never cheated on Francesca."

"Perhaps. But I doubt she'll care when she finds out about all of this." Flores smiled again. He shut off the tape recorder. "The minister wants the distribution list back. He wants things the way they were before you went to Canada. Before you involved yourself in affairs that didn't concern you."

"I didn't kill Antifona."

Flores shrugged. "Who cares? We have photographs of you with her last night. Getting into your car. Kissing. You should never have taken her to the killing ground. And you should have told us you knew her."

"I didn't know her before last night."

"Perhaps not in the carnal sense. But I'm sure you'll understand,

Ramirez, if I don't believe you." Flores turned on the tape recorder. He inserted a new tape and pushed a button.

Ramirez heard the metallic sound of his own voice: "I'm sorry, Antifona. You really need to leave. I can't have you hanging around my apartment. My wife and children will be back soon, and believe me Francesca wouldn't appreciate you being here when she's not home. Besides, you're far too attractive. It's distracting."

"There's another part on that tape where you can't find your pants," said Flores. "And then, of course, there's the conversation in your car. I admit, the lesbian sex sounded hot. It was a nice surprise, finding out that you knew who Antifona Conejo was throughout the entire investigation and didn't tell anyone. It certainly feeds into my theory of your schizophrenic paranoia."

"You planted the bugs?"

"Not personally. But good for you for finding them. I've always said you were a brilliant detective."

"I should have known the minister didn't assign you to our unit to investigate a serial killer."

"Let's just say he wanted a profile that fit the crime he was most concerned with, which was blackmail. He told you he didn't care about *jineteras*. He's a man of his word."

"How did you find Antifona when we weren't able to?"

"There aren't too many *jineteras* with that name," said Flores. "After a few days cleaning up after pigs, believe me, she was happy to work with us."

Ramirez nodded slowly. "You put her in a rehabilitation camp."

Flores smiled. "For obvious reasons, our office is handling the investigation into her death. Imagine, a police inspector who's also a serial killer. The FBI could write an entire study about it. Who knows? Maybe they will." Flores tapped on a photograph. "Look. See the cigarette lying beside the body? It's the one you lit for her last night. It has your DNA all over it. Señora Conejo was prudent

enough to keep it before she gave us a statement about your attempted rape."

Apiro had it right, Ramirez realized. He should have listened to
his friend instead of his ego. "She was a honey-pot."

"Well she *was* very beautiful, Ramirez. Your loyalty to your wife
was the only surprise. After almost a week alone, I could have sworn
you'd take the opportunity to have sex." Flores shrugged. "Of course,
it would have been better for us if you had, but we have enough evidence to proceed with charges without it. Señora Conejo signed the
complaint of lascivious assault just before she, shall we say, gave up
her permanent address. That gives us motive. And her statement is ad-
missible in court even if she can no longer testify in person, poor girl."

Ramirez shook his head. "I still don't understand why you felt
you had to kill her."

"Don't be stupid, Ramirez. She was naïve. She really believed
that she could leave the country. We could hardly have her recanting
her statement after she found out she wasn't going anywhere."

Once the listening device in his apartment picked up her name,
Ramirez realized, Antifona was as good as dead. "She was only nineteen."

"I had orders," said Flores. "I simply executed them."

"Bullshit," said Ramirez, standing up. He was furious. They had
used and murdered an innocent woman for political gamesman-
ship. He grabbed the older man by his jacket lapels. "You're part of
the inner circle."

"If you really believe that, don't you think you should take your
hands off me?"

Ramirez reluctantly let go. Flores brushed himself off and
smoothed his rumpled clothes.

"How much did you pay her?" But Ramirez already knew the
answer. Some new clothes. The promise of an exit permit.

A bad policeman, Dr. Yeung said. Manuel Flores.

58

"Once you turn the distribution list over, Ramirez, this profile will be destroyed. Juan Otero will be charged with murdering his sister-in-law as well as his wife. Of course, I'll have to revise a few facts here and there in my report to fit him instead of you, and the police holding-cell records will need to be altered by a day or two, but you know how things work."

Flores straightened his shirt collar. "You've always misunderstood the minister, you know. He's not interested in child pornography. He's only trying to protect the people who are. Rumours are one thing; it's proof that makes them dangerous. You're far more dangerous to this government than any dissident. What did you expect him to do?"

"Who murdered her—you?"

"Not me, Ramirez. My killing days ended decades ago. I have a clear conscience."

"That usually reflects a bad memory."

The psychiatrist smiled. "You know at Castellanos they used to douse the dissidents with water, for better electrical conduction. Those are the people you're dealing with. Give him back the list. You're a good detective. You should be doing your job, not wading around in politics. It's not healthy; you really are under a great deal of stress, you know. That's my professional opinion. The minister is a dangerous man to have as an enemy. But at least you have something to trade. And he wants *all* the copies."

Doused them with water. Ramirez put the final pieces of the puzzle in place: the real reason that Manuel Flores was back in Cuba and who he was working with. "I don't think so," he said, and handed the report back to Flores.

"Don't be stupid, Ramirez. How long do you think you'll survive in jail?"

"You should ask yourself the same question."

"You'll never prove I was involved in Antifona's murder. All the evidence leads to you."

"Not Antifona's death," said Ramirez. "The premeditated murder of an Italian curator. That's the real reason Antifona's dead, isn't it? She knew what the real Lorenzo Testa looked like. They were going to be engaged."

The paintings were as important to him as his own children. That's what Dominique Gatti had said. But Lorenzo Testa wasn't a father. According to Mama Loa, he wanted to get married so he could have children. He wasn't an Iraqi tortured for information; he was a man who held the key to millions of dollars' worth of art.

"Detective Espinoza is at the airport now," said Ramirez. "He called me just before I came here. It's funny; Señor Testa seems to have changed his appearance quite dramatically in the course of a few days. Espinoza can't find a flight into Havana with a passenger named Dominique Gatti, either, but I'm assuming she and the man who is pretending to be Señor Testa came here from Guantánamo Bay. Are they American CIA? Señora Gatti, or whoever she really is, wore the uniform well, I must say. In the panic over a bomb, people saw what they expected to see. They thought she was a man. So did I. It sounds like, occasionally, so does she."

Flores kept his face composed, but he shifted slightly in his seat. Nassara was right, thought Ramirez. *Follow the money.*

"You planned this with the CIA for months," said Ramirez. "A conspiracy to steal priceless Italian masterpieces. The CIA is always happy to embarrass Cuba, and if it can find a way to get money that's off the books to fund its secret operations, I'm sure it doesn't shy away. And you need money too, lots of it, if you're going to get that new treatment for your cancer. That's what we always hear about America, how expensive their health care is."

"You credit me with a great deal of complexity, Ramirez," said Flores, but Ramirez read fear in the older man's face.

"You certainly had me thinking along certain lines, Dr. Flores. Graffiti, political protests, damaged artworks, I could have run around in circles for days. But it's the only way to steal art from a place like Cuba, isn't it? Deface paintings that have been brought into the country legitimately and then demand their removal for repairs so you can take them wherever you like. But to do that, you had to kidnap the real Lorenzo Testa and make sure he gave you the information you needed.

"When he told you about his girlfriend, Antifona Conejo, you sent Dominique Gatti to find out if she was going to be a problem. Then you had the brilliant idea of killing Antifona and framing me so I'd be out of the picture, no pun intended. It almost worked. But I can assure you, those paintings will never make it to Guantánamo Bay, I'm guessing that's where they were really headed. And neither will the imposters."

"You breached a direct order from the minister. He'll have your job."

"Do you think so?" said Ramirez. He reached in his pocket and put the listening device on the coffee table. "This is one of the bugs

I found. Which means that Cuban Intelligence has been listening to our conversation. I don't think either of the Castros will be happy to find out that the entire time you were supposed to be working on Luis Posada's trial, you were actually plotting an art heist with the American CIA."

Ramirez picked up the listening device and threw it on the ground. He stood up and crushed it with his shoe. "Now that's gone, perhaps we can speak a little more freely."

The old man blanched. "What do you want, Ramirez?"

"I'm tired of the minister's brinkmanship. You're going to call him and tell him the mission was successful. Tell him that I gave you the CD from Sanchez's laptop with the distribution list on it, but regrettably there was an accident. You wanted to make sure I was telling the truth. You accidentally erased it, like Nixon's secretary."

He dialed the minister's number and handed Flores his cell phone. Flores made the call and hung up.

"What will happen now?" the older man asked. His face was ashen.

"That's up to Cuban Intelligence. As far as I'm concerned, you already have a death sentence. No money means no more treatments, and they'll never let you leave Cuba again. How long do you have left? A few weeks? A few months? That's if they don't put you in a psychiatric institution to rot. I think you've been suffering from delusions of capitalism. Imagine what it would be like to spend your last days at Mazorra or Castellanos. You might even run into some of your old patients. But don't worry, most of them are sane."

Ramirez turned to go. But before he left Flores's apartment to walk back downstairs, he picked up the profiler's report. When he got to his car, he held it with the very tips of his fingers as he put a match to it, making sure he wouldn't get burned.

59

Charlie Pike sat in the front seat of Sheldon Waubasking's truck. "That's why you beat up Billy so bad in remand, isn't it?" said Pike. "You found out about Molly."

Sheldon nodded, ashamed. "He called her a slut because she got pregnant. He had no right to do that. I should have told someone back then what Chesley did to her."

"Don't beat yourself up now. We were just kids."

That's how it started, thought Pike. Stories of incest that hid in the woods, in the bedrooms, behind walls.

"That Maylene Kesler, bringing all that stuff up. Did that guy Adam Neville really kill her?"

Pike shook his head. He turned to face his friend. "No. But you know who did, don't you, Sheldon. You recognized those tire marks. That's why you showed them to me. You wanted me to think they were all-seasons instead of just real old and worn. Same as those shoe prints. They weren't from a woman walking up to the truck door and back to the highway. They were from a woman getting out of her truck and walking back to it later."

Sheldon fell silent. He knew all right, thought Pike, but Sheldon wouldn't tell. He'd go to jail before he'd say who in his community was guilty of murder.

But Pike had it figured out. Celia Jones had said it herself. It didn't matter whether they were white, red, or yellow: when it came to getting into someone's car, women were afraid of men. But not of other women.

"I said another little prayer for her today," the killer had said. *Another* prayer for Maylene Kesler. It had taken Pike a while before he realized that meant there was a first one.

———

Freda Wabigoon answered the door. Her shoulders sagged when she saw him.

"I know why you're here, Charlie. Sit down in the kitchen; I'll make us some tea. I'm alone today. All the boys are at school. You're not in a hurry, are you?"

"You know I have to caution you before you say anything else, Freda. You have the right to remain silent. Anything you say can and will be used against you in a court of law. You have the right to a lawyer. If you can't afford one, one will be provided to you."

"I don't need a lawyer. I know what I did. And I know what Chesley did too." Freda sighed. "That woman, that lady doctor, she had Chesley's blood tests from way back in the 1970s. That's when they first tested him for mercury. And she had Pauley's too. After Molly ran away, she called me because I was Pauley's legal guardian."

Freda started to weep.

"Tell me how you did it," said Pike. He sat down beside her. He saw a box of Kleenex on the coffee table and handed her one.

"I said I'd meet her at the clinic," she said, blowing her nose. "She explained it all to me there. She wanted me to know she was going to report what she found. She said she had to; it's the law. She wouldn't listen when I told her Billy would be ruined if that story got out about his dad and his sister, that he'd never be elected chief again, would never be regional chief. And there are so many media up this way now. You know what it's like here, Charlie. People talk. She had no heart at all, that woman. It was like she was made out of ice."

"Incest is a crime," said Pike. "It's in the Criminal Code. She probably thought she didn't have a choice."

"What about our laws, Charlie? You always have a choice. Nothing good was going to come out of her reporting that to the police; it was only going to hurt a lot of innocent people. But she was stubborn. I tried so hard, but I couldn't make her listen. She was just the same as all those nuns at residential school who treated us like we didn't matter. So I told her she'd better come home with me, so she could tell Pauley herself. She said she had a rental and it didn't have very good winter tires. I said we could take my truck instead. The weather was still bad. It had just stopped snowing. I pulled over to the side of the road as soon as we got on the reserve, away from the highway. I told her I was having problems with the engine. I put up the hood, put some red pylons out. But I forgot them when I drove away, I was so upset."

The red pylons, Pike thought. He never thought to ask Sheldon where he got them.

"I pulled my axe out of the back and I told her to walk in front of me into the woods. I grabbed her from behind when we got inside. I'm still strong, Charlie. Despite the diabetes."

Years of pulling nets in the bay.

"I said a little prayer for her after. I burned some tobacco. Then I chopped out a grave, and I put the brush on top of her, to protect her from the animals."

We always bury our dead.

"Where did the axe come from?"

"It's the one I use for ice fishing. It's in the back of the truck now, where it always is. What are you going to do to me, Charlie?"

"I have to take you in, Freda. That's first-degree murder."

"What's the sentence for that? Will they hang me?"

Pike shook his head. "They don't hang people anymore. Life imprisonment is twenty-five years. Maybe they'll agree to second degree if you admit what you did. The judge will decide how long before you get parole. Could be ten, twenty years."

"Twenty years?" She nodded, wiped a tear from her eye. "That's a long time. I'll be old when I get out. Okay. Let me go say goodbye to Pauley. You tell Bill what happened, okay? Tell him not to worry."

"He knows lots of good lawyers, Freda."

She smiled sadly. "A few too many, if you ask me."

She stood up and walked down the hallway before Charlie Pike remembered that Pauley Oshig was at school.

He jumped to his feet and began to run after her. He heard the shotgun blast before he made it down the hall.

60

Inspector Ramirez met up with Detective Espinoza at the airport. The young detective was grinning. "You were right, Inspector. They hadn't booked a flight at all. Patrol found them loading the paintings into a van, and arrested them. The driver says they offered him a thousand U.S. dollars to take them to Guantánamo. The museum had no way of knowing they weren't headed for the airport. Or that Señor Testa was an imposter. He's been wearing Testa's clothes all week. No one at the museum had ever seen the real Señor Testa in person. They dealt with him only by email, and occasionally by phone."

"Good work, Fernando. Do we have any idea who Dominique Gatti is?"

"None. As I told you on the phone, she didn't fly into Havana—she's not on the airport surveillance tapes. Do you really think she came from Guantánamo Bay? It's not easy to get through the checkpoints. Maybe she's an American."

Ramirez thought for a moment, remembering his dream. He shook his head. "Wait here for a minute," he said to Espinoza, and walked over to one of the airport clerks.

"*Hola*," he said, showing her his badge. "Is there anyone here who speaks Italian?"

"Sonia does," the woman said. "She's on her break. I'll go get her."

A few minutes later, the other clerk materialized beside the first one. "How can I help you?" she asked.

"The name Dominique Gatti. Do those words mean anything special in Italian?"

"Not really," she said, wrinkling her forehead. "Dominique is just a name. Gatti is a common name too, but it can mean someone who is very agile, like a cat."

Ramirez nodded. "*Gracias*, Señora." He walked back to Espinoza, thinking.

Manuel Flores had said the organized killer enjoyed leaving clues out in the open. Maybe "Gatti" was Dr. Flores's little joke. Ramirez recalled Hector Apiro telling him about the Cuban doctors sent to foreign countries and the children kept behind to make sure they'd return. Castro would never let a valuable resource like Manuel Flores go to the United States for medical treatment without ensuring he'd be available whenever Castro needed him. And despite being in the middle of treatment for a deadly cancer in New York, Flores had come back.

"I think she could be Manuel Flores's daughter."

"That makes sense, Inspector," said Espinoza. "He told me she was living near the base at Guantánamo, and that she was a language teacher and a gymnast. That would explain how she was able to get in and out of the building so quickly."

"People see what they expect to see. The tourists saw a policeman that day because the person they saw wore a policeman's uniform. We assumed she was Italian, because she spoke the language and because that's what she told us." Ramirez shook his head at how easily they'd been misled; how effectively Manuel Flores had predisposed them to believe what he wanted them to think was true.

"When you interrogate her, lie to her. Tell her that Manuel Flores is dead; it may unnerve her and help you with questioning. By the way, Natasha found an incident report filed by a foot patrolman. He saw Antifona Conejo standing outside the Hotel Nacional on February 14 with a foreign woman. Ask Natasha if she can get hold of the patrolman to see if the woman she was with is Señora Gatti. If he identifies her, you can use that to question her as well. If he doesn't, pretend he did."

"You don't want to interrogate these two yourself?"

"No need," said Ramirez.

If they were CIA operatives, Ramirez doubted they'd say anything incriminating. But they didn't have to. The two prisoners could be useful pawns in the diplomatic war of words being waged in Geneva. The man impersonating Lorenzo Testa might be of interest to the prosecutors in the torture trial about to start in Rome. If so, the Italians might be persuaded to keep the matter of the vandalism at the museum quiet.

Ramirez was sure the Cuban emissaries would find a way to work things out. Negotiations, he'd learned, involved the art of diplomacy. It worked well enough, as long as you had something of value to exchange. This time they did.

"It will be good experience for you, Fernando." Ramirez clapped his hand on Espinoza's back. "I'm sure you'll do well."

Ramirez had started to walk away when Espinoza called him back. "Oh, Inspector, I almost forgot. Dominique Gatti was wearing this gold chain. I think it belonged to Señor Testa. Once a thief, always a thief, yes?"

Espinoza handed Ramirez a plastic exhibit bag. It held a thick gold braid.

Mama Loa was waiting for Ramirez next to his car in the parking lot. She sat on a small patch of grass beside the iron fence, her swollen legs folded beneath her.

"She's dead now, isn't she," she said. "I see her, Antifona, in my dreams last night. She's running in the woods, scared. She calls out my name; she wants me to help. She say she made a bad mistake; her *lwa* is angry. Nothing I can do in a dream. That pretty girl." She shook her head. "Some *houngans*, they claim they can bring back the dead. Me, I think it's better to leave them alone."

"Yes," Ramirez said. "She's dead. I'm sorry. I somehow dragged her into this."

Antifona's ghost had come from the future to help him with his investigation into her sister's and boyfriend's deaths. Perhaps she hoped to change her fate as well. But the future was already written, as his grandmother often said. Sometimes, thought Ramirez, it was easier to rewrite the past.

"The gods must have wanted her. You can't blame yourself. But now both my goddaughters are gone. Sit beside me for a minute," Mama Loa said, moving aside to make room for him on the concrete curb. The tears welled in her eyes; she wiped them away. "Tell me why."

Ramirez told the old black woman about the failed art heist and the reason Antifona's foreign boyfriend hadn't contacted her. But he had no explanation for LaNeva Otero's death. It was pure, random evil.

He reached into his jacket pocket and removed the plastic exhibit bag. He opened it and handed Mama Loa the gold chain. "Here, I think you should have this. Maybe you can sell it and use the money to find a place to live. A place where your goddaughters can escape the men who hurt them."

She nodded her head. She held the chain in her fingers and closed her eyes. "I can see it like I'm there. They get him at the airport. They tell him Antifona needs him, that she's in trouble. They take him to an old part of the city, so old it's still haunted by ghosts. They tie him up. They make him breathe water until he answers their questions. Who else knows you? Antifona, she got a cell phone? What's the number? He has to tell; he's scared so bad. They say if he tells them, he'll be safe, but they kill him anyway. He dies ashamed of himself, that he didn't protect her."

She opened her eyes and gripped Ramirez's fingers with her wizened hand.

"Now he can't cross to the other side. I think he blames himself that she's dead. He needs to know that things are okay with them, that Antifona understands. You have to tell her what he done, that he tried. Yeah, I know she's dead. But that's just her body. The rest of her's still out there, waiting. She's trapped too." She stood up and straightened her skirt. "I got to go now. I got two funerals to plan." She walked away, stepping lightly despite her massive weight.

"Mama Loa," Ramirez called after her. "I saw those things. It's like I was there when he died. I was dreaming. But I *was* that man. I was inside his head. How can that be?"

She turned her head and looked at him sadly. "Spend enough time with the dead, you start to think the way they do. It's a gift, I guess. For some, it's a curse."

61

"*I can't believe that Adam Neville* tried to frame Sheldon with murder," said Celia Jones. They were standing in her parents' driveway, looking over the snowdrifts. Jones was bundled in a parka, but Charlie Pike seemed oblivious to the cold. His only concession to the weather was that his hands were in his pockets. "Or that he's the Highway Strangler. How in God's name did you figure that out?"

"I only saw Sheldon violent once, Celia, and that was a long time ago. Besides, there *was* someone who saw Adam spray Luminol on Maylene Kesler's body in those woods."

"Pauley Oshig?"

"No, he wasn't there when that happened," said Pike. "He headed straight for the band office, just like he said. He was too afraid to hang around in the forest. He knew Bill would be angry enough at him for skipping school. He told me who let him know what they saw. I just didn't pay enough attention."

"There was another witness in the woods that morning? But who?"

"More than one; a whole bunch of them. Doesn't matter, Celia. They wouldn't be able to pick Adam out of a police lineup anyway." Pike smiled and shook his head. He could never explain to Celia that crows were people too.

"Mercury, that's what Maylene Kesler found in those tests," he said, changing the subject. "Everyone's levels are off the charts around here, including your mother's. That's what I came to tell you. That could be why her symptoms are getting worse. Chelation therapy, that can help. I read a medical article about it." He didn't tell Jones how he got it. "You and your dad might want to check that out."

"There's mercury in the drinking water?" Jones said. "Oh my God, she's been drinking gallons of tea every day. I'll get on it right away. Thanks for telling me. You know, I'm going to talk to Alex about having my parents move in with us in Ottawa. My mom needs medical care she can't get here. But cripes, Charlie, mercury? That could explain her confusion, the disorientation, everything."

Pike nodded. Mercury poisoning could account for a lot of things. It might even explain why Dr. Kesler had told Molly Oshig that her son might not have FAS at all, why she had written on Pauley's file that he should be evaluated for autism.

"Bill's planning to go to the media. Be interesting to see if the mill finally gets shut down once the government finds out there are white people around here at risk too." Although they might already know, he thought, remembering the sign at the airport warning people not to drink the water.

"So stupid," Jones said, shaking her head. "Fingers crossed. When do you head back to Ottawa?"

"Later today. But I have a wake to go to first. There was another suicide on the reserve yesterday."

Pike didn't tell her it was Freda Wabigoon or about the incest. He didn't plan to put it in his report to O'Malley either. After all, Freda had been right. The Anishnabe had their own laws. When it came right down to it, what happened on-reserve was no one else's business.

"Well, I guess I'll see you at the office in a few days, Charlie. You did a helluva job. The media never even got hold of this story. I have to tell you, I'm almost dreading going back to Ottawa. Alex and I have to figure out this situation with Beatriz. We're still thinking about whether we should apply for her to get refugee status. I'm worried about Children's Aid stepping in. Everyone says they'll put her in foster care."

"It messes you up, being taken away from everything you know," said Pike. "I've been in that system. It's a revolving door. Most of my friends were in foster care too. Bunch of white social workers didn't like the way that Indians raised their kids. The little ones were always running around, playing. To someone who didn't know better, it might have seemed like they weren't being looked after, but there was always someone keeping an eye on them." He turned to look at Jones directly. "You know, it's not that hard to get a birth certificate, if that's all you need."

"You mean a fake one? I'm a lawyer. I can't break the law."

"People on my mom's side, the Mohawks, they travel on their own passports. I like to think of it as respecting *our* laws, not breaking someone else's."

"I don't know, Charlie," said Jones, stamping her feet to keep warm. "I get what you mean. But what about the rule of law?"

"Whose law? Cuban laws say she's yours already, don't they? Canada's laws would send her back to a country where she could die alone. Seems pretty simple to me. Jail cells down south are full of people who could get you a birth certificate. A passport's even easier. Once you get the birth certificate, all you need is a guarantor to say they've known her for two years."

"Who would do that? Beatriz only got here two months ago."

"The list of guarantors includes First Nation police officers."

Jones searched his eyes. "You're staying here, aren't you, Charlie?" The snow caught in the fur of her hood.

"Not right away. I have some commitments in Ottawa. But Bill and some of the other chiefs are talking about setting up a new police force to replace the APF. I was thinking I might apply. This may not be my home anymore, Celia. But it's where I belong."

62

Inspector Ramirez knocked on Hector Apiro's office door in the medical tower. He held a box filled with exhibits from the two women's murders. When Apiro called out for him to come in, he pushed the door open to find Maria Vasquez seated beside Apiro, sipping delicately from a glass of rum. Apiro had pink lipstick on his cheek.

"*Hola*, Hector, Maria."

"Please, Ricardo, come in, sit down, have a drink. My goodness, you've had quite a day. I ran into Detective Espinoza at headquarters. He told me what happened."

Ramirez put the box down while Apiro rooted around in his papers for another glass. He filled it with Havana Club and handed it to Ramirez.

"I was astounded to learn that Manuel Flores was involved in all of this. How was he going to sell the paintings? I would imagine there's a very small market for the illicit trade in Italian masterpieces."

"I think the Cuban families who originally owned them planned to file a legal action in the U.S. courts as soon as the paintings landed in Guantánamo Bay. They were going to argue that the American courts had jurisdiction because the paintings were on American soil. The cost of restoring the paintings would be nothing compared to their true value." Ramirez smiled. "I hope you don't mind, Maria, but I had hoped to pick Hector's brain for a few minutes about some women's murders we're investigating."

"Maria knows about them, Ricardo. She might be able to help."

Ramirez nodded. "The thing is, Manuel Flores was behind Antifona Conejo's murder, but that still leaves the others. I've released Juan Otero from custody. The only thing I'm sure of is that he wasn't involved. Detective Espinoza and Detective Delgado are cross-referencing hotel and rental car records to see if there was a foreigner of interest in Havana at the relevant times. I wanted to go back through the exhibits to see if we missed anything. Any insights you might have, Maria, would be helpful."

"Of course," said Maria. "I knew LaNeva, you know. She was my friend."

Ramirez opened the first box of exhibits and removed all the individually bagged items from Prima Verrier's purse. There was an identification card, a tube of lipstick, and a box of condoms, brand name "Impulse." He put them on Apiro's battered desk.

Maria reached for the box of condoms. "You can't get this brand here easily," she said. "The only condoms we have are from China, and they break." She pointed to another exhibit bag that held condoms from LaNeva's purse. "Same with these ones. They're Trojans."

"I should have noticed that before," said Ramirez. He felt angry with himself for missing it. He thought for a moment. "Up to now, I've assumed that all the items in the victims' purses belonged to them. But what if they were left behind by the killer? Manuel Flores talked about how much pleasure the murderer might take from leaving the obvious out in the open. What if everything we found at these crime scenes was put there deliberately?"

Apiro nodded thoughtfully. "That means re-evaluating the significance of every item from each crime scene."

"What about the Trojans?" Ramirez asked.

"It's interesting imagery when you put it in the context of the apple we found in LaNeva's stomach," said Apiro. "Adam and Eve tasted an apple and gave up immortality. Aphrodite bribed Paris of Troy with an apple and caused the Trojan war."

"All right, then what about this cigarette butt?" said Ramirez. "Silk Cut brand?"

"Ah," said Apiro. "Those were sold here years ago. They were supposed to be lower in tar, so they took longer to kill you. I remember the advertising campaign had scissors that cut through silk. This was back in the days when we still had advertisements, Maria. These were aggressive ads. Phallic shapes. Purple silk that looked almost vaginal, but which was slashed. There was one that had a row of surgical scissors lined up with the blades splayed open, as if they were cabaret dancers."

"It sounds like the men who created that advertising campaign hated women," said Maria. She shuddered.

"Perhaps the surgical scissors are supposed to mean something," said Apiro, "although I can't imagine what. You know, Ricardo, there was something at the crime scene that I didn't appreciate the significance of before. This thin wooden stick in Antifona's purse?" He held up the bag. "It's not for manicures."

"No," said Maria. "It's from a child's lollipop."

"Maria tells me that a 'lollipop' is slang for oral sex."

"Maybe he wants to make sure we know they are prostitutes," Ramirez said. "But trying to understand this man is almost impossible. We might as well examine the entrails of a chicken under the full moon. I thought of doing that, actually."

Apiro chuckled. "Well, there is something that's been bothering me, Ricardo. In Russia, there are stories of Baba Yaga, the guardian of the Waters of Death. She lives in a hut in the woods that has chicken legs and moves around by itself. She uses a broom to sweep away all traces of her path, to keep strangers away. The only shoe prints we've found so far have been from women's shoes, Ricardo. Never a man's."

"You think he sweeps away his shoe prints?" asked Ramirez.

"Either that or he flies away. Maybe it isn't only what he leaves behind that's important, but what he removes." Apiro lit his pipe.

"I think you're right," said Ramirez. "There are multiple clues. Because Prima *was* the first one. And the name, LaNeva, sounds like 'nevar,' which means 'snow' in English. Perhaps he makes contact with his victims before he kills them. It's possible he chooses who to kill based on little more than their names."

"It worries me," said Maria. "I have a friend, Nevara, who had a client who promised to bring her stockings."

"I hope I'm wrong." Ramirez shook his head. "I don't know if we're on to something or wasting our time." He reached into the box for the final item, a lipstick.

"What about this, Maria?"

She examined it closely through the plastic exhibit bag. "It's brand new. See, the seal hasn't even been broken. The name should be on the bottom." She held the lipstick up to the light, squinting to read the fine print on the label. "It's called Indian Red."

"The only truly red Indians were in Canada," said Apiro, drawing on his pipe. "The Beothuks of Newfoundland. They used red ochre in their burial practices. But they were hunted to extinction. There was a bounty on their heads."

"Snow. Indians. Apples from Quebec. The killer has to be Canadian," Ramirez decided.

"If you're right, there could be thousands of suspects," said Apiro. "A million Canadians come here every winter. The killer has probably already left the country."

"I know," said Ramirez, frustrated.

Maria looked at her watch. "I'm sorry, I have to leave. I'm meeting a friend this afternoon. We're going to the zoo."

"Thanks for your help, Maria. It's much appreciated." Ramirez's cell phone rang. "Excuse me," he said, and held it to his ear. It was Detective Espinoza.

"We found a Canadian who registered at the Hotel Telégrafo last year and again this year at the same time as our two victims were killed. His name is Adam Neville. He's from Winnipeg, in Manitoba, Canada. He and his wife, Denise Labelle, stayed there from February 10 to March 2 last year. They registered again on February first this year. He checked out a week ago, but his wife is still there. Hotel staff say she left for a few days but kept the room. She rented a vehicle from Havanautos last year and this year. I have the computer printouts."

"Excellent, Fernando. Fax me that information, will you? I'm in Dr. Apiro's office right now. I'll wait." Ramirez got the number from Apiro and repeated it to Espinoza.

"They found a suspect," he said after he hung up. "A Canadian. Adam Neville. You may have been right about Adam and Eve, Hector. I think we've got him. I need to notify the Canadian authorities. I'm not sure who exactly to contact, but I know who can tell me."

Ramirez dialed the switchboard and asked to be put through to Chief Miles O'Malley in Ottawa.

Inspector Ramirez put down the phone after O'Malley said goodbye. "Well, that's interesting, Hector. Chief O'Malley says that this man, Adam Neville, is already in custody. He's a forensic pathologist, suspected of murdering prostitutes in Canada. They call him the Highway Strangler. Charlie Pike arrested him in Northern Ontario in connection with a recent death there." He explained what O'Malley had told him. "Celia Jones told me about this Highway Strangler when we spoke earlier this week. I should have paid more attention. Chief O'Malley said to call Charlie Pike directly if we have any questions."

"A pathologist was the murderer?" said Apiro, frowning. "That doesn't speak well for the profession."

"It explains why there was never any forensic evidence left behind." Ramirez lit a cigar.

"Maria will be relieved. I'll tell her about the arrest as soon as she gets back from the zoo."

"I used to like the zoo," said Ramirez. He exhaled, watching the smoke waft lazily to the ceiling. "Not much to see there these days, though, is there? A bunch of old lions. Seems like a rather sad place to spend an afternoon."

Apiro nodded. "I know. But apparently her girlfriend really wanted to see it. She's visiting from Canada."

"Well, I'll be glad to close these two files once and for all," said Ramirez. "Chief O'Malley is going to send me a copy of Charlie Pike's report as soon as he gets it. Then I can wrap up my cold case. Señora Verrier's family will be glad to know their ordeal is finally over." He paused for a moment. "Tell me, Hector, have you ever heard of someone having an apparitional experience? Manual Flores mentioned the term to me."

Apiro shook his head and smiled. "You could say that anyone who goes to a Catholic Church and eats a wafer believing it to be the body of Christ is having one. There are a lot of otherwise very rational people who believe in things that are scientifically impossible because they are experiencing auditory and visual hallucinations. Children are particularly vulnerable when it comes to believing things that aren't real. So it's a polite way for psychiatrists to characterize people as mentally healthy even when it's evident that what they say they've seen or heard can't possibly exist in real life. In what context did he use it?"

The fax machine in Apiro's office began to churn. The pathologist stood up to retrieve the papers that curled out of it, his question forgotten. "Ah, here you are, Ricardo. It's the information you asked for from Detective Espinoza." He handed the printouts to Ramirez. "I'll need to update my forensic report for you as well. The technicians found something odd—a bit of an anomaly—but I suppose it doesn't matter anymore. I meant to tell you, and in all the excitement I forgot."

"What was that, Hector?"

"Well, it's odd. They tested the lipstick on the two cigarette butts from the crime scenes. They found saliva, but it wasn't a match for either of the two dead women."

"Adam Neville's?"

"No, and that's what's strange. It can't be. It's saliva from a woman. And whoever's it is, it's the same woman. It took the lab a while to analyze the DNA; we were out of the supplies we needed. It comes from another *jinetera*, I suppose."

Ramirez considered this. "Well, maybe not. Detective Espinoza said it was Adam Neville's wife who arranged the car rentals." He quickly scanned through the fax pages. "Denise Labelle. She rented a red Peugeot on February 12 in Pinar del Río, but she hasn't returned it. " He looked at Apiro, raising his eyebrows. "Labelle? That's a French name, isn't it?"

"Those apples came from Quebec," said Apiro. "Maybe that clue wasn't only meant to refer to snow."

Ramirez grabbed the phone and called Charlie Pike's cell number. After a few rings, Pike picked up. The line was brittle with static.

"Hey, Rick. How are you? Sorry, my phone's not working all that well. I'm up north at the moment."

Ramirez explained what he'd found.

"Denise Labelle?" said Pike. "Sure, that's Adam Neville's wife. She kept her last name. Married women have to do that in Quebec; it's the law."

"You know, Charlie, maybe it wasn't the husband who committed these crimes," said Ramirez. "It could have been the wife. Perhaps that's why he tried to frame someone in Canada for a similar crime. Not to protect himself, but to create an alibi for her."

"Well, Denise knows how to process evidence. She used to work in a crime lab, but she's been off for quite a while on disability. Adam told me that she's back to normal now, though. Worth checking into, for sure. I'll call the Winnipeg City Police; get someone to go over to their home and pick her up for questioning." A pause on the end of the line. "Oh, shit, Rick. Denise Labelle isn't in Canada right now. Adam told me she's off mountain climbing somewhere in South America. In Pinar del Mar, I think he said."

"That's not in South America," said Ramirez. "That's here in Cuba."

63

Maria Vasquez waited outside the hotel for her client. A burly security guard walked towards her, about to tell her to move on when her client came out through the revolving glass doors.

"Now, you leave her alone, she's waiting for me," Denise Labelle said, wagging her finger at him. The security guard shook his head and sidled away.

"I've rented a car," she said to Maria. "A day at the zoo. Doesn't that sound grand?"

"Are you able to spend that long on your feet?" asked Maria, looking at the woman's cane.

"You mean this?" said Labelle. "Don't worry; I'll be fine. Here, I brought something for you. All the way from home." She handed Maria a large plastic bag.

"But this is lovely," said Maria, pulling out a pink leather purse from inside the bag. She folded the plastic bag carefully; they were hard to find. "Really, you shouldn't have." She admired the purse in the reflection of the hotel window, shifting the handle to her shoulder. "It's so hard to get nice purses here."

They walked slowly to the parking lot across from the hotel. Labelle pointed to her rental car, a red Peugeot. She opened the door and tossed her cane in the back seat along with a paper bag.

"Look inside," Labelle said, smiling. She climbed into the driver's seat and put the key in the ignition. "I got some other things for you too, from the duty-free shop at the airport."

Maria got in and pulled the door closed. She opened the purse. Inside was a gold compact with a small mirror, as well as a lipstick, condoms, and a pack of cigarettes, Parliament brand.

"The lipstick's your shade of pink. I remember you telling me how hard it is to get lipstick here."

"*Gracias*," said Maria. "It's a beautiful colour." She turned the lipstick to look at the name on the bottom. Last Tango.

"Lovely," said Labelle. "You'll look absolutely lovely when I take your picture."

———

"It used to be a wonderful zoo," said Maria, as Labelle paid the admission price of two tourist pesos each. "Many of the animals live the way they do in the wild. They're not caged up."

They walked past dilapidated concession stands, most deserted. Some children swung on noisy metal swings. A peacock scrawed nearby, holding its bright plumage upright like a woman's fan. "That's a male," said Maria. "The females are brown and quite plain. He's showing off."

"Men," said Labelle. She laughed. "We should sit somewhere and have a bite to eat. I had the hotel make a lunch for us. It's in the paper bag."

They walked slowly past the enclosure for the rhinoceroses, looking for a place to sit. Labelle leaned heavily on Maria's arm, picking her way carefully with the cane. They found a wooden bench overlooking the island built for monkeys. Across from them was a lion pit with huge rocks. A scrawny lion perched on top of one, carefully watching an ibis graze in a field on the other side of the fence.

"It seems so cruel," said Labelle. "To keep a predator trapped like that. Letting him see his prey every day but not letting him kill it."

"I'm sure they're reasonably well fed," said Maria. "Probably better than we are at times."

Labelle shook her head sadly. "It's not the same."

———

They ate the sandwiches the hotel had provided, drank the juice, finished the pears. "They call this variety Clapp in North America," said Labelle. "They're delicious, aren't they? The hotel got them this morning; I always check to see if they have fresh fruit from home."

They began their tour. A notice on an exhibit in the birdhouse explained that some of the more unique species couldn't be bred with birds at other zoos because of disease.

"There are only a few Cuban parakeets left," said Maria. "I hate to see endangered species. It's so sad."

"My family's like that," said Labelle. "I'm the last of the line. I was an only child. My mother and father died years ago. They didn't have any brothers or sisters, so that's it. When I'm dead, there won't be any more Labelles."

"I'm so sorry to hear that," said Maria. "But you're married, yes?"

"It's just the two of us."

"You don't have any children?"

"Oh, no," said Labelle. "My husband . . ." She sighed. "It's hard to explain, but you've been so kind to me. I feel like I can tell you anything. We've had our problems." She fell silent for a moment.

"Do you want to talk about it?" said Maria, taking her hand.

"We used to have a wonderful relationship." Labelle lowered her voice. "And a really great sex life too." She looked around to make sure no one overheard. "He liked me to get dressed up. Put on stockings, high heels. Sometimes I'd pretend to be a French maid, or he'd be the pizza delivery man. Having fun, you know? The sex was fantastic. And then I got pregnant."

They walked to the snake house and stopped to examine the python cage. The giant snake watched them, lazily flicking its tongue.

"I didn't know it, but I had chlamydia. You've heard of it? It's a sexually transmitted disease. One of the bad ones. But sometimes there are no symptoms. That was the case with me. I ended up with an ectopic pregnancy. That's when the baby develops outside the uterus. It almost killed me, the internal hemorrhaging. I had a blood clot. It caused a stroke. I'm still recovering from it. That's why I have to use this cane to get around. And of course the pregnancy was over. We can never have children."

"Oh my," said Maria. "That sounds so terrible. But how . . . ?"

"The chlamydia? My husband gave it to me. He didn't know he had it either. Some doctor." She laughed, but there was no humour in her voice. "And that's not the worst thing he did."

Maria said nothing, not sure how to respond.

"I found out he was sleeping with prostitutes," said Labelle. "That's how he got infected. Here I was, trying so hard to live up to his sexual fantasies, and he was acting them out for real."

"But you stayed with him."

"Of course," said Labelle. "I love Adam. He's the most exciting man I've ever known. We met mountain climbing, you know. I . . ." She hesitated. "We used to love climbing together. The rush. There are only a limited number of ways to get that kind of high. He was here with me a few weeks ago. I wanted him to stay. But he said he had to go back to work. I didn't believe him."

"You don't blame him for what happened to you?"

"No," she said bitterly. "I blame *them*."

To get back to the city, they took Airport Road.

"I'm sorry, Maria," Labelle said suddenly, "I have to stop and pee. Can I go into the woods? Is it safe here?"

"Of course," said Maria.

Labelle parked. She stepped out, stretched, and retrieved her metal cane from the back seat of the car. She opened her purse and removed a metal-pronged tip that she screwed to the end.

"It's an ice tip. I used to use it when I was climbing. I find it helps me walk a little better when the surface is uneven. Can you come with me? Keep an eye out to make sure no one sees me? Sometimes I need a little help."

"Of course," said Maria. She stepped out of the car.

"I don't suppose you have any toilet paper with you?"

Maria shook her head. "It's hard to get here."

"Well, I guess I can use one of these, then. Damn. I don't have many left."

Labelle reached into her purse and pulled out a nylon stocking. A black one, Maria noticed. With a long seam that ran down the back.

"You're not limping anymore," said Maria, as they walked into the woods. The hair on the back of her neck stood up when she saw the yellow caution tape strung between the trees.

A new purse, a brand new lipstick, nylons. Hector had warned her to be careful, but she never expected the killer to be a woman. Maria cast her eyes desperately searching for help. But no one could see them in the trees; they were too far from the road.

"I'm sorry, Denise. I forgot something in the car. I'll be right back."

Labelle prodded her in the side with the needle-sharp tip of the cane. "You do what I tell you, or I'll stick you like a pig. I'll end your life right here, I swear to God."

Maria looked around frantically.

"No, I'm not limping anymore," said Labelle. "I lied. I recovered. But it's your fault I'll never have children. For a few dollars, a lipstick, a pair of pantyhose, you stupid, careless bitches will spread your legs for anyone. No one uses protection in this goddamn country. The girls here are like the whores in Canada. They kiss, they use their tongues."

"I don't know what you mean. I'm clean. I'm always careful with my clients. I live with a doctor."

"My own husband won't have sex with me now, not even with condoms. Doesn't matter what I do. I can tart myself up and he won't even look at me. See these stockings? I ordered them all the way from England, trying to look sexy. The only women he has sex with now are women like you."

"I'm sorry that this happened to you. But the problems in your marriage have nothing to do with me."

"They have everything to do with you. Keep walking."

Labelle prodded Maria sharply with the cane, forcing her deeper under the forest canopy.

"You don't understand; you have this all wrong."

"You're a whore, just like the others. Women like you ruined my life."

"But I've never met your husband. Trust me, I pose no threat to you. I'm not like other women, believe me."

"Don't think you can charm your way out of this."

She pushed Maria again as they entered the clearing. "My husband is so fucking stupid. He's a medical examiner. He investigates murders all the time. He's been at every one of my crime scenes. I thought that was one way we could spend time together, if he was going to claim he had to work every night. I left clues. They were all dark-skinned women, the women I killed, and it's light powder in the compacts I left behind. You think he would have noticed it was chalk."

"Chalk?"

"For mountain climbing. We use it on our fingers to get a good grip. I don't know how many times he'd come home from an autopsy and tell me what he found, and he still didn't realize it was me. He'd even show me the photographs from the crime scenes. I thought for sure he'd figure it out when we got to Cuba and I did it again, but there was nothing in the goddamned media about the deaths. Then I realized it didn't matter. I wasn't doing it for him anymore. I was doing it for me. We're here. Get down on the ground."

"No. You'll kill me."

"I'll kill you right now if you don't."

Maria looked around for a weapon. There were no broken tree limbs, no sticks, no twigs. There was nothing in the purse that she could use. She couldn't defend herself with lipstick or condoms and the purse wasn't heavy enough to make a dent. She'd made the mistake of wearing sandals for the long walk around the zoo instead of her usual stilettos.

"Please don't do this," she begged. "You are making a terrible mistake."

"You stupid bitch," Labelle said and pushed Maria down. She put her full weight on Maria's back, then wrapped her arm tightly around her throat.

64

"But Ricardo," said Apiro, hopping off his chair. "Denise. That is the name of Maria's friend, the Canadian woman who is going to the zoo with her today."

"Are you sure?"

Apiro's eyes widened. "She's been giving Maria presents all week."

"Hector, Maria could be in real danger. Does she have a cell phone?"

"An illegal one, yes, of course." Apiro dialed the number. "There's no answer. Ricardo, those two women who were murdered were found not far from the zoo."

"Then let's get going."

Apiro ran behind Ramirez down the stairs, his short legs pumping as they headed to the parking lot. Ramirez jumped in his car and started the ignition. Apiro strapped himself in. "Please, drive quickly, Ricardo. As fast as you can."

They raced down Airport Road, dodging cars, bikes, stray dogs. Ramirez swerved to avoid hitting a man pushing a cart full of watermelons across the highway.

"Will she take Maria back to the same place?" asked Apiro.

"I hope so," said Ramirez. "If she doesn't, they could be anywhere."

———

"There's the Peugeot," Apiro said, pointing to a red car parked on the shoulder. "Look at the plate." The maroon plate had a "T" for *turista*. "Quick, stop the car."

Ramirez skidded to a halt. He and Apiro jumped out and cautiously approached the rental car. Ramirez removed his gun from his shoulder holster. He peered inside, but the vehicle was empty.

"That's Maria's tote bag on the back seat," Apiro said, his voice tight with stress.

"They must be in the woods. Wait here, Hector. We have no idea what kind of weapon this woman may have, but we know she's extremely dangerous."

"Believe me, so am I right now," said Apiro. "I'm going with you."

They entered the woods slowly. Ramirez held his gun out as they approached the yellow caution tape, steadying it with both hands. What happened next ended in seconds, but Ramirez would replay it later in his mind like the museum surveillance tape, rewinding the images over and over.

Maria lay on her stomach beneath the blue mahoe trees. A woman straddled her body, her forearm pulled tight around Maria's throat. A metal cane rested beside Maria's limp body.

Apiro ran forward and lunged for the cane. He grabbed it just as the woman looked up, before Ramirez could stop him. He swung the cane in an arc. It made a sickening thud as it connected with the side of the woman's head.

"Hector, you'll kill her! Don't hit her again," Ramirez shouted, jamming his gun in his holster and running forward. It took all his strength to pry the cane from Apiro's fingers. But afterwards he wondered if he should have stopped him at all.

65

They sat in the dingy hallway of the emergency room at the hospital. The fluorescent lights flickered. Apiro looked deflated, even smaller than unusual. "First, do no harm. That's the oath I took, Ricardo." He held his large head in his hands, tears in his eyes. "I was so angry. I wanted to kill her. I fractured her skull."

"I would have done the same thing if it was Francesca lying on the ground, my friend, believe me," said Ramirez.

"If I had hit her again, she would have died."

"But you didn't, and she didn't. And Maria's alive. That's all that matters."

"I suppose you'll have to charge me with aggravated assault or attempted murder. How long will I spend in jail?"

"For what?" said Ramirez. He put his hand on Apiro's shoulder. "The prisoner is unsteady on her feet. She needs a cane. She fell as she was getting into my car to accompany us to headquarters for questioning. She hit her head on the road. It happens."

"I can't falsify a medical report, Ricardo. You know that."

"You don't have to, Hector." Ramirez smiled. "I can. Besides, that's the story I've already told the emergency physician. I should at least be consistent. Believe me, no one will contradict it, not when it comes to a cold-blooded killer like this one."

Ramirez gave his friend's shoulder a squeeze. "Detective Espinoza radioed me a few minutes ago. They found nothing incriminating in the rental car, but Señora Labelle had a digital camera in her purse with photographs of LaNeva Otero. They're searching her hotel room right now. Espinoza says they've found another purse there as well. He is going to see if Juan Otero recognizes it. I think Denise Labelle gave each of her victims a new purse and took theirs as souvenirs. You were right. It wasn't only what she left behind at the crime scenes that was important, but also what she removed."

The emergency physician approached them. Apiro leaped to his feet. "How is Maria? Is she all right?"

"She's awake." He smiled. "Go ahead, Dr. Apiro. You can see her now."

Apiro rushed down the corridor.

The physician turned to Ramirez. "She'll have a sore throat for a few days. She'll have to sip liquids through a straw. And suck on chips of ice, if she can find any. But she'll be fine." He lowered his voice. "Inspector Ramirez, are you aware that this victim is transgendered? Her hyoid bone is much larger than that of a woman. That may have helped her survive this attack. Was this the reason for the assault?"

"No. I don't think her attacker had any idea about her gender. Most people wouldn't," said Ramirez. "There's no need to say anything about this to Dr. Apiro. And if you can avoid putting any reference to it in your report, I'd appreciate it. As you can see"—he inclined his head down the hall—"they're emotionally involved."

"Dr. Apiro doesn't know?"

"I'm sure he does, but he doesn't need to know that I do. Besides,

I'll have to file a copy of your report with the Canadian authorities. Maria's assailant won't be going to trial in Cuba, but she faces serious charges in Canada. The Minister of the Interior has instructed that she be returned there immediately. He wants her own people to deal with her. I'd like to see Maria's private medical information kept out of those reports."

The minister had no more interest in a nearly dead *jinetera* than he had in a dead one—he wanted the problem gone, particularly when a Cuban trial for the murder of two *jineteras* and the attempted murder of another would publicly expose Manuel Flores's treason. But Ramirez didn't want to give him another ground for blackmail.

The physician shrugged. "I don't have to mention it. It's not relevant."

Ramirez thanked him and walked down the dingy hallway. He poked his head into Maria's room. She was propped up on the bed, looking pale and vulnerable. Her neck was badly bruised. Apiro was standing beside her, holding her slender hand in his large one.

"Will you be all right if I leave you here with Maria, Hector? I have to go to the train station to pick up my family this evening. Detective Espinoza will be over shortly, if you need anything. I really should get going. There are a few things I need to do before Francesca and the children get home."

"Of course, *asere*," said Apiro. "Ricardo, I'm so grateful. I can't tell you how much I owe you. How much we both owe you."

Maria tried to speak, but the only sound she made was a croak. She put a hand to her throat and shrugged helplessly.

Ramirez smiled. "I'm glad it all worked out. You're a lucky man, Hector, to have found a woman like Maria. Most men I know would envy you."

66

The elder held **Pagidaendijigewin,** *the ritual* of the dead. He placed a small pile of tobacco in a clamshell and lit it with a match. He smudged everyone present at Freda Wabigoon's wake, cleansing the air, their spirits. He waved an eagle feather above the clamshell, sending smoke over each person's face and chest. The smoke would carry their words and prayers skyward to *Gitche Manitou,* the great unknown.

Outside the gymnasium, the sky was a cold, bright, clear blue. There were no storm clouds to be seen. The sky gods had settled down.

"The souls of the dead, on their journey to the great meadow, must walk a narrow path across a river," the elder said in English. "Those who are hurtful to others always fall." His voice softened as he switched to Ojibway.

"*Mam'oon o'w, giwii-wiidooka.* We say goodbye today to a beloved wife, mother, and daughter. She followed the path of life.

She honoured our brothers: the wolf, the snail, the bear, the white-fish, the eagle, and the trout. She understood that nature is our teacher."

He put the pipe down and reached for his small drum. He sang travelling songs as he thumped it with his hand.

When the prayers and songs were over, the elder spoke directly to the spirit of Freda Wabigoon. He told her what to expect in her travels, and how to behave when she reached the lands of souls. "I know your spirit hears me, Freda. Be careful as you walk. Watch for the blue light, and listen for running water. Those are your guides. In four days, my sister, you will leave us. *K'd'ninguzhimim, wauwkweeng k'd'izhau.*" To the land of souls, you are bound.

When the elder was finished, he handed Bill Wabigoon a small piece of folded birch bark that contained a braid of Freda's hair.

As people mingled, Charlie Pike solemnly shook Pauley Oshig's thin hand. Someone had smeared charcoal on the boy's forehead to keep Freda's spirit from taking him with her if she got lonely.

Pike gave Molly Oshig a hug. He walked over to Chief Wabigoon to say goodbye. "I'm sorry for your loss, Bill."

Wabigoon nodded and wiped away tears. "I'm going to miss her, Charlie. She was a good woman. Your auntie was a lot of help, get-ting things ready. She gave us some little birch baskets that we put inside the casket. Freda don't need much food where she's going, but you know how it is. She's wearing her moccasins."

Pike nodded. The Anishnabe believed that spirits needed to be fed on their journey to *Gaagige Minawaanigoziwining*, the land of ev-erlasting happiness. The tiny baskets were filled with food. The dead wore moccasins so that their footprints melded with those of their ancestors on the path. Not shoe prints, thought Pike. Footprints.

"She was proud of you, Bill. She told me so."

Wabigoon took a deep breath and nodded gratefully. "Will you stay for the feast? Moose stew. Macaroni and corn soup, and some whitefish they pulled from the bay today. Freda would have liked that. Pretty much everyone will be there to send her on her way. We'll be burning tobacco all week to light up her journey."

"No, I can't, Bill, much as I'd like to," Pike said. As soon as he said it, he realized he was genuinely sorry he couldn't stay. "I have a plane to catch in a few hours. But it was good to see you again." He was surprised to discover he meant that too.

Bill Wabigoon smiled as if he'd read Charlie's mind. "You call me when you get back to Ottawa. I'm going to need your help with that police force we're planning. We have lots to talk about, you and me. And Sheldon too."

"I'll do that," said Pike. He walked over to where Sheldon Waubasking was standing. He clapped his friend on the back. "Came to say goodbye, Sheldon. I got to get going."

"Hey, it's not goodbye, Charlie. You'll be back," Sheldon said, grinning. "You can't stay for the feast? You know what they call a wake in Ojibway, eh? Tim Hortons."

Pike laughed. He saw the elder packing up his belongings and remembered the pouch of tobacco in his pocket. He pulled it out and walked over to the elder. He handed him the tobacco.

"*Miigwetch*," the elder said, and Pike realized it was the elder from the sweat lodge.

"Can I ask you something? You mentioned a blue light in the service. What did you mean?"

"The traditional people believe that on the journey to the land of souls, the spirit has two guides. There's a blue light that glows to show the way, and there's the sound of the river. You're supposed to keep the blue light in front of you and the river to your left, so you can stay on a straight path and not get tempted to go astray."

Maybe it wasn't Luminol that Pauley saw, thought Pike. Maybe whatever it was that made the boy different let him see things that others couldn't, the same way it let him speak with birds.

"Do you really think she'll go to a better place?" he asked.

"Not all of them do," the elder said. "Some of them decide to stay in this world, so they can help their friends and family. You can see them sometimes in the northern lights when they're dancing."

Pike thanked the elder. He walked over to where his auntie Alma waited. She was bundled up in her warm hat and mittens. A blanket covered her ruined legs. Outside, he pushed her wheelchair through the snow. The wheels carved parallel tracks as they made their way up the hill to the graveyard to pay their respects to his father.

Hundreds of glossy black crows followed them as Alma directed him to the spot. The birds settled silently into the pine trees above them.

Pike ran his fingers around the beaded cuff bracelet on his wrist. "Go back to your people," the old man had told him in Ottawa. "That's where you belong. Mine are *Anaandeg*, on my mother's side. We have big families."

Anaandeg, Pike thought. Yes, it was a big family, crows, and getting bigger all the time. The trees were getting crowded. Maybe that was the reason the crows had started walking. Or maybe they were turning back into people.

Pike made sure his auntie was tucked comfortably under her blanket, then left her alone for a few minutes while he looked out at Manomin Bay. The steel-blue water glinted gold where patches of ice captured the light. The way the dark water gleamed, it almost looked like mercury.

His auntie was right. They had buried his father in a beautiful spot, overlooking that part of the bay where his grandfather had drowned. Pike stood for a long time, thinking about his mother and his father. He let his anger slowly release, easing the tightness in his chest he'd carried for so long. He finally returned to his auntie's wheelchair. As he pushed her down the hill to the elders' lodge, the crows flew off, one by one.

67

Mabel Nahwegahbow moved stiffly, arthritis twisting her knees.

"You know, Charlie, I think I have a photograph of those children, those little boys. They took it the day an official from the church visited the school. They all got dressed up, like the Pope himself was going to be there. That's why I remember it so well. That one little boy you were talking about, yes, I remember him too. He drowned in the lake the very next day."

She walked to a cabinet that held china and figurines in the upper part and opened a drawer. She removed a pile of photographs and brushed the top one gently.

"I loved those little children, you know. I tried to speak Ojibway to them, but we weren't supposed to, and if we did, we got punished. Can't tell you how many times those nuns got me with a ruler. And I wasn't even a student by then; I was the kitchen help."

She handed him the photo. "This one." She pointed. "On the end of that row in the front. The little one in front of the priest.

That's the boy that drowned. I guess he thought he could make it across the harbour and get home, but the ice gave way. He wasn't very old, maybe seven. Oh, my, I remember the principal was really mad. He said that we shouldn't tell anyone, that he'd take care of it. But I saw the older boys outside with shovels that night, digging a hole in the ground." She wiped away a tear. "I was only fifteen myself, you know. I'd finished my fourth grade, so they made me work in the kitchen. There was nothing I could do to protect any of those little children. I still feel guilty about that."

"Do you know his name—the boy who drowned?"

"His English name was Joseph, but the other boys called him Manajiwin. That's how I knew who you were looking for as soon as you mentioned it. Do you know what it means in our language?"

"Respect," said Pike.

"That's right." The old woman sighed. "There was one nun who was always after him, poor little Joe. Oh, she was bad. She'd grab him by the ear and twist it hard till he cried. Show some respect, she'd say whenever she scolded him. I think the other boys thought if they called him that, the sister could see respect whenever she looked at him and maybe she'd stop hurting him."

"What about his brothers? Can you remember anything about them?"

"Oh, my, let me think. There were four of them. Peter was the oldest. He must have been nine or ten. Then came Joseph, the little one who drowned. Then Thomas. And John was the littlest. He was maybe five." She smiled. "The older boys called him Long John, after Long John Silver, the pirate, because he had really long hair when he first came to school. The teachers cut it all off, all that beautiful hair. That frightened us, because we only cut our hair when someone died.

"They loved puns, all the children. They made up names for all the nuns and the priests. 'Big Foot' for Father Lafete. That made me laugh to myself whenever they whispered it, because that priest certainly did have big feet, I must say. And I remember they called that visiting priest 'Little Ray of Sunshine' when he came too, but I can't remember why. He was the one that came to the school the day that Joe drowned. He's in that picture. That's little Joe he's standing behind. Funny what you remember after all these years, isn't it?"

Pike looked at the photograph. There were three rows of Ojibway children lined up on benches, girls and boys. The boys' hair was cut short and they wore awkward, ill-fitting suits. Some looked like they'd been squirming when the camera captured their images. The girls had long skirts, their hair plaited. They sat passively, resigned.

A young priest stood at the end of the first row, his hands resting lightly on the shoulder of the small boy Mabel had identified as Joseph, the boy that drowned. The priest was Ray Callendes. He was the only person smiling.

"Did Peter have a nickname too?"

Mabel looked at the ceiling for a minute, thinking. "They called him Peter Rabbit, now that I think of it, because he'd steal vegetables from the garden, but he always got caught."

"Was that his last name, Rabbit?"

"Oh, no, I don't think so. There are some Rabbits around Manitoulin Island, but that's pretty far south. And I've met some Rabbit Skin people too, but they were all Cree. These boys spoke the same language as us. Not from Sandy Lake or Manomin Bay, but somewhere not too far; we had the same accent. I remember whenever they called him Rabbit, he'd smile. A sweet little boy, you know. Whenever he smiled, he lit right up."

Pike thought of the old man who called him son, and the damage caused to him by the priest who stood at the end of the row, his hands resting casually on the shoulders of the child he'd already chosen as his next victim. Angry tears stung Pike's eyes.

"He had really long hair too, when he started school," Mabel added. "That's the other reason they called him Peter Rabbit, come to think of it. It was another pun. I think his last name was Hare."

"Do you know what happened to the others, to Thomas and John?" Pike asked. "Are they still alive?"

"I'm sorry, I don't, Charlie. I stopped working at the school when I turned sixteen. I haven't thought about those little boys for years."

As Pike got up to leave, the old woman spoke again, haltingly, as if trying to decide how much she could trust him. "I heard they found human remains back there, Charlie. Last spring. Behind the school."

"Who found them?"

"Some parents from Pelican Lake whose children went missing a long, long time ago. Back in the seventies. They've been looking for them for years. They started digging out back and they found some buttons, same as the ones that were on everyone's school uniforms. They kept on going until they found bones. The elders said they were human, so they buried them in the graveyard at their reserve. The traditional way, four days later."

"They're supposed to call the coroner when they find human remains so they can be examined by an expert," Pike said, exhaling. "Did they do any forensic testing? Do they know whose bones they were?"

She looked at him sadly. "The elders don't need some white scientist to tell them what human bones look like, Charlie. They know what comes from an animal and what doesn't. Besides, it doesn't matter. We always bury our dead."

Pike nodded slowly, his mind whirling. "How many did they find?"

"Sixteen, is what I heard."

"Sixteen bones?"

"No, Charlie. Sixteen children."

68

Inspector Ramirez pushed open the door to the Chinese restaurant. Before he went to pick up his family at the train station, he wanted to try to contact Antifona Conejo, and there was only one way he could think of to do that. He no longer trusted anything that Manuel Flores had told him about his visions. Besides, whatever they were, they were hardly subconscious. Ramirez approached the same waitress who served him when he was there with Dr. Yeung.

"Excuse me, I'm looking for the 'ask rice' woman. The old woman that was working here the other day?"

The woman looked puzzled and shook her head. "We have no old women employed in this restaurant. All our servers are young."

Ramirez looked around the room. The waitresses were Cuban, wearing tight satin dresses with high collars. "She's Chinese. Maybe in her seventies or even older. She has a necklace made of gold coins around her neck."

"Oh, I know who you mean now. There is an old woman with a

necklace like that. She runs the *kiosko* that sells paper dragons and Chinese kites. Out the front door, down the street, on your right. She comes in for green tea in the afternoon."

Ramirez walked outside and saw the small kiosk. Red lanterns swung from its four corners. As he approached, he recognized her immediately. The cluster of coins still hung around her neck. Her face was creased with spiderweb lines.

"Dr. Yeung said you'd be back," she said, and bowed to him. "She flew back to China this morning, but she left this for you." She reached below the counter and handed him a package.

"You speak Spanish," he said, surprised.

"I was born here, Señor." She smiled. "My grandmother was Chinese."

"I need to talk to the hungry ghost again. Can you help me?"

"Me?" She covered her mouth as she laughed. "Oh, no. I'm not an 'ask rice' woman."

"So the whole thing was a scam? The empty place setting, the chopsticks? But why?"

The old woman smiled. "You misunderstand the reason I laughed. I am not the 'ask rice' woman. That's Dr. Yeung."

Ramirez realized that when Dr. Yeung had been talking to the old woman, she'd been giving her instructions, paying for whatever was in the package. He opened it cautiously. He half expected to find a vial of white grubs inside. Instead, there was a paper airplane, a paper suitcase, and paper credit cards, as well as paper dresses, paper high heels, cardboard tubes of lipstick, even paper condoms.

There was also a note from Dr. Yeung, scripted in tidy calligraphy:

To the Chinese, there is no greater good than to bury stray bones. Lu Tung-pin, the Immortal, exorcises demons. You can ask the hungry ghosts to stay away, if you wish, by using these. You can burn ghost money for a long life too, but you have to buy your own. The choice is yours.

"What is ghost money?" he asked the vendor.

"'Hell money' is what some call it," the old woman said. "But I like to think of it as heaven money. It's bad luck to give it to someone who's alive. It's funny, the company in China that makes it, their motto is to please customers in the next life. How much do you want? Ten billion? It only costs a few pesos. Heaven is cheap."

Ramirez gave her a handful of domestic pesos and she handed him a stack of bills. One denomination was for a million dollars. On the back of the note was a picture of the Bank of Hell.

"Do you have any paper exit permits?"

The old woman laughed. "Ghosts don't need them. They come and go wherever they want, whenever they want. Time isn't something that concerns them, only us. Now, make sure to hold these in both hands when you put them in the fire. You have children? The little ones like the paper cars."

69

Charlie Pike phoned Chief O'Malley from the airport. The clerk insisted Pike use her phone, waving off his protests that the call would be long distance. "Don't worry about it, hon."

"The Cuban authorities have been in touch with us already about Denise Labelle," said O'Malley. "The RCMP are going down to pick her up and bring her back to Winnipeg for prosecution. As soon as Adam Neville heard she was in custody, that was enough for him to start talking about cutting a deal. The Crown says he has to plead guilty and agree to testify against her; otherwise, they can't force him to, because of spousal immunity. There's no evidence connecting her to any of the crimes without his evidence. It's a good deal for him. A few years in jail instead of life. He'll lose his medical licence, of course; that's part of the package."

"Did he say why he did it? Why he framed Sheldon?"

"He claims he didn't know Denise had anything to do with these murders until he found her fingerprints on a compact in Gloria

TwoQuill's purse a few days before they went on their holidays. He says he was stunned. He left Cuba early to get away from her while he decided what to do. When he saw Maylene Kesler's body, he realized he could make it look like the Highway Strangler had killed her too, and maybe protect Denise while he sorted things out. He decided to frame Sheldon when the opportunity presented itself. He thought you'd jump at the chance to close these files. He didn't realize that you and Sheldon have a history."

"Do you believe him? It could have been the two of them that did this together."

O'Malley shrugged. "I expect they'll point fingers at each other. It worked for Homolka and Bernardo."

"I still don't understand why she did it."

"And you know what, Charlie? We probably never will. She's as crazy as a coot, from what I can tell. Killing those women so she could get her husband's attention? Frankly, the bigger problem it creates for us is with the dozens of murders she *didn't* commit. Any half-decent defence lawyer is going to point to her whenever the task force turns up a suspect. I'm already trying to figure out how many convictions in Manitoba are going to be opened up because of Neville's willingness to tamper with evidence." He sighed. "Anyway, Charlie, it was good work you did up there. Well done, lad."

Pike looked out the airport window as the bush plane taxied in. "I need to get going in a few minutes, Chief. My plane just landed. By the way, I think I found out the old man's name. I'm pretty sure it's Peter Hare. How did he make out while I was away? Is he all right?"

O'Malley smiled. "Now, don't you worry; I've been taking care of Mr. Hare, and I got him to tell me his name while you were gone. We found him a spot in palliative care. They've started him on some damn good pain relief. For the first time in a long while, he's feeling better."

Pike was astonished. "How'd you get him into a hospital without any identification? And how did you find out his name?"

"Well, now, you know how persuasive I can be, Charlie. I told him I'd promised you I'd look after him, and that I had to do that properly or I'd lose face. He didn't have an OHIP card. I don't think he'd ever applied for health care. But your friend Chief Bill Wabigoon helped me work all that out. He called the Deputy Minister of Health and threatened to hold a press conference if an Ojibway elder froze to death because of some missing paperwork. The Odawa Friendship Centre is going to keep an eye on Mr. Hare too. They're going to send someone over to talk to him about filing an Indian residential school claim. Apparently, he's entitled to some money for each year he was there, although it seems he doesn't want to say much about what happened."

"That means a lot to me," Pike said. "You looking out for him." He wiped his wet eyes with the back of his hand.

"It was the least I could do for you, son."

70

The train was due to arrive in forty minutes. Inspector Ramirez couldn't wait to see his wife, his children, to hear all about Edel's games, to see the empty space in Estella's smile where her baby tooth had fallen out.

The station wasn't far from the ocean. He parked the car on a side street, retrieved the package of paper goods, and walked down to the beach. He removed his shoes and picked his way gingerly across the hot sand until he found a quiet spot away from any tourists. He kneeled down and dug a shallow pit with his fingers.

He felt Antifona's presence before he saw her. She stood, facing the ocean, a cigarette held loosely in her fingers. She looked longingly towards Florida, to the future she would never have.

"I'm sorry, Antifona," Ramirez said. He felt an overwhelming sense of guilt. He stood and brushed the white sand from his pants. "I should never have picked you up that night. I made you a target."

She held his eyes until he looked away. This ghostly traveller had come back to the past, not so much to help him with his investigation as to repair a relationship that was more important to her than her own life. The old woman was right: time had no meaning to the dead, only the living. But even for the dead, it seemed that love transcended time.

Ramirez thought about Dr. Yeung's instructions. A long life—yes, of course, he wanted that. But he also wanted to never be in another situation where his visions resulted in someone's death the way they had with Antifona. He thought for a moment about what to wish for. No more apparitions? A return to a happy marriage?

Without his ghosts, his life would go back to normal. He could stop questioning his health. Francesca would worry about him less.

———

Ramirez squatted on the sand. He held the paper money in both hands, the way the old woman had instructed. He put it down in loose stacks in the hole he'd dug, then the other paper goods. He set aside the tiny paper car he'd purchased for Edel. He wondered what the exchange rate was in heaven, what favours would be owed.

He lit a match and watched the edges of the bills curl and catch fire. He stood up. Flakes of grey ash were captured by the evening breeze as the bits of paper went up in smoke and drifted skyward.

Antifona hiked up her skirt and waded into the ocean. The water lapped against her smooth brown thighs. She raised an eyebrow, inviting Ramirez to join her. He shook his head.

"It wasn't Lorenzo's fault that he didn't show up," Ramirez said. "The same men that killed you tortured him to death. He tried as hard as he could to protect you. That's all he could think about, despite the pain. He planned to marry you; he even told them so. I think he's out there, somewhere, hoping you'll forgive him, so he can join you on the other side."

Antifona's shoulders relaxed. She smiled. She backed into the ocean, farther and farther, until the waves swept around her waist.

She blew Ramirez a kiss and tossed her cigarette into the water. Then she turned away from him. He watched her walk into the ocean until her head disappeared from view.

The waves brought the cigarette butt to Ramirez's feet, dragging it up and down the sand. He threw the butt on the embers, where it sizzled.

He stamped out the small pyre. Then he walked back to his car, eager to see his family.

ACKNOWLEDGMENTS

It's not an easy thing to switch publishers mid-series. I owe a huge debt of thanks to Chris Bucci for somehow managing to pull that off, and to Kevin Hanson of Simon & Schuster Canada for taking the bait. Simon & Schuster has been an absolute joy to work with and, while Alison Clarke is no longer with them, she made me feel right at home. I'm deeply grateful.

My father, Roddie Blair, to whom this book is dedicated, died in the fall of 2013, just shy of his ninety-eighth birthday. He always had a book in his hand. He didn't care what the genre was as long as it was well written. I'll never forget arriving at his funeral service in Aurora to find flowers from Simon & Schuster, thanks to Alison. It's that kind of thoughtfulness that characterizes, and continues to characterize, the entire organization. It's extraordinary, in these often dark days for publishers, to find one with such a big heart and boundless optimism. I know exactly how lucky I am.

I had always wanted to write a book about an art heist and that's how this story originally started; although, as usual, the characters decided to take things in a different direction.

But because of the efforts of some wonderful friends—Ottawa artist Sharon VanStarkenburg; Sharon Louden, senior critic for the New York Academy of Art; and David Thomas—around twenty talented artists have offered to create works of art based on their impressions of *Hungry Ghosts*. We're going to hold an art exhibition as part of the book launch. These artists range from those who work with encaustic to watercolour and from glass art to graffiti. I can't wait to see what they come up with. It's going to be amazing. Thank you, all.

I also want to thank my external readers, Debbie Hantusch, Bill Schaper, and Debbie Levy, for pointing out plot gaps and holes in the story without reducing me to a puddle of insecurity. Thanks also to Guillermo Martinez-Zalce, who helped me out whenever I wasn't sure of a Spanish word's meaning or spelling. I owe a huge debt of gratitude to Alexandra Sanchez for her guidance in all things Cuban. Thanks also to former CSI and fellow author Tom Adair for helping me research the forensic use of blowflies.

Alex Schultz, my brilliant editor, worked his usual magic. This is our third book together now; I can't imagine doing this with anyone else. I very much appreciate that Simon & Schuster allowed us to carry on that relationship. Any errors left after Alex's rigorous editing are mine and mine alone.

One final note. Shortly after I finished writing *Hungry Ghosts*, in October 2012, there was a story in the Ottawa media about a crow named Walter that was rescued as a baby by an Ottawa family. Walter developed a very special relationship with their young son, who insisted that he and Walter often talked together. Walter often accompanied him to school and kept a watchful eye from the treetops. Sometimes, the boy said when he was sad, he would tell Walter his secrets because he knew Walter wouldn't tell anyone else.

Just sayin'.